CW01367525

The Cloisters Of Canterbury

A Novel By

ROBERT DEAN BAIR

To Olivia,
Our love
Robert Dean Bair

ArcheBooks Publishing

The Cloisters of Canterbury

By

ROBERT DEAN BAIR

Copyright © 2006 by Robert Dean Bair

ISBN: 1-59507-163-6

ArcheBooks Publishing Incorporated

www.archebooks.com

9101 W. Sahara Ave.

Suite 105-112

Las Vegas, NV 89117

All rights reserved, including the right to reproduce this book or portions thereof in any form whatsoever. For information about this book, please contact ArcheBooks at publisher@ArcheBooks.com.

This book is entirely a work of fiction. The names, characters, places, and incidents depicted herein are either products of the author's imagination or are used fictitiously. Any resemblance to actual events or locales or persons, living or dead, is entirely coincidental.

First Edition: 2006

In Memory

The Reverend Canon Ferdie W. Phillips, M.C., B.A.
The Canterbury Cathedral
Canterbury, England

A percentage of the royalties from this novel have been pledged to the H. LEE MOFFITT CANCER CENTER & RESEARCH INSTITUTE, Tampa, Florida

Dedication

This book is dedicated to those men and women who serve in our nation's intelligence community, and especially those who have taken their secrets to their graves. They dedicate their lives and many times give their lives for the safety of a grateful nation. They and their families make unknown sacrifices and never experience a normal life. They continue to fight terrorism, leaks and corruption today.

Appreciation

For the endless love of my parents,
William and Mona J. Bair

That special person, my loving wife, Mary Dell Tinsley, my friend, a gifted artist, a dedicated and caring teacher, who has been supportive wherever I might be and for reading my manuscripts, correcting and wondering but not asking.

Acknowledgements

Burl Meachum taught me how lonely life can be.

Thanks to James P. Allen for his insight and belief in me.

A special thanks to Joseph "Scottie" Davidson for opening endless doors.

To Robert Gelinas, my publisher and gifted editor, whose tireless efforts benefit so many.

And a special thanks to my agent, Barbara Casey, for her encouragement and friendship.

The Cloisters
Of Canterbury

Robert Dean Bair

Introduction

The United States of America was in a financial depression and still trying to heal from the wounds of the Civil War and World War One. With these things ever present in the minds of Americans on Memorial Day, they gathered around graves honoring those who had died while rifle shots and sorrowful tones from a bugler's horn sounded on a distant hill.

Government leaders tried desperately to avoid the war in Europe by supplying England with military supplies and equipment. But when the Japanese attacked Pearl Harbor on December 7, 1941, the United States had no other choice but to declare war on Japan and enter the war in Europe. The mobilization of the nation's resources to provide weapons for war was unprecedented: scrap metal and paper drives; gasoline, automobiles, tires, food, clothing and shoes, and treasured coffee—nothing escaped rationing. Many people worked two jobs...women joined the men in the factories...farmers left their fields at dark to work at night in army tank plants. Gone was the sight of men begging for a piece of bread or standing around a blazing fire in a metal barrel on a street corner. Everyone wanted to do what they could to help in the war effort.

The Cloisters of Canterbury

A nation watched their love ones, sons, daughters, brothers, sisters and fathers, board troop trains that would take them to the battle fields. 400,000 would not return. Gold stars were hung in the windows of houses on the streets across the nation, telling all that a loved one had been lost. Funerals and memorial services were held in each of the States for the fallen, and folded American flags were presented to the grieving mothers and wives.

Rumors of atrocities suddenly became reality when photographs of concentration camps in Germany and Poland liberated by Allied forces were printed on the front pages of newspapers and shown in the news-reels at local move theatres. Many were outraged; they wondered why such horrible things had been hidden from them when they learned their government—the United States of America—had knowledge of the treatment of the Jews. Their concern grew. What was going on behind the closed doors of the government offices?

•

This story is an eye-witness account of courage exhibited by ordinary people with deep convictions, honor, patriotism, and integrity. They risked their lives to fight corruption, treason and murder during the months leading to the end of World War II and thereafter.

Rob Royal was a member of the Special Troops stationed at U.S. First Army Headquarters at Fort Jay on Governor's Island in New York Harbor, assigned to the Communication Section of Military Intelligence. The Commander of the First Army, Four-Star General William Courtney, ordered Royal to report to President Harry S. Truman at the White House in Washington. After Royal completed a confidential assignment for the President of the United States, his life was forever changed. As a result, and despite high security, an attempt was made on his life.

Royal was recruited by a *group* of ordinary citizens who were not part of the government. The covert Group had concerns about the effectiveness of the government's intelligence organizations and gathered information from many points of the world for the President of the United States and certain members of Congress. They were ordinary people who volunteered to do extraordinary things for their country.

Rob Royal was one of the ordinary people.

This is his story. These are his words.

Chapter 1

THE WHITE HOUSE

It was a beautiful fall October day in New York.

Just before noon, I was looking out a window of the First Army military intelligence office at the Statue of Liberty when General William Courtney's staff car stopped in front of the building. I watched Harry, the general's driver, get out of the car and open the door for the general, who had just returned from a meeting in Washington. Everyone was aware when the general was off Governor's Island, but there was always enough brass on the island such that no one ever slacked off in his or her duties. It didn't make a lot of difference whether he was there or not, except that when walking by his office you didn't worry about him suddenly coming out, or the rare occasion when he walked past your open office door and your feet were resting on top of the desk.

The general was only in the building for a few minutes when I was startled by the ringing of my telephone. I picked up the receiver, and before I could speak, the firm voice of the general's secretary said, "The general will see you now."

The Cloisters of Canterbury

Instantly I stood at attention as if he was in the room. I remembered the general telling me, "If my secretary tells you to do something, it's the same as if *I did!*"

I hurried. No, I ran down the stairs and only slowed when I was in front of the military policeman standing guard at the entrance to the general's outer office. The look on the MP's face was obvious that he had been alerted by the sound of my running down the steps and it turned into a smile; he probably assumed that I was in trouble for something.

The general's secretary stood behind her desk. She always made me feel that she knew everything about me, even the color of my under shorts—and they'd better be khaki. She walked to the general's door and knocked.

"Come in," came the reply. She opened the door and I walked to the front of the general's desk and saluted.

The general said, "Stand at ease."

I did.

The general looked up from his desk. "I have just returned from a meeting with President Truman at the White House. He has requested that you report to him today, as soon as possible. You are to fly from the island airstrip within the hour. This is a confidential meeting. You are not to discuss the trip, or your meeting with the president, with anyone except me. Report to me when you return, do you understand?"

"Yes, sir." I saluted.

"That's all." The general returned his attention to his desk without returning my salute, which was not unusual.

I turned and walked out of the office, pausing in front of his secretary's desk.

She looked up with her normal stern look. "Harry is waiting at the side entrance."

I left the office, strode past the MP and almost missed the smirk on his face.

Harry was behind the wheel of the general's car, the right front door of the car stood open; I promptly got in and closed the door. There was no conversation between us as he drove directly to the airstrip.

Why did the president want to see me at the White House? My mind considered all possibilities without coming to a positive conclusion, not even a hint.

A Piper, a single-engine, high-wing, two-passenger airplane was waiting at the airstrip. The engine of the small plane seemed to labor as we flew past the Statue of Liberty. I thought about Wilbur Wright when he made the first over-water flight from Governor's Island around the Statue of Liberty in 1909, wondering how the little engine in his plane sounded.

It was a short flight to Mitchell Field. When we landed, the pilot taxied to a waiting C-46 cargo plane with its engines running. The pilot and co-pilot, staff sergeant, plus an Army medical flight surgeon were the only other passengers. As soon as I was on board the staff sergeant closed the door and the plane started to move.

The landing at Andrews Field was smooth. The plane taxied off the landing strip to a group of hangers and before the pilot shut down the engines, the staff sergeant had the plane's door open. A military staff car pulled up; the driver got out and walked to the plane. The staff sergeant motioned to me. I moved to the door and dropped to the ground. The driver escorted me to the car.

The driver had obviously driven from Andrews to the White House many times. When we arrived at the gate, a guard instructed the driver to park and wait. A Secret Service agent escorted me into the White House. This particular visit to the White House was much different from my previous visit when I was part of a public tour.

Another Secret Service agent opened the door to the Oval Office. The agent announced, "Mr. President, Warrant Officer Royal is here."

President Truman was seated behind his desk. "Come in, Mr. Royal."

I approached the president's desk. He stood and extended his hand. His grip was firm. The president pointed to an armchair in front of the desk. "Have a seat, young man."

"Thank you, Mr. President."

He didn't waste any time. "When I was in the Senate, I chaired a committee investigating military contracts. When I became president after President Roosevelt's death, my concerns continued about the investigations. In fact, I still have major concerns.

"I received a report from General Courtney about the two German prisoners' escape attempt in a small plane from the Fort Jay airstrip on Governor's Island on New Year's Eve. He told me of your involvement in preventing the former German Luftwaffe pilots from escaping. When he told me that you were from Xenia, Ohio, near Dayton, the name of a military contractor in Dayton came to mind. I have been receiving some disturbing information about the company.

"I suggested to the general that you be sent to investigate S & M Precision Machine Company—to look around so to speak. They have

The Cloisters of Canterbury

received contracts to manufacture replacement parts for military aircraft. The government provided the funds for building about 100,000 square feet of building, fenced the property which was owned by the president of the company, and we also paid for the machinery and equipment for manufacturing the parts."

The president paused, "It smells like there's a 'rat in the woodpile' down there. When you return to Fort Jay, you're going to receive a fourteen day furlough to go home, during which time I want you to nose around, see what you can learn and report back to the general—but spend some time with your family. This envelope has the information you will need. But remember, this is hush-hush. There is also a telephone number in there that you should use in case of an emergency." The president stood and walked around to the front of his desk. "That was a fine job you did New Year's Eve."

I said, "Thank you, Mr. President."

The president shook my hand and walked with me to the door. I had not been in the office for more than ten minutes. The same driver returned me to Andrews where the C-46 was waiting for the flight back to Mitchell. As soon as we landed I boarded the waiting Piper and was flown back to Governor's Island.

Harry was waiting in the general's staff car at the Governor's Island airstrip when the pilot taxied to the guard shack. He drove me to the side entrance of the First Army Headquarters' building. I went directly to the general's office. His secretary was standing behind her desk. "Mr. Royal, here are your furlough papers."

"Thank you. It looks like I may be home for an early Thanksgiving."

I returned to the communication office and began putting things on my desk in order. Just as I was leaving, Army Sergeant Major Murphy came in and handed me a duffel bag. "You might need this. Have a safe trip."

"Thanks, Sergeant."

At the barracks I checked the train schedule. There was a train leaving for Dayton out of Grand Central at 10:15. I called the general's secretary and told her my plans.

Harry was waiting with the general's staff car in front of the barracks when I came out. "Rob, the general's secretary told me you had a train to catch."

As soon as I arrived at Grand Central Station, I called my parents and told them of my furlough, and that I would arrive in Dayton the following morning at 7:20. There were several vacant seats on the train.

I located two seats that would allow me to sleep. It was going to be a long night.

•

My father met the train at the Dayton station the next morning. When we got to the house Mugs, my Boston terrier, greeted me, and mother had breakfast ready. That evening, Angel, my sister, and I walked down the street to a drugstore with a soda fountain, marble counter top and stools in front. We used to hang out there in high school; it was just like the old days.

On the walk home, I asked Angel for a favor. "Angel, there are several names on this list and if it is possible I would like to know if they own any property or have spent any time in the local jail."

Angel was a clerk in the Montgomery County Records office and had access to all of the public records. She looked at the list and at me but asked no questions. "That's not a problem."

I enjoyed spending time with my family and eating all of the food Mother remembered that I liked. We looked at old photographs and talked until midnight. I slept until the smell of bacon drifted up to my room. Like so many mornings over the years, Mother opened the door to the back stairs and sent Mugs up to wake me. Old Mugs hadn't forgotten. He jumped onto the bed and licked my face just as he had done since he was only a few months old. After being sure that I was awake he jumped off the bed and returned downstairs to wait for his morning walk.

Chapter 2

CONFIDENTIAL ASSIGNMENT

After breakfast I borrowed my dad's car, a black 1941 Ford Tudor, and drove into Dayton to the Montgomery County Courthouse, to the Records office where Angel greeted me. Angel handed me a folded piece of paper without saying anything. I folded it again and placed it in my jacket pocket.

I hugged her and said, "Angel, I'll see you at home about six o'clock. Mother is having fried chicken, mashed potatoes, gravy and apple pie for dessert, don't be late."

Sitting in the car, I removed the paper from my jacket pocket. It was the list I had given Angel, and after each of the names, except one, she had written "No Record." The one exception was the name Frank A. Salvatore. His name appeared as the owner on two real estate deeds. There were no records of the S & M Precision Machine Company. However, I knew that Salvatore had signed the government contracts as president of the company.

Salvatore purchased ten acres, listing his address in Trenton, New Jersey, in June of 1939, from the estate of a deceased county judge. The land was part of a farm that had been owned by the judge for many years and the administrator of the estate, the judge's only son, whose address was in a bank building in Trenton, New Jersey. The estate had subdivided the property and sold ten parcels of ten acres each along a road named after the judge. Angel's notes indicated that there were ten more parcels not sold. The subject's property was the last one on the north side of the road.

Salvatore also owned a house in Oakwood, a suburb of Dayton, Ohio. Purchased in November of 1940, the address of record was the same Trenton, New Jersey, address as the other property. There was no record of mortgages, liens, marriage, divorce, births, lawsuits, judgments, or voting history. She listed the telephone numbers for Frank Salvatore and the S & M Precision Machine Company. Oh yes, Angel's information was certainly going to be helpful.

•

I finally located S & M Precision Machine Company on a narrow gravel road off State Road 4. On both sides of the road there were cement block buildings, except for one building that was an old wooden barn probably part of the original farm. It had been modified and appeared to be used for storage; metal racks with angle iron were visible from the open barn door. All of the other properties had gravel parking lots with cars parked in orderly rows.

The names on the buildings indicated that they were occupied by various types of service and manufacturing companies. There were nine buildings including the old barn, and the one at the end of the road fit Angel's information.

I drove to the end of the road. On the left side was a fenced parcel of land and a cement block building with a sign on the front, S & M Precision Machine Company. There were no cars parked in front or in the gravel parking lot.

At different times during the next several days and nights I drove down that gravel road looking at the S & M building. It was apparent that something was not right. It was surrounded by a chain link fence. A twenty-foot wide gate was secured with a chain and padlock that opened into a vacant gravel parking lot. The front of the building had one door and no windows. All of the glass in the windows on both sides of the building and in the skylights was painted white, preventing anyone from looking inside. I observed the building at various hours, day and night; I never saw a watchman. At night there was a faint light

The Cloisters of Canterbury

visible from the windows in the building. There were no signs of any activity, no employees reporting for work, no trucks arriving with materials or picking up out-going shipments.

I also took the opportunity to visit two local freight-trucking companies; both indicated that they had not delivered or picked up anything at the S & M Precision Machine Company.

I stopped at one of the other buildings on the road, the last one before a vacant property and the S & M Precision Machine building at the end of the road, and entered the door marked "Office." It was a small room about ten by ten feet. On a small table lay several employment applications.

A woman with graying brown hair and brown eyes opened the sliding glass window. "May I help you?"

"Are you hiring?"

"Yes, milling machine operators for the third shift," was her answer.

I picked up one of the applications from the table and said, "I might be interested. I was looking for the S & M Precision Machine Company. Stopped at the office down the road, but there was no one around."

The woman replied, "There is nothing going on down there. In fact, it never opened after the building was completed. I've been working here since before they built it, and I haven't seen anything going on except for the red Buick that parks in front of the building for short periods."

Strange, no one knew of any employment at the company since the building was completed. No wonder the president and others found it suspicious.

"What are you paying mill operators?"

"It depends upon your experience, and there are additional hourly benefits for the third shift. Starting rate is $1.50 an hour for experienced, with a ten-cent night bonus."

"What do you manufacture?"

"We have several government contracts."

"I'll take an application, look around, and might come back." I never found out what they manufactured.

Back in Dayton, I located Frank Salvatore's house in Oakwood, and drove around the neighborhood. It was a nice neighborhood with large lots and mature maple and oak trees. The homes were Georgian style, two-story brick, with attached two-car garages. I parked in front of the third house on the opposite side of the street from the Salvatore house, walked up to the door, and rang the doorbell.

No answer. I tried again; still no response. I walked down the steps to the sidewalk and up to the next house and rang the doorbell. It opened after the first ring, and a pleasant woman holding a black and white cat opened the door with a smile.

She said, "The Moore family is not home; they are visiting her sister in Cincinnati."

It was obvious that she had been watching me and probably knew about everything and everyone in the neighborhood.

"I am not looking for the Moore family. I am looking for Frank Salvatore."

The woman then pointed to the house across the street and said, "Mr. Salvatore lives in that house, but they are not home either. Mr. Salvatore plays a lot of golf, but I'm not sure where. He leaves the house in the morning with white or plaid knickers and various colors of socks and caps on his head like golfers do. He and his wife eat out most of the time. She is a pretty redhead and much younger. They have had a "C" Gasoline Ration Stamp on their red Buick convertible's windshield all the time during the war, so they didn't have to worry about gasoline and she doesn't even drive."

It certainly was obvious that this woman didn't particularly care for her neighbor—her eyes saying more than what came out of her mouth. No one seemed to know where Salvatore came from. They moved into the house after a widow of a local attorney joined her husband in the local cemetery.

•

Every day of my furlough I drove past the Oakwood house and the S & M Precision Machine Company building. One afternoon I saw the aforementioned red Buick convertible parked in front of the building, and two days later the car was in the driveway of the Oakwood house. Unfortunately, I had not seen anyone arriving or leaving the house.

One evening, after dark, I parked my dad's car three blocks from the Salvatore house and walked past it several times. There was light seeping through the edges of the draperies in the front windows. I even walked up the steps onto the front porch, but was not able to see through the openings. I returned to the car and left.

Four nights before I was to return to Governor's Island, dark clouds in the sky covered the new moon. I just hoped that it wouldn't rain or snow; the temperature was barely above freezing. I figured it was time

The Cloisters of Canterbury

for a look inside of the S & M building.

I drove down the gravel road and parked the Ford about a half-mile away in the parking lot of a tool and die shop that was operating 24 hours a day. The night shift workers had just returned to work after their lunch break, so I didn't think anyone would take notice of one more car.

I wore a pair of bib overalls, jump boots and a well-worn army khaki shirt, a field jacket, a knit army cap and a pair of canvas gloves from my dad's workbench in the garage. Other than the jump boots, I was dressed just like one of the factory workers.

The twenty feet of 3/8-inch rope wrapped around my upper torso made me look a lot heavier, but it wasn't very comfortable. I broke into a sweat walking the half-mile even with the temperature in the thirties. As I made my way along the road, I picked up several rocks from the side of the road and put them in my jacket pockets. About fifty yards from the building I moved off the road a few feet, stopped and looked at the luminous dial on my wristwatch; it was 3:15 a.m. There was just a dim light shining from the windows of the building and no cars, as usual.

I looked back up the road—no sign of traffic. It was quiet except for the sounds of machinery from one of the factories with an open door.

After watching and listening for about ten minutes, I stood by a tree just across from the front of the S & M building, unbuttoned the field jacket, removed the rope from around my waist, and made a loop about two feet in diameter.

I took another look down the road—still no traffic or new sounds.

I crossed the road to the front of the building. After five or six tries, I was able to hook the loop of rope on an angle iron brace of the sign that extended above the roof.

I looked down the road again—still clear.

Using both hands I climbed up and stood on top of the 10-foot fence, paused for a moment, took a deep breath and clambered onto the edge of the roof. So far, so good.

I walked along the roof until I reached the middle of the building, selected one of the skylights and looked around. It was about as quiet as I could have asked and the moon was still cloud-covered.

I took a rock about the size of a golf ball from my field jacket and broke the glass in the skylight. I tossed the rest of the stones onto the roof so if someone looked around later they would blame it on some kids. I removed just enough glass for my head to fit in the opening and get a good look. Single light bulbs on electric cords hung down about six feet from the rafters every twenty feet in the middle of the building providing a clear view of the building from one end to the other.

I was not sure what to expect, but what I saw surprised me—the building was completely empty. There was not one piece of equipment, no material, not even a broom. The concrete floor was bare except for the rock and glass that had fallen from the skylight.

Removing more glass allowed me to put both hands into the opening. From my jacket, I removed the camera that Murphy in Intelligence had included in the duffel bag. Lowering the camera with both hands, I put my head through the opening and took a sequence of eight pictures. The camera was capable of taking pictures with less light than was available, so I was not concerned about failing to have evidence that the building was vacant. It would be up to the Army's photo lab to develop the film. When finished, I sat down to catch my breath; perspiration rolled down my face.

I heard the sound of a car coming in the distance. I quietly moved to the edge of the roof to view the road, laying down flat on the roof and waiting. The car pulled up in front of the building and stopped. A door opened and closed, then another door opened and closed. I heard footsteps on the gravel and two distinct voices. They were not visible, I heard the front door of the building open and close, cutting off the sound of the voices. I looked at my watch; it was five minutes after four in the morning.

Twenty minutes passed. The front door opened and closed again. Footsteps on the gravel seemed to last longer than when they arrived. There was a sound, but not like a car door, more like a car's trunk lid, more sounds of feet on gravel, a car door opening and closing. I waited for the second car door to open and close but it didn't. The car motor turned but didn't start. The engine back-fired and then the motor finally started, gravel flew from the tires. It was leaving in one big hurry.

I looked over the edge of the roof just as the clouds in the sky uncovered the slit of the new moon; the car's dash lights reflected on only one person—the driver of the Buick convertible. Now where was the second person? Had they seen the glass and rock on the floor? A night watchman just coming on duty? I hadn't seen anything that would indicate that a guard even existed. A guard for what? There wasn't anything to watch or protect!

Was the person looking around for the rock thrower? There was a noise from the other side of the roof; a person's head emerged from a skylight and then a beam from a flashlight started sweeping across the roof.

I had left the rope on the roof at the front of the building planning to leave from there. That was no longer an option. The ground sloped into a ditch on the right side of the building, but that was a thirty-foot drop. I wondered about the rear of the building. The gravel of the parking lot on the left was flat, but there was no way to get past the head sticking up from the skylight.

A man was climbing onto the roof from the skylight.

I started running along the right edge of the roof staying away from the skylights, hoping to reach the back of the building where I could jump. Suddenly something hit the roof to my left and then the sound of a gunshot. It wasn't a 45—something smaller, but it wouldn't make any difference if it hit me.

How I wished for a 45, or something, and was sorry that I had been instructed not to carry a weapon. I fell to the roof's hard surface and rolled closer to the edge with the intention of dropping off the roof regardless of the distance. There was a crashing sound of glass and words spoken in a foreign language that I didn't understand. More breaking glass and a blood-chilling scream followed by a thud.

I listened, hearing nothing, got up on one knee, looked and listened again—nothing.

Thinking that whoever was shooting at me had fallen through the skylight and was no longer a danger, I got up and walked slowly toward the skylight and looked through the opening. Indeed, a man was down there on the concrete floor. He had dark hair, wore a dark suit, and was laying on his right side. From his left ear to the left side of his mouth was a wide cut. Blood was flowing into his eye and over his nose that was almost flat against his left cheek. There was no movement and not a sound.

I said out loud, "This guy is dead."

I paused for a moment to think. The man in the Buick convertible could be on his way back with help. Why leave? Why not call the police? Then again, what was put into the trunk of the car? A skylight broken by a rock shouldn't be a reason to panic. Maybe the man was still alive. I was sure that if he was still alive he couldn't identify me; the beam from his flashlight never found my face.

Walking to the back right corner of the building's roof, I looked over the edge, wishing for a ladder, a tree, or maybe even some paratrooper training. All I had were jump boots, but it was time to be somewhere else. If I jumped and broke my neck or leg, or was found dead, President Truman had assured me that the flag on the White House would not be lowered. Well, at least I had enjoyed about two weeks of my mother's cooking and had a nice visit with my family. Slept in my old bed and Mugs had greeted me in the mornings.

I moved closer to the edge of the roof, took several deep breaths and jumped. I hit the ground on both feet and rolled over onto my right side. After a few moments, I realized that life was still with me and I could feel no pain. I moved my head, it worked, and my arms didn't shout at me. When I attempted to get up my legs worked. Thank God for Sergeant Major Alan Murphy. The old Irishman always sent his charges out well equipped. He had included the jump boots in the bag.

Now, how to get out of a fenced area.

I walked along the side fence to the corner where the fence ran along the back of property. The corner post was larger than the line posts and had several strands of wire twisted together running on an angle to a metal stake in the ground bracing the post.

I removed my field jacket and put the camera into a pocket of my overalls. Several times I attempted to hook the field jacket onto the top of the corner post. Sweat ran down from my forehead into my eyes. It started to rain, and the slit of light from the new moon was still covered by dark clouds. Finally, the jacket hooked on the top of the corner post. I pulled myself up with the jacket using the bracing wire to support my feet. Just as I made the last pull a ripping noise of the jacket broke the silence. I swung my right leg over the top of the fence, held onto the jacket and fell over the other side; the jacket tore loose from the fence post just before I landed on my right hip on the wet ground. Out of breath, with sweat running down my face, I lay motionless on the ground.

The rain was turning to snow.

I got up, put on my jacket, and walked along the fence at the rear of the property. It was more difficult, but would provide adequate cover in case the man in the Buick or someone else drove down the road. The weeds along the fence were slippery from the snow. My feet tangled in the undergrowth and I fell to the ground every few feet. Reaching the end of the fence, I decided that the best option was to cross the adjacent field on an angle, keeping away from the road for as long as possible.

My path across the field would have been a better obstacle course than the Army used—unseen logs and ditches filled with water, I located all of them. Arriving at the edge of the road, wet and covered with

The Cloisters of Canterbury

mud, the torn field jacket provided very little warmth or protection from the snow that continued to increase and was now blowing against my wet face. I had been sweating, but now I was cold and shivering.

I paused in the ditch beside the road praying that there would be no cars. The noise of a car would give me time to fall into the ditch that had collected several inches of water. There would be no choice but the ditch. Car headlights would expose a wet, mud-covered person, and a local driver would probably stop and offer me a ride. I didn't need that.

I crossed the road and counted the snow-covered cars from the entrance and located my dad's car. I had not locked it. Looking around once more I slid my mud-covered body under the steering wheel, thinking that my dad was going to have a fit. The seat covers would help, but not enough. I reached under the seat for the keys where I always placed them. When using dad's car, I never wanted to wake him with a telephone call in the middle of the night because I had lost the keys while night fishing or on some other adventure.

I looked at my watch and drove out of the factory's parking lot. The car's windshield wipers moved the snow slowly. I reached Route 4 and made a left turn toward Dayton. I couldn't stop thinking of the man covered with blood on the floor of the building. The snow was still coming down; the wipers provided a small opening, barely enough to see the road.

On the right side of the road there were lights, and after passing it, I realized that it was a gas station. There were no car lights in front and none from the rear. Slowly I made a u-turn in the middle of the road and returned to the gas station. The small Sinclair station had two pumps out front. I stopped the car in front of the pumps, opened the car door and got out. Snow covered the seat before I was able to close the door.

There was a light inside the small building of the station; a man was sitting near a potbelly stove attempting to stay warm. When I opened the door, the man jumped out of the chair; there was a surprised look on his face.

I said, "I want five gallons of gas and do you have a telephone?"

The man pointed to a phone hanging on the wall.

I dialed the operator and asked for the sheriff's office. After eight or more rings a sleepy voice said, "Sheriff's office."

"I'm the night watchman at S & M Precision Machine Company. Someone tried to break in and fell through a skylight."

"What's your telephone number?"

"The phone's not working. I'm calling from a gas station."

I clicked the receiver several times and said, "Can't hear you," and hung up.

The man returned from pumping my gas, said that it would be eighty cents, five gallons at sixteen cents a gallon.

I gave him a dollar. "Thanks for the use of the telephone."

The man returned to the chair and potbelly stove and started rubbing his hands together.

Forty minutes later, I pulled the Ford in behind my dad's shop. I opened the trunk of the car and removed a duffel bag with a change of clothes. On the ring that held the car key was a key to the small rear door of the shop. I turned on the light in the lavatory, hung a change of clothes on two nails on the wall. I pulled several rags from a bag by the door and returned to the car and removed all of the visible mud from the car seat.

I looked at my wristwatch. It was 7:15, which meant Dad would be walking in the front door at eight sharp. I had told my parents that I would be visiting friends in Springfield and might stay overnight. Not having the car wasn't a problem since dad walked to the shop most days.

I didn't have to return the car until sometime later in the day, so there was time to recheck for any mud that had been missed. In the lavatory I removed all of my clothes, shivering. The cold water was a shock as I washed the mud off my face and hands, put on GI khaki under shorts and shirt, an old flannel shirt and Army fatigue pants, clean socks and my jump boots. I would miss the destroyed field jacket. I knew the supply sergeant at Fort Jay would issue me another one, but I would have to pay for it. I rolled up all the wet and muddy clothes, put them in the duffel bag, and checked my clean-up job.

I went into the office and sat down in the chair. I opened my billfold and removed a slip of paper with the emergency phone number the president had given me. I picked up the telephone, dialed the operator, and placed a collect call to the Houston, Texas, number. I was sure that the events at S & M Precision Machine would be classified as an emergency. President Truman's concern that there was a "rat in the woodpile" was justified; in fact, there was probably a "pack of rats" running around.

After counting twenty rings, I started to wonder if it was the wrong number when a sleepy man's voice responded, "It's too early in Texas to go coon hunting."

The operator said, "Will you accept a collect call?"

The voice from Texas said, "Yes."

The Cloisters of Canterbury

I said, "I am from Missouri, show me." Just as instructed.

His response was, "Tell me about it."

I did not know the man or the voice, only that the call was answered, just as the president said it would be. I gave the details about S & M Precision Machine: empty building, no employees, details of the visit to the building, gunshot on the roof, the man falling through the skylight, his apparent condition and the report to the sheriff's office by telephone. I told him about the man leaving in the red Buick and my plan to visit the Salvatore neighborhood and see what else I could learn.

"Be careful, and call me if you learn anything more."

The receiver clicked. I wondered who he was. He sort of sounded like a Texan, but what would you expect when calling a Houston telephone number.

I checked around; didn't see any mud on the desk or floor. I turned the light off and went out the back door, locked it and double-checked it. I put the duffel bag in the trunk. The clothes would have to be disposed of before returning home. I drove around the block and on to my parent's house. When I got home, Mother was comfortably seated in a chair reading. I kissed her on her forehead.

"How about bacon and eggs?" she said. Mother placed a plate on the table with two eggs sunny side up, and four strips of bacon, two slices buttered toast and homemade strawberry preserves. She joined me with two cups of coffee and a pitcher of cream. She looked at me with that knowing look. "It looks like you didn't get any sleep last night."

I just smiled.

•

After breakfast, I drove into Dayton and stopped at the courthouse to have a chat with Angel. I wanted to see if anyone had been making any comments. If so, Angel would tell me. With the activities at S & M Precision Machine during the night, there just might be some talk at the courthouse. Secrets were rarely kept in county or city offices.

When I walked into the Records office, everyone looked up; my appearance must not have been normal.

Angel came over, leaned on the counter and looked at me. "Looks like you need some sleep."

Ignoring her remark, I asked, "How are things at the house?"

"No problems," was her answer.

I drove to Oakwood to see if there was any activity at Salvatore's house. The sun had not emerged from behind the clouds and it was still snowing lightly. In front of several houses people were shoveling snow from their walks. Soon they would be covered with more snow; it seemed like a lot of wasted effort. I noticed the woman who had been so informative a few days before sweeping the snow from her front steps with a broom.

I stopped in front of her house and got out of the car. "There certainly has been a change in the weather."

"That is not all of the changes."

"What's that?"

"Just after five o'clock this morning our dog started barking and woke us up. My husband, Ralph, went downstairs, looked out the front window and saw lights on in the Salvatore house. I was a little slow joining my husband with all the lights out in the house. We watched the man and woman running back and forth to their Buick convertible with what appeared to be clothes over their arms, putting them in the trunk and inside the car. We watched for several minutes and then the lights went out in the house and they drove away, sliding all over the slippery street. It has always been so quiet and peaceful in our neighborhood. We never have had anything disturbing until those people moved in."

"I am sorry to have missed Mr. Salvatore. I wanted to talk with him about a building that he owns. I'll have to come back some other time."

"We won't miss them if they never came back," she said.

•

As soon as I was out of the neighborhood I started looking for a telephone. I needed to call the Texan. Several minutes later, I spotted a drugstore on a corner. There was a phone booth just inside the door. I closed the phone booth door, dialed the operator, and placed another collect call.

The same voice answered, "It's too early in Texas to go coon hunting."

"I am from Missouri, show me."

"Tell me about it," the man said in a slow Texan drawl.

I gave him a complete rundown on the activities at Salvatore's house

The Cloisters of Canterbury

during the early morning hours.

The Texan verified the license number on the red Buick convertible that I had previously given to him. I told him that it was still snowing in southern Ohio, northern Kentucky and that the Dayton paper had reported the snow was even heavier in northern Ohio and Michigan.

"Rob, where will you be for the next twenty-four hours?"

"At my parents' house, the same telephone number."

The Texan hung up the telephone.

I removed the snow from the windows of the car and drove back to my parents' house. When I walked through the door from the garage into the mudroom, the aroma of Mother's kitchen told me that she had been busy most of the day. Cinnamon was a guarantee of homemade apple pie and, yes, a turkey in the oven. Mother and Angel were setting the table in the dining room where we always had our evening meals, as well as Sundays at noon after church.

Mother handed me a telegram with a sad look on her face, "It arrived a few minutes ago."

I kissed her on the forehead and took the telegram, opened it, and read it aloud. "You are ordered to report for duty by 1800 hours, 21 November. You have reservations on Eastern Airlines leaving at 1000 hours from Dayton airport to New York LaGuardia. You will be expected." It was from General William Courtney.

My mother was obviously concerned.

I said cheerfully, "Nothing to worry about, just a change in my plans. I get to fly rather than having a long train ride. Let's eat."

We had a wonderful early Thanksgiving meal, turkey, dressing, mashed potatoes, gravy, green beans, and Mother's great pumpkin pie for desert. The apple pie would be for a bedtime snack. We sat around the table, Mother, Dad, Angel and me, talking about many previous family holidays until just before midnight. Dad said that he would drive me to the airport in the morning, and in view of the heavy snow, he recommended that we should leave in the morning by eight. Mother and Angel started to clear the dining room table.

"Come on, Mugs." He followed me to my old bedroom and curled up next to the bed where he slept while I packed my bags to leave. Other nights, Mugs would sleep near the back door on his pillow. Mugs always seemed to know what was going on. I didn't sleep much that night. I kept thinking how lucky I was to have such a loving home.

•

After breakfast the next morning, I finished dressing in my Army uniform and rechecked my bag. I picked up the envelope that contained my report. I placed the camera with the evidence of the empty building into my shirt pocket. Mugs followed me downstairs. I kissed Mother and Angel goodbye; there were tears in their eyes. Dad was in the car with the motor running. It was evident that he had shoveled some snow while I was upstairs.

It stopped snowing sometime during the night and the highway department trucks had scraped the snow to the sides of the roads and spread salt. The drive to Dayton airport was not nearly as slow as expected. We arrived at the airport just before nine. Dad pulled up in front of the terminal. I retrieved my bag from the backseat and with envelope in hand, walked around the car and said goodbye to my dad.

He said, "Safe journey, you are in God's care."

"Thanks, Dad."

I watched him drive away until he was out of sight, then walked into the terminal to the Eastern Airlines counter. As promised, my ticket was waiting. Now I only had an hour to wait.

•

When the plane landed at New York LaGuardia, the general's staff car with the four stars on the front license plate was waiting on the tarmac for me. Harry had the front passenger's door open.

As we drove off the tarmac and onto the street, I asked, "Harry, how are you able to drive onto the field?"

Without blinking an eye Harry said, "The four stars on the front of the general's car open all gates. How was your trip?"

"Swell. I had a nice visit with my parents and sister, and an early Thanksgiving dinner yesterday."

Harry drove to First Army Headquarters and let me out at the side entrance. I went directly to Army Sergeant Major Murphy's office and gave him the camera. I had not removed the film.

"Rob, I have been instructed to return the prints to you as soon as the film is developed."

I walked down the stairs, returned the MP's salute in front of the general's office and went in.

His secretary looked up. "He has been expecting you." She called the general and motioned for me to go in. I approached his desk and saluted.

The Cloisters of Canterbury

The general returned my salute and motioned for me to an armchair.

"Give me a verbal report on your assignment."

I read the details from my report.

When I was finished, the general said, "As soon as the photographs are ready, Harry will take you to the airstrip. A plane is on standby to fly you to Mitchell. You will fly into Andrews and a car will be waiting to take you to the White House. President Truman has been alerted. You are to hand the report and photographs to him and to no one else. He will be leaving for a meeting as soon as he has your report. The car will return you to Andrews, and then you will fly back here as you have before."

The general added, "Remember your instructions—you are not to discuss this assignment or anything about it with anyone except the president and me."

"I understand, sir."

"Good job, Rob."

I stood, saluted. "Thank you, sir." I walked to the door as General Courtney's secretary opened it.

•

Back at my desk there were a number of folders in my mailbox. Others had reviewed most of the mail while I was away but left several for me to review so that I would be informed. Some were transmissions from England.

Three hours after leaving the general's office there was a knock on my door. It was Sergeant Major Murphy with the developed pictures.

"How did they come out?"

"Six of the eight were clear and made good prints."

He gave me the photographs and the negatives for the photographs in an envelope. I examined the negatives and returned them to the envelope. Then I looked at the photographs. Indeed, six frames were clear and made good prints. The photographs clearly showed that the S & M Precision Machine building was vacant; nothing was on the floor of the building. On the back of the photographs, an ink stamp had been provided for information: date, location, description, photographer, and who developed and printed. As previously instructed, I initialed them, but did not provide my full name. The photo lab person had already signed them. In the event the photographs were presented as evidence in a trial and I was subpoenaed as a witness, I could identify the photographs. However, it was intended that I never be called as a witness.

"Thanks, sergeant, and especially for the contents in the duffle bag."

"Any time, Rob."

As soon as the sergeant left the office, I called the general's secretary and advised her that I was ready for the trip to Washington.

She said, "Harry will be at the side entrance when you arrive."

Five minutes later I was in the right seat of the single engine Piper airplane. We landed at Mitchell Field and taxied directly to the C-46 waiting for the flight to Andrews. We landed in less than two hours.

When we arrived at the White House gate, as expected, a Secret Service agent verified my ID and told the MPs in the jeep to wait at the gate. Security seemed tighter than before. The agent got in the front passenger's seat of the staff car and told the driver to proceed to the front door of the White House. I was escorted to the door of the Oval Office; it was opened immediately from inside by another agent.

President Truman said, "Come in, Rob."

By the time I reached the front of President Truman's desk, the president was standing. I handed him the sealed envelope with my report on S & M Precision Machine Company, along with the photographs and the negatives of the photos.

The president shook my hand. "Thank you very much. This is a great service to the country."

"It has been an honor, Mr. President."

I turned and walked out of the Oval Office and followed the waiting Secret Service agent back to the staff car. The trip to Andrews was the opposite of my trip in. I smiled at the attention that I was getting. At the gate to Andrews, MPs waved us through, and we drove to the C-46 that was waiting with its propellers turning. I got in the plane and before my seatbelt was fastened, the door was closed and the plane moved to the runway. Even though the trip was routine for some people, it kept my adrenaline pumping. With the special treatment, nobody could have done it faster.

As soon as the C-46 landed at Mitchell Field, the pilot taxied to a hanger where the Piper was waiting. I walked twenty feet, got into the right seat of the small plane and was back in the air on the way to Governor's Island.

The sun was setting when we flew past the Statue of Liberty. I really didn't like landing on the short grass airstrip on Governor's Island at night. The pilot approached Governor's Island, landed and taxied to the tie-down in front of the guard shack.

The Cloisters of Canterbury

Harry was waiting in the general's staff car for me. My trip had been well coordinated.

It had all started here...on this grass airstrip in a blinding snow storm that eventful New Year's Eve. If I had not been on guard duty that night, where would I be?

Chapter 3

New Year's Eve

There is a view of the Statue of Liberty from Fort Jay on Governor's Island in the New York Harbor twenty-four hours a day except when fog blankets the harbor. The eerie sounds of foghorns haunt the air, and the bells of the channel marker buoys clang continuously. Winter snowstorms can move in from the Atlantic Ocean causing the Statue to disappear, and within a few hours, dump several feet of snow on Governor's Island. After the snow melts, then refreezes, the narrow road that runs around the island becomes a hazard to all. Only a rail of metal pipe and a few rocks prevent slipping into the frigid water of the harbor.

I remembered that the weather did not stop the Fort Jay military police from patrolling the island in jeeps, with windshield wipers making no more than a feeble effort in removing the freezing snow.

It was especially cold on that New Year's Eve President Truman referred to when giving me the S & M assignment. I had just returned from Communications School at Fort Wadsworth on Staten Island. Rain, snow and rough water made the Staten Island Ferry ride to lower

The Cloisters of Canterbury

Manhattan anything but enjoyable. How relieved I was when I saw the Army staff car and driver from First Army Headquarters motor pool waiting for me at the ferry station. In the best of weather, carrying a barracks bag from the Staten Island Ferry to the Governor's Island Ferry was never very high on my list of travel options. Having a driver waiting in a staff car was one of several advantages of my assignment in Special Troops at First Army Headquarters.

The driver told me that he had a major to pickup at Grand Central Station and that he would drop me at the Governor's Island ferry before picking up the major. I thanked him for the ride and carried my barracks bag on to the Governor's Island ferry just as it was leaving.

I was glad that the ferry to Governor's Island was only about a ten-minute ride; the weather was deteriorating fast. The wind had increased and the snow prevented seeing the island. An MP in a jeep gave me a lift to my barracks. The impressive two-story brick building always reminded me of a college campus.

I carried my bag up the steps through the snow into the barracks. What weather to welcome in a New Year! I shook off the snow that had collected on my coat, kicked my boots against the metal radiator by the front door and proceeded to climb the steps to my room. Living conditions were good: a single room, bunk, a double metal wall locker and footlocker, a small desk with a lamp, even a matching chair. There was a stuffed chair that was satisfactory for reading, but I had very little time for reading. A bath was next door, just like home. However, one of the most enjoyable comforts of the quarters, other than not having a roommate, was the window that provided the view of New York Harbor and the Statue of Liberty. There was a lot of boat traffic—Staten Island and Ellis Island ferries, and ocean freighters twenty-four hours a day.

Some nights when I was unable to sleep, I looked out the window at the boat traffic and tried to visualize Fort Jay during the American Revolution. George Washington declared Fort Jay the strongest fort in the American colonies. Americans defended their land against the British in the War of 1812, firing French-made 20- and 35-pound canons from Castle Williams at the British ships entering the harbor.

I unpacked my barracks bag and neatly hung as much in the metal locker as it would hold. The rest went into the footlocker. Yes, this was much better than a wooden barracks with twenty or more snoring bodies.

A knock on the door brought me back to reality. I opened the door and was surprised to see Captain Alan Dickie who had been my commanding officer in MP training at Fort Dix, New Jersey, and now was the commanding officer of the Fort Jay Military Police Company.

Without the normal military salute, Dickie said, "How was communication school? And have you eaten dinner yet?"

I knew that the captain had something else on his mind. I replied, "School was better than most, and I haven't eaten."

"Get your jacket and we'll go to the PX."

I put on a field jacket over my Ike jacket, pulled on an overseas cap and followed Dickie down the stairs. We went out in the snow and into the waiting staff car. We arrived at the PX and both ordered a hamburger and a glass of milk.

Captain Dickie gave me his winning smile, "Had a conversation with Captain Earl Smallwood, the CO at the Fort Wadsworth School, and he told me that you were on duty a few weekends ago while he and his English bride went into town to celebrate their wedding anniversary—and that you saved his backside in the crazy ward at the hospital. What happened?"

"Nothing really, just some patients overpowered the ward attendants and I talked them into releasing the attendants. The sound of a Browning 45 automatic's slide convinced them. They weren't *that* crazy!"

"That's what I heard, and that you had things cleaned up, and they were sleeping when he returned. Most of all you prevented a major problem."

It seemed to me that it was time to find out what Dickie really had on his mind. He had paid for the hamburgers and milk, which was unusual. Normally each person paid for his own meal.

I looked at Dickie's smiling face. "Well, what's on your mind?"

"We're short of manpower tonight, with men off on holiday passes and with the weather requiring extra patrols. Technically, you are not due back on duty until Monday, and you are not required to take MP duty with your current assignment. Nevertheless, I could use some help tonight. Could we say midnight until four at the airstrip? Best duty on the island. Sit in the nice warm shack. You can even take a pot of coffee from the officers' mess and keep it warm on the stove."

Governor's Island rarely had security problems; no one had ever escaped from Willie's Castle. It was a dungeon, double iron entrance gates, outside windows with steel bars and no glass, wood shutters in winter. Whenever I walked past the prison, it always reminded me of the European dungeon scenes in the movies. There were rumors that

The Cloisters of Canterbury

they hung prisoners behind its walls during the Civil War. No one had ever escaped the island by swimming due to a strong current of water between the island and the Bowery of lower Manhattan.

The ferry was the only way off the island and military police were on duty aboard the ferry as well as both boarding points. The only other possible escape route was from the airstrip and that wouldn't be possible, especially with the snow blowing horizontally at twenty miles an hour.

The prisoners were confined to Willie's Castle, except for the trustees, who had work assignments as janitors and tended the coal furnaces in the buildings around the clock. Some were German prisoners of war and they never had it so good. Those who kept the fires going had a cot near the furnaces and were allowed to sleep as long as the fires never died out. They also had the privilege of shoveling snow off the walks and roads.

I agreed to take the airstrip duty midnight until 4 a.m.

During the war, several high-wing single engine airplanes were at the Governor's Island airstrip. The planes were for air patrols looking for German submarines over the Atlantic Ocean off the Long Island shore, at the entrance to New York Harbor, and in the Hudson River. One of the air patrols did spot a German sub off Long Island. Other sightings were reported but not confirmed. The planes now flew staff to Mitchell Field and other airfields. One thing for sure, the planes would not be flying this stormy New Year's Eve.

Captain Dickie made me feel like I had volunteered. He could have given me a direct order, but with my agreement, it eliminated some paper work for him in his report.

"The sergeant of the guard will pick you up at 11:30, and oh, yeah, thanks."

We exchanged salutes; I stepped out of the staff car into a couple feet of snow. Captain Dickie was a good officer and a nice man. I had a lot of respect for him. I kicked the snow off my boots at the front door, removed the field jacket, shook the snow off, and went up to my room. I set the alarm for ten-thirty. That would give me about three hours of sleep. I stretched out on the bunk and the next thing I heard was the clanging of the alarm.

I pulled on long underwear pants and shirt and hoped that the woolen shirt and pants, and woolen socks in combat boots would help me stay warm. I put on a long wool overcoat and fastened a web belt with a holstered Browning 45 automatic attached around my waist. As always, I slid the 45 from its holster and removed the clip; it was full, checked the chamber, replaced the clip and put the 45 back into the holster. Putting on a wool scarf, knit cap and gloves, I was ready for a cold windy ride in the jeep to the airstrip.

At 11:25 I was waiting outside the barracks. The snow was still falling. The wind continued blowing the snow into drifts against buildings, cars and any object that protruded above the ground. I did not see the jeep coming but heard the motor laboring. Its headlights became visible just as the sergeant of the guard stopped twenty feet in front of the building. The ride to the airstrip was slow; even with the jeep's four-wheel drive we slid on and off the road. The spinning tires screamed over the howling wind. Snow had accumulated over three feet and some of the drifts were six or more feet high. The sergeant of the guard knew the direction. Carefully avoiding all areas higher than the road, he drove between buildings and snow-covered humps that looked liked parked cars.

We arrived at the airstrip at midnight. I stepped out of the jeep into three feet of snow; it was almost impossible to walk. The guard that I was relieving came out of the shack and gave me his carbine. I opened the chamber; it was empty, and then checked to see that the clip was full.

The sergeant said, "We'll see you later."

The normal inspection would be once every hour and usually a surprise inspection sometime during a tour. I was sure that Captain Dickie would make more than one surprise inspection.

After the sergeant of the guard drove off, I went into the shack and checked the potbelly stove to be sure it was burning. It had a nice bed of coals, but I added another shovel anyway. Looking out of the glass in the door, it was impossible to see the single-engine planes—everything was white. My first thought was that no one would attempt to fly one of them on a night like this, not even one of the German prisoners who had been pilots in the Luftwaffe. The first rule when taking over a duty post was to make an inspection. I checked the stove again; it would burn more than an hour with the damper set. I buttoned up the long overcoat, returned the belt and 45 to my waist, pulled the wool knit cap down, and grabbed the carbine and flashlight. Opening the door, I stepped out into the blowing snow.

The first plane was always tied down about thirty yards from the guard shack. I trudged through three feet of snow and before covering fifteen feet sweat was pouring down my face. Even the snow was not cooling me down. I unbuttoned the top button of the overcoat and loosened the scarf from around my neck. Continuing a few feet more, I tripped over a plane's tie-down rope and fell into the snow headfirst, carbine and all; my profanity should have melted the snow. This was not a good idea. After some more choice words that only I heard, I regained my footing and located the tie-down rope to use it to guide me to the plane. Standing next to the plane's fuselage, I felt for the plane's door latch, and after several tries, the door opened. I directed the flashlight into the plane to check it and closed the door. With my hand on the plane, I worked my way along the fuselage, under the propeller and under the wing. Then I checked the port tie-down; it was secure.

I went to the next plane and went through the same procedure. It was secure, too. It was difficult to locate the third plane. I had lost all sense of direction and but finally located it by falling over another tie-down. After opening the door, I pulled myself into the right seat and closed the door. It was time for a break; I had been out there over an hour.

On a normal night, the sergeant of the guard and the officer of the day would have already made their inspection. If they had tonight and I was not in the guard shack, they should be driving around in the jeep looking for me. If they did not find me, they would radio back to the guardhouse and order a search. In this case, they would find me out in the blizzard doing my duty. I remembered that Captain Dickie had said, "It was the best duty of the night." After all, I had as much as volunteered, forgetting the rule, "Never volunteer for anything in the Army."

I climbed out of the plane, closed the door and checked the tie-downs. The snow was not coming down as heavy, but the fourth and last plane was still not visible.

Plowing through the snow in the direction that should lead me to the last plane, I again tripped over a tie-down. This time I was not in a hurry to get up. Rolling over on my left side, I started to get up—but something caught my eye.

In the window of the right door there was a red glow, and then it disappeared. I waited. It reappeared and disappeared again, then in a few moments reappeared. There was no question about it...someone was in the plane smoking a cigarette, but who?

I stood up, loosened the leather sling on the carbine, and slung it over my left shoulder. I removed the 45 from its holster with my right hand, pulled the slide back, putting a cartridge into the chamber, and took the safety off with my thumb. The flashlight was in my left hand.

Opening the plane's door was going to be difficult with the flashlight, but I expected the door to open easy since whoever was in the plane would have used the door and the latch would not be frozen. I moved slowly toward the plane; I did not want to fall against the plane and lose the element of surprise. Reaching the side of the plane just to the rear of the right door, I waited, heard nothing, and did not see the glow of the cigarette again.

I took one more deep breath and then opened the door, turned the flashlight on and pointed it into the plane. There were two men in the plane, one in the left pilot's seat and one in the right observer's seat. I would never know who was more surprised, the occupants or me. All I heard was a lot of German flowing from their mouths. The only thing that I understood was "No Shoot." They put their hands on the top of their heads.

At that point, I was no longer hot and sweating, but shivering in my boots. I shouted, "Don't move, don't move, keep hands on head!"

I stepped back slowly, the 45 pointed at the first man's head, and glanced in the direction of where the guard shack should be. I couldn't see anything through the snow, but prayed that the sergeant of the guard and Captain Dickie were looking for me. I held the 45 away from the doorway of the plane, pointed it over my head away from the plane's wing, and fired two shots into the air. It sounded like a cannon; I returned the 45 in the direction of the men.

Both shouted, "No shoot! No shoot! No shoot!"

Within a few minutes, the sound of a siren penetrated the air and grew louder with every second. A jeep pulled up in front of the plane, lights flashing, and in a matter of seconds, two more jeeps arrived. Captain Dickie, the sergeant of the guard and six MPs surrounded the plane, 45s and carbines pointing at the plane. Captain Dickie's German was sufficient for the two German prisoners to understand. They came out of the plane. It was obvious that one German would need a change of pants. Both trouser legs were wet below his knees; even in the cold, it probably was not bothering him. The MPs took the prisoners back to Willie's Castle.

As Captain Dickie and I watched, two of the MPs searched the plane. They recovered a bag that contained civilian clothing, two hundred dollars in United States currency, two hundred in Canadian currency, and two US passports, birth certificates, and maps of the United States and Canada. There was going to be a lot of explaining and heads rolling before this investigation was over. Someone had certainly

The Cloisters of Canterbury

been helping them.

I was relieved from my post by one of the MPs, and I rode with Captain Dickie and the sergeant of the guard to Willie's Castle.

Captain Dickie, who was riding in the right front seat, looked back at me and said, "I told you that the airstrip was the best post."

The sergeant of the guard carefully maneuvered the jeep through the snow. Captain Dickie remarked, "Reminds me of many days in Belgium and Germany." A few minutes later the jeep slid into a ditch, front wheels buried and snow covering the hood.

"Sergeant, where are you from?" Dickie shouted.

"Northern Michigan," the sergeant answered.

After shifting the gears from forward to reverse several times, the sergeant backed out of the ditch.

"Thank God for four-wheel drive," replied Captain Dickie.

The sergeant looked at Dickie. "Don't I get credit for anything?"

We arrived at Willie's Castle, the snow increasing again. I never thought that I would be glad to be inside the ancient prison walls. Around a beat-up desk that must have been as old as the prison, I gave Captain Dickie a detailed report of the activities at the airstrip.

The prisoners were interrogated most of the night and New Year's Day by First Army military intelligence officers. The prisoners, Fritz Bartels and Morris Hinkle, had been fighter pilots in the German Luftwaffe. They had been planning their escape for several months, expecting everything to be quiet on New Year's Eve. They planned to overpower the guard on duty at the airstrip after midnight, but the snowstorm had interfered with the plan. They then decided to wait until the snow stopped and the airstrip was clear before attempting to overpower the guard and fly the plane to Canada. Circled on the Canadian map was a private airport near Niagara Falls.

Intelligence officers learned from their interrogation that a cook in the headquarters company mess hall had aided the prisoners. When the military police went to the man's barracks and to the mess hall, he was not located. Several days later, his body was recovered from the New York harbor near Ellis Island.

I realized that my training had been responsible for not panicking, but I never expected to have such an experience, certainly not on Governor's Island on New Year's Eve in a blinding snowstorm.

•

After sleeping most of New Year's Day, I reported for duty at the communications office and started reviewing documents that arrived from England during the holidays. On the second day before lunch Captain Dickie came into the communications office and stood with his volunteer smile on his face.

Remembering his previous visit that resulted in volunteering for duty on the airstrip I said, "No, thank you."

Without changing expressions, Captain Dickie said, "Follow me."

"Yes sir!" I stood up and followed him, two paces to his rear, down the hall to the stairs and down to the first floor. The MP honor guard stood at attention as we walked into the office.

The general's door was open, the secretary never looked up, and we walked through the door and stopped two paces in front of the general's desk.

We saluted, and the captain said, "Captain Dickie and Sergeant Royal reporting as ordered, sir."

The general stood, returned our salutes and walked around to the front of his desk. "Sergeant Royal, it is my privilege to advise you of your promotion to warrant officer." The general placed the bar of a warrant officer in my left hand and shook my right hand.

The general continued, "Your dedication to duty under adverse conditions prevented the escape of two German prisoners who would have become a threat to the security of the United States and Canada." The general stepped back and saluted; I returned his salute.

Captain Dickie said, "May I pin your bar on your collar, Mr. Royal?"

"Yes, sir."

He pinned the warrant officer's bar on my shirt collar. He then grasped the sergeant's stripes on my right sleeve with his fingers and tore them off, and then did the same to the stripes on the left. The stripes had not been sewn on well; the threads broke with little effort. Capt. Dickie stepped back and saluted. I returned the salute.

Dickie then said, "Congratulations, Mister Royal."

The general said in a stern voice, "It is of the most vital importance that nothing about the German prisoner escape attempt be told or relayed to anyone other than the investigating officers and those in this room. There is a major concern that there will be German soldiers attempting to enter the United States and Canada. Some of them may be on lists for war crimes. It is vital that the American press and citizens not become alarmed. Is that understood?"

"Yes, sir," I replied.

The Cloisters of Canterbury

"Dismissed," the general said and returned to his chair.

We saluted, turned and left the office.

Walking back to the communications office Dickie said, "Now, aren't you glad that you volunteered?"

For the next nine months I continued the daily task of reading documents. British intelligence sent messages and newspaper articles, most of them unimportant. I was convinced that this was not the way I was going to spend the rest of my life.

Now, having completed the special assignment for President Truman concerning the S & M Precision Machine Company, I was even more convinced.

Chapter 4

Subpoena

One morning I received a document with a small envelope attached, Personal: Warrant Officer Rob Royal. I opened it; it was from Bifford Wallace in London.

```
     You need to save your dollars and
come for a holiday.
     Biff.
```

I read Biff's note the second time. It would be nice to meet Biff in person. I had been reading documents from him and exchanging cable messages with him in London for a long time.

A knock came on my open office door. A man in a gray business suit spoke, "Are you Rob Royal?"

I didn't know him. "Yes, what can I do for you?"

The man came in, closing the door. He removed a small leather wallet from an inside pocket of his suit coat and opened it revealing a United States marshal's badge. "I am US Marshal Swanson."

The Cloisters of Canterbury

I motioned for him to be seated in the wooden armchair next to the desk.

The marshal sat down then handed me a folded document.

I looked at the marshal as I unfolded the paper. It was a subpoena to appear as a witness in the United States vs. Frank C. Salvatore and S & M Precision Machine Company in the United States Federal Court at Newark, New Jersey, on July 10, in five days. After completing the assignment for President Truman I had been told that I would not be called as a witness.

The marshal explained that the United States attorney had just made the decision to call me as a witness. Someone would contact me with details and that I would be using an alias.

"I'll have to clear this with my superiors."

"The general has already been advised," the marshal responded.

As soon as the marshal left, the telephone rang. It was the general's secretary. "Please come to the office." That was the first call I had received from her saying "please."

The MP honor guard at the entrance to the general's office smiled when I walked past him into the office. The general's secretary opened his door and motioned for me to go in.

I approached General Courtney's desk and saluted.

"At ease, have a chair. I have talked with the president about the subpoena and he's mad as hell! They were supposed to protect you! You have no other choice now. You have been cleared from duty, just follow the instruction of the U.S. marshal, and be careful, Rob."

I returned to my office and didn't review any more documents the rest of the day, just looked out the window at the Statue of Liberty and wondered what was next. The following days were far from productive; I waited for my instructions from the US marshals.

•

The morning of July 9, I received a call from Marshal Swanson. He told me to pack civilian clothes in a bag and that they would meet me when I got off the Governor's Island ferry at five o'clock.

I left the office at three o'clock and stopped at the general's office for my leave papers. It wasn't necessary that I have them to leave the island, but just in case there was a problem I received a five-day furlough. Returning to my room I packed civilian clothes and headed to the ferry terminal. When I got off the ferry, a dark green Plymouth four-door sedan stopped in front of me. It was Marshal Swanson. I opened the rear door, put my bag in and climbed into the front passenger's seat.

The marshal said that we would stay at a Howard Johnson Motel and Restaurant south of Newark near Elizabeth, New Jersey, and that I should use the name of Rodger Hutton when I checked into the motel.

"Why Rodger Hutton?"

"Just made it up, that way just you and I know. You should be comfortable writing R-O and the rest should flow easy."

That sounded like a reasonable answer and I shouldn't have trouble signing the motel's register.

We made a stop for gas just after entering New Jersey. The marshal told me to take my bag into the restroom and change into civilian clothes. I was to put my uniform in the bag. I followed the instructions. Two hours later we arrived at the motel. The office was in the restaurant, which made it convenient. We checked in; our rooms were adjoining with a connecting door that had locks on both sides.

The marshal said, "This is the plan for tomorrow. We will get up at six, put our bags in the trunk of the car, have breakfast and check out. We'll leave at seven o'clock sharp. There will be a black Buick Special four-door sedan with U.S. marshals in it parked next to our car that will pick us up. Don't open your door tonight for anyone except me and leave the door connecting our rooms unlocked. Have a good night."

I knew that it was not about to be a good night. I took a shower and laid my civilian clothes out for the next day. I finally went to sleep. The knock on the connecting door was too soon.

We ordered breakfast but did not speak during the meal. I kept looking at my wristwatch. Five minutes before seven we paid the check and were walking to the car just as the black Buick pulled in next to our Plymouth. I was introduced to the marshals in the Buick.

During the drive to Newark they told me the driver would pull the Buick up in front of the federal building. The marshal in the right front seat and the one in the right rear seat would get out of the car and I would follow right behind him. I was to walk between the two marshals up the steps into the federal building. The plan seemed simple enough but they repeated it several times.

Traffic wasn't heavy. We stopped at several red lights and arrived in front of the federal building at 9:45 a.m. When the driver stopped the Buick in front of the building, the two marshals got out of the car and I followed as instructed. There were several people ahead of us walking up the steps entering the federal building. We had walked up no more than

The Cloisters of Canterbury

three steps when the sound of gun fire drowned out all other sounds. I was pushed to the ground by the marshal on my left. I saw the marshal on my right kneeling, firing his revolver to our left.

There was more gunfire from other directions. The marshal that pushed me to the ground partially covered me. When the gunfire stopped, I waited for the marshal to move. When he did not, I moved from under him. I looked at his face. His eyes were wide open; blood was seeping from a hole just under his right eye down his face. I felt his neck for a pulse; there was none. More blood was coming from a large hole in the back of the marshal's head, covering my pants. One of the marshals quickly checked me and then pushed me back down on the ground. He tried to find a pulse on his brother officer.

He shook his head from side to side and yelled, "Get an ambulance."

People were screaming and calling for help.

I looked to the left. There was a body on the ground with several policemen looking at it. There were three other bodies lying on the steps.

More policemen arrived, along with ambulances and their deafening sirens. The air was full of the smell of gunpowder. Ambulance attendants lifted the fallen marshal onto a stretcher and carried him to an ambulance. They closed the door and it sped away with its siren screaming.

A marshal and several policemen encircled me and started walking me toward the federal building entrance once more. I glanced down at the man lying on the steps with blood flowing from his gunshot wounds.

"Stop, I know that man," I said. "He was the one that fell through the roof of the building in Dayton." The scar on his face from his left ear to the corner of his mouth was red and still very visible.

"Are you sure?" a marshal asked.

"I have seen that face in my dreams ever since looking down through the skylight at him on the floor of that building in Dayton."

The marshal talked with a police captain and then they continued to escort me into the federal building and into an office where two men who identified themselves as United States attorneys and a woman court reporter entered. The attorneys questioned me. The court reporter recorded my brief statement identifying the dead man, and I attested that my statement was factual. The government had verified that the building in Dayton was empty. There had been no reason to subpoena me and it had cost the life of the U.S. Marshal. After they left the office, a policeman came in with a pair of pants and gave them to me. A marshal walked with me to a restroom where I removed the bloody ones I wore, washed my legs, and put on the clean pants, a couple sizes too large. Just like Army basic training; pants were always too large.

I waited with the marshal for over two hours. I was finally taken out a door into a waiting car and rode with three U.S. marshals to the Governor's Island ferry terminal. When the ferry arrived from the island, they drove onto the ferry and returned to the island without waiting for any other cars or passengers.

When we arrived at my barracks Captain Dickie, who was the officer of the day, greeted us. He told me that the general had received a report about the shooting in Newark and that he would talk with me in the morning. I was confined to my barracks with two MPs posted outside my room.

Captain Dickie returned later with food from the officer's mess. While eating I told Dickie all the events of the previous forty-eight hours, and the precautions that the U.S. marshals had taken. Still a "leak" had to have come from within the government. The assassin had to have received some specific information in order to be waiting for me to appear. The decision to subpoena me had been made at the last minute, no more than five days before the trial; but a lot could happen in five days.

•

The following morning, Captain Dickie arrived at my room with breakfast. After I finished eating, Dickie and one of the MPs escorted me to the general's office. We walked past the MP honor guard; the general's secretary was waiting at the general's door.

"Are you all right, Mr. Royal?" she asked.

"Yes, I'm fine," I assured her.

She opened the door and motioned me into the office.

Captain Dickie and I approached the general's desk and saluted.

The general pointed to the armchairs in front of his desk. "At ease. Please sit down."

Dickie and I sat down.

"I have talked with President Truman this morning and he is really madder than hell, and said that he would get to the bottom of it, and that he was tired of the leaks coming out of the government."

General Courtney informed me that I was being transferred to Fort Devens for the next few weeks. Before leaving, I would receive a differ-

The Cloisters of Canterbury

ent identity, and that Captain Dickie and Sergeant Major Murphy would make the arrangements. The president also made the point that the federal judge and U.S. attorneys would be proceeding with the trial of Salvatore. I would not appear as a witness.

Dickie and I left the general and went directly to Murphy' office.

"Well, seems like we need to change your appearance. Take off your jacket and shirt and have a seat in this chair by the window." Murphy had a smile on his face.

I sat down in the chair. Murphy placed an apron over me just like in a barbershop. The next thing I heard was the sound of electric barber clippers and then felt pressure of the clippers on my head as Murphy removed all of my blond hair. When he was satisfied with that, Murphy used a straightedge razor and shaved my head. I was now bald as the day I was born.

I looked at Captain Dickie; he had a great big grin on his face. "You look like a cue ball."

Murphy handed me a mirror. I looked into it and said, "I knew that volunteering for duty on the airstrip on New Year's Eve was a mistake. Just think, none of this would have taken place if I hadn't."

Murphy handed me a pair of captain's bars. "You are now Captain William Burrows, United States Signal Corps, attached to Fort Devens until further notice. Just remember not to give anyone orders while at Fort Devens. You will have a desk in a small office, a telephone, and will receive a daily mail pouch. You will continue processing documents for First Army Intelligence. We don't have time to train you for anything else."

•

The following morning Captain Dickie and a military policeman drove me to the Governor's Island Ferry. When I arrived at the ferry I looked at the Statue of Liberty and wondered when I would be able to see her again.

At Fort Devens I stayed in a wooden barracks close to the mess hall. My room had a bunk and wall locker and an office adjacent to it with a desk, a lamp, in and out mail trays, a telephone, a chair, and a locking four-drawer file cabinet. At the far end of the first floor was a lavatory and shower. The rest of the space was empty. On the second floor, there were several offices occupied by an Army signal unit.

For several months I received a daily mail pouch from First Army at

Governor's Island. I read the documents, made notes, returned the documents to the pouch and exchanged it for another one when the courier arrived.

I had considered my activities on Governor's Island boring but this "duty" was unbelievable. I had very little contact with anyone except when going through the line at the mess hall. I attempted to be friendly, but it was almost as if everyone had been ordered to stay away from me. My shaved head probably didn't help. I did go into Boston in civilian clothes on several weekends to watch Ted Williams play baseball with the Red Socks.

Late one afternoon several months after arriving at Fort Devens, I received a phone call from General Courtney's secretary.

"The general is sending a car for you to return to Governor's Island; it will be at Fort Devens by nine tomorrow morning. We will be happy to have you back. And report to the general as soon as you arrive."

Chapter 5

RECRUITED

The next morning I waited in front of the wooden barracks, my home for the last several months, when the staff car arrived
 I missed Governor's Island and welcomed the sight of the Statue of Liberty on the ferry ride. The driver stopped at the side door of First Army Headquarters. I carried my bag inside and left it by the door.

I was home.

Passing the MP honor guard and stepping into the secretary's office, missing was her icy stare, replaced with a pleasant smile. She said, "Welcome back, Mr. Royal."

She walked to the general's door and opened it; then, without speaking, motioned for me to go in.

As usual, I walked to the front of the general's desk and saluted.

He said, "At ease," and pointed to the armchair in front of his desk.

"I want you to know that the trial in federal court has come to a close. All parties have been convicted, sentenced and are in prison. You may not be aware that there were some details withheld from the public. Several federal employees were involved in the conspiracy and provided sufficient evidence for the conviction of Salvatore. There were only two deaths from the attempt upon your life—the United States marshal that gave his life protecting you and the man who attempted to kill you. Two other marshals received minor wounds and they are recovering.

"You can now remove the captain's bars and return to your warrant officer rank. It has been suggested that you continue to wear your hair short but not bald, and Sgt. Murphy has arranged for you to wear eyeglasses. It would be wise that you stay out of public places for a while. You never know who might still be out there. Rob, I want you to know I am sorry that you had this experience."

I nodded, but said nothing.

He added, "President Truman has requested that you go to Washington tomorrow. Arrangements have been made for you to fly from the strip to Mitchell then Andrews. A driver will be expecting you."

I knew the meeting was over; I saluted and left the office.

•

Dinner alone at the officer's mess allowed me to wonder what President Truman wanted this time. I didn't want conversation. I returned to my room still wondering what the president had planned for me. I set my alarm clock for six, but it was another night with very little sleep. The general had not given me any indication what my new orders were all about, only that the meeting would be confidential. I woke before the alarm sounded, took a shower, dressed and was waiting in front of the building when Harry arrived with the general's staff car at 6:30.

As soon as we landed at Andrews and taxied off the runway to a hanger, an Army staff car drove up next to the plane. The sergeant opened the plane's door and I jumped to the ground and walked to the car where the driver was standing by the open right rear door. The same driver had driven me to the White House months before. I was certainly getting the special treatment again.

The driver said, "Morning, did you have a good flight?"

"A good flight, thank you."

We proceeded to the White House. As soon as the car stopped at the gate, two military policemen approached the car and opened the door. I stepped out and was escorted to the front door of the White House. A Secret Service agent from inside opened the door.

A secretary looked up at me. "The president is expecting you."

One of the Secret Service agents escorted me to the door of the Oval

Office and knocked.

A voice from within said, "Come in."

The agent opened the door and motioned for me to enter.

Seated behind a highly polished mahogany desk sat President Truman. He stood up, walked around the desk and extended his right hand. I hesitated for a split second, and took the president's outstretched hand. His grip was firm just as I remembered from my previous visits. The president wore a broad smile on his face.

He returned to his chair behind the desk and pointed to a chair. "Please sit down. Your general told me that you had some qualifications and character for that assignment. You do not know the mixed emotions I had reading your report and looking at the photographs of the empty building in Dayton. I am glad for the opportunity now to thank you personally."

I returned a polite smile.

"Your investigation has enabled the government to recover almost two million dollars. Salvatore got forty years, but he probably will be out in fifteen. They should have hung the SOB. It was unbelievable how they put together the conspiracy, authorized invoices, and made payments. All in all there were seven people involved."

President Truman paused and looked at me, "I am deeply sorry that there was an attempt on your life. I am so grateful that you were not injured or killed. The death of the U.S. marshal was a tragedy that should not have happened if it had not been for another leak within our government. These leaks must stop!"

"Indeed, sir," I said.

"Now, let's talk about why I have asked you to come to the White House. A number of good Americans have had some concerns about activities within our government. For many years, even before the death of President Roosevelt, there were problems with the citizens' money being spent unwisely, which I am sure you are well aware. In addition, there are concerns about some other departments within our government. I am not going to talk about the specifics.

"There is a man in the next room that represents a group of private citizens. He wants to talk with you about how you can assist our nation. I only ask that you listen to him, you may have heard his name and possibly seen his picture in a newspaper. He is an honest man. To my knowledge, all of the members in his group are of the highest character. Listen carefully to what he says to you. It is important to the nation. If you agree to be a part of what they are undertaking, you will be contributing part of your life to a worthwhile cause. You will never receive any recognition for that service—only you and others who become associated with this group and your God will know."

"Mr. President, there is something that you should know, I am not a Democrat."

President Truman tilted his head back and looked into my eyes. There was a slight frown on his face. "I don't give a damn what your politics are...just as long as you are honest."

President Truman rose from his chair, walked around the desk, and shook my hand as we walked to a door across the room. The president opened the door and walked through.

I followed.

"Clarence Doud, I would like for you to meet Rob Royal, the man that we have spoken about." The president turned to me. "Listen hard, and make your decision. We will not speak about this again. Good luck." The president left through the door from which we had entered.

Doud rose from his desk chair. A tall man over six feet with gray wavy hair and a face that was well-tanned, he appeared not to have an ounce of fat on his body, only a few lines under his eyes. He walked around the desk and shook my hand with a grip of strength and control. With his steel gray eyes, Doud looked at me, giving me the feeling that he was observing my very soul.

"Mr. Royal, you've been recommended to a group of American citizens by President Truman, General Courtney, the principal of your high school, and a banker who knew you from your youth when you were delivering newspapers in the morning before going to school."

I was surprised. I recognized his voice. He was the Texan that I talked with on the telephone when on the assignment for the president.

Doud said, "Let's be comfortable and use the chairs around the coffee table. There is fresh coffee, all military people drink coffee, but maybe I should not have assumed that you are like all other military people. You may smoke your pipe—we have learned that there are times when you are preparing to make a decision you sit back and enjoy a good Turkish tobacco. In fact, that is also one of my enjoyments in life along with a little scotch and branch, as the president refers to it with his bourbon. As you have guessed, we are aware that scotch is your choice, and of the man that introduced it to you in the Neil House in Columbus, Ohio, several years ago."

I looked at Doud and smiled. "You must have been a Boy Scout—Always Be Prepared."

The Cloisters of Canterbury

"Indeed, Mr. Royal. You see, the Group I speak of has concerns about some things that are taking place in our government. You know that President Truman chaired a committee involving questionable government contracts when he was in the House of Representatives before he became our president. We are aware of the assignment that you completed for the president that related to government contracts, and I want to commend you for the manner in which you completed that assignment. The results of your efforts are far-reaching and are having a major impact on many."

"Thank you," I nodded.

"There are other concerns about leaks by individuals in some departments within the government. Many have mishandled information relating to individual citizens and with our British friends. We expect individuals from Germany, Italy and Russia to enter the United States through England and Canada. They may have relatives living here. It is possible that they will be hiding from their war crimes. It is a foregone conclusion that in many cases we will have to pay informants for the names and locations of these individuals.

"When the name of an individual becomes suspect, the name will be delivered to the Group by one of our couriers, such as you, if you elect to be a member. The controlling members of the Group will give the names to individuals within the United States and British governments that are known to be trustworthy and are supportive of our mission."

Mr. Doud stopped talking and placed his hands on the arms of the chair. The veins on the back of them stood out from the force of his grip, but his voice remained even. "There will be occasions when you will be requested to not only identify an individual, but verify their residence and other information."

He looked into my eyes. "We know that you are capable from your performance on the assignment given you by the president. We deem that it is important that the Group operate until a time when the president is able to establish a new agency or department within the government that will have the responsibility for such operations. This new department will not have any association with the existing intelligence organizations. It is possible that such a department could become a reality in the near future. However, there is a possibility that this Group of private citizens will elect to continue their activities indefinitely."

"Indefinitely?" I asked.

He gave a slight shrug. "Those who become associated with the

Group will have the opportunity to sever their relationship at any time.

"I see," I said, but wasn't certain that was true at that point.

"Consider the logic of having members who are gainfully employed, living for all practical purposes a normal life, taking vacations, traveling, involved in social activities within their community, not associated with the government in any perceptible way, and who on certain occasions simply act as couriers. It has its advantages. Unlike our intelligence organizations that are under surveillance by each other, as well as those of other nations."

Doud paused, looked down at his hands folded on the desk as in prayer. "It is our intent and objective to investigate these areas of concern, not using any investigative organization that now exists or any others that may be structured by the government. We also intend to share information with a similar group in Great Britain. Members of these groups have had close personal, business and government relationships for many years. All have had the same basic worries.

"We are selecting and attempting to recruit a number of individuals to be couriers of information and of cash or securities that will be used for paying informants for information. You also might be requested to observe the activities of individuals and transmit your findings to designated persons. Our couriers will carry out their assignments while proceeding with their normal lives. I am repeating that because your life will never be normal. You will engage in gainful employment, operate your own business, or elect to obtain a college education. The Group will not attempt to influence you in determining your life's work.

"Those who agree to become a part of this secret program will be required to take an oath of confidentiality about the Group and their activities and the names of all that become known to them. You will not disclose your activities to anyone. This includes all members of your family: parents, brothers, sisters, grandparents, uncles, aunts, girlfriends and wives, all employers, business associates and friends, including ministers, priests, bankers and lawyers. I want to make this point very clear. One of the most difficult tasks facing you and others that make the decision to become a member of the Group will be your relationship with your family, especially with a spouse.

"It will not be easy to live, in a matter of speaking, two lives. It is the consensus of the Group that each member must live a life that in all outward appearances is that of a normal citizen. The Group will not direct you into any specific field or occupation. You must be willing to travel when requested and vacation like any ordinary citizen. The life

The Cloisters of Canterbury

that you choose, as with each individual, will be dully considered in the assignments that you are given.

"Again, we want you to realize the strain and pressure this involvement will have on your personal life. Some will be more freely able to travel and carry out their assignments than others. You will be required to be away from your family while on activities for the Group. You will be required to provide misleading information about your activities and this will be difficult. You will have experiences and visit places that can never be shared, with anyone.

"We realize that during an individual's life, conditions will change. The type of assignments given will also be changed to adapt to those conditions whenever possible.

"At some time after these selected individuals make the decision to join the Group, and agree to all its terms and conditions, they will proceed with their lives until they are contacted. That time is unknown. It may be weeks or months. Under a subterfuge that fits into their lives, they will receive training and instructions for various assignments. If you make the decision to become a member of the Group, you will be discharged from the Army at the convenience of the government. Do you have any questions?"

I paused before answering. My mind was having difficulty with everything Doud had been saying. "Not at the present time."

"I'll clear up some obvious questions. You will receive cash advances so that you will always have sufficient funds for all expenses. A twenty-five thousand dollar life insurance policy will be provided and held in trust by a bank. You will have the right to name and change the beneficiary, and specify the condition of the trust and its disbursement.

"So long as you engage in any activity for the Group within a period of five years, you will have active status. At the end of any five-year period in which you have not been active you will be on reserve status, subject to call, unless you advise the Group that you are no longer available to accept assignments.

"It is possible that the Group may have the need for service of mature individuals—only time will tell. However, you are to keep your oath until your final breath.

"The trustee will determine that you are alive on January 1st and July 1st of each year. If you have not notified them on or before these dates, they will verify that you are still living or deceased. In the event you are missing for one year, the terms and conditions that you have established in the trust will be honored.

"When you are contacted to start your training you will receive full instructions as to how future contacts will be made, provisions for your compensation and reimbursing your expenses. You will receive instructions for all routine communications and emergencies.

"At times, you may be a courier delivering and picking up parcels within the United States and Great Britain. This Group of private citizens and some within the government believe that accurate information is required for making the right decisions. Some believe that the existing organizations within the government are not providing the information needed by the President of the United States and Congress. Their performance indicates that they have other interests."

"How much time do I have to make a decision?"

"At the end of one week, if you agree to join the Group, you are to advise General Courtney that you want to be discharged from the military as soon as possible. If you decide not to proceed, advise the general that you want to continue your military service. General Courtney will understand.

"After we have received your answer, and if it is positive, you will be contacted and a meeting will be arranged for any further questions. During training, you will receive instructions in methods and tactics that will be useful in your assignments."

I assume from the slightly pensive expression on my face he added, "We want you to know that at no time will you be asked to perform any illegal activity against the United States or any other country. You must also understand that there *will* be those who will try to interfere with the Group's objectives. Therefore, it is only fair and realistic to tell you that there could and will be danger for your life. Safety will have a lot to do with your skills. You will carry nothing that would identify you with the Group or anyone within the Group. You will have no authority to carry a weapon."

That wasn't a comforting thought. Then again, he didn't say there was any prohibition of weapons if the situation warranted.

He smiled. "Mr. Royal, I more than realize you have a great deal to consider. We hope that your decision will be positive." Doud stood up.

The meeting was over.

As we shook hands I said, "Thank you, sir. It *is* a lot to consider."

Doud opened a door that led directly to the hall. A Secret Service agent escorted me to the front door. The staff car and driver were waiting at the gate to take me back to Andrews.

I remembered very little of the flight back to Governor's Island. Just before walking into my barracks I turned and looked at the Statue of Liberty. The sun was shining directly on Lady Liberty. The sound of the waves against the island's shore welcomed me back. I would miss this place if I joined the Group.

•

Three days later, I was reading articles from a London newspaper when I received a call from the general's secretary stating that the general wanted to see me after lunch, at one o'clock sharp. I agreed without taking a breath.

At 12:50 I appeared before the general's secretary and she offered me a chair. I received one look from her that was without expression. Staring at the clock on the wall behind her desk while waiting for a meeting with the general had become part of my routine.

When the minute hand reached 12:58, she said, "The general will see you now, Mr. Royal."

I was already walking toward the general's office when she spoke the first word. I had been there before.

When the general said one o'clock that meant in front of his desk. She knocked lightly on the door, opened it, and motioned for me to go in.

General Courtney said, "At ease."

Slight chance, I thought.

"Have you made your decision?"

I wasn't expecting a call to his office for the decision so soon, but I didn't hesitate.

"The decision is yes, barring any information that might be revealed at the next meeting."

"I am pleased. What are you going to do when you're discharged?"

It was easy for me to reply. "I intend to enroll in college, not sure which one."

The general leaned back in his chair, thinking. "You know if you agree to be part of the Group it could be some time before you are given an assignment. Consider staying in the service here at First Army, enroll at Columbia, attend classes during the day and continue with your current assignment. We can arrange for you to head the night team. Think about that and run it by your friend at your next meeting. If they have no problem with it, I am sure that G-2 would be glad to have you around."

He indicated that the meeting was over when he said, "Thanks for stopping by." He had never said that before. It was always, "That will be all."

I saluted and left, closing the door behind me. I looked at the general's secretary, still no expression on her face. Just before leaving I paused, walked back to the front of the secretary's desk.

She looked up and said, "Yes?"

"I want to thank you for coordinating all of my trips. You have certainly made my life easier, and I do appreciate it. You are the most efficient person I have ever known."

There was a new light in her eyes. She really had a very important and demanding position. I had judged her unfairly.

Chapter 6

The Group

During the four weeks after I told the general of my decision to join the Group and wanted my discharge, the number of documents received on my desk more than doubled. Most were from England and marked "Priority." Everyone in the office was working ten and twelve hours a day, seven days a week. There were some complaints, but it helped me keep my mind busy while waiting for a call from the Group. They were to schedule a meeting in New York for finalizing my agreement.

On Friday morning of the fifth week, the general's secretary called and asked me to stop by the office some time after lunch. This was certainly different from all previous calls that had been orders to appear *Now!* This wasn't an order to see the general. I joined others in the office for lunch at the headquarters' mess. The warrant officer promotion had some additional benefits; I could eat in either the enlisted men's or officer's mess. The food wasn't any different; the kitchen was located between the two mess halls. The same cooks prepared the food, but they served the enlisted men on metal trays and the officers on china.

I would be the first one to admit that the food in the enlisted men's mess on Governor's Island was different from any other mess hall experience. Living in brick buildings with a well cared for lawn, a game room with pool and ping-pong tables, and a library was different from wooden barracks in the middle of a dirt or sand field.

After lunch, I walked to First Army Headquarters. The expression on the face of the MP honor guard told me that the general was in his office. I opened the door and the secretary looked up from her desk. "Good afternoon, Mr. Royal."

Wonders would never cease. "Good afternoon."

She handed me a sealed, plain white envelope. I looked at the envelope. It was not military or government; there was no return address and no postmark.

```
              CONFIDENTIAL
         Warrant Officer Rob Royal
         U.S. First Army Headquarters
         Fort Jay, Governor's Island, New York
```

I looked at the envelope and then at her.

"The general had a visitor this morning and when he left I was asked to give this to you."

She then gave me another envelope. This one was a government envelope. Inside was a furlough for six weeks effective at 0800 hours Saturday the following day.

"The general asked me to tell you that should there be a need, you should call this office, and also to report here when you return from furlough."

"Thank you." I left the office. The atmosphere certainly had changed.

I returned to my desk before opening the other envelope. It was from Doud. I was to meet him the following day at the Waldorf Astoria Hotel in New York at noon. He would be waiting in the lobby. I wasn't scheduled to work Saturday or Sunday for a change. The meeting would probably be to finalize things with the Group. With the six-week furlough it was more than likely, if everything went well at the meeting, the next six weeks would be training some place.

I started reading documents. I wanted to read as many as possible

The Cloisters of Canterbury

before leaving. A secretary from G-2 came in just before 4:00 and told me that she was aware of my furlough and would give any documents not read to someone else.

It was after 6:00 before I read the last article from a London newspaper and cleared my desk. Passing General Courtney's office I knew that the general had already left, the MP honor guard was reading a book. An MP was stationed twenty-four hours a day, seven days a week in front of the office.

I went to my quarters and started to organize clothing for the furlough. I wasn't sure what the dress code would be, but would probably learn that at the Waldorf.

After dinner at the officer's mess I returned to my room. As was my habit, I laid out the uniform for the next day, showered, set the alarm and was sleeping in a matter of minutes, as if I had not a worry in the world.

•

When I walked into the Waldorf Hotel lobby, Doud got up from a chair and came to greet me. It was exactly noon. We shook hands and returned to the same group of chairs where Doud had been waiting.

"Rob, I am sorry that we haven't been able to schedule our meeting sooner. I've been in London for a couple of weeks and we have been finalizing arrangements for the Group's six weeks of training that you'll start this coming Monday unless you have changed your mind. But first, you must have the opportunity to ask any questions that you might have."

I looked at him. Doud appeared to be waiting for me to say something. "I have no further questions. I would be interested in the oath that I am required to take."

"The oath will be read to the Group of twenty on the first night of training. If at that time anyone has a problem, he or she will be free to leave. Let me assure you that there will be nothing objectionable. Do you have a problem with that?"

"That's agreeable."

Doud withdrew a folded sheet of paper from an inside pocket of his suit coat and handed it to me.

I opened it. It was the oath. Doud had a smile on his face. I wondered if this was part of their game. It read:

> I agree to uphold the Constitution of
> the United States of America. I will
> not reveal to anyone my association
> with the Group or the activities of the
> Group or the name of anyone associated
> with the Group. So help me God.

There was nothing objectionable. I handed the paper back to Doud.

"Tomorrow morning at 10:15 you are to take a bus from the Greyhound bus terminal to Washington, D.C. When you arrive, you will be met by this man." He showed me a photograph of a man wearing a chauffeur's uniform. "When you recognize him, tell him that you want to be taken to the Club." Doud put the photograph back in the same inside pocket with the oath.

"You will be taken to the place for your training. I'll see you on Monday. I almost forgot; wear civilian dress clothes, and bring a trench coat and hat. Do not bring any military clothing with you. I suggest that you stop at Macy's and purchase a small non-military bag, if you do not already have one, to carry combat or jump boots, your toothbrush, socks and shorts. All other clothing will be issued."

We shook hands and I walked out of the Waldorf onto the street. My thoughts turned to questions. This was a different atmosphere, the meeting was non-personal, just two people meeting, nothing friendly. Doud's eyes constantly moved, surveying everyone and everything during the meeting. I had the feeling that my training had already started.

While waiting for the ferry to return from Governor's Island, a rusty old tugboat pushed a barge up the Hudson River against the river's current. The river never stopped flowing; its direction never changed. I thought of my life; tomorrow it was certain to be going in a new direction.

Leaving the ferry, I walked past Castle Williams—"Willie's Castle"—wondering where the two German prisoners might be. Would they ever see their homeland again?

It was going to be easy packing for the six-week furlough now after the instructions. The small suitcase from the wall locker held everything. Setting the alarm for six, I attempted to sleep.

•

The Cloisters of Canterbury

I put on a gray worsted suit, white shirt and was tying a black knit tie when the alarm sounded. Picking up my trench coat, felt hat, and the suitcase, I walked out of the room and down the stairs to the street. I checked in the suit coat pocket for my furlough papers and walked toward the ferry.

When I arrived at the Penn Station subway station, I walked up the steps and out of the door to the bus station. After purchasing a one-way ticket for Washington, D.C., I picked up a copy of a *New York Times*, a cup of coffee and a donut. The bus was scheduled to leave at 10:15; that gave me over two hours to read the paper. An empty bench near a wall opposite the exit door to the bus parking would do just fine. It had been several weeks since I had the opportunity just to sit and read the newspapers. That was rather unusual; I had been reading the morning papers for years, until becoming part of the Army routine.

A loud voice from a speaker announced that the 10:15 bus for Washington, D.C., was boarding. I found a seat on the left side, about halfway back on the bus. The bus made several stops on the way. When it arrived at the station in Washington, I walked into the station, and, indeed, a man in a chauffeur's uniform wearing a cap was standing by the exit door. There was no doubt in my mind; he was the man in the photograph that Doud had shown me.

Approaching the chauffeur, I said, "I would like to be taken to the Club."

"Yes sir, I have been expecting you." He reached for my bag. "Please follow me, sir."

In a parking place across the driveway, the man opened the left rear door of a black Packard four-door sedan. I got in; the driver closed the door, and then placed my bag in the trunk.

When we drove over the bridge across the Potomac River, he said, "We are now in Virginia and will arrive at the farm in about two hours.

Now I knew my next six-weeks would be on a farm in Virginia. I really wanted to say, "If they expect me to milk the cows, they will be surprised." I decided that smart-alecky remarks would be best unsaid.

The drive through the Virginia rolling hills was not impressive; the leaves had long since fallen from most of the trees, and except for the green of pine and spruce trees and some of the fields, everything was brown. The driver slowed the car and made a turn off the paved highway onto a narrow rolling gravel road. The ditches on both sides of the road were full of dead weeds, and dead vines covered the wire and wooden fence.

After driving on the gravel road for over forty minutes, the driver slowed again and turned in at a gravel driveway. A cedar rail fence lined both sides of the drive. Green fields sprawled beyond the fence. The road was almost a roller coaster, it would dip and nothing was visible ahead except the gravel just a few feet in front of the car. Then the road made a sharp turn to the right. After a straight stretch of about fifty yards, there was a closed, chain-link gate with a small building just past it on the left.

The driver stopped and a man appeared from the building dressed in a faded denim jacket carrying a rifle. It appeared that he recognized the car and the driver. The driver pulled the headlight switch on and off three times. The man with the rifle opened the gate and the driver drove forward and stopped.

The man looked into the car at the driver and then at me. He said nothing but waved us on. Another man stood in the open doorway of the building, dressed the same, also holding a rifle.

We continued down the winding driveway for a hundred yards or more and around another curve to where there stood a large, gray ranch house, with white trim, closed black shutters on the windows and an aged cedar shingled roof. Several other buildings sat farther back. The house and buildings were close to a mile from the road.

In a fenced area adjacent to a building there appeared to be a stable. Two dark brown horses were leaning over a rail fence looking in our direction as if they were observing the visitors. There were no other signs of life, animal or human, and no vehicles in sight.

The chauffer drove the car around the circular drive and stopped at the front door. He got out of the car, opened the left rear door for me, then removed my bag from the trunk and walked to the front door. I followed. A man in a black waistcoat, white shirt, black bow tie and striped gray trousers opened the door just as we reached it. He had to be the butler.

"Welcome. You must be Mr. Royal. I am James, Mr. Doud's houseman. He asked me to make you comfortable.

"The others have already arrived and are in their rooms. If you'll follow me I'll acquaint you with the facilities."

The ranch house's living room was forty by sixty feet and looked like an expensive lodge. On one end of the room, a stone fireplace covered half of the forty-foot wall, extending to the top of the cathedral ceiling. There were several brown leather chairs grouped together to easily accommodate forty or more people. French doors opened into a dining room with a long table, twenty places set for dinner. On both sides of the table along the walls were buffets with serving dishes in place.

I followed James through double-swing doors into the kitchen outfitted with stainless steel stoves and refrigerators, sinks, and food preparation tables that one would expect in a large restaurant or hotel. We returned to the dining room. This was the best training camp I had ever seen.

"You will be served your meals here."

Following James back into the living room and through another door and down a long hall past six bedrooms and several closed doors I attempted to memorize everything. At the end of the hall was another room, twenty by forty feet. It had oak flooring and three Oriental carpets. There were no windows in the room, just bookcases from floor to ceiling, and a large oak executive desk with an over-stuffed brown leather chair behind it. In front of the desk were four matching leather armchairs. There was a massive rectangular oak conference table with twelve armchairs at the other side of the room. There were two closed doors on the wall behind the desk.

"This is Mr. Doud's office."

This was an unusual office, no windows and enough books for a public library in a small town.

We walked halfway back down the hall where James opened a door leading into a well-lit hall, and at the end was another door that led outdoors. Outside I realized that we were at the back of the house facing three buildings.

The buildings on the left and on the right appeared to be rows of stables. The buildings were connected to a large barn building that was more than three times as high as the stables, forming a horseshoe. A fence with a gate provided a paddock and horse training area, enclosing the open area between the three buildings.

"The building on the left and the building on the right that appear to be stables are in fact not stables except for the four box stalls on the far end of the right building," explained James. "Along the outside walls under the overhanging roof are several rooms; each room has a window and the door that appears to be the entrance to the stall is in fact the outside entrance to the room. There is also an interior door to each room. In the left building there are twenty sleeping rooms, ten on each side of a long room; that is a multiple purpose area. In the other building, there are sixteen rooms in addition to the four box stalls for horses.

"Before I take you to your quarters, let's go into the building that joins the two stables at the far end."

James opened a gate in the fence to the outdoor riding arena. It was evident that horses had been in the area earlier in the day and the stable man hadn't made his clean up round. With a key on a chain attached to his belt, James unlocked a door into the large, middle building. Its outer appearance was typical of a barn on most horse farms and could have been an inside training arena. He turned on lights that flooded the building's interior. It may have been training and riding arena at one time, but now it was an auditorium with comfortable bleacher seats on two sides, platforms and stages. Numerous spotlights and speakers for a sound system were hanging from the ceiling. There were no windows. There were emergency exit signs with red lights over the two doors with panic bars on the rear wall.

"At your briefing you will be instructed in the use of the emergency exits."

On the same wall were targets; the building was used for gun training. There was a loft over half of the building that was being used for storage of hay and straw. In the area without a loft, a number of ropes were hanging from a large wooden beam. I didn't need an explanation for the use of the ropes. It hadn't been very many months since my last hand-over-hand rope training exercise at Fort Wadsworth.

James opened a door that provided access into the stable with twenty rooms. In the space between the two rows of rooms that would have been used to groom and saddle horses there was a row of desks in the middle. I counted twenty, and at both ends there was a desk on a platform raised from the floor. On top of each desk was a telegraph key for sending Morse code.

At the far end of the large building, James opened a door and entered. It was like most Army supply rooms; behind the counter was a man, probably in his fifties, with a yellow cloth measuring tape around his neck just as I had seen in the alterations room in a men's clothing store. In an Army supply room, you would never have seen a tape measure; clothing issues came in two sizes—too big and too small.

James said, "He will take your measurements for various items of clothing and they will be delivered to your room. The uniform of the day will be navy blue trousers and a sweater over a light blue shirt." As we were leaving James gave the man my room number, no name.

I followed James back to the stable. He stopped at the fifth door, on the right of the building, and opened the door, turned on the lights

The Cloisters of Canterbury

with a wall switch just inside. There were two bunk beds, two wall lockers, two small desks, one telephone, two chairs and a door into a bath with shower. Towels were on the racks and the beds were made up with navy blue top blankets. The floor was gray tile; the walls and ceiling were a light blue. On the outside wall was a space heater.

"I'll bring your suitcase out later." He looked at his watch. "In a few minutes there will be an announcement on the speakers that everyone should come to the living room in the house. Everyone will be introduced, given a schedule of events, and then dinner will be served."

He handed me a key to the room. "Nice to have you here, and if you need anything, please ask."

"Thank you," I said with a curt nod.

I looked around the room and bath noting that things were clean and not bad. I had stayed in several army barracks that did not come close. The announcement came from the speaker in the room, "Good evening, would everyone please join us in the living room."

As I passed the room next to mine the door opened and a man walked out. I said, "Good evening, I am Rob Royal."

A smile covered the man's face, "I am Bifford Wallace."

We embraced as long-time friends. For several years we had corresponded, exchanged cables and Morse code messages, yet we had never spoken or seen the other's picture.

"Biff, I didn't know that you were going to be with the Group."

"Didn't Doud tell you? He was in London a couple weeks ago and with a little pressure, I agreed to join in the fun. He told me that you were going to be a part of the Group. Rob, this is really going to be an experience!"

•

James greeted everyone at the front door of the house. A self-service bar was set up near the French doors to the dining room. Everyone introduced themselves to each other. There were eighteen men and two women in the group. One of the women, Mindy Gorman, was from Ireland, and Mary Ann McGee, from Toronto, Canada. It was an interesting group, nine Americans, two Canadians, four English, two Scots and three Irish. Everyone looked fit and lean.

During the next two hours, like the others, I talked with everyone. I wanted to connect names with faces, find out where they were from, and learn as much as possible in the next six weeks. Some were more talkative than others. Listening and watching their eyes proved to be very interesting. A few times, I knew that someone was watching me. Without showing disrespect for anyone I slowly glanced around the room until making eye contact with Bifford Wallace; in a split second we communicated. It was if Biff had said, "That's the way." It was almost like the way we had learned each other's rhythm when using Morse code.

The next person I talked with was Mindy Gorman. She told me that she was from Northern Ireland but now lived in Dublin. She had graduated from college with a degree in languages. During the war, she was a civilian employee of the United States Army Air Corps at an airstrip near Belfast. She had snow skied since a child and played tennis. Mindy had no siblings and her parents were deceased, but had several relatives in Ireland. She was studying for an advanced degree and did part-time teaching at a Dublin University. She did not answer my questions about her activities while working for the American Air Corps. My impression was that she was a very bright individual and had a good sense of humor. She said the Gorman Motto was "First and Last in War." All the while that I was talking with her I could feel Biff's eyes on me.

I moved across the room to speak with Mary Ann McGee. She was born in Hamilton, Ontario, Canada. Her father was associated with the Ontario government and was a private pilot. He owned a small seaplane, and had taught her to fly. In the summer, they would fly north to the French River on weekends to fish. Her mother was a retired nurse. When the Canadian Air Force started preparing to send pilots to England, she was a civilian employee in operations. She went to England in early 1942, worked with an English radar unit, and was now employed in the control tower at the Toronto airport. When she was in college in Toronto, she had been in several art classes and while in England, she visited the Tate Museum and became interested in J. M. W. Turner's paintings. That was when she took up painting. She avoided answering further questions about her personal life—another bright woman.

I approached a man standing alone near the fireplace, probably in his early thirties, reddish blond hair, strong features, and about six feet tall. He would probably be difficult to intimidate and didn't break our eye contact as I offered my hand.

The man said, "I am Harold Stanton Clancy."

He had been born on Galway Bay, and then his family moved to Dublin where he attended school. He had been a typesetter for a Dublin newspaper when the war started. He joined the Army and soon was back

The Cloisters of Canterbury

setting type for the British War Office in London. In fact, he was still there. He had been married, his wife died when their daughter was born. His parents were raising her and she still lived with them in Dublin. He went to Dublin on weekends and holidays to be with his daughter. When I asked him if he knew Mindy Gorman from Dublin, he told me that he had just met her.

James opened the French doors leading to the dining room. "Dinner is served, and please look for your place cards at the table."

Just the twenty new members of the Group were at the table. The conversation was interesting, mainly speculation about what they would do for the next six-weeks. I thought that it was an interesting approach, not having anyone present who was already a member of the Group. Just twenty people meeting for the first time, becoming acquainted on their own.

James returned when everyone finished eating. "In the morning at six o'clock an announcement on the speaker in everyone's room will advise you to be in the auditorium at 6:30 for forty-five minutes of physical training. Buffet breakfast will be served in the dining room at 7:30. Look for your name before being seated."

On the way to our rooms, Biff asked, "Rob, what's your impression of the events so far?"

"I think that they have already started training. My meeting with Doud at the Waldorf Astoria was different from our previous meeting. His demeanor was different. When I walked into the hotel, it was as if we had never met before. I waited for him to speak and only responded to his questions. I think he was observing my behavior.

"He showed me a picture of a man for less than a minute, told me that he would meet me at the bus station in Washington and told me how to identify myself to the driver. There was no conversation on the drive to the farm. When I arrived, James gave me a good tour of the facilities. The cocktail party with just the twenty new Group members was interesting. The two women provided more personal information than the men did. Both women appeared to suddenly realize that they were talking too freely and stopped. It may have been how I was asking questions. But what was more interesting, I learned something personal about all of them but no one asked anything about me."

"Rob, when I was watching you, it was obvious that the women were relaxed and enjoying their conversation. Why did they stop? Perhaps they realized what this is all about. Don't think it was anything that you said or did. Harold Clancy, Tom Walsh and several of the others appeared to be relaxed when you were talking with them. Don't worry about it. I think that you have a natural ability to put people at ease."

I thanked Biff, said good night, and went into my room. It had been an exciting day, and morning would arrive soon enough.

Chapter 7

Training

The next morning, as James had advised, at 6:00 sharp came the announcement: "Good morning. PT at 6:30, and breakfast will be served at 7:30 in the dining room." This was followed with military marching music.

A new face greeted us when we arrived at the auditorium. The massive body of muscle wore gray shorts, a tee-shirt with Marine Corps imprinted across the front, and jump boots with a shine, useable as a mirror.

"I am Mike Owens, I will be your physical training and small arms instructor, and we will first do a few exercises to wake up those muscles."

Everyone arrived in the auditorium dressed in navy blue pants and sweaters with combat or jump boots. It was obvious that some were not accustomed to wearing heavy boots, especially when climbing up the ropes hand-over-hand after doing a hundred sit-ups, fifty pushups, and running in place for fifteen minutes. Instruction in some basic self-defense movements allowed them to catch their breaths. This routine became the start of every day, including Sunday. It was a surprise that both of the women appeared to be in better physical condition than the men. They accomplished the twenty-foot, hand-over-hand rope climb as if they had been doing it for a long time.

Doud greeted us as we arrived in the dining room for breakfast. He sat at the head of the table, and at the other end of the table sat a new addition, Roger Weathers. Doud introduced him as the training director for the Group, and that there would be others coming along demonstrating their special skills.

When everyone had served themselves at the buffets and were seated, Roger Weathers stood and started to speak. His voice was clear, firm and authoritative.

"Good morning, ladies and gentlemen. On behalf of the Group I want to welcome you. During the next six weeks you will be exposed to some techniques that will aid you in accomplishing your assignments. Your assignments will be passive in nature, but you will receive training on how to protect yourself. Mike Owens, who you met at PT this morning, may have already started."

He slowly looked at each of us, making eye contact before moving to the next. "There will be meetings in the auditorium when training films are shown. You are not permitted to record or take any written notes. You must learn to remember things that you see and hear. There will be four groups of five for specific demonstrations and training. Each team will select a team leader of their choice. You must learn how to work as a team as well as independently be able to complete an assignment, if required, on your own.

"You will be couriers, your assignments will be to deliver and receive certain packets, envelopes, briefcases and small boxes. The contents will rarely be known to you except when your instructions require you to verify the contents. You will be trained how to identify the contact, safely pass and receive, while observing people and conditions around you. You must know where to look for information needed for your assignment. It is imperative that you learn how to travel safely by air, bus, car, and train, and walking on the street. It will also be necessary for you to know how to be safe when staying in a hotel or house."

After making eye contact again, he continued, "Just to make things a little more interesting, you will receive training in techniques of taking photographs, developing film and enlarging. You will learn how to open a lock in case you have lost your room key. If that does not work, you will learn how to cut a window glass without cutting your hand and waking your spouse."

The Cloisters of Canterbury

He watched our faces and listened to the laughter as he made eye contact yet again.

"All of you are aware that the Group does not authorize you to carry weapons, but you will receive small arms training from Mike Owens for relaxation." He paused, concluding by saying, "We will meet in the auditorium at 8:15."

•

For the next six weeks, each day started at six o'clock with a wake-up call from the speaker followed by various military marching songs. There was a reason for everything—the military music was probably to brainwash us, as well as wake us for the day. PT, breakfast, classes, lunch, more classes, break, an hour cocktail party and dinner were without change. The only thing that changed was the menu.

We watched films demonstrating surveillance and passing documents, observing surroundings, and contacting the Group, taking photographs of people, scenes and documents with several different cameras in various conditions. Developing film was a challenge, printing in a bathroom, in a dark closet and in a horse stall with horse blankets blocking out the light from the door and windows. Preparation was always complicated, as circumstances always changed. Hours were devoted to observing people on the streets in daylight and at night in nearby towns. We moved from one team to another. We repeated some of the same demonstrations and added new ones, learning to adapt to working with others.

We received instruction in using pistols and automatic handguns. They announced individual and team scores at the evening meals. My individual scores with a Browning 45 automatic were always second, with Biff holding first without exception in every weapon.

I was surprised when we were given instructions on how to obtain information about individuals and companies. But, I had difficulty relating the weapon training and learning how to pick locks and cut glass in order to enter a building without a key with respect to only being a courier.

One of the surveillance exercises in Virginia City was our team's most successful. Biff Wallace, Mindy Gorman, Mary Ann McGee, Harold Clancy and I made up the team. We voted Biff as our team leader. The assignment was to observe the activities of another team that was to arrive at a bus terminal and make contact with members of a third team in several locations without detection.

The night before the exercise, our team met and using area maps, we made our plans. With the knowledge we received about opening locks, we acquired clothing from the Group's supply room. Using Mindy and Mary Ann's cosmetics, including heavy use of perfume, we changed our appearances. Harold Clancy dressed and wore makeup as a woman. While waiting in the bus station, two different men attempted to pick him up.

The teams left the farm at different times in cars the other team had not seen before. Biff instructed the driver where to take us in Virginia City. We were able to set up our surveillance and take photographs of all their contacts from 8:00 PM until 2:00 AM without detection. I gave credit for our success to Biff, our team leader. I did not reveal that Biff had been in British Intelligence. I was the only one aware of Biff's experience other than Doud and the Group's control.

On other exercises, the teams were taken into towns where we practiced passing documents in crowded places, bus terminals, bars, restaurants, retail stores and while crossing streets. We were provided a description of an individual and passwords for identifications; other times just something specific about their clothing. We were observed and rated on our performance. There were occasions when the exchange was deliberately interfered with, making it impossible to complete the transfer and then an alternate contact was used. We learned when the contact was impossible to make, how to receive further instructions and when to act on our own.

Eight hours of sleep never existed. Planning for courier exercises in Richmond one day or night, then another city such as Newport News, Norfolk, Virginia Beach and Alexandria the next, was demanding in addition to the daily class schedules.

On the last day of our training, we had some free time. Sitting on the top rail of a wooden fence Biff and I watched men exercising the four horses stabled in the one barn. We discussed our experience during the six weeks. Biff remarked that the training was very good, and that it provided more than would be required to complete most courier assignments. We were just getting off the fence when Doud walked up.

"Biff, the horses must remind you of home."

"Yes, I started riding with my parents when I was just six years old."

"Your team assignments were well planned, and we're very pleased with the performance. Rob, you shall be assigned as the Group's contact

The Cloisters of Canterbury

person with Biff in England. Of course, this is strictly confidential. In the next few months, you will go to London to become better acquainted with Biff. You will establish how you want to work with each other."

I glanced at Biff who was smiling. "Thank you," I said. "It will be a pleasure and certainly educational to spend time with Bifford."

"It will be my pleasure to introduce you to England."

Doud shook our hands and returned to the house.

As we walked to our rooms Biff said, "We will have some fun when you are in England. I don't believe in working all of the time."

•

The cocktail party before dinner that evening was relaxed, everyone realizing that the strenuous training was now completed.

The French doors to the dining room opened, and once again James announced, "Dinner is being served and Mr. Doud will be joining you this evening for dinner. Please remember to check for your names on the table."

We had been doing this at every meal since arriving. Our places at the table changed for every meal. This required some special planning by James. The benefits were far reaching; we had become a team, and the relationships that had formed would be important in the future.

Doud stood. "I want to thank all of you for agreeing to become couriers for the Group. In addition, I want to commend you for your dedication to the training during these past weeks. You have become teams that are capable of performing any assignment that you may be given. We do not know when you will receive a call from the Group. All of you have received the necessary instructions to contact the Group if there is a need, and when you are contacted by the Group you know how to verify that it is indeed the Group."

Doud walked to the buffet on the right, opened a door, and removed a silver tray with several small boxes neatly arranged. He placed the tray in front of him. "The ring that you now receive is to be worn on the third finger of your right hand unless you are communicating with another member of this group. All of you have been given instruction in the use of the ring."

Looking at the small boxes, he started calling the names of everyone from memory in alphabetical orders. The first person was on his left. The person stood, walked to Doud's right. Doud removed the ring from the box and placed it on the third finger of the right hand. Biff and I exchanged looks. Doud did not make one mistake; each ring fit the third finger of the person.

James and his staff returned to the dining room with a cart of filled champagne glasses. When everyone had a glass, Doud gave a toast to our relationship with the Group and stated that we were in God's hands.

The team exchanged goodbyes with each other that evening. We would be leaving at different times the next day and for different places. No two members would be traveling together.

I had acquired the ability to make eye contact with Biff and understand what he was thinking. This was surely going to be an unusual relationship. I was looking forward to making the trip to London.

•

The next morning, there was no PT. Breakfast was at 7:30 as every other day, although some had already left and there were empty places. Biff was gone.

I spoke to Mindy Gorman, and we shook hands. I wondered if we would meet again. As I was returning to the stable, Mary Ann McGee called my name just as she was getting into a car. I walked over to her and we shook hands, wished each other a safe trip.

Then she asked, "How's your tennis game?"

I didn't reply. She was a nice lady, but why did she want to know about my tennis game?

I was to leave at 11:00 AM and was waiting at the front door of the house when my car arrived. I found it to be a most unusual way to have everyone leave.

The drive back to Washington seemed longer than when arriving. It had been an interesting six weeks, and I wondered if this group would ever meet again. I couldn't help but think about the twenty people who were recruited. All had agreed to join a Group that did not exist and become couriers and perform assignments that could have a far-reaching impact on the lives of others.

My chauffeur was the same one who had brought me to the farm. He drove directly to the train station and parked in front where he opened the trunk and removed my bag and handed it to me. "Have a safe journey, sir."

I wondered how many trips he had made to the farm, and who his passengers had been.

The Cloisters of Canterbury

I purchased a one-way ticket to New York. The terminal was busy with people returning to Washington after spending the weekend away from the city. Many government employees returned to their families on weekends after working in various government offices all week.

When I arrived at Grand Central station, I went directly to the subway entrance and boarded a train for the Governor's Island ferry. It was always interesting to watch the boat traffic and look at the Statue of Liberty and the skyline of New York City from the water—a view I was sure would never leave my mind.

•

The next morning the general's secretary greeted me with a smile, "Good morning, Mr. Royal. Did you have an enjoyable furlough? You'll have to tell me all about it."

"It was very enjoyable but it's nice to be back on Governor's Island. The general instructed me to report when I returned."

She said, "Yes, I have it on his calendar for nine this morning. Would you please return a few minutes before?"

I went to the office and looked at my desk. The incoming mail was waiting. I started with the first document, a London newspaper with several articles circled. My name was at the top of the distribution list indicating that someone wanted me to read it.

When I looked at my watch it was time to report to the general.

The secretary greeted me once more with a smile. "The general will be available as soon as he hangs up the telephone." She watched the light on his telephone line and as soon as it went out she called him and motioned for me to go in.

I entered the general's office and saluted.

General Courtney said, "At ease," and motioned for me to have a chair in front of his desk. "How was the furlough?"

"It was an interesting and intense experience, sir."

"I just talked with your friend and he reported that it was a successful training program. Have you made a decision about attending Columbia?"

"Yes, sir, but I think that I need to spend time close to my family. I appreciate your offer. It has been a privilege to serve under you, sir. It is a time that I'll always remember."

"In that case, your discharge will be processed as soon as possible. I want you to know that your services have been appreciated, and that your decision to be a part of this Group has my blessing." The general stood, reached across his desk and shook my hand.

I then stepped back, saluted the general, and it was returned with a slight smile.

When I walked past the general's secretary, she said, "I'll miss you, Mr. Royal."

"Thank you, I will miss all of you and appreciate all you have done for me."

Chapter 8

Goodbye To Governor's Island

The Army had been interesting, but I was now convinced that an Army career was not for me. For the next three days, I arrived at my desk by seven and read documents until six in the evening, leaving only for lunch at the mess hall or the PX.

On Thursday morning, I received a call from the general's secretary. "Your discharge papers are ready, but you need to go to the hospital for a physical at eleven this morning."

The physical took about ten minutes, and then I went to lunch with Army Sergeant Major Murphy at the non-commission officer's club.

After lunch I stopped at the general's office and his secretary told me that my separation papers would be available at nine on Friday. Things were really starting to move fast; when the general wanted something done, it had already happened.

Thursday afternoon Captain Dickie came into my office after returning from a two-week leave. "I can't leave you alone for a minute without you getting into trouble."

"Now what have you heard?"

"I understand that the Army is getting rid of you in a few days. I am sorry to see you leave."

We shook hands.

On his way out Dickie said, "On Friday night, Joan and I would like you to join us for dinner at the officer's club at seven."

"Thank you, I would enjoy that." Since arriving at Fort Jay, I had often joined Dickie and his wife, Joan, for lunch or dinner at the PX, and the officer's club after becoming a warrant officer. They were nice people. I would miss both of them.

Friday morning when I arrived at the office, my discharge papers were sitting on the desk. I read all the documents in the inbox and was finished by 4:30. Then I cleaned out my desk—a number of notes and documents brought back memories, most of which I could never share with anyone. I closed the last emptied drawer and left the office. When I walked past the general's door, the MP came to attention and saluted me. I returned the salute.

The MP said, "I'll miss seeing you around."

"Thank you, it's been an enjoyable experience working with you. I remember some of the posts we shared when we first came to Fort Jay."

Being stationed at Fort Jay on Governor's Island, so rich in history from before the American Revolution and the War of 1812, had been a privilege. How fortunate I had been to receive this assignment.

I showered, put on a clean uniform and went to the officer's club. From inside, piano music and laughter flowed out into the evening. When I opened the door, the piano player stopped and started playing "For He's a Jolly Good Fellow." Captain Dickie was at the piano and more than thirty members of the First Army Headquarters staff were singing.

To say that I was surprised would not express it.

Someone handed me a scotch and water. Sometime later, the club manager announced that dinner was ready to be served. I was seated at the head table with Captain Dickie on my right and his wife, Joan, on my left. During dinner, several stood and gave details of events that involved some of my activities that had not found their way into my military records. According to Captain Dickie, if they had been known I would not be receiving an honorable discharge.

After dinner, Captain Dickie returned to the piano. Joan Dickie asked me to dance. After we danced to a number of songs, Dickie stopped playing and stood up. Everyone got quiet.

Captain Dickie said, "Rob, if you don't stop dancing with my wife,

The Cloisters of Canterbury

you will *not* be receiving an honorable discharge, and you *will* be spending time in Willie's Castle."

Everyone in the club laughed except me. I could feel my face turning red.

It was a good thing that no one was driving home after the party and their bunks were within staggering distance. The MPs patrolling the island were aware of the party and provided transportation for several of the staff.

•

On the ferry from Governor's Island to lower Manhattan, looking at the Statue of Liberty, I wondered if I would ever return to the island. It had been an enjoyable experience, filled with surprises and full of rich memories.

My original plan had been to accept Eastern Airline's offer to work in communications and stay in New York; that is, until I met Doud in President Truman's office. Where would this river of life take me now?

I purchased a one-way ticket home and started to carry both barracks bags to the train when a sailor picked up one of the bags and carried it for me.

The train arrived in Cincinnati at 9:40 AM and my sister, Angel, was waiting to pick me up. While Angel drove home to Xenia, she attempted to get me to say what I intended to do with my life.

I practiced being evasive, but in truth, I really had no idea.

Chapter 9

Normal Life

When I arrived home, I didn't waste much time. I purchased a hunter green 1948 Ford with a tan convertible top from the local Ford dealer, enrolled at the University of Dayton under the GI Bill, and started class on June 5. Next, I opened a post office box close to the university to receive correspondence from the Group. Any free time from class, I helped out at Dad's appliance store.

Living at home was great, sleeping in my old bed and having Mugs wake me in the morning. After breakfast each morning, I drove to the University of Dayton. Most mornings Angel rode with me and I would drop her off at the Montgomery County Clerk of Courts office where she worked from eight to five. I studied at the library after classes until it was time to pick her up.

Every day I dutifully walked to the post office at noon to check my post office box. The only mail I received was a notice from the Group reminding me to notify the Swiss bank that I was still alive by July 1 and January 1. There wasn't a lot of time to think about the Group, but I did wonder when they might have an assignment for me.

The Cloisters of Canterbury

One day I had been busy with midterms and didn't check the post office box. I picked Angel up at the courthouse and as we were leaving Dayton I remembered. "You know, Angel, I didn't check my mail box today."

"Is that where you receive your secret love letters?"

"Now, with my schedule, how would I have time for a love affair?"

I turned around just missing a car, drove to the post office and double-parked in front. Angel waited in the car with the motor running. Much to my surprise there was a white business envelope in the box. I opened the envelope and removed a one-page note.

```
Please call your Group contact.
```

I put the note back in the envelope, put it in my pocket, and returned to the car.

"What a waste of time."

After dinner I went into the library and placed a collect call to my Group contact in Houston.

After three rings, Doud answered the phone. I almost laughed when I heard, "It's too early to coon hunt in Texas."

I replied, "I am from Missouri."

"Go to the Valley Bank in Dayton and ask for John Myers, a vice president there. He will ask you for your driver's license and will touch your ring. He will give you a briefcase and envelope. If you have any questions, call me. Have a safe trip."

Doud hung up the telephone without giving me an opportunity to speak. I was happy to hear from the Group, but was expecting to hear about a trip to England to meet with Bifford Wallace.

•

The following day between classes, I drove to the Valley Bank and asked the receptionist for John Myers. I was directed to his office on the third floor. When I arrived at Myers' office and gave the secretary my name, she appeared to have been expecting me.

She walked to the door of Myers' office and opened it. "Mr. Royal is here to see you."

"Mr. Royal, I have been expecting you." He rose from his chair behind the desk, walked around and shook my hand. "Please sit down and make yourself comfortable."

I removed my driver's license from my wallet and handed it to Myers. He looked at it, and then gave it back to me, pausing just long enough to touch the ring on the third finger of my right hand. Myers walked over to a fireproof metal filling cabinet, turned the dial on the combination lock and opened a drawer containing a black briefcase and a sealed envelope. He placed the briefcase on the floor next to my chair, handed me an envelope, and returned to his chair.

I opened the sealed envelope with the letter opener that Myers had slid across the desk, and removed one page of instructions along with five twenty dollar bills paper clipped to a TWA airline ticket. The ticket was a round-trip ticket from Dayton airport to Pittsburgh, leaving on Saturday, the next morning, at 10:15, and returning that afternoon at 1:45 to Dayton.

I read the instructions to myself:

```
Your assignment is to deliver the
briefcase containing fifty-thousand
dollars in one-hundred dollar bills to
a contact at the Pittsburgh terminal.
The contact is a woman and she will
probably have a male companion travel-
ing with her. They will not be aware
that you are on the same flight. The
woman expects to meet her contact in
the terminal when she arrives at the
gate.
     Inside the briefcase you have just
received is a smaller brown briefcase
that is identical to the one carried by
the woman, except her briefcase will
have a small, three-inch mallard duck
painted on one side.
     Remove the brown briefcase from the
black one and leave the black briefcase
on the plane.
     She will be carrying her briefcase so
that the duck is visible. This will be
the only identification you will have,
except for her description. She will be
wearing a dark blue suit, a white knit
blouse and have shoulder-length gray
hair.
     After making the exchange and the
woman has left, open the brown brief-
case with the mallard duck. Verify that
```

The Cloisters of Canterbury

```
there is a list of names inside and
call me. The only description we have
of the man likely to be with her is
that he is about five-foot-six inches,
one-hundred sixty pounds, and bald,
rarely wears a hat.
```

While John Myers watched, I continued reading the instructions.

```
Memorize the woman's description.
When you are sure that you have it
memorized, tear these instructions into
several pieces, place them in the ash
tray on the desk in front of you, light
them, watch them burn. When they are
completely burned dump the ashes into
the metal wastebasket at the end of the
desk.
```

I read the woman's description three more times, folded the instructions four times, tore the paper five times, and placed the pieces in the ashtray. Myers handed me a box of wooden matches. As instructed, I removed a match, struck it on the box and I held the lighted match to the paper in the ashtray, watching until the fire had consumed the paper and there was no longer a flame. I carefully dumped the ashes into the metal wastepaper basket.

Myers smiled. His eyes told me that this wasn't the first time papers had been burned in the ashtray.

I placed the black briefcase on the desk, opened it, removed the brown briefcase and opened it. There were ten bundles of circulated $100 bills. Myers watched as I removed one bundle and carefully counted fifty $100 bills and counted the remaining nine bundles. Indeed, there was a total of fifty-thousand dollars. I returned the money to the brown briefcase, closed it, and placed it into the worn black briefcase. Myers walked with me to the elevator.

There were three men and a woman on the elevator. I glanced at them, not sure what I was looking for if anything. This was my first courier assignment for the Group. I tightened my grip on the briefcase. This was an elevator in a bank building; there shouldn't be any danger. I moved to the rear of the elevator car in order to be the last one off. On my first courier assignment for the Group, I certainly didn't want to lose the fifty grand.

Exchanging the brown briefcase with the $50,000 in it for another briefcase that was supposed to contain the names and addresses of fifty individuals from Europe who were in the United States illegally seemed like an easy enough assignment. I was concerned about carrying such a large amount of money, and was curious how the contact had acquired the names. I also wondered how the Group determined the value of the names.

At the farm they had said, "For the right amount of money, someone will betray their best friend, a neighbor, and even their mother."

Leaving the bank building I walked directly to the car, put the briefcase in the trunk and locked it. While on the way to the courthouse to pick up Angel, I kept a close eye on the rearview mirror of the car, expecting to see someone following me. When stopping at traffic lights I looked into the cars next to me. At this rate, I was going to be a basket case before morning. I parked and waited for Angel. At five minutes after five, Angel walked out of the door.

"You got here early. I saw you from the window. You must be going out tonight."

"I just didn't stay at the library as long; sometimes it gets boring. Reading in the Army convinced me that the Army was not going to be my career. So far, I haven't opened a textbook that really interests me. It's a wonder that all my grades have been passing. A couple of professors sound like that old record player at Grandpa's when it was running down. It's all I can do to stay awake."

•

Mugs woke me just before six. I dressed, went downstairs, and took him for a walk around the block. When we got back to the house, the sweet aroma of the kitchen greeted me. Fresh baked cinnamon rolls were a Saturday morning event. I told my parents that I was going into Dayton for the day. No questions were asked, and Angel was still in bed.

The Saturday morning traffic was light. Most factory workers didn't work on Saturdays since the end of the war. I arrived at the airport parking lot just before nine, entered the terminal, checked in at the TWA counter, and found the departure gate. The flight was to leave at 10:15. It would only be a forty-five minute wait.

Watching the passengers arriving for the flight, I didn't see anyone that fit the description of the contact. They called for boarding of the flight. I delayed boarding, looking for the contact, but followed a number of passengers to the plane. A stewardess directed me to seat B23. I

The Cloisters of Canterbury

placed the briefcase under my seat.

More passengers walked down the aisle and took their seats. I watched as they became rather irritated when a very large man took an aisle seat three rows in front of me. The man was so overweight that he hung over into the aisle, barely able to get into his seat. Even his head was large and out of proportion to his massive body. The stems on his eyeglasses only reached to the front of his ears, not long enough to hook over his ears; they were tight and his skin folded over them. I could never remember seeing a man this big. Everyone was having difficulty in getting around him.

It was also now impossible to see the passengers seated in front of the big man. I was anxious that if the man stepped into the aisle when the plane landed in Pittsburgh, I would be delayed and miss my contact.

More passengers boarded the plane and it became impossible to see most of them. I could feel my chest muscles tighten. The stewardess walked down the aisle counting passengers. When she got to the big man she hesitated and turned sideways to pass. The expression on her face did not change. She returned to the front of the plane.

Where was the contact?

The plane moved from the terminal, taxied to the runway, and turned into the wind. Engines revved and we were soon airborne. The sound of the landing gear rising into the fuselage was almost as loud as the plane's engines. The stewardess pointed to the exits as she gave her instructions on emergency landings. The pilot stated that the flight from terminal to terminal would take just over an hour and half and that it would be on time.

Across the aisle two women were trying to out-talk each other, both talking at once. I wondered how they were able to understand each other. They were not stopping to listen to the other. It even sounded as if one was finishing the sentence of the other. It was very distracting. I finally decided that the women were afraid of flying. Maybe it was their first flight.

I still had not been able to locate the woman who was supposed to be on the plane. The flight was rough and the pilot asked that everyone remain in their seats. I would have to wait until arriving in Pittsburgh, but really wanted to locate her on the plane beforehand, if possible. The woman was traveling with a bald-headed man, who I suspected was probably her bodyguard.

Looking up and down the aisle of the airplane at the passengers, it was unbelievable the number of bald men on the plane. Most of them matched the description of the woman's companion. The description of the woman in the instructions that I had burned stated that she was tall, five-feet ten inches. How could I tell how tall anyone was with everyone in their seats? She was to be wearing a dark blue suit, a white knit blouse, and have shoulder-length gray hair.

The flight smoothed out but the pilot did not turn off the seatbelt light. I still had not been able to locate the woman when the pilot announced that we were approaching Pittsburgh airport and the cabin crew should prepare for landing. The landing was smooth. The pilot must have been in a hurry; the plane touched down and parked in front of the terminal with the engines stopped in less than ten minutes.

The passengers were also in a hurry. The big fat man was out of his seat blocking the aisle and my vision. I removed the black briefcase from under the seat, placed it on the empty seat and removed the brown briefcase. I then closed the black one and put it back under the seat and would leave it on the plane as instructed.

I was now able to see the passengers walking across the pavement to the terminal entrance. There was only one bald-headed man; the others must have put their hats on. At last, I spotted a woman who fit the description. A tall women, shoulder-length gray hair, dark blue jacket and skirt, a briefcase close to her right side and her left hand was holding onto the arm of a man, height was right, but he was wearing a hat.

Following the couple was the big fat man, who soon blocked my view. I was going to be the last passenger off the plane and didn't know where the woman and man had gone. My heart pounded. She surely wouldn't be in a hurry to pass up the fifty-thousand dollars. When I entered the terminal a woman with a briefcase was standing in the middle of the aisle looking at people approaching from the terminal. A bald-headed man holding his hat was standing twenty or more feet from her looking in the same direction. Clearly, they had not known that their contact with the money had been on the same flight.

I approached the woman from behind. When I was within ten feet I said, "How was the duck hunting?"

She turned with a surprised look on her face. My left hand held the brown briefcase so that it was visible for her. I extended my right hand. When directly in front of her, I placed my right hand on her left elbow, looked directly into her eyes and said, "How was your flight? Mine was rather rough."

She hesitated before replying, "This was my first flight."

"Your flight back tonight will probably be smoother."

The Cloisters of Canterbury

"I hope so," she replied.

Her briefcase had the mallard duck on it. She seemed flustered so I reassured her by saying, "I am going to place my briefcase next to your left foot; place yours next to it. I will hug you and then pick up my briefcase and hand it to you, then pick up the other briefcase and walk away from you."

When I was hugging her the bald-headed man started moving towards us, hat in his hand. By the time he arrived next to us, I had placed the briefcase in her hand, and picked up the other briefcase, once again checking for the mallard duck. The expression on the woman's face was of relief.

The man reached for the briefcase, took it from the woman's hand, his eyes reflecting nothing but determination. They turned and walked toward the main area of the terminal.

I walked in the opposite direction until I located an empty chair, sat down, and opened the briefcase. Paper-clipped together were a number of sheets of yellow-lined tablet paper. I leafed through the pages and counted thirteen pages with four names and addresses per page, except for the last page which had only two names. Fifty names. It didn't look like fifty-thousand dollars worth to me. I put them back in the briefcase, closed it and walked toward the main part of the terminal where I stopped at a telephone booth and placed a collect call to the Group contact. I reported the exchange had been made and there were fifty names on thirteen sheets of yellow tablet paper. I was told to call if the contact departed for any place other than Dayton.

After hanging up the telephone I walked past the airline ticket counters and the departing gates and baggage claim. Deciding that I had missed them, I started into a restroom when I saw the couple going through an Eastern Airline gate—the plane was going to New Orleans. When the plane was in the air, I wrote down the flight number at the Eastern counter and its arrival time in New Orleans.

Once again I located a pay telephone and called my contact to report that the couple had boarded an Eastern flight to New Orleans. I also gave the flight number and scheduled arrival time.

After visiting the restroom, the TWA departure gate seemed like a good place to wait for my flight. The first courier hand-off was complete. My heart was now filled with excitement and pride.

•

My first class on Monday felt twice as long. When it was over I drove to the Valley Bank and went directly to John Myers's office. His secretary told me that Myers was on the telephone and asked me to have a seat. Sit, it was hard enough to stand. I felt like I was glowing. This was my first assignment and it was a success! As soon as the light went out on the telephone line, she called him. The door opened and Myers came out and asked me to come in, then he closed the door.

I gave him the briefcase. Myers took it and put it in the same drawer in the fireproof file that had held the black briefcase on Friday. Then he said, "Did you have a good trip?"

I replied, "Yes."

Myers smiled and said, "Thanks," as he extended his hand. That was it, a cold transaction.

The more I thought about the exchange of the fifty-thousand dollars for the thirteen pieces of lined yellow tablet paper with fifty names and addresses, the more I wondered how the names got on the list. Biff Wallace had revealed the various sources he used in England, but I had not learned the Group's sources in the US. It looked like someone had put the word out: "We buy names, we pay top dollar, $1,000 per name."

The names on the thirteen sheets of paper appeared to be mostly German, a few Italian and a couple that were probably Russian. Their addresses were mostly in Michigan, Ohio, Pennsylvania, Wisconsin, Illinois and Louisiana. Who was providing the names? The appearance of the woman contact didn't provide any clues. Her male companion gave the appearance of someone who could be rough.

However, I was just the courier.

Chapter 10

LONDON 1948

After returning from the first courier assignment for the Group I wondered more and more about the Group's activities. I didn't have any doubts about their purpose, but who was funding the Group? The trip to Pittsburgh had been exciting. In fact, it had been fun!

The training at the farm was certainly useful. I found myself observing everyone on the street and in the cars while waiting for the traffic light to turn from red to green. If a car followed too closely, glancing in the rear mirror every few seconds became automatic. When looking at people, I tried to make eye contact. It was interesting watching their reactions. It became more than a game.

My interest in some college classes increased, especially those that I could visualize using. Studying harder and trying to retain as much as possible did not prevent my mind from thinking about the Group. On several occasions, I found myself observing professors as if they were a contact.

On the evening of June 20th I received a phone call from Doud. After we exchanged our established coon hunting identification he said, "You will be flying to London from New York on July 10th. Your plane ticket will be sent to your post office box. Have a good trip and call me when you return." He never wasted any time when calling.

London! At last!

For the next ten days, I checked the post office box twice a day. My anticipation was evident. I had difficulty sleeping, a loss of appetite, and I found it impossible to concentrate in class. This was not helping me complete my first year of college.

On the tenth day, just before the post office closed, I opened the box. It was empty. Starting to leave the post office, I heard sounds of mail being put into boxes. I returned to the box and found a business-size envelope. I looked around, not sure why; maybe the training at the farm had kicked into my subconscious. I walked out of the post office trying not to show any indication that something unusual was taking place in my life. The trip to Pittsburgh had been exciting, but it didn't come close to my anticipation of making a trip to London. I recalled the meeting with Doud when President Truman introduced him. He said that it might be months before getting an assignment. It could be an undetermined time between assignments. I was told I should just go about my normal life. *Fat chance!* Since then, I had wondered many times what a normal life might be.

When I returned to my Ford convertible I couldn't wait to open the envelope. It contained a round trip airline ticket from Dayton to New York LaGuardia, and a round trip ticket from LaGuardia to London Heathrow, leaving on July 10th and returning on July 20th. Having two tickets would provide for my cover—I would show the family the round trip ticket to New York, but not disclose the trip to England. Inside the one page of instructions were five, one hundred dollar bills, and twenty-five, twenty dollar bills US, plus three-hundred British pounds. I re-counted the money and started to read the instructions.

```
     You are to travel to London and meet
your English contact, Bifford Wallace,
in London under the clock at Victoria
Station between 1:00 PM and 2:00 PM. In
the event contact is not made, leave
Victoria Station and return at 8:00 PM.
If by 11:00 PM you have not made con-
tact, engage a taxi and go to the
Dorchester Hotel. Reservations will
have been made for you. Check in and
```

The Cloisters of Canterbury

send the following message by cable to your contact in the United States: Do not think that I want to live in London.

If you receive no further communications, learn as much as you can about London and return to the US as scheduled and call your friend in Texas. Do not be too concerned about your English contact not meeting you. He has been making certain arrangements for your meeting that will be of importance in the future.

This was the first assignment that would require hiding my activities from the family for several days. I was looking forward to this trip realizing that it would be important to set up details of future contacts with Biff. But the secrecy was different for me. We had always been an honest, open family.

The day before leaving the farm, Doud told me that a cover story would be provided when an assignment required leaving their families, friends and employers. I had been interviewed by Pete Mitchell at Eastern Airlines and been offered a position. Returning for another interview would be justification for a trip to New York. The Group's connection assured me that if anyone called Eastern Airlines, the call would go to Mitchell and he would cover for me. Army Sergeant Major Murphy had referred me to Pete Mitchell at Eastern Airlines and I had seriously considered the job at Eastern until the Group entered my life.

On the drive home from Dayton, I rehearsed the reason for the trip to New York. This was not going to be easy; my mother always knew when the truth was being stretched. I walked into the kitchen, placed the round trip Eastern Airline ticket from Dayton to New York on the table and told the family that Eastern Airlines had further interest. I gave them Pete Mitchell's name and telephone number and told them that I planned to stay with him on Long Island.

•

The next morning Angel and I left for the Dayton airport just after six and we arrived just after seven. I walked into the terminal, presented the round trip ticket to New York, checked my bag, and took a seat across from the counter.

The plane lifted off the runway on time and headed northeast into a bright morning sun. I remembered another flight from the Dayton airport not too long before. Dad had driven me to the airport after a snowstorm in November when I had been on an assignment for President Truman that resulted in the direction my life was now taking.

The flight to New York on an Eastern Airlines DC-3 was pleasant. There were a number of empty seats. The crew was friendly and couldn't have been more attentive. From the window of the airplane I saw the corn and wheat fields, and farmers mowing hay. The farmers on their tractors were mere dots and cattle grazing only specks. I remembered visiting my grandfather's and great grandfather's farms, watching them labor day after day from before daylight until after the sun set, not just to feed their own families but others.

I wondered what the world would do without the farmers. What would the world be like if all those who had died in World War II and all the wars before had not died? Would my efforts prevent the death of others? I had not revealed the purpose of the trip to my family, and I wondered how many half-truths and lies would be required in the future. Yes, Doud tried to make it clear that the most difficult part of becoming a member of the Group would be concealing our activities from our families, friends and especially a spouse.

The DC-3 landed at LaGuardia shortly after eleven that morning. It had been a smooth flight, and it would be several hours of layover before the flight to London. I picked up my bag in baggage claim and carried it to the PAN AM counter, presented my ticket and passport, and received my seat assignment. The flight was to leave at 8:45 that evening. Now all I had to do was locate the restrooms, find somewhere to eat and a place to sit, read, and sleep. I visited the restroom, found a hot dog stand and walked back to the PAN AM counter area.

Finding a chair out of the traffic, I picked up a copy of *The New Yorker* magazine that someone had left on the next chair. After reading several articles, I started my game of observing the people who were coming into the area and checking in at the PAN AM counter. They would be on the same flight; there were no other flights scheduled that night.

There were only men waiting for the flight except for an elderly couple who looked to be in their seventies. They both carried small knit bags and placed them at their feet when they sat down across from me. The woman had a wool shawl over her head with just a little gray hair showing. Her long woolen coat looked out of place for July. Her face

The Cloisters of Canterbury

was wrinkled and her eyes looked tired, but she wasn't wearing glasses.

The man walked with a slight stoop, as if he had carried too many bags in his lifetime. A beaver fedora sat straight on his head; white hair touched the collar of his long woolen coat. It could have been from the same cloth as his wife's coat. He removed his coat and placed it over his knees. His dark black suit showed the shine of age. On the lapel of his suit coat was a Star of David.

The flight from New York was far from smooth; the plane was up and down. I could hear the plane's engines laboring as it recovered from each fall. About an hour away from England, the weather got worse. It was impossible to locate the sun from the window of the plane through the storm. The pilot announced that we would soon be approaching London Heathrow airport. I watched out of the window of the plane hoping to see the shoreline.

It was raining when the plane descended to land at Heathrow; the wind had increased, bouncing the plane around even more. Passengers held on to the armrests of their seats. When the plane touched down, the rain was blowing across the runway in solid sheets so hard the terminal was not visible from the plane. Taxiing to the terminal took forever. All planes were moving slowly in the blinding rain. The plane finally reached the gate. It was another long wait before they opened the door and allowed the passengers to walk down the slippery steps. Attendants handed out umbrellas to passengers as they left the plane for the walk to the terminal entrance.

I was thankful for my trench coat and hat. Several passengers were wearing short coats; they were drenched with the wind blowing cold rain on their legs and up under their coats. Hats not held flew into the air; no one attempted to retrieve them. It was certainly going to be a rainy day in London town. The pilot had said before landing that it was raining all over England, Scotland and Ireland. Nevertheless, I was still looking forward to this adventure.

While waiting inside the terminal, looking out of the window, I was barely able to see the plane and the baggage handlers unloading the bags. I followed the signs to baggage claim and waited for my suitcase. The waiting passengers were wet. The elderly couple that I observed in New York wearing their long woolen coats appeared to be dryer than others.

When the elderly man with the black fedora hat and long wool coat picked up their two bags, he looked at me and said, "Shalom."

My bag arrived, wet but showing no sign of damage. I picked it up and followed those walking in the direction of customs. I put my passport on the counter and was greeted with "Welcome to England" by a man in his mid-forties. He looked at the passport photo and then at me and said, "Have a good visit, Yank," and stamped the passport.

It was not difficult to find the directions to transportation; just follow the wet crowd going out to the lines of buses and taxis. Most of the passengers from the plane were taking the bus. I elected to take a taxi. Being crammed in a bus with wet folks didn't seem too inviting. Besides, I hoped to see more from the taxi windows than from a crowded bus. After walking through the rain and dodging puddles of water to the first taxi in line, a driver lowered the left front window of the taxi.

"Where to, Gov'nor?"

"Victoria Station."

"It's going to be a slow trip with this blimey weather."

I had arrived at Heathrow airport not knowing what to expect. It was obviously not like the airports in the United States. Heathrow had been the Croydon airport, a civil airport for London, until May of 1946. When the plane was approaching the airport, I was unable to see any signs of the war. From the windows of the taxi, buildings were damaged and others that had been leveled during the bombing of Britain were impossible to escape my view. Pictures published in newspapers and in the newsreels at the movie theaters at home did not prepare me for what I saw.

Britain had furnished most of the intelligence information for the Americans for the European theatre of operations. Their intelligence service was well established and reliable. Without it, the war in Europe would not have ended when it did, and the Americans would have had many more casualties. All that I could think about was the poor people of Britain.

How fortunate I was to live in the United States. Yes, many American lives had been lost, but the war hadn't been fought on American soil. I still vividly remembered Sunday, December 7, 1941, when Japan attacked Pearl Harbor. I was at my parents' home just starting to go upstairs when President Roosevelt's voice came over the radio announcing the attack on Pearl Harbor.

This was my first visit to London, but I knew it would not be the last. Looking at the destruction from the taxi and listening to the taxi driver describe how he and his family had survived sounded worse than the news that reached the United States.

The taxi stopped at what appeared to be the main entrance to Victoria Station. I paid the driver and walked into the station. There was no glass in the windows; they were covered with old boards. It was impossible to count all of the pigeons on the floor and flying around inside the station. I walked around and eventually located the big clock where Biff was supposed to meet me. About twenty feet away from the clock where everyone approaching could be seen, I put my suitcase down and sat down on it.

Biff was an interesting man. He grew up in Scotland, had many connections there, not only family, but also friends that he could call on.

On this visit to London, Biff and I were to work out the details of how we were going to operate for the Group between the United States and England. The Group's concern about information leaking from within both governments was alarming.

Biff, through his association with British Intelligence and Scotland Yard, and through his undisclosed sources, would collect names of individuals with certain backgrounds that indicated possible danger to both governments. Biff and I would pass these names and other information that might be of interest to the two governments.

I was to become acquainted with England, especially London, so that I would be comfortable working alone. On occasion Biff would act as my chauffeur or taxi driver providing a good cover for our courier activities. There was a concern for protection of the Group's courier, especially when delivering American dollars to informants for information.

We were to establish various signals, body gestures, and other codes that only Biff and I would know. The rings given us at the farm would provide initial identification with other members of the Group, but other identifying means were required, depending on the assignment.

The concern for not talking in one's sleep was understandable, as well as not consuming excessive alcoholic beverages. The Group probably used the cocktail parties every evening at the farm to observe our drinking habits, although previous background checks had been made before we were recruited.

Biff was also to establish a safe house that I would use when on assignment in London. It was to be located within walking distance of Victoria Station.

As soon as the airlines established better schedules between New York and London, I would make frequent trips from New York to London and back within two to three days, meeting Biff, delivering and picking up information. The Group was to know my location twenty-four hours a day. I had a telephone number to report my daily activities and another number for emergency use only, and a special code for those occasions.

While waiting for Biff to show up, I watched workers removing debris hanging from the ceiling of the station and wondered if they would ever be able to clean the soot and dust that covered the walls and filled every crack and crevice. The workers swept and shoveled everything not attached into wheelbarrows and dumped them in piles. I thought about how clean New York's Grand Central and Penn Stations were, and free from the scars of war. American streets were not lined with bombed and burned-out homes and buildings.

A London police officer stopped in front of me.

I said, "Good afternoon, officer."

He cocked his head to the side with a questionable look, "Where you from, Yank?"

"Ohio," I responded.

A smile came to his face, "That's Indian country?"

"Yes, but a long time ago."

"What are you doing?" he asked.

"I have been watching how hard the men are working. They all seem to be rushing. "

The policeman said, "Yes, they are preparing London for the 14th Olympic Games that will open on July 29th."

My first reaction was how the English people could even think about hosting such an event. The next thought was that it would be impossible for them to be ready. Then I remembered Winston Churchill's statement, "We'll fight them with pitch forks and we'll never, never, never give up." The English people were determined.

The police officer walked away and I continued watching the people in the station. They all appeared to have a purpose, some place to go and wanted to be there on time. Occasionally, one of the workers rolled a cigarette, took a few puffs, knocked the fire off the end, and put the dead cigarette into his jacket pocket. I didn't hear anyone call that it was break time.

I noticed a man coming into view. He paused, and looked slowly around, not letting his eyes stop at any one place or person. He was too far away for me to see the features of his face, but I was almost sure it was Biff. Six weeks at the farm, watching and listening to Biff, I had learned a lot about the man.

The man continued his approach, observing everything around him.

The Cloisters of Canterbury

If need be, this man could describe in detail every person in the station and probably every pigeon. As he came closer, I knew it was Biff.

We made eye contact.

He turned his head to the right for a fraction of a second, changed his direction and walked out the entrance that led to the taxi's queue. I looked at my wristwatch, counted to sixty, stood up, looked around in all directions, picked up my suitcase and walked out the same exit that Biff used.

Biff had acknowledged and given me instructions in that moment just as we had practiced at the farm. I walked past the line of taxis and spotted Biff in the driver's seat of the fourth taxi. I recounted the taxis and walked up to the queue point and stepped in behind the third person in line just before another person arrived.

When I reached the taxi that Biff was driving, we made eye contact.

"Where to, Gov'nor?"

"Dorchester Hotel."

I opened the left rear door of the taxi and set my suitcase on the floor, got in and closed the door. Without saying a word, Biff drove away from the station. We did not speak until Biff had driven as least two blocks.

"How was your flight?"

"Long and rough," I replied.

Biff drove down several blocks, made several turns, then made a right on Belgrade and drove back past Victoria Station. He drove slowly for the next six blocks, naming the streets as we passed, referenced a large open area as a park fronted on three sides by flats, made a right turn on Warwick Way, drove two blocks, made a right turn on Warwick Place North and stopped in front of a row of brick buildings.

I looked out of the car window at the dirty two-story brick building. There were several units, about twenty feet each in width, all connected. There were no windows on the ground floor facing the street. The two doors side by side in front would indicate that there were two units every forty feet or so. In the United States they would be called duplexes.

"Biff, what do we have here?"

"These are flats."

I looked up at the buildings. On the second floor facing the street there were four French-style windows with rusty iron bars covering them. From the street, the roof appeared to be flat. There was evidence of work on these two particular flats; they were cleaner than other buildings. Many buildings in the neighborhood showed no sign of repair—no evidence of bomb damage from the blitz, it was just neglect. I understood that property owners couldn't be expected to do very much maintenance when a bomb could level the building at any time.

I looked both ways down Warwick Way; it certainly was not an upscale neighborhood. Everything was covered with soot from years of coal smoke. In years past, the wooden doors and window trim probably had been white.

Biff turned to me, the expression on his face indicated that he had read my mind.

"This is our safe house. You won't be staying here tonight, but if everything goes well, you will on your next visit, if it's not too soon. When material becomes available, repairs and several modifications are planned. The location is within walking distance of Victoria Station and can be approached from four different directions. The buildings in the neighborhood are mostly flats. These buildings were constructed after World War I. The original proprietors or their families have operated several of the neighborhood shops and pubs since they first opened."

I was relieved that my first night in London was not to be in one of these buildings. The street was cluttered with trash, and on the front step of the building sat a very large brown rat. Several others were exploring the garbage. I didn't know when my next visit would be to London, but I was hoping that it wouldn't be too soon. I hated rats!

Biff led the way up the steps of the safe house. The big brown rat on the step looked at me, then jumped off the step and slowly moved along the sidewalk. Biff opened the door and we went in. In the first room the wooden floors had been refinished, the walls and ceiling painted, and the kitchen was being remodeled. We went back into the large room and up the wooden steps to the second floor. There were two bedrooms separated by a bath, everything was in various stages of repair. We returned to the first floor and went out the front door. The rats had not been disturbed.

Biff started the motor of the old taxi. Black smoke billowed out of the tailpipe as we drove down the street for two blocks, pulled to the curb on the left side of the street and parked in front of a pub.

The smoke-filled pub was dimly lit, almost impossible to see if booths along the wall were empty or not. I heard Biff's voice and followed it to where he was standing by an empty booth. After my eyes adjusted to the lighting, I saw that all of the stools in front of the bar were occupied. At one end of the bar was a glass display case with several different prepared foods. Steam was seeping up around the metal containers.

"Rob, I suggest the shepherd's pie and half-pint of Guinness."

"I've never experienced shepherd's pie or Guinness, but I am willing to try as long as you take the first bite and swallow."

I watched as Biff went to the open space at the bar reserved for ordering. The expression on the bartender's face indicated that Biff had been there before. He returned with a tray, the Guinness and two dinner plates with large servings of shepherd's pie.

"Rob, shepherd's pie is made with lamb, gravy, mixed vegetables with lots of peas and carrots, covered with creamed potatoes, they're mashed potatoes to you Yanks."

I found the shepherd's pie to be a very enjoyable and the Guinness was different and flavorful. I would order both again.

We left the pub and returned to the old black taxi, the black smoke still bellowing out of the exhaust as Biff started my tour of London that would eventually take several days. Whenever coming to London, I would normally be arriving at Victoria from Heathrow and would need to know how to reach several places from Victoria Station. Finding Westminster Abby and the British Foreign Office would not be a problem, but the Bank of England at Old Broad Street and Princess Street would be more difficult.

After four hours of riding around London, Biff said, "It's time to check in at the Dorchester Hotel. It's on Park Lane."

He parked on the street a block from the hotel. We carried our bags to the hotel and checked in. Our rooms were adjoining on the third floor.

At seven, Biff knocked on my door and we returned to the lobby and had dinner in the dining room. After dinner, we walked around the streets of London for over an hour before returning to the hotel.

•

Early the next morning after breakfast Biff said, "We are going to drive to Canterbury, I want you to see the cathedral, but of more importance, I want you to meet Rev. Ferdie Filpin. I met him during the war and we have become friends."

The drive from London through the country southeast of London was a delightful experience. I received a history lesson at every turn in the road. Even if I had studied English history, very little of what Biff was showing and telling me would have been in any textbook.

Biff stopped the car on a hill overlooking a valley. In the distance the Canterbury Cathedral was visible, a breath-taking view. As we stood by the car, Biff talked about the priest that we were to meet. He was born in Wales and educated there. He became a priest, was a chaplain in the Army, and had been in the Canterbury Diocese since the war.

We parked a short distance from the cathedral. There was damage to it during the blitz in 1941, and most of it had not been repaired.

We walked to the Chaucer Hotel on Ivy Lane where Biff had arranged to meet Rev. Filpin at noon. It was five minutes after twelve. The Reverend was waiting at the front door. I was promptly introduced to the priest, who then led the way to a table by the fireplace.

During our meal I learned that Biff had met the priest in early 1941. They had been together several times during the war. In 1945, at Buckingham Palace, King George VI decorated Rev. Filpin with the Military Cross "for conspicuous gallantry in rescuing wounded under heavy mortar and machine-gun fire in Wadi Akarit, Tunisia, in 1943." At the same time, Bifford A. Wallace also received a medal. I did not learn what medal. When I asked Biff about it, he acted as if he had not heard me and proceeded to talk about Canterbury.

After lunch, we were given a personal tour of the cathedral. Rev. Filpin had a fantastic knowledge of church history from the architecture to its most memorable events. He stopped for silent prayers near the place where the knights of King Henry VIII killed Thomas Becket in 1170. The afternoon had gone too fast as Rev. Filpin walked with us back to the car.

What an extraordinary man in an extraordinary place!

•

The following day Biff drove the old taxi to Stonehenge on the Salisbury plain. As we walked around the huge, mystical stones, Biff gave his version of the mystery of how the stones were moved to the place and their purpose.

He said, "My version has not been acknowledged or published yet."

The stones gave me a strange, eerie feeling that I was having trouble shaking off.

In the remaining days, Biff drove me around London pointing out more sights than I could possibly retain. The evenings were devoted to reading names and articles that I would take back to the Group. When we ate in pubs and walked on the streets of London, Biff continued to instruct me in the observations of people and how we would communicate with each other.

Every evening we attended Evensong at Westminster Abby. Biff wanted me to be well acquainted with the Abby, as it would be one of the Group's contact locations. There could be occasions that Biff would not be available and I would have to make contact with others.

We visited the Bank of England where Biff introduced me to an officer in the bank who would provide financial assistance if needed. Another interesting introduction was a man in the British Foreign Office who was available in case of an emergency that could not be addressed by others.

A visit to Jayems tobacco shop on Victoria was a delight. I purchased a Peterson briar pipe and a pound of pipe tobacco recommended by one of Biff's friends employed in the shop for many years.

Overall, my first visit to England had been interesting, informative and rewarding. I would not hesitate to visit London alone. London was more difficult to get around in than New York, but I had a good feel for the directions needed.

•

Biff drove me to Heathrow for my return flight to New York. I got out of the old cab and Biff removed my bag from the boot and handed it to me.

"Have a good flight, friend, I'll see you soon."

"Thanks, Biff, I appreciate this time with you. I hope that I am able to retain what I've seen, and especially what you have shared with me. The visit to Canterbury and meeting Rev. Filpin was a privilege. And, Biff, thanks for the history lessons."

We gave each other a bear hug. I watched Biff drive away and then walked into the terminal, checked in and found a seat near the gate. While waiting I thought about all the many quaint and historic places I had seen.

On the flight back to New York, I slept until the voice of the pilot announced the approach to LaGuardia. I was one of the first passengers off the plane at the gate.

I checked in at the Eastern counter for my flight to Dayton; it would leave in an hour. I called Angel at the records office and asked her to meet me at the airport after work. I waited in a chair near the gate.

When they called for boarding, I watched everyone else board the plane before walking up the steps and found my seat in the fifth row. The seat next to mine was vacant.

On the flight, I started making notes for my report to the Group. In all probability, my next trip to London would be very different. I would fly to London Heathrow airport from New York. Biff would meet me in the terminal, we would exchange information and I would return on the next flight to New York. Biff and I had planned how we would be able to meet for short periods at the airport without arousing any undue suspicion.

With approval of the Group, I would form an import-export company. I would naturally represent the company in exploring business opportunities in England. Solicitor Bifford Wallace would provide legal advice in England. Therefore, frequent visits would be justified.

Angel was waiting in my car in front of the Dayton airport terminal.

I walked around the car and said, "Since there are no dents, it will probably be safe to ride with you. You drive."

On the drive from the airport, I had difficulty answering Angel's questions without being rude. I tried to ask her as many questions about what she had been doing to prevent her from asking questions.

This was not going to be easy.

Chapter 11

Normal Life

After returning to Ohio from London, I found it difficult adjusting to college life. Ten days in England and getting to know Biff Wallace better was not only stimulating, but also a fascinating experience to say the least. Biff's introduction to London gave me a history lesson and a deep appreciation for the English people and the ravages of war on a country. I was sure that the pictures of the dead bodies in the concentration camps would never be erased from my mind. Unfortunately, I was having all of these experiences and would not be able to share them with anyone, which was difficult.

The next days, weeks and months went by quickly.

Attending school year round was something less than enjoyable, but I would graduate in three years. I had received approval from the Group to form the import-export company called Midwest American Imports. I made frequent trips to London, flying from Dayton to New York to London Heathrow and met Biff at the terminal. We exchanged courier pouches and spent a few hours together reviewing the names of the Germans that Biff knew had acquired false documents to enter Canada and the United States.

Other courier trips were even more demanding. After class on Fridays I would drive from Dayton to Chicago and check into the Sheridan Hotel on Michigan Ave. There, I would wait for a telephone call, meet a contact, pick up a briefcase, go to O'Hara airport, fly to San Francisco, meet the contact, exchange pouches or briefcases, fly back to Chicago and then drive back to Dayton. It was exhausting but exciting nevertheless.

After graduation in June, I helped my dad who was encouraging me to continue working with him in the shop. It was his hope that I would some day take over the business. Thankfully, my family never asked any questions about my long weekends. Angel always had that know-it-all look on her face, but she never pressed me for an explanation.

I had several job interviews with companies. However, no one expressed any unusual interest, nor did I find them interesting, except for a consulting firm in Cleveland. They were looking for accountants for their audit department. Graduate school held no interest for me. I certainly did not want to teach. I'd taken several law courses, but was not interested in becoming a lawyer.

One day while working in the appliance store I answered the telephone. A woman asked about a new refrigerator that was on display in the front window of the store. I described it to her and gave her the price.

She replied, "We would like to buy it and have it delivered as soon as possible. We have a new baby and the existing refrigerator is not working."

I asked, "Have you called a serviceman?"

She said, "No, that wasn't necessary. It was really an icebox."

She further indicated that she couldn't leave her baby or bring the baby with her since it had a cold. Her husband wouldn't be home until after seven that evening and the store closed at six. I covered the phone and confirmed with my dad if the refrigerator was available.

I asked the woman if it would be convenient for me to stop by at seven-thirty that evening to complete the sales agreement and arrange for delivery. This was agreeable; she gave me her address and telephone number. The address was in southeast Dayton. An order out of town was not unusual in view of the shortage of new refrigerators. Many stores had waiting lists. In fact, my dad's store normally did, but the last one on the list had cancelled.

I arrived at the address in southeast Dayton. It was a residential neighborhood of older homes. It was starting to get dark, but I had no difficulty locating the numbers above the mailbox on the front of the house. I parked, walked to the door, and announced my arrival with the brass doorknocker. A porch light turned on and the door opened.

An elderly man greeted me with an unemotional face. "Yes?"

I was rather surprised for I had expected a younger man. I gave him the woman's name and the reason I was there. Without a change of expression the elderly man directed me to a side entrance.

I walked around the house and used a similar doorknocker. Another man opened the door which led upstairs to the second floor. The man shook his head slightly and covered his mouth with his fingers.

I recognized him from the farm. He had been in the Group's training. I loudly gave the purpose of my visit.

He introduced himself. "I am Ted Walsh."

I had not connected the woman's last name with the Group. I followed him up the stairs and met his wife, the woman on the telephone. They proudly introduced their infant daughter.

She offered tea, which I accepted. They explained that the man on the first floor was her uncle and that her aunt had recently died. They had agreed to live in the apartment while Ted, who worked for a consulting firm in Cleveland, was on assignment in Dayton at Patterson Field.

I asked, "What's the name of the firm?"

He replied, "James Allen & Associates."

It was the same firm that had interviewed me two months before. Ted's eyes told me that he was aware of my interview.

I asked how they happened to be looking in an appliance store window in Xenia. Ted's wife said that the baby had been restless and would sleep when riding in the car. They had just been driving around the previous Sunday afternoon in Xenia when they noticed the refrigerator in the window of the appliance store. On their way home, Ted had suggested that she call.

Ted was trying to tell me something with his eyes.

I provided some general information about the Frigidaire refrigerator and restated the price that I had given to Ted's wife on the telephone. They agreed that they wanted it. Ted wrote a check for the amount. I thanked them for their purchase and looked at the baby sleeping in her mother's arms. What a beautiful sight.

Ted walked down the stairs with me and to the car. "Rob, I overheard a conversation at the office, and they are going to offer you a job. They are not aware that I know you. And it was not an accident that we stopped at your father's appliance store. Yes, we were going to purchase a refrigerator anyway. The Group is aware of my association with the firm and they should be made aware of their interest in you. And I wanted you to know that I was working for them."

We agreed that if the firm did make me an offer, that I should advise the Group prior to making a decision.

The refrigerator was delivered the next afternoon, and two days later, I stopped to check on it. Ted's wife and baby were just leaving for a walk, and the baby was in a stroller. She told me that the refrigerator was wonderful—no more running out of ice, and that Ted was at a meeting in Cleveland and would be back on Friday.

On the next Friday, I received a letter from James Allen & Associates inviting me to return on the following Monday for another interview. If I still had an interest in a position with them, they would appreciate a telephone call to confirm the meeting. It was now time for me to call the Group and advise them of the contact with Ted Walsh and share the fact that I had been interviewing with the same firm.

I made a collect call to the Group's Houston telephone number. "It's too early to hunt coon in Texas." It was Doud's voice.

"I am from Missouri, show me." It still sounded like a kid's game to me. I gave him all the details about making application with the Cleveland firm and my conversation with Ted Walsh.

Doud asked me to call back the next day.

The following afternoon, I called back and Doud told me that if offered a position that I wanted to accept, the Group would have no objections. However, it was important that I keep him informed.

I made the call to Cleveland and agreed to be there on Monday morning. This would mean driving to Cleveland on Sunday.

•

The drive to Cleveland was long, but I had time to think about many things. I wondered where this particular trip would be leading me.

The meeting with the consulting firm was interesting; two different department managers interviewed me before lunch. Lunch was in a small restaurant near the office building with the two department managers, three staff managers as well as the senior vice president, Joseph Davidson. Conversation was light, but directed to the various assignments they had with several major American corporations within the

The Cloisters of Canterbury

United States and Europe, and with several branches of the United States government. They asked about my early years and military service. I inquired about their various consulting assignments and received informative answers.

After lunch, Davidson informed me that James Allen, president of the firm, wanted to meet me. In the meeting, Mr. Allen expressed his desire that I join the firm and that the staff was interested in having me join their *group*.

Lights went on in my brain—it was the way that Allen said "group," the look in his green eyes, and the way he shook my hand. It reminded me of previous meetings with Doud. I followed Davidson back to his office. He offered me a chair facing a north-west window with a view of Lake Erie.

Davidson sat in a red leather chair behind a mahogany desk. He opened a folder on the top of the desk and removed the documents. "This is a contract that you should read."

The contract provided for employment as a management consultant for a period of one year. It was renewable at the end of twelve months, with the mutual agreement of both parties. When on assignment out of the geographical Cleveland area, a per diem would be paid and a mileage auto allowance. In the event of foreign travel, airfare would be prepaid and all necessary expenses. I would have two weeks paid vacation after the first twelve months of employment. I would be assigned to the audit department in the Cleveland office.

I read the contract over three times. It covered everything—confidentiality, auto insurance coverage, dress code; dark blue or gray suit, white shirt, dark maroon or blue tie, knit ties were acceptable. The provisions for resignation and termination were fair.

Trying not to show my surprise and joy of the terms of the agreement, especially the salary, I told the senior vice president that I was interested in becoming a member of their firm.

Davidson replied that they all would be pleased to hear of my decision and requested that I start on the first day of September. There was no reason why that wouldn't be possible. As I was leaving the office, Davidson asked his secretary to give me the address of several places to consider for temporary housing.

I drove past three of the addresses. When I drove past the fourth, I turned around and pulled into the driveway of a two-story home just two blocks from Lake Erie in Bay Village. I knew that this would be my home.

I knocked on the door, opened by a lovely woman, probably in her early sixties.

She greeted me, "I am Mrs. Gray," as if she was expecting me.

She showed me through her home and upstairs to a nice room on the front of the house with a bath. I paid a month's rent in advance. Just as I was leaving, she said, "Say hello to Shirley."

It was obvious the firm had made prior arrangements, probably with all four places. They certainly were taking good care of me.

I returned to Xenia happy with the world. When I arrived home, my parents, sister and I celebrated. Nevertheless, I knew they would miss me and I would miss them, too.

Chapter 12

CLEVELAND

Arriving in Cleveland on August 30th, I moved into my room at Mrs. Gray's Bay Village house. It would be nice to see Lake Erie every day and hear the surf.

The following day I checked the driving time to the firm's office in the National City Bank building on Euclid Avenue in downtown Cleveland. I drove past the Cleveland Indians baseball stadium where I would have to see a game for my dad, who had been a fan since the team played their first game. I located several places to eat and a dry cleaner that advertised in their window: "Shirts laundered like your mother."

The drive to the office on Monday morning went smoothly. I arrived at 7:30 carrying an empty briefcase into the lobby and rode the elevator to the tenth floor.

The receptionist greeted me, "Good morning, Mr. Royal."

While ushering me to a conference room, she inquired where I was staying, wished me well, and offered her assistance in the office if it was needed. With a smile on her face, she explained to me the office rules.

I thought that she was going to break out laughing when I said, "You mean I can't have a drink with you after work."

"Those are the rule—unless you want to support me."

We both laughed.

Joseph Scott Davidson, senior vice president and manager of the audit group, awaited me. I would soon learn that this man could not only analyze any company's financial and operating statements, he could dissect them. He also knew everything about a company's manufacturing process, from receiving to shipping. I was assigned a small office with a desk, chair, table, and a four-drawer fireproof filing cabinet with a combination lock.

For the next several months, I went with senior consultants on assignments at Cleveland companies. I assisted them by compiling financial and production information that they would use in the analysis of a company's operation. This was a time-consuming task but it gave me invaluable experience. I soon learned to recognize areas of a company that were not efficient and not contributing to their profitability. I had the opportunity to analyze problems and make proposed changes. It really became interesting. I soon learned that becoming acquainted with individuals in the problem areas and asking questions, that their answers sometimes directed me to the solutions. Often there were employees in the companies who knew how to solve the problems, but management would not listen to their suggestions.

•

Arriving at the office on a Monday morning, I found a neat stack of file folders and binders on my desk. Attached to the back of my chair was a note from Joseph Davidson: "Please start analyzing this company. I will be back with you later. Scottie."

To my surprise, I knew of the company; it was located in Springfield, Ohio. I began leafing through the operating reports wondering what I was supposed to be looking for.

Davidson's secretary came in through the open door and said, "President Allen wants to see you in his office."

It reminded me of the four star general on Governor's Island. I followed her down the hall, where she pointed to a door at the end of the plush deep green carpet.

President James K. Allen greeted me with, "Glad to have you aboard, I understand things have been going well." He walked around his desk and pointed to a red leather chair.

He explained, "Scottie has placed information on your desk for you to review. Your assignment will be to go to Springfield, Ohio, and complete an analysis of the Springfield Truck Company's operation. They have a number of problems, mainly production due to the lack of space. It is an old company. It has been manufacturing a quality truck for years. Other truck companies in the country are making plans to expand production, and they need to expand in order to take advantage of the growing truck market.

"Rob, your assignment is to evaluate their existing operations and determine the feasibility of expanding the existing facilities. Within the company there are three factions: one group does not want to do anything, the second wants to expand the existing buildings, the third wants to build a new facility at another location. Analyze the existing operation, determine the problems. Look at their plans for expanding the existing facilities, analyze them and make your recommendations. You'll be in contact with Scottie Davidson on a weekly basis to review your daily field reports."

Allen picked up a folder from a side table, removed several sheets of paper stapled together and a letter size envelope, and handed them to me.

He continued, "This is a list of names and photographs that have been furnished to the Group by your friend, Biff Wallace. Doud returned from London a few days ago, stopped here in Cleveland and gave me the information.

My heart skipped a beat.

"Yes," Allen said, "I am a member of the Group. Doud said for me to give you his best."

I shook my head in wonder. "I am not surprised. Over the past few weeks there have been two or three things that made me think that it might be possible."

Allen smiled. "You have an appointment with Arnold Reasonier, the treasurer of the truck company next Monday at 10:00 AM. He will give you access to all of the company records. When you analyze their work force, you will have access to their employee files. This will give you an opportunity to look for the names of those on the list and the photographs should be of help. In the event that you identify one of the wanted men, call Doud immediately."

I was surprised to receive the assignment. I had been with the consulting firm only a few months, but during that time I had made some proposals while working with the senior consultants. Many of the proposals had resulted from asking questions and simply applying common sense. So far I had found the consulting business a fascinating experience, something new and different in each of the companies.

"When should I leave for Springfield?"

"Leave in the morning, locate a comfortable place to stay, look around town, and go to the company on Monday morning for the ten o'clock appointment."

Things were starting to get exciting. My employment by the firm had been in concert with the Group after all. I understood why the Group wanted to keep their operations out of the government. The travel and some of the events had been new experiences. The fact that the Group was making deposits in a Swiss bank account that they had established for me was also interesting. I returned to my office and closed the door, moved files from the desk to the file cabinet. I left the office for lunch alone. I needed privacy to find a pay telephone and call Doud with the details of the assignment.

There was a telephone in the lobby of the National City Bank building that offered sufficient privacy. Doud answered my collect call with, "It's too early to hunt coon in Texas."

I replied, "I am from Missouri, show me."

"Tell me about it."

I gave Doud the details of the assignment. He replied, "Keep me advised of your address, telephone number and any changes. Remember, you are employed as a consultant, a regular normal job. The fact that Allen is a member of the Group has no bearing on your consulting position. However, report any unusual activities to me until directed otherwise. You are free to call if you need to talk."

I decided to pass on lunch, and returned to the office, opened the combination lock on the file, removed the files that would be needed in Springfield, and put them in an expandable briefcase. There was a knock on the door.

"Come in."

It was James Allen, "Just wanted to wish you luck. I am sure that you'll do well. Call me if you need anything and I'll see you in about ten days, and by the way, our friend Doud called and said that you were checking me out." He smiled, shook my hand, and left.

I left a short time later. On my way out, Allen's secretary handed me a sealed business envelope and said, "Have a safe trip and be sure that you call and tell me where you will be staying."

The four o'clock traffic had just started to pick up. When I arrived in Bay Village, I reduced the car's speed and looked out on Lake Erie;

The Cloisters of Canterbury

there was a north wind and the waves were breaking on the shore. I made a left turn away from the lake and pulled into Mrs. Gray's drive. When I got out of the car, I could still hear the breaking waves. There were dark clouds over Lake Erie, a storm coming out of Canada. Sometimes the storms off the lake could penetrate deep into Ohio.

Mrs. Gray greeted me as I opened the front door. I told her that the company was sending me out of town and I was not sure for how long and so I paid her another month's rent. After packing a leather two-suitor bag and a smaller matching bag, I was on my way in twenty minutes.

I was actually looking forward to this assignment, and intended to drive all the way to Springfield that night so I would be out of the snow belt just in case the weather took a turn for the worse.

Chapter 13

Springfield

I finally arrived in Springfield. Route 68 became Limestone Street and I slowed down when passing O'Brian's Tavern, a favorite hangout for Wittenberg College students. It was a good place to eat, and I stopped there on several occasions in years past when visiting friends at Wittenberg. I parked in front of the Shawnee Hotel at the corner of Limestone and East Main Street.

The hotel had been open for many years and was centrally located, ideal for my assignment. I walked in and went to the registration desk, told the desk clerk that I would be in town for several weeks. The clerk told me that the hotel didn't have parking, but that I was welcome to park my car on the street. That wasn't usually a problem unless there was a snowstorm. My third floor room faced west overlooking Limestone. A bellhop took my bags to the room.

I set the alarm clock for six, but was awake shortly after five, had breakfast, and was on my way to the plant by six. I wanted to a get a feel for the activity of the plant early in the morning and observe the employees arriving to start their day. The traffic was heavy and slow on the narrow two-lane street leading to the plant. I found a parking place on the street two blocks from the plant entrance, parked and watched.

Several Springfield city buses were not improving the car traffic, but without the bus system these workers wouldn't have anywhere to park even if they did have a car. Many were walking, carrying metal lunch boxes, passing the slow-moving cars.

When it appeared that all of the employees starting the seven o'clock first shift had arrived, I drove around the neighboring streets. All of the houses were side-by-side, maybe ten feet between them. Without exception, they were framed, two-story, with a porch across the front, built on the side of the hill, off the street by ten or twelve feet. The once white houses were now gray, covered with soot from their coal stoves and from the truck plant, but they didn't begin to compare to what I had seen in London. I should have expected that; London had been accumulating coal soot for several hundred years.

I drove back to the truck plant a few minutes before ten. Going into the main entrance, a receptionist directed me to the treasurer's office on the second floor. The stairs were cupped-out wooden steps, worn from years of wear. Just to the left, at the top of the stairs, a secretary greeted me. I gave her my business card from James Allen & Associates and told her that I had an appointment with Arnold Reasonier. She escorted me down the hall to Reasonier's secretary and gave her my card, who, in turn, telephoned the treasurer, went to the door, and opened it.

"Please go in."

Reasonier stood and walked from behind his desk, shook my hand and offered me a chair in front of his desk. We had some general conversation, whereupon I told him that I would like to start by walking through the plant.

"First let's get you set up in an office." We passed several offices with secretaries at desks in front of them. He stopped in front of one and said, "Miss Watkins, this is Mr. Royal from James Allen & Associates. He will be with us for several weeks, and I would like you to assist him in every way. He will be using the office next to Mr. Speer."

She stood. "Nice to meet you, sir. The office has been made ready. If there is anything you need, please let me know."

We returned to the treasurer's office just as Jim Banks, the plant manager, arrived.

I toured the truck plant with the plant manager, who turned out to be most informative. He appeared to know all of the employees, but I soon realized that he was calling them by one of several names—Smith,

Johnson, Jackson, Jones, or Swartz. He didn't call any of them by their first names. Some of the men returned his greeting with; "Good morning, boss." Others would wave or nod their heads. As we walked along the assembly line, Banks spoke to a couple of men by the name of Swartz.

"Do you have many German employees?"

He replied, "Yes, we have a number and some are related, especially the several Swartz employees.

I didn't respond—there wasn't a Swartz on the Group's list of war criminals.

"I would like to observe all operations in the plant, and would like to start in the morning in the receiving department, then the machining, sub-assemblies, the assembly line, and also watch a truck leave the plant."

The plant manager said, "I'll schedule a meeting with all the foremen for eight o'clock tomorrow morning, introduce you, and explain why you're here."

As promised, the following morning the plant manager introduced me to the foremen and assistant foremen. He explained that I would be asking questions about how and why they were doing various things.

One of the men asked, "What's this for?"

The plant manager replied that they were making plans to increase the size of the plant and that I was working with the company's treasurer on the financial planning. This appeared to satisfy the men since expansion would create more jobs and provide security for their own employment.

During the following week I observed every operation in the plant, talked with the department foremen and workers, and asked many questions. Most wanted to talk. This gave me the opportunity to get to know some of the men and learn their names. During their lunch break and before their shifts started, I talked with many of them always asking where they were from. Many were from Ohio, Indiana, and Michigan, but most were from Kentucky and West Virginia. Several would not engage in conversation within the group, but would talk with each other. Their English was limited, but it appeared that they were trying to learn.

I listened to their conversations, what they called each other, and observed their body language. It seemed all of them were willing to talk about their families when asked. I soon learned that many of the men were living in rooms, and when their Friday work shift ended, six or

The Cloisters of Canterbury

more would get into an old car and drive home to Kentucky or West Virginia, returning late on Sunday night, getting a few hours sleep, and report to work on Monday.

Monday production was always less than other days in the week. This was probably due to the workers driving home and returning on the weekend, tired and just working slower. They certainly couldn't get much sleep. The trips home on weekends were in cars that looked like they should be on a scrap pile. Overhearing their conversations I learned that it wasn't unusual for them to have two or three flat tires on their trips. They would stop, jack the car up, remove the tire, take the rubber inner-tube out and glue a patch on it, return it to the tire, and pump it up with a hand pump. Most of the tires had to be fixed in the middle of the night along some dark road, sometimes unpaved. These men had been doing this during all the years of the war.

The conditions these men endured just to feed their families, and returning to see them on the weekend, not just occasionally but every weekend, was unbelievable.

I had often wondered how the United States would have been able to manufacture all the airplanes, tanks, trucks and other materials required for the war effort. Now I knew it was because of the thousands of men and women from Kentucky, West Virginia and other states who had migrated to the cities, driving hundreds of miles, living in horrible conditions to support the war effort, along with those men and women serving in all branches of the military service.

As I continued to review the company's operation, observing the activities in the plant and comparing it with the company operating statements, I soon learned their major problem. The physical plant was in need of repair, and maintenance during World War II was not one of their highest priorities. The government hadn't been buying trucks since the war ended, but the company was selling all the trucks they were capable of manufacturing to American consumers who had not been able to buy a truck since before the war.

I returned to my assigned office and wondered if any of the Germans on the Group's list were employed at the plant. I was expecting to have difficulty in looking at the individual rosters. However, when the plant manager introduced me to Wayne Speer, the employment manager, he could not have been more helpful. I asked to see a list of employees, by department and occupation and their length of service and their production records. Speer introduced me to his secretary, Ruth Watkins, and asked her to assist me.

She said, "I have already met Mr. Royal."

She was in her early thirties, dark wavy hair and brown eyes and a smile that would prevent or win most battles, a very beautiful woman.

I followed her to her office that was next to the employment manager's office and sat in a chair across from her desk.

She asked, "What information will you need?"

I gave her a prepared list.

She looked at the list, "When will you need it?"

"Whenever it's convenient for you."

"Would tomorrow morning at eight be soon enough?"

"That's not necessary. Thursday or Friday will be fine"

Returning to the truck assembly line I walked from the start of the line to the end of the line, the final point where the truck was ready to drive out the door. I talked with a number of the men who had previously explained what they were doing. I had located two men by the name of Swartz; neither looked like the photos. The only time that I had heard them speak was in German to each other. They never joined in the conversations with the other men when I was present. I asked the other men if they ever joined them, and they said that they spoke very little English.

If everything worked as planned, the employment records would provide me with the names of the men in each department. Employment records would show date of birth, place of birth, marital status, dependents, home address, previous employment and addresses, if they were United States citizens and their references. All of this information may or may not be true. Nevertheless, I was interested to see what information was in their files.

The following morning when I arrived at the office at five minutes before eight, Ruth Watkins greeted me.

"All of the information that you requested is on the table in the conference room next to your office." She opened the door and pointed to the stacks of files, each stack identified. She certainly had worked late yesterday to have all this completed.

"There is coffee on the side table. Call me if you need anything else."

"Thanks, Miss Watkins. "

She smiled and left, with her dark brown eyes sparkling. Her perfume lingered. Yes, she probably could prevent a war, but more likely start one.

I poured a cup of coffee, added cream, sat down and started to organize the stacks in the sequence of my planned review. It was not

The Cloisters of Canterbury

necessary. Ruth had placed the stacks on the table exactly in the order of my list. I would be able to keep the files in the conference room until I needed them, allowing me to keep my desk clear.

My request for information was in order of the manufacturing process, starting with receiving of material, warehousing and the first use of the materials. Of course, no one at the truck plant was to know of my association with the Group. Besides, my assignment as a consultant at the truck company was legitimate. With so many German employees, I could not help but wonder if one or more of the men on the list might be working in the plant, but not using their real name.

I looked at the folders and started with my planned analysis, following the procedures that the senior consultants used. I would not change the plan unless there was a logical reason.

After spending several hours analyzing the company's financial and operating statements, I proceeded to labor costs and the personnel in the various departments, starting with the receiving department and warehousing employee files. Most of the employees, with the exception of men returning from military service, had been employed before or at the start of World War II. All except for one in the receiving and warehousing had been born in Springfield or in Clark County, Ohio, and he was from West Virginia.

I continued reading employee files looking for German names as well as their birthplaces. In the engine assembly department and final assembly I had heard a number of men speaking German, so I looked carefully at the files of the men in the two departments. There was one man, John A. Johnson, in the engine assembly group that had a German accent. His English was rather good. When I stopped to talk with the men in the group, Johnson always moved away. I needed to know more about Johnson and to look at the photographs very carefully. I copied the names and addresses of all employees with German names. Trying to determine where they lived, grouping the names by streets.

That afternoon, I left the plant at 4:30 and drove to East Main Street and located the addresses of three employees named Swartz on the list, but was not successful in locating the fourth Swartz or John Johnson. Their records indicated that they lived on East Main Street, but the street numbers for the two were not visible from the car. All of the addresses were within six blocks of the Shawnee Hotel that was on the corner of Main Street and Limestone, where I was staying. For several blocks there were one-story brick buildings that appeared to be residential. The buildings had wooden entrance doors with single glass panels.

The street numbers were on the brick walls over rusting mailboxes. The area was in general need of maintenance and renovation. It reminded me of the buildings on Warwick Way in London.

I knew this was going to take more time than planned. I would have to study the photographs and concentrate on men that resembled them. I kept reminding myself that I was here to do a consulting job.

I drove to the hotel and checked at the desk for messages—there were none. Once in my room, I put the brief case in the closet and fixed the security lock that I had received at the farm to the door. Making sure that all was secure, I left the hotel again and walked past the addresses that had been visible from the car. The street had some litter, but nothing compared to London. This city hadn't been through the ravages of London's bombing. Walking on the north side of Main Street for seven blocks, I passed several men leaning against the walls and standing on the sidewalk, most were smoking. I didn't see any men from the plant.

When I returned to my room after supper, I reviewed the information from the personnel files of the men, showered and went to bed about ten. It probably would have been more productive if I had not gone to bed, my brain couldn't stop thinking about the truck plant. There were obvious problems, but the missing addresses of the employees interfered when I tried to focus on one specific operation. I wondered where they lived. There might be several reasons, some not important, except that the Group's list of the twenty men was always on my mind.

The next morning I called Ruth Watkins at the plant and told her that I wouldn't be in until ten or eleven. I pulled on a sweater instead of my suit coat, locked my briefcase in the closet and went to the dining room. I ordered breakfast from the same waiter who had served me the night before.

I asked him, "Do you ever go home?"

The waiter replied, "I only work twelve hours a day seven days a week."

After breakfast, I walked down East Main Street, past the first address of one of the men, stopped next-door and knocked, but received no answer. I tried the next three, but received no answer. When I was about to knock on the fourth door, a man walked out. His appearance was like so many of the men at the truck plant, bib overhauls, unshaved and not very clean.

I asked, "Does John Johnson and Herman Swartz lived here?"

The man said, "Don't know 'em." His dialect indicated that he was

The Cloisters of Canterbury

probably from Kentucky or West Virginia.

"Is there a landlord or manager?"

"No, a man comes by on Friday evening and Saturday to collect the rent money."

"How many rooms are there in the building?"

"Don't rightly know, never counted 'em. There's the first floor, basement one, and basement two."

"What do you mean, two basements?"

He opened the door and pointed to the stairs and said; "You go down the stairs to the first basement, go along the hall and down more stairs to the second basement."

I learned that the men rented rooms by the week and in some cases, rented beds by the shift. One man slept and when he left another slept in the same bed. The man told me that most of the buildings along the street were the same, and that the only way I could locate anyone was to knock on doors. He was unable to provide me with a name of the owner, but pointed to a card, yellowed from age, thumb tacked to the wall just inside the door. A single light bulb hanging from the ceiling on a cord provided just enough light so it could be read. I copied the telephone number.

Just as I was starting to leave the man suggested, "Just go down the hall and knock on the doors, that's what the police do when they're looking for someone. They got no way out. If you tell them you're not a cop, that you're an insurance man, they'll answer."

Down the street I looked for the address listed for Herman Swartz; pausing for a moment and knocked on the door hoping to learn something. After not receiving a response, I opened the door. The rancid smell of bacon and cigarette smoke was overpowering. I hesitated, not sure that going in was a good idea. A single small light bulb hung from the ceiling by an electric cord, just like the building up the street.

Wishing for a flashlight, I considered lighting a match, but was sure that the smell of natural gas was lingering under the other smells. In all probability it would not have been a problem. The men living in the building were cooking their food on gas hotplates, and if there had been a gas leak the place would have blown up long before.

I knocked on a door.

From within a sleeping man's voice hollered, "Who is it?"

"Insurance man, I am looking for Herman Swartz."

"Don't know him," was the answer.

Tried the next door, knocked, and received the same answer. I knocked on all of the doors on both sides of the hall, receiving either no answer or the same sleepy answer. They all sounded like the same man. Remembering the description of the second basement, I decided that now was as good a time as any to have a look. Something told me that this would not be my last visit. At the end of the hall another light bulb hung from the ceiling barely revealing the stairs going down.

With hesitation, I descended the steps to the bottom. The second basement was the same as the first, except the rancid smells were stronger and it was difficult to breath. How could these men live under such conditions? It was nothing but a firetrap. At the end of the hall, I turned around and retraced my steps, stopping at every door and knocking. The only difference in the answers was the tone of the voice, all were very unhappy about being disturbed.

It was time to find daylight and fresh air.

After my experience in the basements of the building on Main Street, I was concerned about the living conditions of the men. How could it be ignored? Not locating John Johnson's address because the street number didn't exist increased my determination to find out where he lived.

Driving to the truck plant I continued to think of all the answers that were not answers. When I walked into my office, Ruth Watkins was standing by the desk and appeared to be looking for something.

I paused and said, "Good morning, Ruth."

She turned, her face turned slightly pink. "I have some more information for you from Mr. Reasonier, but I wasn't sure where to put it." She handed me a new stack of documents. They were cost estimates for the proposed plant addition.

"Thank you. Do you have a list of local building supply companies and building contractors in the area? I want to review material and construction costs for the proposed addition."

"I am sure that we do. I'll locate them for you."

Was I imagining her embarrassment? The expression on her face alarmed me. There were several clear places on the desktop where she could have put the documents.

Just as she reached the door, I asked. "Would you like to stop for a drink after work?"

She turned, her face had turned a shade redder and her eyes were almost flashing. "I am busy every night!"

I heard the clicking sound of her high-heeled shoes striking the floor all way down the hall. She didn't stop at her desk—by the sound she

The Cloisters of Canterbury

must have gone to the restroom.

Sitting at the desk I looked at the documents she left, but my mind was not on them. There was something about Ruth Watkins; she was sending mixed messages. When I first met her, she came on very strong, blinking her eyes, with a smile that made me look at her more than once. She was selling, but what? Now this explosive reaction was something different. Returning to the papers before me, I was still not able to concentrate.

Several things were bothering me. Employees' addresses were not accurate. Ruth Watkins' embarrassment when I observed her looking at things on the top of the desk. It just didn't make sense. The expression on her face indicated that something else was going on. When I asked her if she would like to stop for a drink, she indicated that I had pushed the wrong button—crossed a line. After her surprised reaction when I walked into the office, I wanted to find out what her reaction would be to creating a personal relationship. I certainly found out in a hurry and became even more concerned about her actions.

I unlocked the combination lock on my briefcase and removed the pictures of the men that were of interest to the Group. I studied each face of the twenty photographs and the names on the back. None of the names on the Group's wanted list were on the truck company's employee roster. None of the employees looked like the photographs, except maybe one: John A. Johnson. He resembled one of them, but the hair was longer and the face was much fuller now. It would have been easy for him to gain a lot of weight.

I turned the picture over: "Hans Mueller, Nazi SS Officer."

I needed to look at Johnson more carefully.

Replacing the pictures back in the briefcase and locking it, I switched gears and looked at the proposed building addition estimate. At five o'clock I put the files in the briefcase, turned out the office light, closed the door, and walked past Ruth Watkins' desk. She was just putting her things away.

"I hope that you weren't offended when I invited you for a drink."

She looked up with a serious look on her face. "You didn't. It's just that my regular would really get angry."

I said good night and left the building, walked to my car and drove past the buildings on East Main Street on the way to the hotel. It looked the same, just men standing or sitting in front of the buildings, smoking cigarettes and talking. After visiting one of the buildings and experiencing the conditions that they were living in, it was no wonder they stood outside.

I reviewed my options. One option that appeared to be necessary was to start observing the buildings on East Main Street. It would not be easy. Most of the cars were beat up old cars; my car would stand out. And one of the employees from the plant would probably recognize it.

Chapter 14

SURVEILLANCE

It was obvious that surveillance was going to be necessary if I was to learn more about these men. Locating John A. Johnson's residence was number one on the list. Every time that I walked through the plant stopping at various locations to observe the workers, most would look at me, smile and sometimes say something. But when I arrived near Johnson's work area, he would put his head down and avoid making eye contact.

I had found that the best time to talk with the men was when they were on a work break. They would gather, smoke and drink coffee, and I could talk with the various groups, ask where they were from, and question them about their families. Many would talk about a child's birthday or hunting experience. Making eye contact with most of the workers was easy. They were just hard-working men, who became much friendlier when I related my factory experiences.

After dinner I changed out of my jacket and tie into a dark brown sweater. On the way out of the hotel, I picked up a newspaper. About a block from the hotel was a Lincoln-Mercury car dealership, and the show room lights were still on. In the adjacent building a veiled woman was standing under the sign in the window: "Palm Reader – Tell Your Fortune." As I passed she lowered the veil on her face, motioned with her hands for me to come in. I continued walking.

Entering the car dealership, I looked at the new Mercury on display. A salesman with a nice smile approached me. "You can drive this one away tonight."

"I am looking for a two-hundred dollar used car for hunting." You could see the disappointment on the salesman's face.

"We don't sell used cars from here. The used car lot is on East Main Street, about ten blocks from Limestone. They stay open until nine o'clock.

"Thanks." I returned to my car.

It was a short drive to the used car lot, just past the brick buildings where some of the plant workers lived, or more accurately, *existed*. I drove onto the used car lot, and before getting out, I saw just the right car, a 1938 black Ford two-door. There were a number of dents on the fenders of the left side, paint was faded, but the tires looked good. If it would start and run. I walked pass the old Ford only giving it a brief look, and slowly continued down two rows of cars. Some were nice-looking cars, but my need was not looks.

A salesman walked out with a cigar is his mouth, removed it long enough to say, "What you looking for?"

"I need a car that's got an engine that will start and run, with good rubber, for a hunting car."

The salesman guided me along the row of cars. I stopped in front of the '38 Ford, opened the door, got in and turned the key. The engine started on the first turn of the starter, a good sign. I walked around the car, more dents and rust, the tires looked good. I kicked one of them and the cigar came out of the salesman's mouth.

"Don't kick too hard, those are recaps." The cigar went back into his mouth.

The engine was still running and sounded good. The speedometer indicated 97,441 miles. The interior was in fair condition, but the previous owner must have been a heavy pipe smoker; the smell was overpowering and the headliner was yellow from pipe smoke. The salesman saw me shaking my head at the headliner.

Out came the cigar. "You said you wanted a car for hunting, not to court a woman."

I walked around the car. "How much?"

The Cloisters of Canterbury

The salesman chewed on his cigar, "Five-hundred dollars."

I responded with, "One hundred fifty," and started walking back to my car.

The salesman countered with, "Four-hundred," and did not remove the cigar.

"Two-hundred," and I continued walking.

The cigar said, "Three-hundred fifty."

I opened the door to my car, turned and said, "Two hundred twenty-five dollars cash, but only if you can arrange for me to park the car in back of the new car show room for the next two weeks."

"It's yours, and I can arrange the parking."

I followed him to the office inside a small wood building.

He sat down behind the only desk, picked up the telephone and made a call. He put the telephone down, "It's all right on the parking, just ask for Ted, the service manager."

He pulled out some papers and I provided him with the information that he requested, and gave him two-hundred twenty-five dollars in cash. He gave me a copy of the sales contract and instructions for titling the car. The receipt he gave me for the money did not have the company's name on it. I had a feeling that this car had not been in the inventory of the Lincoln-Mercury dealer. The salesman was probably selling it for himself. In the car business, it was called "curbing" or something like that. We made arrangements for me to pick up the car the next day. The salesman handed me two sets of keys.

"What did the former owner do for a living?" I asked.

"He sells life insurance. Collects every week, mostly from factory workers. Many live in the firetraps up the street. And also from all the old widows hoping that when they die that there will be enough to bury them."

"What do you mean firetraps?"

He gave me a full description of the buildings that I had visited. He had a name for the owner of the buildings and the insurance salesman that was taking advantage of the poor workers and widows. His remarks would never be heard at a church picnic.

"Thanks."

From behind the cigar came, "Any time."

I remembered what the man in front of one of the buildings had said, "When you knock on the doors, tell them you're an insurance man." He was probably the former owner of the '38 Ford and they were used to having the insurance man knocking on the doors to collect and sell them more life insurance.

It was a sleepless night. I could not help but think about the workers living in those unbelievable conditions. They worked hard while their families lived some place in Kentucky or West Virginia. They paid their weekly insurance premiums, no doubt to pay for their own burials and possibly to leave something extra for their families.

•

The next day I left the plant at five o'clock and could visualize many changes that were going to be required. In my hotel room, I changed into a pair of old gray slacks, a wool shirt and a dark brown sweater, then left the hotel and walked down the Limestone hill, past the gypsy palm reader. I glanced in the window, but she didn't even attempt to lure me in. It must have been the change in clothes. I waved to the salesman looking out the showroom window in the Lincoln-Mercury dealership, and walked around to the rear of the service department. There was the '38 Ford. It started on the first turn of the key. Arranging for discrete parking had been a good idea.

Driving the car around the streets of the downtown area for a while assured me that the old car wasn't too bad, with the exception of the rancid pipe smoke smell. My olfactory senses were very keen. Many times I had been aware of the presence of someone just from the smell of an unlit pipe that they were carrying in a pocket.

There were several old cars parked along Main Street near the brick buildings occupied by the factory workers. Some of the cars hadn't been moved for a long time—windshields were covered with dust, a number of flat tires. I parked the Ford between two cars that appeared to have been driven recently—no flat ties and clean windshields. I could now walk from the hotel, get in the car, and smoke my pipe while observing the arrival and departure of the workers. It was not likely that anyone would pay any attention to me, just another of the many who were using cars to get out of the flophouses for a few hours.

I stayed in the car over four hours looking over a newspaper and drinking a Hires root beer. There was very little activity on the street until it started to rain. From unknown places, men quickly returned to their rooms in the flophouses. After it appeared that all of the men had returned, I locked the old car and walked back to the hotel in the rain.

For the next several nights, I sat in the old car parked across the street from the firetraps watching the men standing around and looking

The Cloisters of Canterbury

for Johnson. I observed nothing unusual, just tired men leaning against the buildings or sitting on the curb, until Friday night when I noticed a muscular guy talking with the men and going in and out of the buildings. It was soon obvious that the man was collecting the rent for the rooms. I watched the man for more than two hours until he started walking west on Main Street. He apparently had made all of the collections for the night.

I got out of the car and followed him from the opposite side of the street for eight blocks. The man walked as if he didn't have a care in the world. He didn't look around and showed no signs of expecting to be robbed. The man finally went in the front door of a two-story, white-frame house. I waited until a light came on in a second floor window and a blind was pulled down. I now knew how they collected the rent.

•

Two days after the incident with Ruth, she was at her desk when I arrived.

"Good morning, Ruth."

She quickly covered her right eye with her hand and said, "Good morning," without raising her head.

What happened to that award-winning smile? I hoped that she wasn't angry because I had asked her to stop for a drink, but something was definitely wrong.

For the next two hours I analyzed production reports, projected sales and the proposed expansion costs. Ruth wasn't at her desk when I left for lunch.

After lunch, I walked through the plant stopping in each department, talking with the foremen. I was becoming a regular visitor and with each visit, they became friendlier. Many of the workers would step into the aisle and exchange a few words with me. Most of them had that same tired look. I still wondered which ones were living in the East Main Street buildings. Although, I also learned that there were other areas as bad or even worse, which was hard to believe.

When I entered the motor assembly area where John A. Johnson worked, I stopped and talked with the foreman, my back was to Johnson. I had a strange feeling that someone was looking at me, the same feeling when a teacher in grade school was looking over my shoulder while I was reading a comic book and not doing my assignment.

I continued chatting with the foreman, watching his eyes, and carefully listening to comments about a quality problem within his department that had been corrected by one of the tool and die makers from the die shop. Suddenly the foreman stopped talking and directed his eyes over my shoulder.

I turned and for the first time made eye contact with John A. Johnson. He stared directly into my eyes for several seconds, then turned and moved away. The cold expression in Johnson's eyes made a chill run down my back. I turned back to the foreman.

"That fellow has a mean streak in him," the foreman explained. "It shows up every once in a while. The men say it's after he has had a run in with his old lady."

I nodded and continued touring the plant. When I returned to my office, Ruth wasn't at her desk, but another woman was in her place.

"Where's Ruth?"

"She had a doctor's appointment."

In the office, I pulled John A. Johnson's employment file. His marital status was single. The foreman had mentioned Johnson having a run in with his old lady. It was very possible that "old lady" didn't necessarily mean a wife. I continued looking through the employment records and located Ruth Watkins' file under Administration. Her age was twenty-eight when hired in 1948, no date of birth, no place of birth, marital status—the single box was checked, previous employment: "WAC" 1942-1946. I wondered where she was from 1946 to 1948.

Now my alarm bell was ringing! The records indicated that she had graduated from a Trenton, New Jersey, high school—no school name or the years she attended—attended Vassar College, no dates. There was no graduation date or relatives or anyone listed to notify in case of an emergency. Her home address was on Fountain Blvd, but no telephone. Two references were listed: a WAC Captain Shannon, Washington, D.C., for an address, and Miss Tuttle, at Vassar College.

There was no indication that anyone had checked her references. Her employment application and records were interesting because there was very little detail. No reference was evident as to who had interviewed or hired her for the secretarial position. I copied the information from her file and carefully returned the file to the stack of administrative employees. I was reluctant to discuss this observation of Ruth's records with the employment manager or anyone else in the company. My assignment was to review the company's operation and make recommendations for improvement. They would probably think looking at a secretary's employment record was stretching things a little.

The Cloisters of Canterbury

I was concerned. The company's employment procedures were excellent. All of the employment applications appeared to be complete and very few questions left unanswered. There were numerous penciled notes on applications, obviously by the person interviewing or hiring. Many had reference letters attached. Questions that were left blank did not apply. Ruth Watkins, the secretary of the employment department manager, and John A. Johnson's employment applications were incomplete. Why?

Opening the files on another group of employees I found that all employment records were complete without exception. Looking at another group of files, again all were complete, annotated with many notes and numerous reference letters. It was obvious that the company's employment records were well organized. So then why were the records of those two individuals incomplete? Who was responsible for their employment? My mind flew in different, frustrated directions.

I picked up my briefcase and left the office at five o'clock. Per my normal routine, I walked to the parking lot, drove directly to the hotel, parked the car in about the same place, and had dinner in the hotel dining room. There was nothing wrong with that, but I figured now might be a good time to practice some of the training from the farm. I decided that driving a different route to the hotel and finding other places to eat would be a good change. But, I'd continue parking in front of the Lincoln-Mercury showroom. It was well lit and convenient.

I remembered men in military intelligence who had worked in the field talk about the hair on the back of their heads standing out when they were in danger, and Biff Wallace had related the exact same thing in London.

I asked Biff how he acquired that sense, and he said, "The first time it happened was in Berlin. My mental alarm sounded, giving me a critical warning that saved my life. I have had the same feeling many times since, and always when there was a danger."

I hadn't had that feeling until Johnson was watching me with those cold, grey eyes.

One thing I became convinced of: John A. Johnson and Hans Mueller were the same person. The address in Johnson's employment records didn't exist. I needed to determine where he was living before notifying the Group that there was the likelihood that one of the men on their wanted list for war crimes was working at the truck plant.

Going to O'Brian's for a sandwich was always a good idea, but my thoughts kept me from tasting the food. When I finished eating, I drove to Fountain Blvd. to look for the address that was on Ruth Watkins' employment records. On both sides of the street were large, two-story brick homes on large lots.

After driving the length of the street twice I located the address—a large English Tudor house, with a driveway on the side leading to a two-car detached garage. Lights were on in the first and second floors of the house. I was concerned because Ruth had covered the right side of her face and did not raise her head when I spoke to her that morning. It was also disconcerting that she had left for a doctor's appointment and didn't return to work. One other thing I learned that day: Ruth Watkins lived in a very nice house. If she didn't return to work soon, I would visit the house. I added the events of the evening to my list of strange questions and few answers.

Returning to the hotel I parked at the curb in front of the Lincoln-Mercury dealership's showroom and locked the car door. As I removed my briefcase from the trunk, the palm reader sitting in the window motioned for me to come in. I shook my head. She smiled.

•

The following day I arrived at the truck plant at 7:30, made my regular morning tour of the plant, making more notes. What recommendations could be made that would improve the plant's operation? Productivity needed to be improved, but morale of the workers would have to change. The plant could stand some general cleaning and painting of the steel structure as well as most of the machinery. There was a need for more storage bins for parts. The workers had difficulty in picking up some of the parts that they needed for assembly. Sometimes the parts were not available and the worker reported it to the foreman, usually after complaining to other workers. The cluttered aisles made it difficult for the forklifts to move through the plant. I heard profanity from the forklift operators above the factory noise whenever they bumped into metal parts bins and had to back up and try again. Lost time and tempers did not make for an efficient operation.

The paint department was unbelievable. They were attempting to remove paint spray and fumes with small exhaust fans mounted in the windows with very little success. The paint spray covered the overhead lights. It was difficult to understand how the painters could breathe or were even able to lay the paint on the trucks and achieve such good quality.

The Cloisters of Canterbury

Walking to the end of the assembly line, I watched a truck move out of the building to the storage yard. Only part of the storage area was gravel; the remaining was dirt and mud from the previous night's rain.

While talking with a foreman standing by the door, I asked, "What happens when it snows?"

"We pull and push through the snow and the mud and hope that the truck transport drivers arrive and move them before they get stuck too deep. The final assembly is always slow due to the lack of front bumpers and door mirrors." From the tone of his voice and his body language, I could tell he wasn't a happy employee. At least from my review of the company's proposed building expansion drawings, I knew that management was aware of the parts storage problems.

The company's analysis of the projected sales increase and the additional production required were realistic. My chief concern, however, was the feasibility of adding the necessary buildings on the existing land when they needed more land for storage of completed trucks and additional parking for employees. More parking would improve the overall morale of the workers and would, in turn, have its effect on efficiency.

After completing the daily field report, I placed it in the briefcase and left the office.

It was only 2:55, but I wanted to wait in the car and watch the first shift workers leaving and follow the bus that John A. Johnson boarded. I needed to locate where Johnson lived. There were twelve city transit buses waiting for the workers. Johnson and four others from the engine department boarded the same bus. It pulled away with another one directly behind it.

The seats on both buses were full, with men standing in the aisle. I followed the second bus, staying back about fifty yards, watching the men exit the buses at each stop. The buses finally made their first stop on East Main Street then proceeded west, stopping at every block. Both buses stopped at the same stops, with men getting off, walking in all directions. Johnson was still on the bus. They would be near the flophouses soon.

The buses stopped at the street corner just before the row of brick buildings where the men lived in the basements. I stopped behind a parked car several yards from the last bus. About thirty men got off and started walking west on Main Street. Several crossed the street. The others continued west, two or three at a time, going into the doors of the brick buildings. Johnson was not one of them. I continued following the buses, but neither of them stopped at Limestone and Main in front of the Shawnee Hotel.

Had I missed Johnson?

When both of the buses stopped at Main and Fountain. Two men got off the last bus and one exited from the first bus—it was Johnson. I delayed moving until a driver behind blew his car horn. I saw Johnson make his way into a small restaurant.

There were no vacant parking places, so I had to park three blocks away and return on foot on the opposite side of the street. Standing on the corner across the street from the restaurant with a newspaper in front of my face, I was able to see that the restaurant had a counter with stools, but all of them were empty. Two men with white aprons stood behind the counter talking with each other, but no sign of Johnson. Just in case he was in the restroom, I waited and watched for twenty minutes, but still no Johnson.

"Had Johnson spotted me?"

I walked across the street, went into the restaurant, sat down on the second stool, and ordered a cup of coffee and a glazed doughnut. While the coffee cooled, I ate the doughnut and glanced around. On the counter next to the cash register was a tray of sandwiches each wrapped in wax paper. Propped next to the tray was a small, hand-printed sign, which read: "Bratwurst 25 cents." It was always dangerous to assume, but I was guessing that Johnson had stopped at the restaurant and bought a good old German bratwurst to take home. I walked back to the car. Johnson might make a stop for a bratwurst every night on his way home, wherever that might be.

Tomorrow I would be waiting when Johnson got off the bus.

I returned to the hotel and parked in front of the palm reader's window. As I removed the briefcase from the trunk, I had a feeling that someone was looking at me. I turned and saw that it was only the gypsy motioning for me to come in. I smiled and shook my head and walked to the side door of the hotel. The elevator always seemed to be waiting with the door open.

Once in the room, I kicked my shoes off and stretched out on the bed. Johnson's movements were confusing. He could have walked back east on Main Street to one of the rooms in the flophouses, but I couldn't picture a German SS officer living in such a place. Johnson always appeared to be clean—very different in appearance from the men from Kentucky and West Virginia. He just was not one of them. I intended to eat in the hotel, change clothes and take the '38 Ford out for several hours. Instead, I was soon fast asleep without changing my clothes.

The Cloisters of Canterbury

When I woke, it was dark outside. I looked at my watch; it was 7:35. I had slept for over two hours and my stomach told me that it was time to eat. I left the room and walked down the stairs to the hotel lobby, took one look into the dining room and decided that O'Brian's Tavern would be a better choice.

The sound of voices and laughter at O'Brian's was refreshing. I remembered a meeting with Doud when he said, "There will be many times when you will need a change of scenery, a fresh look, and get away from the dirt that surrounds you. Do something different, take a drive, go to a movie, and eat in a different restaurant. Go where there are happy people. This was a welcomed change and the ham sandwich was delicious.

After leaving O'Brian's, I decided to drive over to Fountain Blvd. and take another look at the Tudor house where Ruth Watkins lived. I drove several blocks past the house, turned around, and then drove past the Tudor from the other direction. There were "no parking" signs on the street, and I certainly didn't want to pull into her driveway. Eight houses to the north there were three houses side by side with no lights visible from the street. I drove past these houses two more times and on the third pass pulled into the drive of the second house. I turned the car lights off. I still couldn't see any lights on in the house.

I walked back past the Tudor house twice before making the decision that I would go up to the porch, knock and inquire as to Ruth Watkins' health.

As I approached the porch steps, there were faint voices, male and female, coming from inside of the house. I carefully placed each foot on the brick steps, holding my breath until I was next to the door. Light was shining from the window on the right. It was Ruth's voice, of that I was sure, but I couldn't hear what she was saying. The tone of her voice was anything but calm. Moving to the window, I looked between the curtains that were slightly open. I was certain that the hair on the back of my head was standing up. If scared was a feeling, it was all over me. Sitting in a chair was none other than John A. Johnson!

My feet started to move but my body felt like it would never get off the porch. Somehow I reached the sidewalk and must have walked backed to the car, but had no memory of it. The car started on the first try, I backed into the street without lights. After driving down the street for a block, I finally turned on the car's headlights and realized that my clothing was soaked from perspiration.

I returned to the hotel. The walk up the hill to the hotel required more effort than usual. I was unusually tired for some reason. Going into the hotel's Limestone Street entrance, I walked directly to the elevator and pushed the button for the third floor. Alone, my mind was telling me something else. I opened the door to my room, removed my clothes and got into the shower.

I had no idea how long I was under the cool flow of water. I finally sat down in my pajamas at the writing desk and started writing. This is where my training took over in order to arrive at emotionless facts.

> *John A. Johnson, is he "Hans Mueller" a Nazi SS officer wanted for war crimes?*
>
> *The address in his employment records does not exist.*
>
> *His employment records listed previous employment, Mechanic, Army 14 years. What army? No references – Hans Mueller came from Germany.*
>
> *Ruth Watkins' application indicates that she served in the Woman's Army Corps employed two months before Johnson, references not checked.*
>
> *Ruth Watkins lives in a large Tudor house on Fountain Blvd. in a very nice neighborhood.*
>
> *John A. Johnson was in the living room with her. She appeared to have a facial injury.*
>
> *John A. Johnson shows his anger at plant.*
>
> *Johnson's foreman states that the men say "he loses it after having a fight with his old lady."*

Ruth Watkins' residence was very interesting, and called for a visit to the Clark County Records office. Seeing John A. Johnson at Ruth's was most disturbing. What was their connection?

I had seen Ruth driving a light green Desoto four door from the plant parking lot. However, Johnson boarded a Springfield city bus with other men. Johnson worked from 7:00 AM until 3:00 PM, and Watkins' hours were from 8:00 AM to 5:00 PM with an hour for lunch.

The Cloisters of Canterbury

Therefore, it was logical for him to ride the bus.

Nevertheless, I still wanted to check the Springfield police and the Clark County sheriff's records. I wasn't sure what I would find, if anything, but with Johnson's temper, he just might have been arrested in a bar or some other disturbance. It wouldn't be easy checking records for a John Johnson. The plant had more than two-hundred employees named Johnson on the payroll, and how many more lived in Clark County? The odds were that several men named Johnson had been arrested.

Chapter 15

INVESTIGATION

Another short night passed and I was in the hotel restaurant for breakfast before seven. Harold, the friendly waiter, saw me enter and placed a cup of coffee and the Springfield morning newspaper on my usual table, along with his "great to be alive" smile.

I sat down and ordered the usual, and then looked at the headlines: *Nuremberg War Trials Open*. Chills ran down my spine. My stomach tightened as I started reading the article. The war trials would certainly bring justice for many of those responsible for the atrocities in the concentration camps.

In Washington, Doud had told me of the diversity of the Group's founding members. They were Protestant, Catholic, Jewish, heads of major companies, and old-line preeminent American families. Their primary objective was to identify Nazis who had been involved in the Holocaust. War criminals were escaping from Europe through England and Canada into the United States and South America to avoid standing trial for their crimes.

Etched in my mind were photographs of the concentration camps

The Cloisters of Canterbury

received by military intelligence. Now, here I was, deeply involved in bringing one of the guilty into the hands of the prosecutors. There was little doubt in my mind that John A. Johnson was Hans Mueller, a Nazi SS officer wanted for war crimes. Ruth Watkins' and Johnson's relationship alarmed me.

After breakfast, I waited at the door of the Clark County record's office until they opened the door at eight. A kindly woman greeted me with a smile.

I asked, "How can the ownership of real estate be determined?"

Still smiling, "What is the address of the property?"

I gave her the address of the Fountain Boulevard property where Ruth Watkins lived. She wrote the address down and asked me to follow her. She offered me a chair at a table. I watched as she removed a large binder, probably twenty-four by thirty-six inches and four inches thick, from one of the vaults and placed it on the table.

Within a few minutes she turned to the deed to the property. "If you need any help, just ask."

I thanked her and began reading the deed. The deed transferred the property to Ruth Marie Watkins, a single woman, by probate of the Will of Henry Adolph Wiseman and Rachel Marie Wiseman, on September 11, 1944. Who was Henry Adolph Wiseman?

I glanced up; the kindly woman was looking my way. I must have had that "help" look on my face. She rose from her chair and walked to the table. I placed a finger under "Probate of Will." She wrote the name on a piece of paper and left. She returned with another binder the same as the one on the table. After looking at several pages, she got up and went into another room.

It was several minutes before she returned, this time with a packet-type envelope stamped with: "Probate – Henry Adolph Wiseman." She removed the papers and placed them in front of me. They were the original probating documents filed by Glenn G. Hudson, attorney, in Clark County, Ohio, and approved by Elmer Edward Smith, judge in and for Clark County, State of Ohio on September 11, 1944.

The original "Last Will and Testament of Henry Adolph Wiseman and Rachel Marie Wiseman" was executed on January 6, 1940, in Springfield, Clark County, Ohio. They conveyed at their death their entire estate and possessions to their niece, Ruth Marie Watkins. Offered as proof of death was a letter dated 17, July 1944, from Herman Berman, a banker in Zurich, Switzerland. The letter stated that Henry Adolph Wiseman had been arrested in Munich, Germany, by the Nazi

SS, and died 11 March 1943 on a train to Dachau.

Glenn G. Hudson, attorney, prepared an inventory of Henry Adolph and Rachel Wiseman's Estate. The inventory of the estate consisted of the Fountain Blvd house; all furniture and contents; four buildings on East Main Street, Springfield, Ohio; one-hundred shares of common stock in Valley Bank of Dayton; a savings account in the Valley Bank with a balance of $351,760.11 as of the date of the inventory; and a checking account in the same bank with a balance of $29,240.05.

There was a property management contract between Henry Wiseman and Mike Rome for the management of 72 rental units. Rome was to give all rental receipts to Ronald Lock, an accountant, to deposit in the Valley Bank in Dayton. Now, two more names were added to my list: Ronald Lock and Mike Rome. I paused and thought that Mike Rome could have been the man collecting the rent.

•

From the records office I drove to the plant and parked next to Ruth Watkins' car. I wrote down her license plate number and went into the office. Ruth Watkins was at her desk.

"It's nice to see you back, hope you're feeling better."

She raised her head. Her dark brown eyes looked tired. Her makeup didn't completely cover the abrasion on her right cheek.

"Thanks, it's nice to be back."

I went into the office and found the telephone directory. There was no listing for Glenn G. Hudson under lawyers, but there was a G. Hudson on North Fountain Blvd., three house numbers north of Ruth Watkins' address. There was no listing for Mike Rome in the residential listings or business listings; but that could just mean his telephone was listed under a business name. I made a note to try the emergency telephone number listed on the wall of the East Main Street building. Ronald Lock, an accountant, was listed at an address on West Main Street. That could be the address entered by the rent collector. I thought about checking that, but there really wasn't any reason to talk with him, and in all probability, he wouldn't discuss Wiseman's business anyway.

What was Ruth Watkins' relationship with Johnson?

I returned the papers to my briefcase and left the office. It was still early, but I needed to talk with Doud. Ruth was not at her desk. When I reached the parking lot, her car was still there.

I drove north on Fountain Blvd. past Ruth Watkins' English Tudor

The Cloisters of Canterbury

home and stopped in the driveway of the third house beyond Ruth's house—the address for a G. Hudson. Could this be the lawyer's home? The house was set back from the street in line with all of the other houses for several blocks. It was a nice neighborhood. I ascended the four steps, and raised the brass knocker on the door, giving it three gentle knocks.

A soft voice responded, "Just a minute." A woman probably in her late-sixties opened the door. She wore a black dress, white apron and a friendly face.

"Is Ruth Watkins home?"

She turned her head slightly to the side. "I am sorry, young man, you have the wrong address, there's no Ruth Watkins living here." She appeared truly sorry.

"Did she ever live here?"

"No, she lived down the street two houses." She stepped out on the porch and pointed to the Tudor house.

I was sure there was a surprised look on my face.

The lady touched my arm and looked into my eyes. "She was killed in a motor accident in England during the war. She lived with her uncle and aunt, Henry and Rachel Wiseman, for several years after her parents died some place in China—they were missionaries."

Each day something else was revealed, not all of it, just little pieces.

"Are you sure?" Nothing could have prepared me for this shock!

"I have been living here with the Hudsons for over thirty-four years. Glen died a little over six years ago. Now it's just Sarah for me to care for. Sarah is my sister. Glen and Sarah often talked about how sad it was that the Watkins were killed in China and the little girl was left all alone in that strange place. Ruth's mother was Jewish when she fell in love with Rev. Watkins. Rev. Watkins was a Methodist missionary, and when the two of them married, they were sent to China. After they were killed, the church reunited Ruth with her uncle and aunt. Glen was a lawyer, knew Mr. Wiseman, and always spoke well of him. In fact, Glen was Mr. Wiseman's lawyer for many years. I heard Glen tell Sarah that Mr. Wiseman had no other relatives other than a sister in Germany and he would look out for the little girl. He sent her to Vassar, a girl's school in the east, after she graduated from high school. Then when she graduated from Vassar she joined the Woman's Army Auxiliary Corps."

With heart pounding, I asked, "Who lives in the Wiseman house now?"

"The house was sold some time after Glen's death. I don't know who they are—just a man and woman. We don't see much of them. They leave early and return in the evening. They just keep to themselves. Why are you looking for Ruth Watkins?"

"I was asked to stop and see her by some of her friends in the service. They will be saddened to learn of her death."

She had turned on a number of lights in my head, but I still couldn't see.

I was just starting to go down the steps when another thought occurred to me. "Did Ruth attend high school in Springfield?"

"Yes, Springfield High."

I was sure that this nice little lady had overheard many of the Hudsons' conversations. "Did she have any friends in the neighborhood?"

"Why yes, of course. Elizabeth Hummel, she lived next to them on the far side."

"Does Elizabeth live there now?"

"No, Elizabeth became a nurse and worked at Mercy Hospital and then went into the Navy. I heard her mother tell Sarah that she now lives in Denver, Colorado. Ruth Watkins and Elizabeth Hummel were here at the house when both of them were home, just before Ruth went to England. They were such nice girls. Both of them had blue eyes and blonde hair that was fine as silk. They were forever laughing about curlers in their hair every night and sometimes in the afternoon before football and basketball games. They were cheerleaders.

"Won't you sit for a while?" She pointed to two white wicker chairs on the porch. It was a delightful day; the sun was shining on the porch.

I had many more questions, but didn't know how far to go. It was obvious that this dear lady was lonely and very willing to talk. She probably had no one other than her sister to talk with, and who knows, her health might even prevent that.

"How is Mrs. Hudson's health?"

"Her memory and hearing are not what they once were."

"I am sorry. It must be very lonely for you."

"Yes, but I keep busy with the house and meals. We send the laundry out. In the evenings I read a lot."

"What do you read?"

With a smile on her face and twinkle in her eyes, she said, "By the way, my name is Mary Combs, you may call me Mary. I read history books. My father was a history professor at Wittenberg College, so that's probably how I acquired my interest. After my husband didn't return from the First World War, I came to live with my sister."

The Cloisters of Canterbury

"Mary, do you know why Mr. Wiseman was in Germany at the time of his death?"

"Mr. Wiseman went to Zurich, Switzerland, and then to Munich, Germany, hoping to locate his sister and bring her to the United States. After his older sister was killed in China, he told Glen that he just had to try to find her and bring her to the States, with all the talk about what was happening to the Jewish people. Glen received a letter from a man at a bank in Zurich. Mr. Wiseman had known the man for years. He wrote that Mr. Wiseman had been in the bank and was going to go across the Alps with a friend. The friend returned to Zurich and told the banker that Mr. Wiseman had learned that his sister was dead, and that the Nazi SS in Munich had arrested Wiseman because he was a Jew, even though he had a Swiss passport. Then Glen received another letter from the Zurich banker telling of Mr. Wiseman's death on a train. Some time later another letter was received from a lawyer in London about Mr. Wiseman's death in a concentration camp."

"How did Mr. Hudson—Glen—learn of Ruth Watkins' death in England?"

"Glen received all of Mr. Wiseman's mail when he was out of town. A letter came from the United States Army or Air Force to Mr. Wiseman notifying him of Ruth's death in an auto accident near London. Another letter came after Glen made an inquiry to the government explaining the details, but I didn't see the letter."

"Mary, did Glen have a partner in his law office?"

"No, only Rose White, his secretary."

My mind was running faster than I could ask questions. "What happened to all of Glen's office records after his death?"

"Glen had not been feeling well, he was having heart problems. He was so overweight. He didn't want to go to the office every day. About a year before he was killed, he had his desk and chair, and another desk and chair for Rose, and filing cabinets moved here into the library next to the dining room. Rose would stop at the post office, pick up the mail from a box, and arrive here at nine every morning, five days a week."

"Then all of his records are still here? What happened to Rose?" I was moving a little fast.

Without hesitation, Mary answered both of my questions. "Yes, all of his records are in the library or in boxes in the third floor attic, and Rose still lives in town with her husband who's retired from the Army. She stops in every once in a while."

Just one more questioned, "You said Glen was killed?"

"Yes, one morning after Rose arrived with the mail. Rose said after he opened a letter, he put it in his suit coat pocket and told her he had to go to the courthouse. He walked down to the corner bus stop, just as he always did since he stopped driving. When he was getting off the bus at the courthouse, a car didn't stop for the red traffic light and ran over him. He died on the street."

"Mary, do you know if the letter Glen had taken with him was returned?"

"I am sure that it wasn't. At the time Rose said that she hadn't read the letter and wondered about it after the funeral."

It was time to leave. I didn't want to push Mary any further. Mary would be sure to tell Rose White of my visit, and I might want to talk with her. Having too many people aware of my activities might create problems, but I would risk a conversation with Rose White, if necessary. With the way Mary had freely provided answers to the questions and obviously so willing to talk, on Rose's next visit she would be given the details of my visit.

I thanked her for telling me about Ruth Watkins and that I was sure that her friends would be saddened to learn that she had died in England.

When I turned to leave, she reached out and held my hand for a moment. "Come back to see me when you can." The look in her eyes was sincere, a good-bye of two friends after an afternoon visit.

I had been there more than hour. She waved as I backed the car out of the driveway. I would, indeed, stop to see her again, maybe soon.

She had described Ruth Watkins as having blue eyes and blonde hair. The woman at the plant had dark brown eyes. If they were any darker, they would have been black and her hair was nearly a raven black, long with a natural wave.

A visit to the Hummels might prove useful at some point, but not now. They would certainly have pictures of the girls. There would be photographs in the yearbooks at the high school, and very likely at the *Springfield News Sun* newspaper and Vassar College. However, the high school sounded like the first stop.

I needed to get a current picture of this Ruth Watkins at the plant and that would be difficult. There was no way I could walk in and ask Ruth to pose or just walk up take her picture. What I needed was a camera like the one I used in the building when on the assignment for President Truman.

What an afternoon! I was moving on automatic now. Thank goodness that the training at the farm was for the mind as well as the body. I ate, but couldn't remember what, and then showered before collapsing on the bed.

•

I woke early, skipped breakfast, and drove north to Springfield High School. The laughter from the young boys and girls hurrying into the school reminded me of the many mornings that I had rushed to beat the bell before class started. I followed several students through the main door and stopped in front of a large glass-enclosed case. On display were numerous pictures and trophies of the school's athletics teams—football, basketball, baseball and track. On the lower shelf were pictures of the cheerleaders for various years.

There was one gold-framed picture of a cheerleader with a black ribbon draped over it. Under the picture was a plaque: "In Memory of Ruth Marie Watkins." A pretty girl with blonde hair dressed in a green and white cheerleader sweater and ruffled skirt with a smile that would bring joy to all. This was not the Ruth Watkins living in the Tudor house on Fountain Blvd and employed at the truck plant.

Leaving the school, I drove directly to the Springfield Police Department. The woman at the information desk directed me to the records room. I was surprised at the number of racks with large binders, but soon learned that they were not all arrest records. I removed the arrest record binder for the current year, placed it on a small table, and pulled up a chair. I opened the binder to the last page which had the arrest records for the previous Saturday.

The information was hand written in ink: Date, Case Number, Last Name, First name, Initial, Address (street number and name), City, State, Violation, Arresting Officer, Disposition.

I moved my right index finder down the list of names looking for Johnson, John. On the second page a Johnson first appeared. There were four Johnson's listed, but no John Johnson. Continuing down all the pages in the book I found many Johnsons, but not a single John Johnson. I searched into the next year, still nothing.

Just as I was about to give up, I turned to the last page in the December 1948 book. My finger stopped on December 7, 1948. Listed was John Johnson, arrested for intoxication, resisting arrest, address 1542 East Main Street, the same address listed in John Johnson's employment records, the same street address that did not exist. I copied the case number with all the information, and returned the binder to the shelf.

I gave the clerk across the hall the case number and asked her for the file. She looked at the number, and without saying a word, walked across the hall to same room where I had spent the last three hours. She returned and handed me a packet with the case number on it, and before returning to her desk admonished me, "You can't take the file out of this office."

Standing at the counter I withdrew the documents from the packet and read the police officer's report:

> John Johnson was arrested for intoxication and resisting arrest on December 7, 1948, at 11:15 PM in front of 1526 East Main Street. He was staggering in the middle of the street, drinking from a whiskey bottle, shouting profanities and fell to the street. When the officer attempted to place handcuffs on the subject, he swung the whiskey bottle, hitting the officer on his right leg, and continued shouting profanities. He was arrested and taken to the police station.

I thought that it was ironic for this German to get drunk on the anniversary of Pearl Harbor.

> The following morning he appeared in court, entered no-plea, was found guilty, fined $50.00 and cost, and released. Cash. Paid fine and cost.

No reference was made to who provided the money. His personal property removed at the time of his arrest indicated he had four dollars and thirty-three cents, no jewelry nor any other possessions.

I wondered what Johnson was doing on East Main Street, giving the same address as in his employment records. Revisiting East Main Street might be a good idea. I must have missed something. I put the documents back in the packet and returned them to the woman.

"Where would I find the records of a hit-and-run accident that happened just over four years ago? A man was killed."

"What was the name of the man killed?"

"Glenn Hudson, he was a local lawyer who was hit in front of the courthouse and died on the street."

The woman turned without hesitation, walked directly to a row of filing cabinets, opened one drawer, and removed a packet similar to the previous one. She handed it to me.

"Glenn Hudson was a nice man; he was in our office at least once a week when he was active in practicing law."

I removed the documents and read:

> Springfield Police Department Accident Report dated November 10, 1948, at approximately 11:17 AM, white male, stepped from Springfield city bus, at the Bus Stop. He walked in front of the bus. The traffic light was red. The automobile drove past the stopped bus at a high rate of speed, car's right front fender hit the man, and the man was knocked back in front of the bus. The bus driver immediately exited the bus to assist the man. The bus driver identified the man as Glenn Hudson, a regular bus passenger. Springfield city ambulance attendant declared Hudson dead at the scene. The driver of the car did not stop or return to the scene of the accident. Two bus passengers identified the automobile as a 1945 or 1946 Dark Gray Buick four-door.

I continued reading. There was no information about Hudson's personal property. The Coroner's report listed cause of death, multiple head and chest injuries from a hit-and-run auto, dead at the scene.

The next document was very interesting:

> Ohio State Patrol: 1946 Buick 4-door found in ditch on the east side of Route 4, six miles south of the Dayton City limits, no license plate. The Buick had a large dent in the right front fender and the right headlight was shattered. A Dayton auto dealership reported the car stolen before noon on the day of Hudson's death.

I copied the details of the documents and returned them to the woman and left the building in complete disbelief. It was possible for someone to have stolen a car from an auto dealership and was unable to stop at the light. There was no record that the police were pursuing the auto. However, no one in a stolen car would stop at an accident scene. Was this accident merely a tragic coincidence?

There were many more unanswered questions. However, the most important question remained: Who was the woman living in the Tudor house on Fountain Blvd and employed at the truck plant?

Doud needed to know about these facts, but first I wanted to see Glenn Hudson's records of Henry Wiseman.

•

The following morning I arrived at the truck plant, walked through the plant visiting with the foreman in each of the departments, as usual, and spoke to a number of the workers. I stopped in the engine department, and watched the men assembling the truck motors. John A. Johnson was installing pistons into the engine block. He looked up at me and started on the next assembly; he was very efficient. He had obviously worked on gasoline engines before. He showed more skill at the job than the others in the department.

As I walked past Ruth Watkins' desk, she was talking on the telephone. I waved to her and went into my office. For the next three hours, I worked on my report for the Cleveland office. At noon I left for lunch and noticed that Ruth was still talking on the telephone.

I left the plant and drove to O'Brian's Tavern. It was starting to rain. My mind was on Henry Wiseman's files at the deceased attorney's home. As soon as I finished eating, I drove over to the Hudsons' home. I wondered what Mary Combs would say when she saw me again. I knocked on the door and Mary opened it with a smile

"Good afternoon...come in."

"How are you and Mrs. Hudson?"

"We are doing very well, thank you."

"Mary, I wonder if a may look at Mr. Wiseman's files, especially the letter about Ruth Watkins' death. There is something bothering me about her death."

Without hesitating she led me to the library, turned on the light, and pointed to an oak file. "All of Mr. Wiseman's records are in that filing cabinet. Would you like a cup of tea?"

The Cloisters of Canterbury

"That would be very nice, thank you."

I opened the bottom drawer of the five drawer filing cabinet with "W" on the front. The first file was "Henry A. Wiseman Probate." I looked at the labels on the folders: Valley Bank, Main Apartments, Rentals, Insurance Auto, Insurance Fountain Blvd., Insurance Main Street Property and finally, Ruth Marie Watkins.

I removed the Watkins file and placed it on the desk. Mary Combs came back carrying a silver tray with several small sugar cookies, a china teapot, cup and saucer, silver cream pitcher and sugar bowl, and a linen napkin, which she carefully placed on the desk. She poured tea into the cup.

"Thank you, Mary."

She left the room smiling. "Call me if you need anything."

The first document in the Watkins file was the letter from the Army notifying the next of kin of Ruth Watkins' death in an auto accident in London, England. The next letter was Hudson's letter to the government requesting further information. A reply letter from the Eighth Air Force provided details of the accident. It stated that Ruth Watkins was a passenger in a private vehicle driven by Frances Murita on a road near London. Another vehicle struck the car. Murita was thrown from the car. Ruth Watkins was killed upon impact. The other vehicle did not stop. There were no witnesses. Murita provided information to a British constable and the military police from the American Eighth Air Force. I copied the letter into a notebook, dated and initialed it.

I opened the "Henry A. Wiseman Probate" file. It contained a copy of the will that was on file at the Clark County Courthouse. There was also a letter from the Zurich banker advising of his death, the same letter that was in the probate file, and a letter from Alvin C. Waite, a lawyer in London, England, advising that Henry A. Wiseman had died in the concentration camp at Auschwitz, according to death records discovered by the military when they liberated the camp.

I made a note: Conflict in where Wiseman died. Was it Auschwitz or Dachau? Where are the two camps located? I copied the letter into my notebook, dated and initialed it, then turned the original over, initialed and dated it in very small letters. I returned the file to the oak filing cabinet. Having read all of the documents and made hand-written copies, I was ready to call Doud and inform him what I had discovered.

While sitting at the desk drinking a cup of tea without cream or sugar, Mary Combs returned to the library and joined me in the chair next to the desk. I told her that the information helped clear up some of the details of Ruth Watkins' death, and I would be more comfortable now when talking with her friends.

Mary Combs walked me to the door and placed her small hand on my right arm. "Come back soon."

As I drove away, she stood on the porch and waved.

I realized it was also time to call the office in Cleveland and give them a report on the status of my analysis of the truck company. The first draft should be ready late next week. The time devoted to Johnson, and now Ruth Watkins, was interfering with my consulting assignment. I couldn't delay calling Doud any longer and I needed to report what I had learned about Johnson or Mueller and Ruth Watkins. This would be a good weekend to spend with my parents in Xenia.

I drove back to the hotel and parked in front of the Lincoln-Mercury auto dealership. There always seemed to be a parking place in the area. The window with "Read Your Palm Tell Your Fortune" appeared to be cleaner. Once again, the woman with a veil over half of her face was motioning for me to come in. On the back wall I could see a doorway covered by strands of beads.

She dropped the veil from her face, walked to the door, and called out, "You are in great danger, let me help you!"

I stopped, but didn't turn around. What does she know that I don't know? I walked toward the hotel, but couldn't stop thinking that there certainly was danger out there. If John A. Johnson was in fact Hans Mueller, a Nazi SS officer wanted for war crimes, and Ruth Watkins, who was not Watkins but apparently lived with Mueller, both could be dangerous. They were living in a house that had been willed by Henry Adolph Wiseman to his niece. Wiseman died either at Auschwitz or on a train to Dachau. His niece, Ruth Watkins, died in an accident in England. Was the hit-and-run auto killing of Wiseman's lawyer, Glenn Hudson, connected? With all of these deaths, maybe...I should see what the palm reader could offer.

I really wasn't concerned about the alarm sounded by the palm reader. The real danger would be walking behind the curtain of beads. This little gypsy girl's father or husband would have my wallet and maybe my life. It didn't take much to remember when I was an MP, and pulling some of the soldiers out of similar places on Staten Island.

The walk up the hill to the Shawnee Hotel was all the exercise I was getting. I passed the elevator, found a telephone booth and called Joseph Davidson at the company office to advise him of the progress at the truck company.

The Cloisters of Canterbury

After packing a small bag for the weekend, I made certain that all my papers were in the briefcase. When I turned the room key in at the desk, I told the desk clerk that I would be out of town until Sunday evening, but was not checking out.

I was going home for the weekend.

Chapter 16

QUESTIONS?

Driving to my parents' home gave me a chance to think about everything I had learned. I felt there was little doubt about the identity of Hans Mueller. But learning that the woman Hans Mueller was living with had assumed the dead Ruth Watkins' identity could lead to more than just Hans Mueller's arrest and his return to face a war crimes trail. I needed direction from Doud.

What was difficult to understand was why no one had questioned the woman assuming Ruth Watkins' identity. There was also something about the letter from the lawyer in England that was puzzling. The information about the auto accident and death of Ruth Watkins outside of London was vague, as was the letter from the government to Hudson.

I needed positive identification of Wiseman's niece, Ruth Watkins, without disturbing the Springfield neighborhood if possible. If John A. Johnson was arrested, the woman who had assumed Ruth Watkins' identity would take flight. What was their connection? Just lovers? Ruth Watkins' voice gave no indication that she was from Europe, maybe educated in the United States. If she had been educated in England she would still have a trace of an accent.

The Cloisters of Canterbury

As Biff had said, "It's in their blood and seeps out of the mouth when they speak."

I planned to stop in Dayton and call Doud from a pay phone in the lobby of the Belmont Hotel, not wanting to make calls to the Group from telephones in Springfield. Maybe it was an unnecessary concern, but they related some unusual stories at the farm and the experiences of the intelligence officers that returned from the field that more than justified my concern.

Going to the last telephone booth in the row, I gave the operator the number. It was answered on the third ring. "It's too early to hunt coon in Texas."

I replied, "I am from Missouri, show me."

Doud drawled, "Tell me about it."

"I am almost positive that Hans Mueller is working in the truck factory using the name of John A. Johnson and is living with the employment manager's secretary, who has assumed the identity of Ruth Watkins, who was killed in England during the war."

Doud said, "What are you saying?"

I related everything about the real Ruth Watkins, Wiseman's niece, and how I was able to see the Wiseman's records at his deceased attorney's house. Additionally, my concern is that her association with Hans Mueller could lead to others who were involved in the conspiracy. I explained that Glenn G. Hudson, the lawyer who had previously represented Henry Wiseman and probated his will, was dead. That Hudson had moved his law office to his home prior to his death and his records were stored in the home.

Doud expressed the need for pictures of Ruth Watkins and John A. Johnson. He asked where I would be that evening. I told him at my parents' home in Xenia. He asked me to call him back at nine.

I arrived in Xenia just before six. When I opened the door of my parents' home, the aroma of chicken frying and cinnamon from an apple pie in the oven reached me before Mother greeted me with a hug and kiss.

Mother said, "I knew that you would be home in time for dinner."

Dad and Angel were in the kitchen. For years you could set your watch at six when we sat down for dinner in the evening, six days a week—Sundays could vary.

Dinner with my family was one of the most wonderful experiences in my life. We lingered around the table talking until well after eight.

I explained, "I have a call to make at nine, so I have a half hour to wash the dishes."

Angel started removing dishes from the table. "I'll help."

I went into the library, closed the door and placed a collect call to Doud. It was answered on the third ring with the usual greeting and response. Doud told me to continue to develop as much information as I could on the woman who had assumed Ruth Watkins' identity. He also instructed me to look at the Wiseman's files and take pictures of the Wiseman documents with a camera that would be sent to me. It was important to get a photograph of the deceased Ruth Watkins and of the woman calling herself Ruth Watkins.

"Rob, it would be helpful if we had a photograph of the man you believe is Hans Mueller, but be careful. If it is Mueller, he is a dangerous man. He has nothing to lose."

"If Ted Walsh is still at Patterson Field in Dayton why not have him visit me," I suggested. "We could tour the plant and he could take the pictures. At the farm he was the best at photography."

"That's a good idea. We'll send you a camera to General Delivery at the Springfield post office that can be used to photograph the documents and pictures of the man and the woman. After you get all of the pictures, call and we will advise you where the film should be developed.

"Rob, have you talked with Walsh about being your camera man?"

"No. I haven't seen or talked with him since before joining James Allen & Associates."

"On second thought, I don't think that Ted Walsh should visit you and take the pictures. In fact, don't even discuss anything about your assignment with him."

I was disappointed about not being able to use Ted, and concerned about the instruction not to discuss anything with him. I was thankful for the photography training at the farm, and hoped that I remembered enough to do it properly.

Doud ended the telephone call with, "Be careful."

I hung up the phone. This certainly was not the description given by the Group when they recruited me to be a courier. They'd only said: "Just look at the photographs. You might see one of them." Furthermore, Doud's instructions not to discuss anything about my assignment with Walsh really bothered me. We were trained to work as a team at the farm, but Walsh was not part of my assignment. On the other hand, they did say that we would be on our own.

The rest of the weekend I continued to think about what was re-

The Cloisters of Canterbury

quired for the Group and not the consulting assignment. I needed to confirm that John A. Johnson was Hans Mueller before the Group called in the U.S. marshals. They needed a current photograph of Johnson, but it would not be easy to obtain. I wasn't sure how to accomplish it, unless Johnson got arrested for something and was held long enough for the feds to get involved. Maybe they could arrest him for being in the country illegally. Johnson hadn't been driving, so he couldn't be arrested on a traffic violation and I didn't know of any bars that he frequented. The bruise on Ruth's face probably was the result of his temper, but she was not likely to have him arrested. And, of course, I certainly wasn't interested in provoking him myself.

There was no doubt in my mind that the person calling herself Ruth Watkins was not the niece of Henry Adolph Wiseman.

Mary Combs, sister-in-law of Glenn Hudson, who had been Wiseman's lawyer, had been very helpful. I still had not contacted the parents of Elizabeth Hummel, Ruth Watkins' high school friend, and was not sure that it was a good idea. More than likely Mary Combs had talked with them after my visit with her. Having too many people aware of my interest was not a good idea.

A visit to the local newspaper could be productive. They might have printed Ruth Watkins' picture with the news story of her death. The picture in the lobby at the Springfield High School certainly was not the person living in the house.

After the camera arrived from Doud I needed to look at the Wiseman's records again. What had Hudson received that sent him to the courthouse on the last day of his life? Mary Combs would probably allow me to looked at the records again, as well as arrange a meeting with Rose White, Hudson's secretary, if needed.

•

I returned to Springfield on Sunday night after the weekend with my parents and parked in front of the gypsy palm reader's window. When I got out of the car and removed the briefcase and overnight bag, I noticed that the palm reader's window was dark. That was different. Everything else on the street was the same. The walk up the Limestone hill to the hotel was the same. The desk clerk at the Shawnee Hotel was the same when I picked up the room key. But, for some reason I didn't feel the same.

I read the daily field reports for the truck plant and the notes for the

Group; all interesting, but something was missing in both. I remembered a training session at the farm, "Look for what is missing."

My internal alarm clock ended another restless night. I had not been able to get a good night's sleep since arriving in Springfield. The first nights were of anticipation of the assignment—expecting it to be an evaluation of a company's operation and making proposed changes that would assist in meeting their objectives. Granted, I was to be looking for individuals who were of interest to the Group, but didn't expect to have so many complications arise.

Sometime during the night I dreamed about Hudson's death from the hit-and-run car as he walked in front of the Springfield city bus. Was it connected to Mueller and Watkins? It just didn't seem feasible. It had to have been a coincidence, but, oh, how convenient.

On the farm, Ted Walsh had been the outstanding one of the twenty in taking pictures under difficult conditions, and his development and printing skills were impressive. I wanted Ted to visit the truck plant and do the camera work. However, Doud not only changed his mind, he further instructed me not to discuss anything about the assignment with Walsh. This put me all alone, other than telephone conversations. I then remembered what Doud had said when he recruited me: "You may have the occasion of being alone and must make the decision. If it's the wrong one, there will be no one to help you since the Group doesn't exist."

I dressed and walked to the post office. It was barely eight. The General Delivery window was just opening. I gave my name to the elderly male clerk who searched a number of packages until he found the right one. The package was about an eighteen-inch square box, postmarked Fairborn, Ohio, with no return address. I wondered who was in the Fairborn area, possibly someone at Wright or Patterson Field. The Group had far-reaching connections. Ted Walsh was on assignment at Patterson Field just a few miles away. Was that just another coincidence?

Back in my hotel room, I opened the package and removed a box revealing a Minox camera. It was similar to the one that we used for training at the farm and the one I had used on the assignment for President Truman. There were four metal cassettes of film, a Bakelite developing tank, three trays for processing, three bottles of chemicals for developing and printing, a magnifying glass for viewing film, a large number of small clips to hold film and prints to dry, a pair of small tweezers and a metal box marked printer/enlarger. An envelope was marked "photo paper." I also found six envelopes for film storage, and another envelope marked instructions, along with a brief note: "There are forty frames in each cassette."

Thank goodness for the instructions! I wasn't sure that I had remembered them from the farm. After reading the one-page of instructions, I inserted one of the film cassettes into the camera The camera was about half the size of a Mars candy bar. It was concealed when I closed my hand. I practiced taking pictures for several minutes. It would be possible to snap a picture of someone without their knowledge. However, indexing the film for another picture would require hiding the camera from view. Attaching the removable key chain that came with the camera determined the distance that the camera should be from the document. The only other concern was sufficient light; a gooseneck desk lamp was perfect. I put the camera in the inside packet of my suit coat, and left.

•

I drove past the Wiseman house and parked in the driveway of the Hudson home. As soon as the door of the car closed, the front door of the house opened and the smiling face of Mary Combs greeted me. It was like the greeting I received from my mother when returning home. She met me on the porch. It was almost as if she had expected me to give her a hug. I gave her a small bouquet of flowers that I had purchased from the florist on the way over.

"Mary, I would like to have another look at the Wiseman's records. I want to be sure that I haven't missed anything about Ruth Watkins' death."

She smiled, "You're always welcome."

What a lovely lady; although, I was sure that she was very lonely.

In the back of my mind, something kept asking if there was something else in the relationship of Wiseman and his attorney, Glenn Hudson. I had seen the letter to Henry Wiseman notifying him of Ruth Watkins's death in an auto accident near London. At that time, Hudson was aware of Wiseman's death. I was hoping to bring up the subject of Glenn Hudson's death. In our earlier discussion, Mary Combs had not given me any specific details. However, I had since seen the Springfield Police Department's accident report, but had not discovered the letter that had sent Hudson on the bus ride to his death. I wanted to look for anything that had been missed and photograph all of the documents that pertained to Ruth Watkins and Wiseman.

I followed Mary into the library. She turned on the lights and said, "I'll be back in a few minutes."

I opened the file drawer and started going through the files, page by page. Mary returned with a silver tray and tea service and placed it on the desk.

She smiled. "Just call if you need anything."

I looked at each document in the folders. Every document that was of interest I placed on the desk under the gooseneck lamp and took a picture with the Minox camera. After taking a picture of the last document, I heard the front door open, and then the sound of Mary's voice and another woman's. I returned the folders to the filing cabinet, put the camera in my jacket pocket, and had just poured a cup of tea when Mary returned.

"Mr. Royal, this is Rose White, Mr. Hudson's secretary that I told you about. This is Mr. Royal, Rose."

I stood and accepted the woman's hand.

Mary spoke, "Rose, have a chair next to the desk. I'll be right back with some more tea."

Rose White was a petite woman, white hair pulled back in a bun, probably a little older than Mary. Through her eyeglasses, her pale blue eyes revealed a questioning look. She waited for me to speak, surely expecting an explanation for my interest.

"Mary has probably told you that I was asked to inquire about Ruth Watkins by some of her friends in the Woman's Army Corps. When I learned from Mary that she had died in an auto accident, I informed her friends. They've asked me to learn as much as possible about her death. Mary has given me the opportunity to read some of the documents that have provided me a little more information. It certainly is sad to learn of the death of someone so young."

Mary returned with another tray with cups, more tea and several small butter cookies. She poured tea for Rose, added more to my cup and then poured a cup for herself. I pulled another chair up to the desk for Mary.

For the next thirty minutes, I led the conversation to the Wittenberg Campus, Mary's father, the history professor at Wittenberg, and inquired about Rose. Rose's inquiring look in her eyes had not changed. I needed to address her concerns.

"Mrs. White, in reading the letters and talking with Mary about

Ruth and Mr. Hudson, I have been having difficulty getting the death of Mr. Hudson out of my mind. Something must have been very important in the letter that you gave him the morning of his death. I didn't see anything in the file that should have disturbed him."

Rose looked at me and then at Mary, then back at me. Her eyes were penetrating mine, searching and questioning. She began, "After Mr. Hudson opened the letter, I could tell that he was very upset. I had worked for him for over thirty years and knew his moods. The only thing he said was that he should not have probated Wiseman's will."

"Was there anything unusual about the letter that you could see?"

"I opened all of his mail, but this letter was marked personal. It was unusual for him to receive mail marked personal. I remember looking at the envelope when I gave it to him. It was postmarked Dayton, Ohio, and the return address was the Valley Bank in Dayton." Her eyes softened and were no longer penetrating and searching; now they were moist and sad.

"After Mr. Hudson's death were any of his personal things, like his wallet or the letter he had with him, returned to Mrs. Hudson?"

"Mr. Hudson never carried a wallet after he stopped driving. He would usually have a few dollars and some change in his pants pocket. He would cash a check for fifty dollars at the bank when he went to the courthouse. He would put most of it in the right hand drawer of the desk and take money out when he needed it."

Rose got up from her chair and opened the top right drawer revealing a small tin box. On the top was printed in faded letters, Swiss Chocolates.

"Mr. Wiseman gave him the box of chocolates when he returned from a trip to Europe." Rose opened the tin box and removed two ten-dollar bills. There were tears in the eyes of Rose and Mary. It was as if Glen Hudson had walked into the room. At this point it was time for me to leave.

"I am glad to have met you, Mrs. White, and, Mary, thank you so much for the tea and the delightful butter cookies."

I shook hands with Rose, and then walked to the door with Mary. She said, "Please come back soon."

When I started down the porch steps, I stopped and turned. "Mary, how do you shop for groceries?" She replied that they called the market and had them delivered.

As I drove away, Mary stood on the porch waving. It had been an emotional visit, but I had learned that the letter responsible for Glenn

Hudson's fatal bus ride came from the Valley Bank in Dayton. I wondered if John Myers at the Valley Bank who gave me the briefcases for the courier assignments for the Group could provide any information. That was a question for Doud.

I drove directly to the Springfield newspaper office, parked across the street, dodged two cars and hurried through the traffic. The receptionist told me that the circulation department was on the second floor. I was greeted by a man in a wheelchair behind the low counter, probably constructed especially for him.

"I am interested in articles about the death of Ruth Marie Watkins. She was killed in an auto accident in England in June of 1945, but it was not known locally until November 1945."

The man turned his wheelchair around, maneuvered it down an aisle of racks, humming all the way. The man was singing softly, truly, a man who had little to rejoice about, but he could not have been more pleasant. He returned with four newspapers across his lap and placed them on the counter.

One had a picture of Ruth Watkins with the story about her death on the front page and another had her picture when honored at the half-time ceremony of a high school football game. The other two were articles without pictures.

"Do you have copies available?"

"We do not keep extra copies that far back. "

"My I take photographs of them?"

The man looked surprised when I removed the Minox camera from my jacket. "I just need a gooseneck desk light."

The man turned his wheelchair around and said, "Follow me."

I followed him across the hall to a room that had several desks with gooseneck desk lights. He pointed to a desktop that was clear. I placed the first newspaper on the desk, adjusted the lamp, set the camera lens and distance and took two pictures. Then I placed the second paper on the desk and took two pictures of it.

I handed the newspapers to the man. "Thanks for your help."

The man smiled, turned his wheel chair around and resumed his singing as he rolled back to the other room.

•

Arriving at the truck plant at ten o'clock, Ruth Watkins, or whoever she was, was not at her desk. I checked the in-coming mail on my desk—just weekly production reports from the previous week that I would review after my daily tour of the plant. I removed the brown leather notebook from my briefcase to make notes, just like every other day, and then stepped out of view from the doorway to check the Minox camera. It was ready, but was I?

It was interesting to observe the sounds and movement of the men and machinery in the plant. At times there was a rhythm, almost like a song. However, when I listened very closely, each department had its own unique music.

One department has several rows of punch presses; some were in unison with each other, machines punching different sized holes at different speeds, contributing different notes to the music of the factory. The large presses boomed as they formed fenders, door panels and the hoods for the trucks. The forming of each part contributed musical notes in the orchestra. Voices of men, barely heard over the sounds of metal and machines, played the role of the choir.

Continuing the tour, I paused to make notes in my brown leather notebook, small details that could be helpful in formulating my evaluation of the truck plant's operation. Many of the notes reaffirmed previous observations. I talked with the foremen in the departments and engaged in conversations with a number of the workers that I had encountered on previous tours.

While walking around and talking with the men, I continued to look for ways to use the camera. On several occasions, I removed the camera from my jacket pocket and simulated taking pictures while writing in the notebook.

I didn't intend to take any pictures; I just needed to work out moves that would accomplish the objective. Taking pictures of specific individuals without the subject being aware of it was not going to be easy.

When I reached the engine department, John A. Johnson, who was probably Hans Mueller, was assembling a truck motor. While watching him installing the pistons in two motor blocks, he looked up.

I nodded my head up and down and said, "Good work."

Having watched Johnson several times before, it was obvious the he was a good mechanic. I walked away knowing that it would be impossible to take pictures undetected. After finishing my tour I returned to the office. Ruth Watkins was back at her desk.

I went into the office, sat down in the desk chair and tried to figure out how I was ever going to be able to take pictures of Johnson and Watkins.

Chapter 17

Explosion

That evening while having dinner at O'Brian's Tavern, I wondered if another trip to the deceased lawyer's house and a visit with Mary Combs would add anything more. There was always a chance something had been missed in the files. But...would that be too suspect?

After dinner, I returned to the hotel. I enjoyed a reasonably good night's sleep, except for the reoccurring dream of Hudson's death after getting off the bus.

I arrived at the plant the next morning and parked two cars from Ruth Watkins' Desoto—she did keep it clean. In fact, she did a much better job of caring for her car than I did mine. Of course, she might be having John Johnson doing it. I wondered what other household duties Johnson had been assigned, or did he do the assigning? That was more likely.

I walked past Ruth's desk. "Good morning. How was your night?"

"Good morning."

She ignored, "How was your night?" which didn't surprise me. This was better than all the other mornings since her face appeared to have been used as a punching bag. There were no signs of it this morning. Time and makeup had done wonders.

I didn't want to change my routine, so I dropped the briefcase next to the desk, and with my brown notebook and camera, I left the office for the daily tour.

The activity in the plant seemed at a higher level than the previous few days. The tow motors were moving in and out of the production areas without sounding their horns and the profanity was absent. I found it most enjoyable talking with the foremen in the departments, inquiring about the production and asking why certain things were being done as they were. Sometimes when asking why, the replies from the different men became part of my evaluation. Some would say, "We have always done it that way." "Can't be done no other way." "This is better." "Ain't any other way."

I was just entering the motor assembly department when a loud explosion came from the motor test area. Flames and smoke billowed to the ceiling around the engine test area. Men shouting, some obviously in pain, drowned out all the factory noise. Several men were using fire extinguishers. The plant's fire alarm siren was deafening.

I moved out the way of several plant firemen who were pulling a large red tank on wheels with "For Gas and Oil Fires Only" painted in white on the side. Two nurses from the plant's first-aid station ran behind the firemen. The sounds of distant sirens grew louder. I went to an open window and watched a Springfield fire truck arrive at a large door twenty or more feet away, and two ambulances came to a stop next to the fire truck. More sirens shrieked in the distance, getting louder by every second.

Apparently, one of the fifty-gallon gas tanks had exploded. Gasoline showered the oil-soaked floor near the motor test area and quickly spread into the motor assembly area where John Johnson worked.

I watched as seven men were moved from the immediate area by their fellow workers. They were laid on the floor out of danger and the nurses attended them. Firefighters sprayed the flames with foam and several men dipped sand with buckets from fifty-five gallon barrels and threw it onto the flames creeping along the floor. Between the screams of those burned and others shouting orders, it was surprising how orderly they had addressed the emergency—certainly due to previous training for such a fire.

Smoke still lingered in the area after the fire was extinguished. The smell would be a reminder of the explosion for some time. There was little visible evidence of damage to the building. Four truck motors on stands had burned. Fortunately, only one of the fifty-gallon gasoline tanks had exploded. It seemed impossible that the other three tanks had not exploded with the heat and fire around them.

The firemen moved the injured from the building on stretchers to waiting ambulances, where they were transported to the Springfield City Hospital. With all the confusion, I was able to take a number of pictures of the fire area.

When the area was clear, I went into the motor assembly area. Many of the workers had left the building and were standing outside the overhead door used by the firemen. I joined the group and listened to the conversations of the men talking about those injured and speculating as to the cause and who was responsible. Some were blaming a leak from one of the gasoline lines, which was very probable, and that one of inspectors testing the running motors might have been smoking a cigarette, tossed the cigarette on the floor when he was finished, and hadn't put it out when he stepped on it.

John Johnson was not with the group of men. A tall man, over six feet, probably weighing over two-hundred pounds, with red hair, who worked in the same motor assembly area as John Johnson, was standing at the edge of the group.

I approached the man and asked, "Do you know who was injured?"

He was quick to reply, "Harry Rowell, our foreman, and John Johnson were two of them." He continued, "Johnson went into the test area because they were testing an engine that he had assembled and Harry had gone in to get him—he wasn't supposed to be in there. We heard him swearing in Kraut at Harry as they were coming out of the test area when all hell broke lose."

"Do you know how bad they were hurt?"

"No, but that German bastard deserved to be burned, just like all those people the Krauts burned alive during the war."

I looked into the man's eyes. He was angry and probably knew something. "Let's pray that Harry and the rest of them will be all right."

Starting to walk away, I stopped, turned to the man, and asked, "Is Johnson a German name?"

"Johnson's not his real name, and there are others around here not using their God-given names."

"How do you know that?"

"One of the guys, after his parents died, was raised by his grandparents, his mother's parents who had come from Germany after the first big war. They never learned English. All they spoke was German. He still understands these Krauts. He listens when they are sitting around blowing smoke, but they don't know that he understands what they say."

I wanted to know more but didn't want to scare him off. This was real anger, probably due to the foreman, Harry Rowell, being injured. I had talked with Rowell on several occasions and he was a likeable man. Still, while this man was angry, it would probably be the best time to learn as much as possible. I had seen him around, but hadn't talked with him and didn't know his name. I extended my right hand to the man. He had a strong grip.

"I am Rob Royal, what's your name?"

"Art Reilly."

Reilly wasn't a German name and Art was probably as Irish as you could get, red hair and all. I tried to get more information from Art Reilly. "I am here at the plant to make some recommendations for the expansion of the plant."

He responded, "Harry Rowell told us in a shop meeting what was going on."

"Art, what does your friend say that Johnson and his friends talk about?"

"Sometimes about living in Germany before and during the war and that they had lived in Canada for a while. Sometimes about their families that died or are still in Germany. Some of it's a lot of bull."

"Art, how many are not using their right names?"

"There are four men including Johnson and a woman in the office."

He was answering my questions without hesitation. "Where do they live?"

"Three of them live over on Henry Street and that SOB Johnson lives with that woman in the office some place near the hospital."

I wasn't going ask about the woman. I already knew who that might be. Without giving him a chance to think, I said, "Somebody the other day said that he gets all bent out of shape when he's had fight with his old lady."

"Yeah, if he sees someone talking to her he beats her up."

Risking one more question, "Art, what are the names of the other three?"

"Who the hell knows, all of them call themselves Johnson."

It was time to back off. "It has been nice talking with you, Art." It wasn't going to be easy checking the employment records. There were fifty or sixty people named either Johnson or Johnston on the employee payroll records.

As I walked back to the office I observed meetings going on in several offices. Ruth Watkins was not at her desk. Another secretary said that Ruth and the employment manager had gone to the hospital to help identify the men and see how badly they were injured.

I sat at my desk and started to think about the events of the day, wondering what else was going to be involved in this adventure. I was concerned about the condition of the men, and wondered if John Johnson had received burns on his face. That would complicate identification even more.

I had been provided a description of the activities in every department: manpower by occupation, along with production schedules and performance. I opened the folder marked Motor Testing. Motor inspectors selected various engines for testing from the assembled units. It was easy to conclude that an accidental fire was very possible. All it would take was a leak in one of the copper lines running from a gas tank and a cigarette tossed on the floor.

After five, I returned everything to the briefcase and left the plant. O'Brian's Tavern seemed like a good place for dinner and a beer. It had been a difficult day. Remembering someone at the farm saying it would be boring most of the time, other than sitting in the old '38 Ford on Main Street, it had not been boring at all on this assignment.

Driving back to the hotel my mind was spinning in many directions. What if Johnson's face was burned and couldn't be identified? What if he died? Art Reilly said that Johnson was walking in front of the foreman, Harry Rowell, when the explosion took place behind them. It was possible that their faces were not burned.

•

The following morning I was up early. I went downstairs and bought a *Springfield Sun* newspaper at the front desk and started reading it while walking to the dining room. The headlines read: "EXPLOSION AT TRUCK PLANT, ONE DEAD," with one picture from the fire scene on the front page. Harold, my regular waiter, directed me to my regular table. Everything was regular except what was in the paper. I barely spoke to Harold, just said, "The regular."

In the front-page article, according to a hospital spokesperson, "Seven men had been injured in the explosion, some men badly burned, all were taken to Springfield Hospital, one died of his injuries, five others in critical condition, and one only received minor injuries and was expected to be released from the hospital within a few days.

A company official stated that a full investigation was underway. Credit was given to the safety department for the training of the company's workers that prevented the fire from spreading until the Springfield firemen arrived. He praised the company's nurses for providing first aid at the scene and in the ambulances that transported the men to the hospital. He stated that the Springfield Fire Department's quick response prevented any major damages to the plant, and production had resumed on the third shift.

I looked for names. The name of the man who died would not be released until notification of his family. The article's details were not complete. I was well aware of things not in the paper.

The article covered most of the page and continued on the third page. I looked for pictures. There were several more of the fire scene, Springfield fire equipment and firemen, another of ambulances leaving with workers lining both sides of the road, but no pictures of the men.

Harold served my breakfast—eggs, bacon, toast and coffee—without disturbing me. I put the newspaper on the table and ate while rereading the articles. I was anxious to find out who had died. Someone at the plant would certainly know.

•

At the plant parking lot, I parked four spaces from Ruth Watkins' reserved space. Her car was not there—it was 8:20. She was normally at her desk by eight. However, this morning she was probably at the hospital with Johnson, or she may have spent the night there. I was still hoping that she wasn't at a funeral home picking out his casket. If that was the case, someone else would be preparing for a burial if the family had been located. My mind went back in time when I stood at the graves of so many bodies that had been returned from Europe and later standing beside Biff Wallace at several graves of his friends in England.

A woman sat at Ruth Watkins' desk. I asked about Ruth, and the woman told me that she was at the hospital with some of the injured men's families.

"Have they been able to notify the family of the man who died?"

"Yes, Harry Rowell's wife was in Michigan with her sick mother, and she was located last night. She'll be back in Springfield today."

Art Reilly had said yesterday that Rowell was walking behind Johnson at the time of the explosion. That Rowell had gone into the engine test area to get Johnson out of there, and now he was dead. Art Reilly and others were going to be angry and might even be dangerous. Their friend was killed because Johnson had been some place that he didn't belong.

I dropped my briefcase in the office and headed for the engine assembly department to look for Art Reilly.

The factory music was different. The tempo was slower, like a funeral march. There were no smiles on the men's faces. Their movements were in slow motion. They had lost one of their own, a friend for many, and a leader for all. As it so often happened, the value placed on coworkers wasn't realized until they were gone. They weren't necessarily close friends, but they contributed to each other's lives. It was like the man standing on a corner waving to everyone who passed, then one morning he was no longer there. People missed him, but never knew his name, just that he made their days a little better.

I wasn't looking forward to meeting Art Reilly, a redheaded Irishman whose temper had already been revealed. Art's red hair stood above the group of men gathered around him. He was talking rather loudly and emotionally about Harry Rowell's death, blaming John A. Johnson for it when I arrived. The whole group was angry. It wouldn't take much for them to become an unruly mob. The last thing I heard before Gaylord Brown, the general foreman, arrived and told them to get back to work was Art Reilly's angry voice.

"We'll kill that Kraut when he gets out of the hospital. He'll wish he had been killed in the explosion."

My previous conversation with Art Reilly after the explosion had convinced me that Art Reilly didn't like Johnson and the other Germans who were not using their own names. I wouldn't care to have Art Reilly as an enemy. The men moved off in several directions talking with each other. These wouldn't be the last words from Reilly.

Gaylord Brown stood watching the men go back to their jobs.

Having had several conversations with Brown, I asked, "How are the injured men doing?"

He replied, "It's too soon to tell. One or more of them still might not make it. They have been burned over most of their bodies."

"Those men who just went back to work certainly were expressing their anger."

Brown nodded. "Yes, and it's always sad to see nice people get so angry and become dangerous when someone they care about is injured. It's almost like a parent's rage after losing a child."

We walked together to the office area. I asked several questions about the plant's operation. I was getting close to finalizing my report. The more I walked through the plant and looked at their proposed additions, the more convinced I became that they should not expand this plant. It was old already with numerous additions that had proven inefficient. My recommendation was probably going to be that they buy land outside of Springfield, along a highway and a railroad. It should be flat and large enough for future growth. The existing plant was in a valley, on the low side of a hill, with nothing desirable around it. There were just several hundred small houses occupied by the workers, and it wouldn't be a popular decision to level all of the workers' homes. It was going to require some night hours to complete the report.

The explosion speeded up the need to get photographs of Johnson and Watkins. If Johnson got word of the anger of the men in the plant and was able to walk out of the hospital, he would disappear quickly. I wasn't sure about Ruth Watkins. She may have been able to accumulate enough cash from the apartment rents—there certainly hadn't been any money spent on maintenance or repairs. The cash in the bank accounts could make it easy for her to leave town. There were too many unknowns about her. Photographs of Johnson and Watkins were definitely needed.

I returned to the office feeling frustrated. Ruth still wasn't at her desk. I sat down in the chair and put my feet up on the desk. Nothing had really gone smoothly since I arrived. It certainly wasn't anything like the assignments in Cleveland before they sent me out on my own. During the next three hours I reviewed all of the information about the company. My proposal included the justification for building a new plant.

I left the plant for lunch, drove to the hospital, but didn't see Ruth Watkins' Desoto in the parking lot or on the street. Driving back downtown I decided to skip O'Brian's and drive over to Fountain past the Tudor house. Ruth's car was in the driveway. Normally when she was at home it was in the garage. She was probably changing clothes and was not going to be at the house for long. It was impossible to take her picture coming out of the house, and there was no purpose in waiting for her to leave.

I returned to the plant's parking lot and parked on the left of Ruth Watkins' reserved space. I lowered both front windows and waited. It was five minutes until one o'clock, Ruth's normal time to return from lunch when she did go out to eat. Most of the time she brought her lunch in a brown paper bag.

I opened the brown notebook and checked the camera. I hoped that it would appear that I was reading. If she did return to the plant, she would park in her reserved space, exit from the left door and I would try to get her picture. At ten minutes after one I thought that she wasn't coming back to the plant and had probably returned to the hospital.

Just as I was about to give up and get out of the car, the sound of a car motor stopped me. I looked in the rearview mirror and saw Ruth's Desoto pull into the lot. My heart started beating as if I had just run a mile. She parked in her usual space, opened the door and stepped out of the car, and turned looking directly at me. I snapped one picture, moved the slide, took another picture, and hurried out of the car. She did not realize that her picture had been taken.

"Ruth, I understand that you have been at the hospital. How are the injured men doing? I was sorry to learn of Harry Rowell's death. I talked with him several times in the plant and he seemed like a nice person."

Her face looked tired. "They are not doing very well, and, yes, Harry Rowell was a nice man. His wife is having a difficult time."

I left the windows opened in the car and while walking with Ruth into the plant I told her about entering the engine test area when the explosion took place and how all of the employees reacted to help the injured men and extinguish the fire.

Wayne Speer, the employment manager, called Ruth into his office as we passed. After taking Ruth's picture and rushing to walk with her into the plant, I had left my briefcase in the trunk of the car. I was just going back to get it when Ruth Watkins came into my office.

"Mr. Speer wants to see you in his office."

"Now?"

"Yes, I told him that you were in the engine test department at the time of the explosion."

I walked down the hall to Speer's office. The door was open.

Speer was talking on the telephone. He motioned for me to come in and pointed to a chair. While waiting for Speer to complete his telephone conversation, I looked at the display on the office wall: Speer's diploma from Wittenberg College in Springfield centered on one wall, with a number of pictures of Speer in a football uniform and a football in his hands. There were other pictures and awards from various civic organizations. On another wall were several pictures of Speer, his wife and five children—a nice looking family.

Speer said on the telephone, "I'll be at the hospital within the hour," and hung up.

"Ruth told me that you were in the engine test department at the time of the explosion."

I related everything as well as the conversations with the men after the fire and watched Speer's eyes when I told him about Art Reilly's comments about the Krauts. I was sure that Speer was a German name and doubted that he was Jewish. One of the family pictures on the wall in the office showed the family seated on the steps of a church that I recognized as a Lutheran church in Springfield. Speer's eyes and body language did not change.

Speer asked me to write down what I had seen while it was fresh in my mind for the accident investigating team. I agreed, but did not mention taking pictures of the fire scene.

Speer got up from his chair and said, "I must go to the hospital."

"May I go along?"

Speer paused, "I see no reason why not."

When we walked from the office to the parking lot, I noticed for the first time that Speer's right knee was stiff. I hadn't been aware of it before. During previous conversations with Speer he was always seated behind his desk.

While Speer drove us to the hospital, I used the opportunity to learn more about him. I learned he was born in Urbana, Ohio, his father was a city policeman, he played football in high school and college—Wittenberg College. In the last game of his senior year, he received a knee injury. It never healed properly and was stiff. He was classified 4F, so he didn't serve in the military service during the war. He started to work for the truck company in the employment office when he graduated from Wittenberg.

During the remainder of the trip my mind raced. Speer had been in Springfield when many events had taken place that would have made the Springfield newspaper. Attorney Glenn Hudson's death from the hit and run auto. Henry Wiseman's death in a concentration camp should have been in the local newspaper. The death of a popular Springfield High School graduate killed in an auto accident in England. It was difficult for me to think that Speer hadn't read the local paper. I knew that Ruth Watkins' death had made the front page.

How could Speer hire a woman by the name of Ruth Watkins when there were articles in the local paper about her death? How was it possible for Speer not to connect the Fountain Blvd. address to Mr. Wiseman and Ruth Watkins? It certainly seemed that he might have questioned Ruth Watkins. I wondered what answers she might have provided. Her application was far from complete. However, she was a beautiful woman with a smile and voice that could talk you into or out of just about anything.

Speer, as the employment manager, would certainly have hired his own secretary, the one and only Ruth Watkins. I decided I would not get into any conversations about Ruth Watkins or John A. Johnson with Wayne Speer. Instead, I asked Speer how the men were doing and he replied not well—they expected another one to die.

"I talked with Harry Rowell several times. He was very helpful about the department's operation. He was likeable; I hate to think of him dying from burns."

Speer responded, "He did receive some burns on his legs, but that didn't kill him. It was a piece of metal from the explosion that pierced the back of his head, like a bullet."

Speer parked his car next to the curb in front of the hospital. Speer knew where to go. We went directly to the surgery floor. I followed him, listening as he talked with a nurse that appeared to be in charge of the floor. She responded to Speer's questions about each of the men with details of their condition. She explained that Steve Holmes' condition had deteriorated, they did not expect him to make it through the night, and that his family was in the waiting room at the end of the hall.

The last man that Speer inquired about was John Johnson. She told him that his burns were first and second degree, confined to the area above both ankles to just below the knee, and had first and second degree burns on both hands, probably received attempting to put the fire out on his legs. They were keeping him sedated; but he should fully recover and be discharged from the hospital in three weeks or sooner.

Speer was showing deep concern about all the men. He asked the nurse if he could just look in on them. She said yes, except for the two who were critical. They were being isolated.

The nurse started down the hall and motioned for Speer to follow.

Speer said to me, "Would you like to go with me?"

"Yes, after seeing these men burning, I didn't expect to see any of them alive."

The nurse opened the door to the first room with men in the two beds. Their arms and legs were covered with moist bandages held off their beds by slings on cables. They were both sleeping. The nurse walked up to each man, turned and walked back to the door. Speer looked at the men and moved to the door. With the Minox camera in my hand I looked at their faces. Johnson was not one of them.

The next room was the same as the first, two beds, two men, moist bandages on their arms and legs. Except, one man's arms were not bandaged, just his hands. The nurse looked at both men, Speer followed. I looked at the first man and the second man. It was Johnson. With my back to the door I took two pictures of John A. Johnson, put the camera back in my suit coat pocket and left the room. Speer was twenty feet down the hall.

Returning to the nurses' station, I asked the nurse if there was a coffee shop in the hospital. She directed me to the first floor. I asked her to tell Mr. Speer that I would wait for him there.

I found the coffee shop and sat down to wait for Speer. The explosion had caused one death, possibly two more, and four others burned but expected to recover. Was this an accident or murder? Who was responsible?

John A. Johnson was in the engine test area where he didn't belong. Harry Rowell ordered him out of the area. Johnson was swearing at Rowell as he followed Johnson out of the test area. Gasoline was leaking onto the floor from the gas tank used to test the truck engines, someone tossed a cigarette that ignited the fire, the tank exploded, and a piece of metal entered the back of Harry Rowell's head. He died. Two other men that were testing the engine near the fifty-gallon gasoline tank received severe burns and were in critical condition. In my own analytical way, I continued to ponder the facts.

John A. Johnson did smoke cigarettes and toss them on the floor, but he usually stepped on them to be sure the fire was out. On the day of the accident, Johnson had a conversation with the men testing an engine that he had assembled. Were there problems with the engine? Had the men doing the testing told him to get out? In either case, John A. Johnson was known to have a temper and a short fuse. Then his foreman, Harry Rowell, ordered Johnson out of the test area. Johnson was angry and was heard swearing at Rowell. These facts led to the thought that in all probability John A. Johnson was smoking a cigarette, tossed it on the floor still burning, and did not step on it.

I needed to develop the film and see if the pictures of John A. Johnson and Ruth Watkins would help provide verification of their identities. When the men in the plant learned more details about the explosion and the cause of Harry Rowell's death, Johnson's life could be very short. This could prevent the Group from providing the information for Johnson's arrest. Then there was still the concern that Johnson would run as soon as they stopped sedating him. Any of these events could force Ruth Watkins to make a move that would prevent the Group from discovering her involvement.

Now my thoughts returned to why Wayne Speer hired Ruth Watkins. From all information that I had learned, she was not the Ruth Watkins that inherited the Wiseman estate. How did Speer fit in the puzzle? Did he hire her because of her beauty and charm?

There were still the unknown facts about Ruth Watkins' auto accident in England and Wiseman's death. The English lawyer certified Wiseman's death at the Auschwitz concentration camp, but the Swiss banker indicated that he died on a train going to the Dachau concentration camp. I remembered reading documents and seeing photographs of the concentration camps taken when Americans, British and the Soviets liberated them. I was sure that Auschwitz was in Poland and Dachau was near Munich, Germany. If the Nazis SS in Munich arrested Wiseman, why would they take him to a concentration camp in Poland? Something was wrong, but where was this leading?

It was too convenient for Hudson to die from a hit-and-run auto accident. When was Ruth Watkins' identity stolen and when did Hans Mueller arrive on the scene? There were too many questions without answers. I knew that more information was necessary before the Group could take action. Unfortunately, whenever I found an answer to one question, I ended up with two more questions.

I had finished two cups of coffee when Wayne Speer came into the coffee shop after talking with the family of the man in critical condition. His face appeared that he had aged twenty years in the last hour.

He walked up to me and said, "Steve Holmes just died."

"Do you want a cup of coffee?"

"No, I need a drink, but I need to get back to the office."

We walked to the car and drove back to plant in silence.

When we arrived, Speer went into the plant. I went to my car and drove back to my regular parking place in front of the gypsy palm reader's window. I had been able to park within thirty-feet of the palm reader every night since arriving in Springfield. As usual, the gypsy motioned for me to come in. I shook my head and said no, and went up the hill to the Shawnee Hotel. This time I skipped the elevator and walked up the stairs to my room.

Chapter 18

EVIDENCE

Developing the film was my top priority. I hoped that the pictures would come out well. I unlocked the travel lock from the closet door, removed the developing equipment, and put it on the nightstand. After reading the instructions over three times, I closed the blinds on the windows and turned the light on in the bathroom.

It was not a difficult process. I turned the bathroom light off, removed the cassette from the camera, inserted it into the developing tank, and poured the pre-measured developing solution into the tank. I closed the tank and slowly turned the knob that transferred the film from the cassette into the tank. I looked at my wristwatch—it would take awhile.

When the time was up, I opened the tank, held it under the cold water faucet and allowed a slow stream of cold water to rinse the film in the tank. After removing the filmstrip, I placed a clip on both ends of it, and fastened one clip to a string that I had previously attached to the shower curtain rod. The other clip weighted the film so it would hang straight down to dry.

It was a few minutes after six, time to eat.

After dinner, I returned to the room. The strip of film was still hanging from the string attached to the shower curtain rod by the clip. I wasn't sure why I would think that the film wouldn't be there, but there had been so many surprises lately. I would make prints of Johnson, Watkins, the fire scene, the newspaper articles of Ruth Watkins' death, and the Wiseman documents. I wanted to be sure they were readable. If the documents were not clear, I still had two cassettes of film to try again.

I went into the bedroom and removed the shade from the table lamp. Holding the film near the light bulb and using the magnifying glass that came with the camera, I was able to see that all of the frames had images.

Sitting in a chair at the small writing desk near the window, I began cutting the individual frames, placing them in the film envelopes one at a time. The filmstrip was small, each frame about three-eights of an inch wide. When this was complete, I placed the enlarger on the table and plugged it in. A small light bulb in the printer provided the necessary light so that the image on the film would project onto the photo paper in the bottom of the enlarger. After the paper was exposed, I placed it in tray number one and then number two, then removed it and hung the print to dry with the small clips onto the line running from the showerhead to the towel rod on the opposite wall. I followed the process on each frame of film.

The photographs of Ruth Watkins getting out of her car and John A. Johnson in bed at the hospital were clear and made good prints. They were the most important, but the other shots looked like they would be good, too.

There was nothing more to do now, so I put the travel lock on the bathroom door, put on my jacket, removed my pipe and tobacco from the suitcase, left the room, remembering to check the door. It was locked. As I walked down the two flights of stairs, I remembered at the farm one of the instructors saying, "There will be times when you wished that you were back in basic training, running and doing push-ups." Today was one of those days. I couldn't believe that such thoughts had entered my mind.

I went out the front door of the hotel, turned east on Main Street, and packed my Peterson pipe with some of the pipe tobacco Biff Wallace had sent me for Christmas. The aroma filled my mind with good memories. I looked down the street and saw the '38 Ford parked on the opposite side of the street about a hundred yards away. I thought it

The Cloisters of Canterbury

might be a good idea to check it.

After crossing the street, I walked slowly east. Men were still sitting on the curb and leaning on the building. I walked past the car, noting that all the tires still had air in them. The glass in the windows had not been broken, just several more days of industrial dust. I continued walking for several blocks, turned and retraced my steps. I couldn't help but be concerned about the living conditions in the flophouses. If I could get some pictures inside the buildings with the Minox camera, I could send photographs to the newspaper before leaving town. First, however, I needed to clear up Ruth Watkins' involvement.

I returned to the hotel and went directly to my room. Even before taking off my coat, I unlocked the travel lock from the bathroom door, turned all the lights in the room off, and opened the bathroom door. Covering the flashlight lens with a handkerchief, I looked at the hanging photos. The photos of the Wiseman documents were clear but would require additional enlargement by the experts. The pictures of the explosion scene were also clear. A man in pain was on the floor being treated by a nurse kneeling at his side. Another picture showed flames on the floor, the fire department and ambulances, all very clear.

The next two were of Ruth Watkins getting out of her car in the plant parking lot, and the photos of the *Springfield Sun* pictures of the real Ruth Watkins were good.

The best of all the photos were the two of John A. Johnson, or Hans Mueller. He had been sedated; posed pictures could not have been better. I knew the pictures of Johnson would verify that he was Hans Mueller, the German SS officer wanted for war crimes. I opened my suitcase, pulled apart the lining on one end and removed the envelope with photographs of the wanted men. I looked at the picture of Hans Mueller. There was a scar under his left eye and another scar on his chin. Identical scars showed up in the photos that had just been printed of Johnson.

Ruth Watkins was another matter. The pictures certainly would verify that she was not Henry Wiseman's niece, but who was she? Wiseman's niece had been killed in an auto accident in England.

I prepared my notes before calling Doud. Tomorrow I would print additional copies of the pictures. The negatives and one copy of the prints would go to the Group and they would arrange for larger and better prints.

•

Just before six o'clock the next morning, I turned the light on and could not have been more pleased. The prints were dry and clear. I removed them and placed them on the bed. I took a shower, shaved, dressed and started the same printing process again, making two prints of each negative, hanging them on the line in bathroom. This time my efforts went faster.

It was time for breakfast. I descended the two flights of stairs with the feeling of success, almost bouncing into the dining room, and greeted Harold before he had a chance to open his mouth.

"Aren't you the cheery one this morning, sir."

I really liked Harold, but I had a problem with him calling me "sir." Harold had to be thirty years older than I. However, the real extreme was in London, when the taxi drivers and the attendants in the restrooms called me "Governor."

Biff told me, "It's the price you pay when they think you have money and you might leave them some of it. However, you are to pronounce it 'Gov'nor.'"

I had my regular breakfast and didn't waste a lot of time. I needed to go to a pay telephone outside the hotel and call Doud in Texas. The telephones in the hotel room went through the hotel switchboard and I was not sure about the two telephones in the hotel lobby. It was best that hotel employees didn't see me using the pay phones—little things made people get interested.

I walked down the Limestone hill to the post office, where there were several pay telephones in the lobby. I went into the last telephone booth in the row, dialed the operator and placed a collect call to Doud.

"Will you accept a call from your Missouri Coon Hunter?"

Doud said, "Yes. What's going on?"

I advised him of the explosion at the plant; that Johnson, who was Hans Mueller, was injured and in the hospital, but would recover and be discharged soon, and could walk out of the hospital at any time if there was a need. I told him about the death of the foreman, Harry Rowell. The anger in the plant was dangerous, and there were threats to kill Johnson as he was probably responsible for the explosion. I also told him that the pictures came out clear, showing all of Johnson's facial scars, and that the pictures were a perfect match of Hans Mueller.

I reminded Doud of Ruth Watkins and her unknown connection with Johnson. "When they arrest Johnson, Ruth Watkins should be arrested at the same time. It appears that she has sufficient funds to make flight a real probability."

The Cloisters of Canterbury

Doud asked me to call back at seven that evening for further instructions. I went back to the hotel to check the photos. They weren't dry, so I picked up my briefcase, put the travel lock back in place and hung the "Do Not Disturb" sign on the door to the room.

I waved at the gypsy palm reader as I got into my car. When I arrived at the plant parking lot, Ruth Watkins' Desoto was in her reserved parking space.

Ruth was at her desk.

I stopped. "Good morning, Ruth, how are the men in the hospital?"

"Another died, as you learned when you were at the hospital with Mr. Speer yesterday. Mr. Speer said that you were going to write up what you had seen about the explosion and when you complete it, I am to type it for you to review and sign."

"I'll do that before taking my tour of the plant."

I went into the office. Ruth didn't miss very much—Speer had probably updated her. I sat down, placed a piece of carbon paper in a legal pad, and proceeded to write down all the details of what I had seen and heard at the explosion. When I was finished, I picked up my notebook, put my camera in my pocket, then took the report to Ruth.

"I hope you can read my writing."

Ruth glanced at the papers. "I am sure there will be no problem."

Her eyes looked tried. Lines showed on her face that had not been visible before. She was obviously under a great deal of stress.

I started my daily tour of the plant, but the music still wasn't there. The machinery and men were all running at about half speed, the sound of men's voices was absent. When I stopped to observe the men working, they didn't look up and give me the nod of their head or attempt to speak. These men were saddened by the loss of two of their co-workers and, in many cases, their friends.

When I arrived in the engine assembly area there was no productivity. Seven or eight men stood in a group listening to the tall redhead. Art Reilly was telling the men how the accident had taken place.

"That Kraut Johnson was angry because the men in the test unit complained that one of the motors he had assembled wasn't running right. Harry Rowell went in and ran him out. He didn't belong in there. We all know Johnson had a cigarette in his ugly face all the time, would flip the butt on the floor. He flipped one on the floor starting the fire. The explosion sent a piece of metal into the back of Harry's head killing him. Now, Steve Holmes is dead. Who's going to feed his six kids and his old lady—she's sickly, can't work."

I continued walking through the plant, but found there was very little activity. If someone didn't quiet Art Reilly down, there was going to be bloodshed. On my return from the final assembly area, the general foreman, Gaylord Brown, was talking to the men. I stopped to listen.

"We have lost two good friends, and they will be missed. But you men must not do something that you'll regret the rest of your lives. Wait for the accident investigators to complete their investigation. We all want to know how this accident could have happened. After all, the safety measures were in place. Now these men's families need your help."

Art Reilly's loud voice stopped Brown from continuing. "Let's start taking up a collection for their families. We've got to bury the men and help feed their kids."

It was surprising how this angry Irishman moved from wanting to hang someone from a tree to wanting to feed the dead men's families and having concern about their final resting place. I wondered how long this change of heart would last. I hoped that the Group could act and get John A. Johnson arrested and behind bars before Reilly and others committed a lynching.

When I returned to the office, Ruth handed me the statement, neatly typed, double spaced on legal size paper, and titled, "Mr. Rob Royal's Observation of Explosion." I read through the pages. On the last page was a line for my signature and date.

"A professional job. I would not have expected less," I said.

She looked up, her eyes showed appreciation. "Thank you."

After signing and dating the last page, I gave it back to her.

"I was happy to do it." She handed me a copy of the papers, "For your records."

"Thanks. With so much going on, would you like to have dinner with me tonight?"

"That would be nice, but I don't dare. Thank you for asking."

I walked to my car and drove to O'Brian's for dinner, all the while replaying Ruth's words, the look in her eyes and her body language. There was so much that I did not know. My speculation ran from how a lovely single woman was trapped in some bazaar situation held by this German to masterminding a fraud. Was it possible that she was responsible for the hit-and-run death of attorney Glenn Hudson and the death of Wiseman's niece?

At the farm they had told us repeatedly, "You must always think that what you want to see is not there. People are not what they appear to be, only what they want you to think they are. A person's eyes can tell you many things, sometimes only what they want you to know. Tell a secret to a woman, and the world will soon know. Sleep in your own bed, alone. Question everything you read or hear and be careful of what you see." There were so many lessons learned at the farm, lessons I wouldn't forget.

Ruth's eyes had sent different signals to me. The first meeting was almost flirtatious. Then she showed fear after her face had been used as a punching bag. Today she wanted to have dinner, but that quickly changed to fear with a look of, "I don't dare."

Chapter 19

Another Death

Arriving at O'Brian's, I seated myself in a booth, ordered, and ate my meal without remembering anything about it. I couldn't stop thinking about what had taken place in the last several weeks. After paying the check, I drove south on Limestone and parked across the street from the post office. I didn't bother to walk to the corner to cross, just jaywalked.

I went to the bank of telephones and placed a call to Doud. When the operator asked, "Will you accept a collect call from Coon Hunter?" He said, "Yes." We still used our regular exchange of identification.

Doud started, "Are you ready to give the Cleveland office your consulting report?"

"Yes."

Doud continued, "Leave early Wednesday morning for Cleveland so that you can meet with Jim Allen. Take your pictures and negatives. Give them to him, but keep the second copy of the prints. Give him your written report on Johnson and Watkins. He will start things moving on Johnson if he concurs that your photos match the ones Biff Wallace gave us of Hans Mueller.

The Cloisters of Canterbury

"And, Rob, plan on going to Vassar College on Thursday to verify that Ruth Watkins, the niece, did attend Vassar—she probably did. However, more importantly, take the photo of the woman calling herself Ruth Watkins and attempt to verify if this other woman did or did not attend Vassar. That is the plan for now. Do you have any questions?"

I replied, "None at this time."

"In addition, there's another thing you need to know. Ted Walsh was killed last night in an auto accident. We don't have all the details, but Jim Allen has someone in Dayton investigating for the Group. I felt you would want to know. He was an asset to the Group."

I was genuinely shocked. "I'm really sorry to hear that. I liked him, met his wife, and saw their baby before joining the consulting firm. They purchased a refrigerator from my father's appliance store in Xenia."

"I remember your report, and can also understand why you wanted Ted to do the photo work in Springfield. Sometimes we have to call things based on what we know and think is best for the Group."

I was stunned and walked back to the car in a daze. Ted was dead, killed in an auto accident. I hadn't thought quick enough to ask Doud if I could call Ted's wife. My mind raced, I was to leave early in the morning for Cleveland and then on Friday go to Vassar College.

The information that I had learned from the Wiseman records and talking with Mary Combs was that Wiseman sent his niece to Vassar College, and she did, in fact, graduate. The important thing was to learn if the woman now calling herself Ruth Watkins was the person who attended Vassar, as she stated on her employment application. Understanding that I was the most qualified to compare the photographs, it was going to be difficult at best to identify the mystery woman.

It was after ten, but I knew I would get very little sleep that night. I parked in front of the gypsy palm reader's window. She waved, but didn't invite me in.

The walk up Limestone hill was unusually steep, the culmination of a stressful day and learning of Ted Walsh's death. I wanted to go see his wife but knew that was not possible. We were told not to make contact with any other Group member or their families unless it was part of the assignment. "You are expected to walk alone."

The elevator ride up to the third floor and my room was slow. I removed the travel security lock from the bathroom and saw that the photos were dry. I unclipped them from the line, placed them in individual envelopes and labeled them. I packed the small suitcase and the briefcase with the photos and reports, laid clothes out for the next morning, took a shower, and set my alarm. I also called the hotel front desk to ask for a 3:45 AM wake-up call, and made a point to advise the desk clerk that I wasn't checking out, but would be out of town for several days.

In spite of all of the events, I didn't waste time falling asleep and didn't wake until the alarm sounded and the telephone rang, both at the same time. I almost went into a panic from the noise. I had been dreaming of an auto accident and was perspiring. My hair was soaking wet, as if just stepping out of a shower.

I had rarely ever had dreams until the man fell through the roof in Dayton, and now my subconscious was probably thinking of Ted Walsh. I went to the bathroom, stepped into the shower for a couple minutes, dried, dressed, and went over to the open window. The morning newspapers were being dropped in bundles by the front door of the drugstore across the street.

I locked the room, carried my bag and briefcase to the elevator. I gave the room key to the night desk clerk and reminded him that I was not checking out.

The night clerk said, "I have made a note and put it in the manager's box and marked the logbook."

I picked up the Springfield and Dayton papers from the rack and paid the desk clerk. Outside, the streets were quiet, except for the sound of a car some place in the distance. Walking down the Limestone hill was easier than the climb up the previous night. It was too early for the palm reader. After putting the briefcase and bag in the trunk, I started the car, and was soon in the country, with no traffic on the road. In a pasture a farmer was already out herding his cows toward the barn for their morning milking.

The sun was starting to rise in the east. It was almost six. I slowed to pass an Amish man in his horse-drawn buggy. A school bus was coming across a side road to my right. There would be others on the road at this time of day. Traffic in Bellefontaine was starting to move. When I stopped for a red traffic light, there was a police officer leaning against the front of a bank.

When I stopped for gas and to use the restroom, an elderly man who hadn't shaved for a day or more came out of the station. I asked him to fill it up. I paid and continued driving north. I couldn't stop thinking about Ted. Everything reminded me of him and his family. I passed a funeral home and wondered if she had made any arrangements yet.

I pulled to the curb in front of a large, three-story home on a corner, shut the car's motor off, reached in the back seat and retrieved the two newspapers I had purchased in Springfield that morning. I looked at the Springfield paper. There was nothing in it about an accident. I unfolded the Dayton paper. Spread across the front page were the headlines, "DAYTON MAN KILLED IN AUTO ACCIDENT." Beneath the caption was a picture of a car that had burned.

I read the article:

> According to witnesses, the local man's car was forced off the road by another automobile. It was learned that Theodore S. Walsh, age 29, of Dayton, was returning from a business meeting in Yellow Springs shortly after 8:00 PM. when a car approached his car from the rear at a high rate of speed, having passed the cars of two witnesses.
>
> As the car pulled next to Walsh's car, it appeared that the car deliberately forced Walsh off the road into a ditch, causing the car to roll over five times. The cars following stopped to help. When two men reached the Walsh car, they discovered Mr. Walsh had been thrown from the car and was dead.
>
> There was a fire in the car. The men moved Walsh's body away from the car just before the gas tank exploded. Walsh leaves his wife and eleven-month-old daughter. He was a veteran of World War II and employed as a consulting engineer with a Cleveland, Ohio, firm at the time of his death. The accident is under investigation by the Montgomery County Sheriff's office and Ohio State Patrol.

I re-read the story, feeling both saddened and angry. Why would anyone deliberately run a car off the road? Ted had told me that he was on an assignment in Dayton at Patterson Field evaluating an inventory control problem, but he had not indicated that he was doing anything for the Group. My mind did a replay. Doud had considered having Ted visit the Springfield truck plant to take the photos, and then changed his mind. He told me not to discuss anything about my assignment with Ted under any conditions. I remembered that the camera package had a Fairborn, Ohio, postmark. Fairborn is near Patterson Field. I assumed that Ted had mailed me the camera since he was on assignment at Patterson Field, but the Group had many connections.

It was a few minutes more before I restarted the car and continued to drive north. During the next four hours of driving, I continued to run the events through my mind again and again. I assumed things were dangerous, but it had always been second nature for me to assume, question, evaluate, weigh, and look for answers to all of the possibilities. I found it difficult not to look at people and ask myself who they really were and wonder what they were hiding. At the farm when they were playing their mind games, given only bits and pieces of certain events, I found that my mind went into high gear, and I had been more successful in solving the various problems than most of the group, except for Biff Wallace. Doud said that Allen had someone in Dayton looking into Ted Walsh's accident. It would be interesting to hear what James Allen found out.

I arrived in Cleveland and parked in the parking lot two blocks from the National City Bank Building. After removing the briefcase from the trunk, I carried it in my left hand and the Dayton newspaper in my right hand. Was I getting paranoid? I looked forward to talking to James Allen. Maybe he had more information about Ted.

When I walked into the office, Sally, the receptionist, said, "Nice to see you back in town. Mr. Allen is waiting for you in his office."

"Thanks. It is nice to be back."

I walked to the north corner office at the end of the hall and went in. Allen's secretary covered the telephone mouthpiece with her hand and said, "Go on in, Mr. Allen is waiting."

As I reached the office, Allen opened the door. We shook hands.

Allen started talking, "First I want you to know how sorry all of us are about Ted Walsh's death. We know that when people spend time together as you and Ted and the others have, there are relationships created. I know how team spirit is created. It's as they say, 'Once a Marine, always a Marine.'

"When Doud put this particular group together, the selection of the individuals was the main ingredient. The reports from the farm were outstanding. There has never been any question that all twenty of you believe in the Group's purpose."

Allen continued, "Rob, I want you to know that Doud and all of us in control of the Group appreciate what you have accomplished on the assignment in Springfield. We recognize the importance of those findings. In addition, your preliminary consulting reports indicate that your analysis and recommendations are professional and will be endorsed by the firm to the client."

The Cloisters of Canterbury

"Thank you. It has been an interesting assignment."

"The firm's operating staff here has no knowledge that you and Ted Walsh have been anything other than management consultants."

I replayed that last statement in my mind—*That you and Ted Walsh have been anything other than management consultants.* Ted Walsh must have been involved in something. Could it have been responsible for his death?

"Let's take a look at the photos that you made down there."

I removed the envelopes from my briefcase and opened the envelope marked, "John A. Johnson." Then I removed from another envelope the picture of Hans Mueller that had been sent to the Group by Biff Wallace in England. I placed them side by side on the desk in front of Allen.

Allen opened a drawer in his desk, removed a magnifying glass, and looked at the two photos. He studied the photos for several minutes.

"There is no way that the man, John A. Johnson, is not Hans Mueller who is wanted for war crimes. Rob this is excellent work. When we have the photos enlarged, we will be able get the federal judge to issue an arrest warrant and the U.S. marshal will make the arrest. This will be done before any other agency is advised. We don't want any leaks."

Allen continued, "Timing is very important. We also need to address Mueller's relationship with the Ruth Watkins woman." He moved the photos to one side of his desk.

I removed the photographs of the two newspaper clippings with the real Ruth Watkins' picture. The articles were about her death in England. I placed them in a row in front of Allen along with the two photos of the woman using Ruth Watkins' name taken in the truck plant parking lot in Springfield.

Allen looked at all of the pictures known to be Wiseman's niece. He picked up the last two photos and looked at them with the magnifying glass. He began making observations: "Head shape different, shape of eyes different, shape of mouth different, texture of hair different, hair color different, but they do change the color."

"Mr. Allen, we have documents that would convince anyone that Wiseman's niece is dead. The question is who is the woman who has claimed the Wiseman estate? How did she accomplish it? What is her connection with Hans Mueller?

"Furthermore, it seems very convenient for Wiseman's lawyer to have been killed just when the woman made claim to the Wiseman's estate. Right before his death, he received a letter from the Valley Bank in Dayton that must have pertained to Ruth Watkins. I was unable to locate that letter. I haven't talked with anyone at the Valley Bank, but could the Group's friend, John Myers, at the bank help?"

Allen looked at me. "That's a possibility."

I continued, "In addition to this puzzle, how did the woman accomplish her employment? Employment records indicate that this woman worked in the employment office when Hans Mueller was employed. Is that a coincidence? The fact that Mueller and this woman are living in the Wiseman Tudor home in Springfield certainly cannot be a coincidence. More alarming is the fact that there are several men using the name Johnson who are German, and reportedly not using their God-given names. Another concern is how the woman was hired, but I think that the employment manager, Speer, was taken in by her. She comes on strong and is quite beautiful. It is easy to think that she turned on the charm."

Allen rose from his chair, walked over to the window and looked out on Lake Erie for several minutes. He turned and shook his head and returned to his desk.

"Rob, I am in agreement with you that there is more to this than it appears on the surface. We need to know if this woman attended Vassar, and did she meet Wiseman's niece there, become friends, learn all the details about Wiseman, and learn of Ruth Watkins' death in the auto accident in England, then developed the plan to assume her identity. Or did the two women become acquainted in the WAC?"

Allen took a deep breath. "Your report indicated questions about the London lawyer's involvement with certifying Henry Wiseman's death in a concentration camp. There is the possibility that he is somehow involved since there is a conflict of information about Wiseman's death. We need to know more about him.

"Rob, my secretary has your consulting report. Review it, have her make any changes necessary, and then take it down to the field staff for them to review. Scottie Davidson is waiting to read it and I am sure they will have questions for you. After you are finished with them come back and check with my secretary. She will tell you when I need to talk with you again. Rob, I want to commend you, the work is outstanding."

"Thank you. I can't say it has all been fun, but I really didn't expect it to be."

On my way out, Allen's secretary handed me a typed copy of my analysis and recommendations. I sat down in a chair next to her desk and read it. It had been a good idea to mail the report to Cleveland in advance of my arrival.

The Cloisters of Canterbury

I proceeded down to the next floor to the field review staff's offices and talked with several members of the staff that I had worked with before going to Springfield. Vice-President Scottie Davidson said that he had read my report, and that it looked good. The staff was looking at the numbers again, and he would review it with me later in the day.

I knew they would probably tear it apart, but I was too tired to worry about that. I could always sell appliances for my dad, but then I remembered that my contract was for one year, with only a couple of things providing for termination, and I had not been guilty of either.

It was now after three in the afternoon and I had still not eaten breakfast or lunch. I went back up to Allen's secretary and told her that I was going out for a sandwich.

I left the building and walked east on Euclid Ave. Fall was in the air, the wind was coming out of Canada across Lake Erie. The tree leaves would be changing soon and the trip to Poughkeepsie, New York, would offer some beautiful fall colors. It had been several years since my last visit to upstate New York in the fall. I stopped in a delicatessen three blocks from the bank building, ordered a roast beef sandwich. It was out of character for me, but I ate the sandwich while walking back to the office. When I returned to the office, the receptionist told me that Mr. Allen's secretary had a message for me. I walked down the hall to Allen's office.

"Mr. Allen is waiting for you. The door is open, go in."

"Come in, Rob, close the door and join me at the conference table." Allen was sitting at the conference table next to the north window with a beautiful view of Lake Erie.

I joined him. "It certainly would be difficult to hold the attention of anyone in a meeting around this table."

"I rarely have meetings. This is for show and my pleasure."

I was about to reply when he informed me, "Rob, I've talked with Doud, and we have agreed on a plan for your trip to Vassar. Tomorrow you will fly from the Cleveland airport to New York LaGuardia. Take a taxi to Vassar College in Poughkeepsie, New York. It will be a two-to-three-hour drive. As a representative of this firm, you will be there to verify information on Ruth Watkins's application for employment with this firm. A picture of the woman that has assumed Watkins identity will be with the application. It will be the photo that you took of the woman in the parking lot in Springfield, cropped and enlarged. The application and photograph will be ready before you leave this evening. What do you think of the plan?"

"That certainly eliminates my concern about approaching the people at Vassar. It will also give me an opportunity to ask to see photos of their graduating classes and yearbooks if they exist."

"When you return from Poughkeepsie, go to Trenton, New Jersey, and visit Trenton High School. Using the application and photograph see what else you can learn. Rob, as you suggested, the woman may have listed the high school that she had actually attended on her employment application at the truck plant. It's a long shot, but worth checking."

He resumed his instructions with an additional sparkle in his eyes, "After completing your investigation in Trenton, we need you to go to Fort Jay on Governor's Island, a place that you are well acquainted with. Go to headquarters and ask to see your old friend, Army Sergeant Major Alan Murphy. He will be expecting you. Give him copies of both women's photographs. We are having several copies made. He will arrange to have both pictures viewed by members of the Women's Army Corps that were with the Eighth Air Force in England, as well as in their training unit in the States. Maybe we will learn something about this woman's claim to have served in the military. We have also asked the sergeant to secure information on Ruth Watkins' death in the auto accident in England."

"It looks like I'll be doing some traveling. What's the latest on Ted Walsh's death?"

Allen looked me in the eyes. "We have nothing new at this time, but you'll know when there's anything you should know."

I didn't care for that answer. I now was more convinced than ever that Ted had been doing something more than a routine consulting assignment at Patterson Field in Dayton.

"Rob, the field people have finished with your report and are ready to review it with you. It sounds like they are in agreement with your recommendations. Go down and listen to what they have to say. When you're finished, come back. The photographs and the application should be here by then."

I stopped at the secretary's desk. "What telephone can I use to call Mrs. Gray in Bay Village?"

"Use the telephone in the conference room. Mrs. Gray called the other day asking about you, she said it wasn't about your rent, that you had paid two months in advance. She just wanted to know if you were all right."

"She's really nice, just like a mother. I appreciate you giving me her name for a place to live."

The Cloisters of Canterbury

I called Mrs. Gray and told her that I would be there before dark.

"I'll be glad to see you," she said before hanging up the phone.

I recalled how many nice people I had met over the years. They made up for the some of the unsavory characters that had crossed my path.

Scottie Davidson who was responsible for field operations motioned for me to come into his office. When I walked in, Davidson ended his telephone conversation and offered a chair in front of his desk.

"Rob, we have reviewed your analysis and recommendations, and there is nothing that needs to be changed. Good job. Your recommendation that they acquire a large flat piece of land north of Springfield on the main highway and next to the New York Central Railroad's north and south line is the only practical decision they can make. There is a good labor market and with the projected increase in the demand for trucks, it is an opportunity that should be profitable. Ford and General Motors are planning new truck plants outside of Michigan in more favorable labor markets.

"Your field report also stated that the treasurer, Arnold Reasonier, would be out of town for the next two weeks. Mr. Allen wants to make the presentation, so we will wait until Reasonier returns."

Davidson stood, shook my hand. "Good job. Nice having you aboard."

Returning to Allen's office, I couldn't help but wonder how much members of the consulting firm knew about the Group's activities.

Someone must have alerted Allen's secretary that I had just stepped out of the elevator. When I arrived at his office, she was standing by Allen's open office door and told me to have a chair, that Mr. Allen would be right back.

I didn't sit down, but stood by the window and watched flocks of ducks landing offshore on Lake Erie. There were dark clouds blowing across the lake from Canada, the wind was increasing, the waves were starting to roll towards the shore. Lake Erie was the shallowest of the Great Lakes and got extremely rough when the storms blew through. I remembered several occasions when storms had forced me to shore while fishing on Lake Erie.

Allen walked in and pulled out two chairs at the conference table. He removed several copies of enlarged photos from an envelope and placed them on the table. Professional photo lab people could do wonders. Using the film that I had developed, they had made clear prints providing much more detail than my efforts in the bathroom.

Allen gave me six copies of the pictures of John A. Johnson and the woman claiming to be Ruth Watkins, and six copies of the pictures from the Springfield newspaper that were known to be Wiseman's niece.

He handed me one of the consulting firm's applications, just like the one I completed when applying at the firm. The name on the application was Ruth Marie Watkins; her address was the Tudor house on North Fountain Blvd, Springfield, Ohio. All the information from her application from the truck plant was included: Trenton High School, Vassar College, served in the WAC, the same references listed. The application was signed Ruth M. Watkins and dated twenty days before. Above the line for applicant's signature was the statement: "This authorizes James Allen & Associates and their representatives to inquire and have access to all information of previous employers, learning institutions and references provided."

"This should open the doors," I said. "It will be interesting where this leads us."

Allen put the photos and application in two separate envelopes, then gave me another envelope. I opened it, removed a round trip airline ticket from Cleveland's Hopkins airport to New York LaGuardia, leaving the next day at 8:40 in the morning. I then removed fifteen one hundred dollar bills.

I looked at Allen and jokingly said, "Think that this will be enough?"

"Before you leave, tell me what you think about your association with the Group."

I pushed my chair back from the conference table, stood up, walked to the window and looked at Lake Erie once more. The water was becoming increasingly more dangerous for anyone in a small boat on the water; the clouds coming over the water from Canada were darker than earlier.

I turned around and looked him in the eye. "I have not changed my mind about agreeing with the purpose and the objectives of the Group to locate anyone responsible for their war crimes in Europe. I also recognize the need for the President of the United States and Congress to have the facts when they make their decisions. My personal concern about leaks within the government should be obvious. The need for the Group has only become *more* real for me with the events in Springfield. I have no doubt that there are individuals with motives unknown to me who have and will continue to injure and kill to accomplish their goals. I am sure that fraud, dishonesty, and more murders will be uncovered when this ends." I sighed and walked back over to the conference table, feeling the full implications of my involvement in the Group.

I added, "When I was recruited by President Truman to investigate the possibility of fraud by a military contractor, danger and bodies laid in the wake. And when US Marshals escorted me to appear as a witness in federal court, an attempt was made on my life, and a US Marshal was killed.

"Now, I am certain that there are individuals who would not think twice about running over me with a car, or putting a knife in my back in one of those dark basements in Springfield if they learned of my activities. Doud warned of possible accidents that might be deliberate. At the farm, they told us that our mistakes would be buried with us, and there would be no one there for us since the Group does not exist. I understand and continue to believe in the cause." I paused for a moment and then said, "But, I still have concerns about Ted Walsh's death."

Allen stood and extended his hand, "Rob, what you're doing is right. Continue to look into their eyes, watch their body language, listen carefully, and place your trust in yourself. Have a safe and productive journey. You will be all right. Call Doud and report daily. He will keep me advised."

I left the office and still hadn't learned any more about Ted Walsh's death.

Allen's secretary said, "Do take some time for you."

"Thanks, I'll see you on my return." The look in her eyes and the tone of her voice told me that she was in the loop.

The elevator descended to the street level. I walked to my car. The temperature was dropping, and an early frost was in the air.

Chapter 20

Vassar

The sun was setting when I arrived in Bay Village and pulled into the drive at Mrs. Gray's house two blocks from the lake. She was looking out of the window.

Mrs. Gray opened the door, "It's nice to have you back in town."

"Thank you, I am glad to be back, even if it's just for a short while."

I sat my bag and briefcase down by the stairs and joined her in the living room. She asked me if I would like some tea, which sounded like a delightful idea. As we enjoyed our tea, she told me about her children and recent visits from her grandchildren. They had fun at the beach with a small sailing boat that belonged to one of her friends.

I carried my bag and briefcase up to my room. She had placed some flowers from her garden on the dresser, the last rose of summer. The nice people of the world justified the Group's activities.

After a shower, I packed a bag for the trip and was soon fast asleep. Thunder woke me several times during the night, but I soon returned to sleep.

Wide awake at seven, shaved, and dressed, I carried my bag and briefcase downstairs. When I went out of the front door, Mrs. Grey was

The Cloisters of Canterbury

sweeping the leaves off the walk. I reminded her of my flight to New York and that I would be back in three or four days.

She smiled, "Have a safe trip, I have never been in an airplane. Just might try it some time."

Cleveland's airport was on the southwest side of the city. I didn't have to drive through a lot of traffic from Bay Village. Shirley, at the office, had given me a shortcut with good directions, turn by turn, which saved a lot of time. Just before reaching the airport, I stopped for breakfast and checked in thirty minutes before the flight was to leave.

It was a smooth flight all the way into LaGuardia. The wait in baggage claim was brief, everything was on time. I carried my bag to a line of taxicabs in front of the terminal. After attempting to engage five taxi drivers for the trip to Poughkeepsie, I finally found a cabbie interested. We agreed on a round trip price, plus so much for every hour that the taxi driver had to wait, and I agreed to pay for all the gas and meals.

We had just cleared the traffic around the airport when the cabbie asked, "Where do you want to go in Poughkeepsie?"

"Vassar College." I watched the man's reaction.

"That's the girl's school, isn't it?"

"That's what I have been told."

The smile on the driver's face gave the impression that he was going to enjoy the trip.

It was a pleasant drive along the Hudson River. We arrived at Vassar College campus just before two. After assuring the driver that I was not going to enroll, and just to keep him happy, I removed a hundred dollar bill from my wallet. His mouth dropped open when I tore it in two and gave him one half of the bill.

"This half is yours. When I return, I'll give you the other half in addition to the fare we have agreed to."

The driver laughed, "Hey, I wouldn't leave you up here with all these young girls."

I had heard of people tearing a hundred dollar bill and giving a taxi driver half of it in order to guarantee that the driver would wait for them, but it had never occurred to me to do such a thing. In the first place, I rarely ever had a hundred dollar bill, and, secondly, I had never needed a taxi to wait for me.

I walked into a building that looked like it would be the administration building. I was correct—just inside the door was an information desk. I told the receptionist that I wanted to verify that a student had graduated from Vassar. She was pleasant and directed me to an office at the end of a hall. I couldn't help but wonder why the offices I was looking for were always at the end of the hall.

The door was open. I walked in and an older woman greeted me. I gave her my business card and showed her the application with the photo of the woman in Springfield using the name Ruth Watkins.

She looked at the picture, then at the application that indicated she had graduated in 1942.

"First I'll look for her name in the alumni directory." She removed a book from a shelf, returned it to the shelf, removed another, returned it to the shelf, and removed a third book. She leafed through several pages, stopped at a page near the back of the book, ran her index finger down the list of names. "Here she is, Ruth Marie Watkins, enrolled September 1938 and graduated June 1942.

"That's great, now do you have pictures of students, class pictures or yearbooks?"

"We certainly do, Vassar has always been proud of our students. Many have become famous in their years after graduating."

"Would it be possible to look at the Class of 1942?"

"You certainly may. It will only take a minute." She walked across the room to a row of bookcases with glass doors. She opened one of doors, quickly removed a book, glanced at its leather cover and returned to her desk.

She opened the book, turned to the page where the students' pictures started in alphabetical order. There were four students' pictures per page.

She turned to the start of the W's, turned two pages, put a finger under a girl's picture, looked at the picture attached to the application, then said, "There must be a mistake. The picture of Ruth Marie Watkins doesn't resemble the picture you have, and she's the only Watkins in the class."

She turned the book so I could have a clear look at the picture. There she was, a blonde, small features, not resembling the picture attached to the application in any way.

"See, your woman is not our Ruth." The woman had a questioning look on her face. I removed the picture known to be the niece of Henry Wiseman from my jacket pocket and placed it on top of the yearbook next to the picture of Ruth Marie Watkins in the yearbook.

The woman gasped. "That picture is our Ruth Watkins."

I explained, "When this woman in the photograph made an application with our consulting firm, she was interviewed by several of the firm's officers and senior partners. They were most favorably impressed. Those who interviewed her had a number of meetings in order to review their evaluations. The interest in her is very high. Academic achievement and experience are very important, but the most important factor is character.

"You see, our clients, some of the largest and most prestigious corporations in the United States and Europe, provide us with sensitive and confidential information about their firms and employees. Therefore, our staff must have unquestionable integrity. Betrayal of our clients' trust is not acceptable. The firm is very careful in verifying background information about individuals before offering a position. That's why I have flown from Cleveland to New York and hired a taxi to bring me here."

The woman stood, "Please excuse me. Vassar's administrator needs to be made aware of this problem. Our girls have unquestionable integrity."

I removed the Minox camera from my coat pocket and took two pictures of the open yearbook and walked to the bookcases where the woman had retrieved the 1942 yearbook. It appeared that Vassar had yearbooks of some type since it was founded in 1861. Returning to the table I started to determine the years that Wiseman's niece could have become acquainted with the woman in question. She enrolled in September 1938 and graduated in June of 1942. Therefore, I needed to look at the yearbooks for 1939 through 1946 just to cover the possibility of a chance meeting if Wiseman's niece had returned to visit Vassar.

The next possibility was the woman in question might have been associated with Vassar as an employee. Unless the woman was a friend of someone at Vassar and visiting, but that was a far reach.

The woman returned and told me that Vassar's administrator and staff were very concerned and would like to meet with me.

I followed the woman to the administrator's office and was introduced to the administrator, three other women, all in their fifties or older, and a man, who was an attorney. I wasn't sure if this was going to be a friendly meeting. All of their faces were strained.

"We, at James Allen & Associates, certainly realize that Vassar College has no responsibility in this matter. However, you can understand our concern, why we would like to know who this woman might really be. How was she able to assume the identity of Ruth Marie Watkins? Was she a student at Vassar, or maybe a member of Vassar's staff?"

The administrator spoke, "We realize that Vassar has no liability, but we are concerned that someone is claiming that they are a graduate of Vassar College when they are not. The staff members here have been at Vassar before Ruth Watkins enrolled in September 1938. Vassar is a small school, we know our students—all of us remember Ruth Watkins. In fact, we learned of her death in England." The faces of all the staff members except the lawyer indicated agreement. I showed them the application.

The administrator was quick to reply. "This person was never on the staff of Vassar." Again, everyone nodded in agreement.

"I appreciate your cooperation, verifying that this woman had not been a student has prevented our firm from making a mistake that could have created grave problems for us. I am sure that our firm will be happy to notify you of any information that we obtain about the woman if you would like."

The administrator said, "We would certainly be interested and would appreciate learning the outcome." She looked at the lawyer.

He spoke his first and only word, "Yes."

I was thinking that this was an unusual meeting when a lawyer had been present and had not dominated the conversation.

"On the application she has given a 'Miss Tuttle' as a reference at Vassar."

Without hesitating, the administrator said, "We have never had anyone on our staff by the name of Tuttle."

"In order to eliminate the possibility that this woman was not at Vassar using another name, would it be possible to look at other yearbooks?"

The administrator spoke, "Miss Stevens will assist you in every way. We appreciate that you have made us aware of this problem."

"Thank you for the assistance." I followed Miss Stevens to her office and gave her the list of the years 1938-1946. She removed the books from the bookcase and placed them on a table. I looked through the yearbooks, year after year, but didn't find a picture that even came close to resembling the woman claiming to be Ruth Watkins.

I thanked Miss Stevens and returned to the taxi. My inquiry had taken over three hours. The driver was sitting on the front fender of the taxi smoking a cigarette, one of several evidenced by the number on the ground by his feet.

The driver said, "Need to call my wife. I am going to be later than usual. When she learns that I am up here at Vassar watching the skirts she may have a question or two for me."

I pulled out the piece of the hundred-dollar bill. "Do you still have

The Cloisters of Canterbury

the other half?"

The driver held it up. "You bet." I gave him an un-torn one hundred dollar bill. The driver smiled and gave me his half of the one-hundred dollar bill.

"Now when you call your wife you can tell her you'll buy her that new fall outfit."

The driver stopped at the first gas station. While the attendant was filling the tank, the driver went inside the station and called his wife. I paid for the gas.

There was no conversation for over an hour, just the driver whistling various songs. I was thinking about what I had just learned. I had verified that Ruth Watkins did attend Vassar and graduate, and was confident that the impostor had not attended Vassar during the same period. Furthermore, her age ruled out attending at any other time. I was also wondering what would be learned at Trenton High School. The Group had considered turning over the information that had been uncovered about Ruth Watkins and the Wiseman estate to a local judge in Springfield, but that might prevent learning her connection with Hans Mueller. We had more digging to do.

The drive from Poughkeepsie to Newburgh and West Point was enjoyable. The trees were changing from green to various shades of red, yellow, a few hinting of brown, all of which would be falling soon. As the evening approached the cab driver suggested an Italian restaurant in Yonkers. It was a good choice.

"Traffic is less going to Manhattan this way through Yonkers. I've driven this way before."

I was happy that I wasn't driving.

We were back in New York in front of the Astor Hotel just before nine o'clock. I paid the driver for his services before getting out of the taxi. It had been a profitable day for the cabbie, and he had made it possible for me to accomplish an important part of the trip and save a lot of time.

Chapter 21

Trenton, New Jersey

It was a restless night. Nightmares disturbed me off and on until the sound of the alarm clock started my day at seven. I quickly dressed, left the room and dropped the room key at the front desk in less than a half hour. I carried the briefcase with the pictures and documents that I would need. It was time for a stop at the *Chock Full o' Nuts* coffee shop for a good cup of coffee, skipping breakfast.

New York City was different from any other city. Things were constantly going on, and it was a great place to watch people. I had always enjoyed it, whether riding on the subway, waiting for a traffic light to change, or riding a train or ferry. Grand Central Station in particular was a good people-watching place.

I purchased a round trip ticket to Trenton and boarded just as the train started to move. I arrived in Trenton and hailed a taxi that took me to Trenton High School. The sound of student voices was loud. But how could anyone expect it to be otherwise during the change of classes in any school. I followed the signs to the office. I approached a woman sitting at a desk and asked her where I could verify that a person had graduated from Trenton High School.

The Cloisters of Canterbury

"You need to write to the school requesting verification that the person has attended."

This was not what I had in mind. I explained that I was with a firm in Cleveland, Ohio, and that they we were very much interested in this woman for an important position. The company had considered it so important, that they had me fly from Cleveland to New York to verify that she had attended Trenton High School. I gave her my business card, and showed her the application with the picture attached. I stood looking at her, trying to reflect my disappointment.

She looked at the business card and the photograph attached to the application.

"Have a seat and I'll see if someone can help you."

The woman returned a few minutes later and asked me to follow her. We walked to an office at the end of a hall. I was introduced to a woman whose personality made me think that we should have written for verification, but that wasn't going to solve the immediate problem. She offered me a chair next to her desk. She looked at the picture, read the application, then looked at me. Without changing her expression or saying a word, she rose from her desk and walked to a row of filing cabinets. She returned with a printed list of names. I read the top line, 1938 Trenton High School Graduates. She turned a group of pages over, then one at a time until she reached the W's.

She looked at a number of pages. With an odd jerking movement of her head the woman said, "Ruth Marie Watkins did not graduate from Trenton High School in 1938."

I hesitated a few seconds before speaking, "I wonder if perhaps she made an error on her application, entered the wrong year?"

The woman looked at me. "How am I supposed to know that?"

I was not getting anywhere. Trying to be pleasant, I explained that the firm was very interested in hiring the woman, but it was important that we verify all information provided on her application.

Knowing before arriving that Ruth Marie Watkins had not graduated from Trenton High School, I wanted to find out if the woman who had completed the application at the truck plant had used the right high school, but not her right name. I decided that there was nothing to lose.

"Yesterday I visited Vassar College at Poughkeepsie, New York, to verify that she had graduated from there. I learned that she had not, but that a Ruth Marie Watkins did graduate from Vassar. The pictures in Vassar's yearbook clearly confirmed that this applicant was assuming someone else's name and identity. I want to assure you that I sincerely appreciate your time. I'm sure you understand the importance of verification of information. Do you have a copy of Trenton High School's 1938 year book?"

The woman said, "Why?"

"I just wondered if by chance the woman had attended Trenton High School using her own name and when she filled out the application she used the high school that she did, in fact, attend, never thinking that anyone would take the time to verify it. She has made a very good impression on several members of our firm."

The woman sighed. She was brighter than her personality would let me believe. Without speaking, she rose from the chair and left the office. A few minutes later, she returned with the 1938 Year Book. She placed the book in front of me, still not saying a word. I opened the book and started turning the pages, looking at the faces of each student. I was getting a lost feeling, until almost through the M's I stopped. A face jumped out at me.

Beneath the photo was: Frances Ann Murita.

The woman seated next to me was looking at every page. She "gasped" and when I looked up, her face had turned red. I was afraid that she was having a heart attack. She held her breath and finally started to breath. Slowly the red color of her face started to fade.

I knew that the woman had recognized the photo in the yearbook. "Do you remember this young lady when she was a student here at Trenton High School?"

She avoided making eye contact with me, but looked at the picture and the student in the yearbook several times. Her breathing became heavy again. It was obvious that something was disturbing her.

"Yes, I remember her. She's the daughter of a local businessman. The family is well known."

"Do you recall hearing anything about her after she graduated from Trenton?"

She replied without hesitating, "No, I don't read the papers."

I thought that her answer was unusual...maybe telling me to check the newspapers. I then asked, "Do you have a copy of this yearbook that I can buy?"

"I don't think so, but I'll ask." She hurried out of the office.

I removed the Minox camera from my pocket, set the exposure and took three pictures of the open book.

The woman returned after several minutes. "I am sorry but the

The Cloisters of Canterbury

school orders the books after the students place their orders and so there are rarely extra copies unless someone fails to pick up their book."

I wasn't surprised. I had the feeling that she had left the office to tell someone about what she had learned. The woman's reaction turned on my alarm. Now that I had a name, I needed to learn more about Frances Murita, but I didn't want the staff at Trenton High School to know how much interest I had.

I thanked the woman and left the school.

As I waited for a taxi in front of the school, I suddenly remembered that in the letter Attorney Hudson had received about Ruth Watkins' death in England, the driver of the car had been Frances Murita!

It was another twenty or thirty minutes until an unoccupied taxi stopped. I asked the driver to take me to the post office. The driver talked nonstop about some ball player that I had never heard of.

"Do you know of a local businessman by the name of Murita?"

The taxi driver stopped talking, and then said, "Yeah."

"What kind of business is he in?"

The driver was slow to respond, "Trucking, warehouses, and some others."

The taxi stopped in front of the post office. Just as I started to get out of the taxi, a passing car's engine backfired. I dropped to the floor of the taxi and hesitated for several seconds before getting up. The taxi driver looked at me in a strange way. I looked out of the taxi in all directions before getting out.

In the post office I located the pay telephones, opened the telephone directory and started looking for Murita in the business section. I soon found Murita Trucking and Storage listed. Back outside the post office, I hailed the first taxi that was empty and asked the driver to take me to Murita Trucking and Storage. The driver didn't ask for a street address, indicating to me that the taxi driver already knew the name and location.

Some fifteen minutes later, I observed a line of old brick buildings with metal roofs. Parked in a fenced area were several trucks, semi and straight beds, with Murita Trucking and Storage printed on their sides. The driver slowed in front of a brick building that appeared to be the office. A sign across the front said, "Murita Trucking and Storage."

"Don't stop, I just checked my watch and I must be at the *Trenton Times* for an advertising deadline in fifteen minutes, can we make it?"

"No problem, it's on Perry."

"Have you lived in Trenton for long?"

"I was born and raised here, and been here all my life except for several years at Fort Dix."

"That must have been good duty. You could come home about every night."

"There were some pluses and minus. I missed seeing some other parts of the world. When people ask, I always tell them I was in the islands, "Manhattan, Long Island, Staten Island and Governor's Island."

"Were you stationed on Governor's Island?"

"No, I was in the military police and we took some AWOL soldiers to Willie's Castle once. After spending time in that old dungeon, they probably never went AWOL again."

I didn't reveal my Governor's Island experiences.

"What are you doing in Trenton; you're not from around here?" he asked

It was always a problem when engaging people in conversations. It led to answering their questions.

"I sell advertising so I call on different companies and newspapers." I was going to take another risk. "When did you graduate from high school?"

"In 1940. Didn't have the grades or the money for college, so I enlisted in 1941 just before Pearl Harbor. Went to Fort Dix and was in a training unit. I expected to be shipped overseas, but someone liked the way that I trained the new recruits."

The driver was relaxed and freely talking.

"What do you know about the Murita trucking people?"

The driver laid on the car's horn and made a quick evasive move to avoid a car that pulled in front of the taxi. After the car in front of him made a left turn without signaling, the driver gave him the horn again.

"Murita has been around for a long time, running a trucking and storage company. They also have several rental buildings in town. One of the girls was a couple years ahead of me in high school, good looking, and a cheerleader. She always had one of her dad's cars at school, guys chased her."

I was not about to ask her name. "What happened to her?"

The driver made another evasive action. He was a good driver, probably due to the military police driver training in addition to driving a taxi for several years.

"She joined the WAC and I never heard anything more about her. She was out of my league anyway. She just might not have wanted to come back to Trenton after her uncle was sent to prison and everyone was talking about it."

The taxi stopped at a railroad crossing and waited for a freight train to pass. The driver lit a cigarette and offered me one. I declined and took my pipe out and filled it with tobacco, and using the old army Zippo, lit the pipe.

After puffing on the pipe and thinking a few minutes, I said, "What did the uncle do to get jail time?"

"He was involved in some kind of fraud with a military contract in Ohio. It got bad in Newark during the trial. Several men shot, and two killed. There was a lot in the newspaper."

Hearing this, I inhaled, which I never did, and choked.

The driver looked back at me, "Are you all right?"

After I stopped coughing, I said, "Yes, I know better than to inhale on a pipe. I was watching the train and listening to you and forgot to take the pipe out of my mouth before breathing."

We arrived at the newspaper office in twenty-five minutes. The driver said, "I am sorry, didn't expect that slow freight train."

I gave the driver the amount on the meter plus an extra five. Inside the *Trenton Times* office on Perry Street, I asked the receptionist, "Where are your archives?"

She directed me to the second floor.

When I entered the archives room, I told the receptionist that I was a writer and was looking for major stories in the last five years. Wasn't sure what I was looking for, just looking. She directed me to racks of papers, filed by date, starting in January of each year.

She said, "Have fun, nothing unusual takes place around here."

I clearly remembered my assignment for President Truman—the president of S & M Machine, in Dayton, Ohio, had been from Trenton, New Jersey. Returning to New Jersey was bothering me.

Starting with the November 1945 issues, I turned over each day, one at a time, until November 23, headlines: "Frank C. Salvatore Arrested." I read the article:

> Frank C. Salvatore, President of S & M Precision Machine, Dayton, Ohio, was arrested at the Holland Tunnel, Detroit, Michigan, by U.S. marshals with a federal warrant, charged with fraud involving United States military contracts. Salvatore was a former Trenton, New Jersey, resident and partner with his brother-in-law, Anthony G. Murita in the Murita Trucking and Storage Company, a lo-

cal firm. Murita was reported not to have been involved in the Dayton Company.

I read the article over several times and could not believe the connection. I copied the details that pertained to the brothers in my notebook, then removed the July 1947 newspapers, stacked them on the table and started looking at front pages. When I reached the July 10 paper the headline jump out at me: "U.S. MARSHALS KILL GUNMAN"

I read the article:

> On the steps of the federal building in Newark today, a United States Marshal shot and killed Hector L. Condenzia who was attempting to kill an unknown witness that U.S. marshals were escorting to the federal court hearing of Frank C. Salvatore, President of S & M Machine, Dayton, Ohio. Salvatore has been charged, with fraud in the government's military contracts with S & M Machine. Condenzia is known to be an associate of Salvatore. Both are former Trenton residents.

I made several entries in my notebook. I returned the papers and placed the October papers on the table.

I stopped at the October 20 edition and started reading the headlines: "SALVATORE CONVICTED IN FEDERAL COURT."

> Frank C. Salvatore was convicted of military contract fraud today in federal court. He received a forty-year prison sentence in a federal prison. Salvatore, President of S & M Machine in Dayton, Ohio, received federal funds to construct a building on land that he owned. He also received federal funds to purchase machine tools for manufacturing parts. S & M Machine received contracts from the government and received payment for parts that his company did not manufacture.
>
> Testimony and evidence submitted in the hearings stated: "S & M Machine did not use the federal money to purchase the machine tools. In fact, S & M Machine never purchased any machinery." Investigators found the building in Dayton, Ohio, empty. There was no evidence that the building was ever used except for the office.

The Cloisters of Canterbury

The most unbelievable part of the fraud was that S & M Machine submitted invoices for parts that they never delivered. It was even more difficult to understand how S & M Precision Machine had received payments for four-hundred-forty-three invoices totaling $3,345,123.59. The federal investigation uncovered a conspiracy involving persons working in the receiving department of a government warehouse and in the accounting office.

Undisclosed sources have stated that Frank C. Salvatore refused to cooperate with the government and has not provided any information. The three million dollars received from the government has not been located.

The information was public record, but I copied most of the article for my report. I returned the newspapers to the files, walked outside and welcomed the fresh air.

The third passing taxi stopped for me.

"Take me to the train station." There was no conversation. I couldn't stop thinking about everything I had just learned. I had chills down my back—not that family again! My feelings ran from joy, having found out that Ruth was Frances, to fright and terror knowing that this family tried to kill me once. What a day! The hair on the back of my head and neck was straight and tingling.

Frances Murita had assumed Ruth Watkins' identity and claimed the Wiseman estate. How did she acquire the information to accomplish the fraud? There was no connection at Vassar College. Frances Murita had attended Trenton High School, and as I suspected, it had been her mistake when she assumed Ruth Watkins' identity and listed her actual high school. If she hadn't, I probably wouldn't have discovered her real name.

I wondered if the visit with Army Sergeant Major Murphy would lead to information about her service in the WAC and her association with the real Ruth Watkins.

However, what really troubled me was in learning that Francis Murita's uncle was Frank C. Salvatore, the man now serving time in a federal prison due to my investigation for President Truman. The fact that her father, Anthony G. Murita, had been a business partner of Salvatore in the trucking business, but not involved in the Dayton Company, was interesting, and also the apparent reason why he had not been arrested. My heart began to pound just thinking about the incident, and of my nightmares of Hector Condenzia's attempt to kill me in front of the federal court in Newark, New Jersey. Now connecting the families to the real Ruth Watkins brought the danger back. Where would it lead?

It was time for me to get out of Trenton and advise the Group of the latest developments, especially the Salvatore connection. I was sure that everyone on the train was looking at me. I also knew that my being paranoid would keep me alive.

As soon as the train arrived in New York, I located a pay telephone and placed a collect call to Doud. When he accepted the call and we played our verification game, I gave him the information about the woman, and that her uncle was Frank G. Salvatore, the man in federal prison. I didn't need to tell Doud any more about Salvatore. He was well aware of my involvement, and was also surprised to learn of the relationship. He agreed that we should continue with our effort to learn the connection between Ruth Watkins and Frances Murita.

It was after eight when I walked into the Astor Hotel. The lights from the street illuminated my room. Somehow after locating the room and looking around, I felt a little safer. I walked to the window and looked down at the people on the street below. They appeared not to have a care in the world, but I knew that was not the case. Everyone had something to worry about, but they hadn't walked in my shoes that day.

As I began to relax, I closed the drapes and undressed. A hot shower felt good. I stood there much longer than normal as the steam billowed around me. I felt the grime of the world slip away. There wasn't anything more to do until the next day. Sleep overtook my tired mind within minutes.

Chapter 22

RETURN TO GOVERNOR'S ISLAND

At six-thirty, I was wide awake, dressed and walking to the subway for the trip to Governor's Island. I was energized and ready for another day.

The subway was full of rushing people on their way to work. I had ridden the subway between Times Square and the Governor's Island ferry many times. Nothing had changed, watching a man push his way through the mass of people to get on a car just as the door closed. I boarded the next train and when it passed three stations down the line that same man, who was in such a rush, was standing against a wall. I had watched the same event many times before. I often wondered what motivated people to rush and then wait down the track. The man certainly hadn't gained anything except the wrath of the people he had pushed out of his way.

While waiting for the Governor's Island Ferry to return from the island, I looked at the water between the shore and the island. It always seemed angry, even in nice weather. The massive rope lines secured the ferry to the pilings after bouncing off several times.

I told the MP on duty at the ferry that Army Sergeant Major Murphy was expecting me at Army headquarters. I waited with three enlisted men and a captain.

As the ferry plowed its way through the rough water to the island, I looked once again at the Statue of Liberty, remembering the many times I had seen the beautiful site. Walking from the ferry past Willie's Castle, the landmark that always greeted people arriving to the island, and seeing the headquarters building, brought back pleasant memories. Somehow, it was like going home and it brought a smile to my face.

A sergeant at a desk just inside the main door greeted me.

"I am Rob Royal. Army Sergeant Major Murphy is expecting me."

The sergeant picked up the telephone, dialed and said, "Rob Royal is here to see you."

He hung up the phone. "The sergeant major will meet you at the top of the stairs."

I walked up the polished marble steps, listening to the sound of my heels like so many times before. Sergeant Murphy greeted me at the top of the stairs. We shook hands and he patted me on the back. We walked down the hall to the sergeant's office.

"Rob, it's been some time since you returned from the assignment for the president, and from what I have been told, you have your nose in another mess. How do you do it? You're such a quiet lad."

"I have no idea. I get this nice management consulting job—a rather enjoyable lifestyle. Then I receive an assignment that should be a normal business experience."

I related the details that he needed about Mueller, Murita and Watkins. I gave him the photographs of the two women with their names printed on the back.

"Excuse me, I'll put some people on this immediately and we'll take a walk."

He returned, removed his overseas cap from a coat rack by the door, and placed it squarely on his head. He motioned for me to follow him without speaking. We walked down the stairs and out of the building. When we were fifty or more feet from the building, the sergeant major said. "I received a call from your friend in Texas last night. He gave me the details of your visit to Poughkeepsie and Trenton.

"The Group is very concerned about the relationship between this Frances Murita and her uncle, Frank Salvatore. We have never been able to find out how Hector Condenzia learned that you were to be a witness in Frank Salvatore's trial in Newark Federal Court. How was he able to get the information and make the attempt on your life? There had to be a leak within the government that a witness was to arrive in Newark, and specifically who it was.

"Your mistake was notifying the police that Condenzia was on the floor in the building in Dayton after he fell through the skylight. Is it possible that you were not aware that Condenzia had a good look at you in Dayton when you were on the assignment for the president? Not to alarm you, but Condenzia has two brothers, and Frank Salvatore has a large family. The Group knows that these people never forget."

I shook my head in dismay. "Sergeant, anything is possible. The night Condenzia fell through the skylight it was pitch black. The moon was behind dark clouds all the time I was at the plant that night. When I heard a noise on the roof, I dropped flat. I was on the opposite side of the ridge of the roof. There had to be a leak from inside the government that a witness was going to appear. Yes, they could have even learned my name. It is also possible that Condenzia saw me snooping around in Salvatore's Oakwood neighborhood or driving on the road to the plant."

I was at liberty to talk in general terms with the sergeant major. To my knowledge he was the only person in the military, other than General Courtney, who had a connection with the Group. We walked down to the water's edge, looking out at the Statue of Liberty.

Murphy said, "I am going to visit with some people about the matter we discussed and I'll call you at your hotel."

"Thanks, Sarge, I appreciate your help."

"Walk carefully, Rob. Remember that sometimes you can't take prisoners, and you are known to that family."

•

The ferry was about to leave when I arrived. Back at the subway station, there were fewer people than earlier that morning. Near Times Square a number of women stood near the curb offering their companionship. I went into the Astor Hotel and stopped at a telephone booth to call Doud. We exchanged the same old identification and I told Doud that Sergeant Murphy was checking with friends about Watkins' and Murita's service in the WAC and would call me the next day.

"Rob, be careful, and call me after you talk with the sergeant, regardless of the time."

When Doud recruited me, he said that life would never be the same, and that there would be difficult times. I was beginning to understand the warning. An attempt had been made on my life, and I was getting closer to some of the same people. There was a sense of excitement, but this was not the fun kind.

I picked up my room key at the front desk and checked for messages. The elevator to the fourth floor moved in slow motion. In fact, everything around was in slow motion.

It was another normal night, very little sleep, reviewing the activities of the day, yesterday and all the days before. The reoccurring dreams brought the screams of the man as he fell through the skylight and landed on the concrete floor. I saw myself looking through the skylight at the bleeding man on the floor of the building. I saw myself driving through the snow, stopping at the gas station, using the telephone to report that there had been an accident. Then the sergeant major told me it was a mistake, "*Sometimes you take no prisoners, no prisoners, no prisoners, no prisoners...*"

I heard the sergeant's words in my mind, again and again, "*...no prisoners, no prisoners...*" I still thought making the call was the right thing to do. But, I really wanted to know how I was identified.

What other mistakes had I made? At the farm they said, "Mistakes are buried with those that make them as someone shovels dirt over you." There were so many statements, quotes and warnings given. Now they seemed to come back to haunt me. Was it my mistake that almost got me killed or was there a government leak? So far, I had been able to live with it. When I woke after six in the morning, my pajamas were wet with perspiration.

I got out of bed, did fifty push-ups and fifty sit-ups, and took a hot and then cold shower. Nothing was on the schedule for the day other than to wait for the sergeant major's telephone call. I left the hotel and walked to Central Park, stopped and watched the ice skaters at Rockefeller Center for a few minutes. I found myself looking over my shoulder, so I returned to the hotel room and started reviewing my notes.

When I was in London, Biff Wallace told me, "Never be too comfortable about what you have learned. There is always something missing. You may never find it, but you must continue to search."

The telephone in the room rang.

"Rob, it's Sergeant Murphy. I am in the lobby, may I come up?"

"Come on up, Sergeant."

I gathered up the papers and had just retrieved the last one when there was a knock on the door. I opened the door. The sergeant major charged in, just about running me over.

The Cloisters of Canterbury

I offered him a chair and I sat on the bed. Reading the expression on the sergeant's face, I knew that he had information that was important to the puzzle.

Sergeant Murphy explained, "In 1942 the Woman's Army Auxiliary Corps was formed. It was not part of the Army, and they didn't have all the regulations and record requirements of the Army, but they had a historian that started recording information. Sometime between July and September 1943, the WAAC received Army status and became the Woman's Army Corps. From that time on there were no centralized records. The records of women in the WAC were maintained by their unit assignments."

The sergeant continued, "I did confirm that Ruth Marie Watkins and Frances Ann Murita both joined the WAAC within days of each other and were in the same basic training unit at Fort Riley, and later were stationed at Fort Devens. The historian's records were unusual, many events, birthday parties and observations were included, more like a personal diary. One entry provided an important clue, 'Frances Murita and Ruth Watkins are never apart, day or night.' When the WAAC became the Woman's Army Corps, members of the WAAC didn't have to rejoin to become members of the Woman's Army Corps, but Watkins and Murita both signed on.

"They were both assigned to the European theater, Eighth Air Force in England. This is where information gets cloudy, but it is always good to have friends. I called an old friend, Major Hamilton Stevens. He was an administrative officer in the Eighth Air Force in England. He served with the unit that Watkins and Murita were assigned to until after it returned to the States.

"Watkins and Murita were secretaries in the Eight Air Force administration office for a while until Murita became a driver. They were inseparable on the base and always went on leave together, mostly to London. No one saw them with any men until the last several months when Murita acquired a civilian male friend, but they always included Watkins when they were off base. They usually met him at The Cork Pub not far from the base. On a number of occasions, they returned to the base in an old black Hillman two-door. Watkins would leave the car and Murita would stay in the car for a period. There was always speculation by the MP's at the gate, both British and American, about what went on in the car."

The sergeant stopped, looked at his notebook again. "Just before midnight, on June 7, 1945, a car stopped at the airbase gate. A woman in a Woman's Army Corps uniform got out of the car, screaming, 'There's been an accident.' The car drove away.

"It was Frances Murita. The British and American MPs tried to calm her down, and attempted to learn the location of the accident. They fully expected it to be near the base. They were unsuccessful in calming her, so one of them called the officer of the day. He arrived in a jeep with its siren blasting, followed by an ambulance with its siren on—everyone expected an emergency.

"Finally, between sobs, she told them, 'A lorry came out of a side road and hit us. Ruth is dead and I was thrown from the car.' The duty officer asked her where the accident had taken place, and Frances Murita told him it had happened just outside of London, they were on their way back to the air base. When the duty officer asked when it had happened, she said, 'This morning, several hours ago.'

"The Duty Officer told the ambulance crew to take Murita to the base hospital and that he would follow. Murita screamed, 'I am not going to any hospital, I am not hurt.'

"The MPs assisted the ambulance driver and his partner. Murita was then crying and kicking. They put her on the cot in the ambulance and restrained her with straps.

"When the ambulance arrived at the base hospital, she was wheeled into an examination room. The duty officer arrived, briefed the doctor on duty. The doctor examined her, and then a nurse stuck a needle in her right arm. She was soon asleep.

"The duty officer called the administration office and learned that Frances Murita and Ruth Watkins had been on a three-day pass for London and were due back that midnight. There had not been a report to the base of any accident. The British counterpart to the American duty officer started making calls. The next morning he received a call from the London police telling him that there had been an accident and that there had been a death. A British officer and an American officer went to the London police station. They were told that Ruth Marie Watkins, age 25, an American Army Corps member, was killed in an auto accident early on the morning of 7 June on Chertsey Parish Road. Her body was in the rear seat, the front of her head was crushed above her eyes, and there was a minimum amount of blood. Her body was taken to the coroner.

"At the accident sight another member of the American Woman's Army Corps identified as Frances Ann Murita, age 25, told police that she was driving the car when a lorry pulled from a side road hitting them and drove away without stopping. She stated that she was thrown from the car. When asked if she was injured she said that she was not.

"The war in Europe was just over. Hitler had committed suicide, service people were given three- and four-day passes. Frances Murita and Ruth Watkins had been on a three-day pass and signed out for London. They were due back at midnight on the night of the accident. Murita awoke several hours later after receiving the shot in her arm. When questioned she said she was driving a Hillman car belonging to her friend, Thomas Harris, who lived in Essex. He loaned her the car. They were on their way back to the airbase when a lorry came out of the side road, hit them broadside and did not stop.

"Murita stated that she had been had thrown from the car and when asked where she landed, she said she didn't remember. But, according to Major Stevens, the accident report indicated that she had not received any injuries and there was only a small amount of dirt on her clothing. She was wearing a skirt, and her legs weren't scraped and her stockings weren't even torn.

"If Watkins was riding in the front left passenger seat at the time of impact, when the lorry struck the Hillman squarely on the left side, how did her body get in the rear seat?

"Major Stevens said that there were questions about the injury to Watkins' head. There was no visible point of impact in the car for such an injury. According to Major Stevens, the investigating officer was unable to break Murita's story.

"An Eighth Air Force officer interviewed a constable from a village near the airbase who said they received a report that the Hillman had been stolen. It hadn't been driven for several years because it needed engine repair. When the owner enlisted in the Navy, he parked the car in a shed next to his mother's cottage. The owner's mother had been in Wales caring for a sick member of her family since before the war. When she returned home, her son's car was gone. She knew that her son had not returned from sea duty with the Navy so she reported the Hillman as stolen to the local constable. The constable said that he didn't get too concerned about the old Hillman since it had seen better days and wasn't of much value.

"The constable reported that he made inquires of the neighbors and learned that a man had been living in the cottage. One day a neighbor from down the road saw him working on the Hillman and he stopped to talk to him. The man working on the car said that he was a friend of the owners and he was going to repair the car for them. For several months, the man was at the cottage and driving the Hillman. The neighbors were not sure when the man moved away. But there was one thing the constable said they agreed about, the man was not from the UK, and his English was not very good.

"Another issue that was never answered—Murita's friend, Thomas Harris, was never located and his description was given to the bartenders and owners of pubs in the area. At The Cork Pub, a bartender remembered a black, two-door Hillman, its male driver and two American service women."

I asked Murphy, "Sergeant, there is more than one point in Murita's story that should have alerted the investigators. The accident was supposed to have taken place early on the morning of June 7. How early? Was it still dark? Murita said they were on their way back to the air base. They were not due back from their leave until midnight on the seventh. Ask any service person, they never return from leave early. What were they doing out on this country road early in the morning? I wonder where Murita was after the early morning accident until she arrived at the base just before midnight, and what was she doing? Someone dropped the ball in this investigation."

"I know." The sergeant major nodded his head in agreement. "But I have a signed statement from Major Stevens that details all that I have just told you."

"Sergeant, did Major Stevens give you any reason why a more thorough investigation had not been made?"

"The Major told me that he and several others were not in agreement with ending the investigation, but the Eighth Air Force had received their orders to pack up and everyone wanted to go home. The English police had closed their investigation."

"Sergeant, we now have a dead woman, a member of Woman's Army Corps, killed in an unsolved accident. The only witness returns to the States, assumes the dead woman's identity, claims her inheritance and is living with a German Nazi wanted for war crimes. I understand that under the circumstances, another dead person might not be important, but I just don't believe that it's right. If those responsible for the investigation had performed their duty at the time of the accident, what would have happened?"

Murphy shook his head. "I certainly don't know."

I walked Sergeant Murphy to the Times Square subway station and returned to the Astor lobby and placed a collect call to Doud. It rang four times. We exchanged our regular identification, and during the next hour, I repeated the information that the sergeant major had just given me. Doud didn't interrupt or say anything until I stopped talking.

"Rob, I have been making some notes and will talk with Allen. Return to Cleveland as scheduled. Be careful."

Chapter 23

Report To The Group

The next morning I checked out of the hotel and took a taxi to LaGuardia. The information that the sergeant major had obtained from Major Stevens bothered me. Why hadn't there been more of an investigation of the accident?

I arrived at LaGuardia an hour before my scheduled flight. At the ticket counter I checked the suitcase and carried my briefcase. When they called for boarding, I found my seat on the right side of the plane. It was the third row, next to the window—easy on and easy off.

The flight landed at the Cleveland airport five minutes ahead of schedule. I was the first off the plane, but my bag was one of the last to arrive at baggage claim. When I walked out of the terminal to my car, it seemed that the temperature had dropped. There was a feel of snow in the air, maybe before morning. I put the briefcase and suitcase in the trunk and drove into Cleveland. Inside the National City Bank building the receptionist welcomed me. I walked down the hall exchanging greetings with several members of the staff.

Allen's secretary asked, "How was your trip? You are expected, go right in."

The Cloisters of Canterbury

The door opened just as I reached it.

James Allen had his hand out. "Good afternoon, Rob, how was your trip?"

"Good flight and a productive trip." I was surprised to see Doud sitting in Allen's office since I had talked with him on the telephone the morning before, and he was in Texas. Doud stood and we shook hands.

"Nice to see you, Rob. It's been some time," he said.

"Yes, it has been a while. I certainly didn't expect to see you here in Cleveland today."

"Allen and I had further conversations and we decided that we needed to review the information with you and make some decisions in light of the latest developments."

We walked over to the conference table. This morning's closed draperies hid the beautiful view of Lake Erie.

"You must want to keep me focused, shutting out Lake Erie." I quipped.

They laughed, knowing that they all had made comments about keeping anyone's attention at meetings with the view from there.

James Allen began, "Rob, we would like for you to go over everything that you have uncovered."

I removed the daily field reports from my briefcase and placed them on the conference table. I had submitted many daily field reports and made many reports by telephone, but this would be my first presentation to Doud and Allen together. This meeting did not bother me. I knew that my field reports were complete in every possible detail.

With my back to the closed draperies, Doud sat to my left at the end of the table and Allen was on my right at the end of the table, making it impossible to observe the faces of both men at the same time. It was one of the tactics learned at the farm, two people asking questions, taking turns, not allowing me to see the reaction of both men at the same time.

I started from the beginning of the assignment in Springfield, and everything through my meeting with the Army Sergeant Major Murphy. Doud and Allen both took notes as I talked. It took over three hours to complete the presentation—without a break. I turned over the last day's field report, pushed my chair back from the table, turned and looked at the draped window blocking my view of Lake Erie.

When I turned back around, Doud and Allen were smiling, and as if by a signal, they both clapped their hands together and spoke in unison, "Well done."

Doud stood. "Rob, tell us what is still needed."

I had no problem responding to the question. I had been thinking about it for a long time and had made a list, crossing off things that had been learned or were no longer of importance and adding to the list additional questions as they became apparent.

I removed a folder from my briefcase, placed it on the table, and opened the folder, announcing, "My summary will address the issues.

"John A. Johnson is Hans Mueller a German Nazi SS officer wanted for war crimes. He should be arrested before he has the opportunity to walk out of the Springfield hospital.

"The woman in Springfield using Ruth Watkins' identity is Frances Ann Murita. She is guilty of harboring a fugitive, fraud, embezzlement, and might be an accomplice in the murder of Ruth Watkins in England. There is sufficient evidence for her arrest, which should take place simultaneously with Mueller's arrest.

"These two arrests will not close the matter in my mind. I believe that determining how Frances Murita accomplished these acts is important, as well as what her association is with Hans Mueller. I also think we should learn more about the English solicitor who certified Henry A. Wiseman's death. In addition, we should learn more about Ruth Watkins' death."

I paused. "This is probably reaching a little too far, but the death of Wiseman's lawyer, Glenn Hudson, by a hit-and-run driver as he stepped off the bus in Springfield was just too convenient. His secretary remembers that he had received a personal letter on that day, and that he was on the way to the courthouse. She said that the letter was from the Valley Bank. Wiseman had accounts in the bank. Did the letter tell Hudson that Ruth Watkins had appeared and obtained control of the bank accounts? We don't know. Hudson had been notified that Ruth Watkins had died in an auto accident in England. I have not contacted anyone at Valley Bank. In view of my previous contacts with John Myers at the bank for the Group, I knew that approval was required before visiting him."

I took a deep breath and continued, "I believe that a few more days at the truck plant is needed to clear the suspicion of several other German men. None of their appearances comes close to matching any of the photographs. They are going to be subject to possible hostile acts by the other employees. Their nationality has convicted them. I do not think that the employment manager was involved in any of the activities. Frances Murita has the ability to turn on the charm and accomplish almost anything. I think we need to learn about the other four German men just for their safety. They have not been involved in my investigation, but I still would like to spend a few days at the plant before Mueller and Murita are arrested."

Allen had not spoken until now. "Let's have lunch and come back, review what you have presented, and agree on a plan to bring this to a close."

"Good idea," said Doud, "and, Allen, it's time you take us to the Cleveland Country Club for lunch."

"That's one way Doud can avoid buying lunch," Allen responded.

•

When we returned from lunch at the Cleveland Country Club, we immediately went back to Allen's office and sat down at the conference table, but this time Doud and Allen sat across from me.

Doud began, "I think that the information you have uncovered will be sufficient to present to the federal court, and warrants should be issued for the arrest of Hans Mueller and Frances Murita. I also have the same concerns you have about Murita's connection with Mueller. How was she able to assume Ruth Watkins' identity? She must have had help. However, I have a greater concern that she may have been involved, if not responsible, for Watkins' death in the car accident. I am in agreement with your evaluation of the investigation of the accident. It was not complete and leaves too many unanswered questions."

He paused and continued, "We need to learn more about the accident in England and the lawyer that was involved with Wiseman. Rob, take the next available flight to London. We will send a cable to Biff Wallace and have him meet you. Take all the information and photographs with you. The assignment will be for you and Biff to investigate the Watkins accident and check out the lawyer that corresponded with Wiseman's lawyer. Biff has not been briefed, Rob. You can do that and he will know what to do. If Murita can be connected to Watkins' death, I would like to have that information when the Group presents the evidence to a federal judge."

Allen walked across the room, opened the draperies, and looked out at Lake Erie. "I agree with Doud, by keeping with the Group's policy of limiting the number of people having access to the information in each assignment, it should reduce the possibility of leaks. We have not forgotten the leak that almost cost your life in the military contractor assignment for the president. Time is also a major concern for all of us. You have worked with Biff Wallace. You know his background and his access to information. Share all your information with him. Just the three of us in this room and Sergeant Murphy are privileged to the details of your assignment. Therefore, Rob, it's only logical for you to make the trip. Do you have any questions?"

"No questions."

Allen smiled and left the room without speaking.

Doud walked to the window and looked out on Lake Erie for a few minutes then returned to the conference table. "Rob, the connection between Hans Mueller and Frances Murita is difficult to understand. Hans Mueller, a Nazi SS officer wanted for war crimes, leaves Germany. Did he arrive in England during the time Frances Murita and Ruth Watkins were with the Woman's Army Corps? Did they meet in England? Or was it after Mueller went to Canada, then to the United States, and located in Springfield, Ohio? Your report indicates that based on his employment application, he should not have been employed, except that Frances Murita was probably responsible for hiring him. At some point in time, they started living together. When was this conspiracy conceived? She must have received help.

"The fact that Frances Murita's uncle is in prison for his illegal activities seems to have nothing to do with this, but it might indicate that Frances had some early training, and probably some help from her family that motivated her to become involved. Your involvement in developing the information for the conviction of her uncle was coincidental. However, we want to caution you, these people are not nice and they will stop at nothing to accomplish their goals and protect their family. They don't forget, Rob, you *must* be careful."

Allen returned, "Rob, you have a reservation on TWA leaving Cleveland tomorrow morning for New York, and on to London Heathrow tomorrow evening. We will send a cable to Biff Wallace, have him meet you and advise him that he will be briefed by you. When you leave, Shirley will give you an envelope with your flight information and funds for the plane tickets that have been made in your name and a little extra for some Balvenie for you and Biff."

"Rob, I remember telling you that it would not always be boring." Doud smiled and shook my hand. "Good luck and have a safe trip."

•

The Cloisters of Canterbury

It was still snowing when I walked from the office to the parking lot. I cleared the snow from the windshield of the car and drove out of the lot. The snow was really starting to collect on Euclid Avenue. I drove west to Bay Village normally looking out at Lake Erie, but the brake lights of cars ahead of me had my full attention.

Mrs. Gray was sweeping the snow from the front steps of her house when I pulled in the drive; it didn't matter that the steps would be covered with snow again within the next hour or less. I took the broom from her and swept the snow off the sidewalk from the front steps to the street. She was a nice lady and had a good sense of humor.

When I went inside, she had fixed me a ham sandwich, a cup of hot chocolate and some homemade cookies. I really appreciated it on this cold snowy night.

Chapter 24

LONDON 1953

I repacked my suitcase for the trip to London, and included a dark gray wool sweater, trench coat and leather gloves. I went over my field notes and made a summary that I would review with Biff. If time permitted, I would give him all of my field notes to read. Setting the alarm clock for six, but probably not needing it, I didn't want to oversleep with a plane to catch, especially when there would be snow on the road to the Cleveland airport.

I dreamed that night that I was in England. It was night. I was alone standing in deep snow in the center of the stones at Stonehenge. It was quiet and still, the moon shone bright, casting eerie shadows of the stones on the snow.

I spoke aloud, "What am I doing out here all alone."

A voice came down from the sky, "You're not alone, you have never been alone, and you will always be cloistered."

I woke up and sat on the edge of the bed for some time. I had only been to Stonehenge once, and that was when I was in England with Biff. I did not understand the voice's message or its meaning.

What was *cloistered*?

The Cloisters of Canterbury

I walked across the room to the bedroom window and looked out. It was still snowing, there was only a streetlight illuminating the snow. I glanced at the alarm clock; it was four o'clock in the morning. I knew I should get more sleep, but I stayed in a state of half-awake and half-asleep.

My mind continued to ask, *What is cloistered? What was the meaning of the dream?*

I sat up in bed the moment the alarm sounded. It had been a strange night. I dressed, left the room, descended the stairs and went out the front door as quietly as possible.

The trip to the airport took longer than usual. I parked the car in the airport parking lot and walked through over six inches of snow. There were passengers at the TWA ticket counter checking in for the New York flight that would leave in two hours.

After checking in, I located a coffee shop, ordered coffee and donuts, and read the headlines of *The Cleveland Plain Dealer* newspaper that someone had left on the table. "Snow Storm Blankets Great Lakes," "Chicago—Detroit Airports Closed."

My flight was to make a stop in Pittsburgh before continuing to New York LaGuardia. If the snowstorm moved farther east, there could be a problem in Pittsburgh. The article also stated that Newark and New York were still open. I had missed a few flights due to weather, but I didn't want to miss this flight to London. I continued reading the newspaper until they called for boarding. The flight left Cleveland on time, landed in Pittsburgh and continued to New York without any delays. The flight to London was to leave at 9:00 PM. It was noon, and would be a long wait.

For the next several hours, I played my old waiting game looking at individuals and attempting to make eye contact with people. I wondered what they were hiding from the world.

They called for boarding forty minutes before scheduled departure time. My seat was next to the window and I placed the briefcase under the seat in front of me. The seat next to me was vacant. I asked for a pillow and blanket from the stewardess and prepared to sleep as soon as we were airborne. My many trips to London had taught me to get as much sleep during the flight as possible so that when arriving in London I was well rested and ready to start the day.

When the plane reached cruising altitude, the pilot announced that we would be flying north over Greenland. Looking out of the window, I saw only a distant light on the ground. I put the seat back, pillow under my head, pulled the blanket up and was asleep within minutes. The next thing I heard was the pilot's voice announcing that we were approaching Ireland's Gander Shannon airport and requesting passengers to return their seats to the upright position.

I looked out of the window. A light dusting of snow covered the ground. Large flocks of sheep were grazing on the side of a hill. I had never seen so many stone fences before, running along the roads, separating the fields.

The plane touched down and taxied to the terminal. Three passengers descended the plane's stairs. The plane taxied back to the runway. It turned, headed north and was airborne again very quickly. The pilot announced that we would be landing at London Heathrow in an hour.

I had slept from New York to Shannon. When I walked down the steps from the plane into the cool London air, I felt rested. I located my suitcase at baggage claim and went to customs. I presented my passport to a tired-looking man who glanced at me and the photo in the passport and then asked, "What's the purpose of your visit?"

"Visiting a special friend."

"Have a good visit."

"Thank you, I plan to visit as often as possible."

I walked out of the Heathrow terminal. Standing next to a dark blue Jaguar XK120 coupe stood Bifford Wallace smiling from ear to ear. The casual observer would think that we were two friends greeting each other.

Biff gave me a bear hug and said, "It's been too long, old friend."

"It's great to be back in England, Biff."

Biff put my suitcase in the boot, started the car and we drove away from the terminal.

"This is a sporty car for a conservative Brit, where's the old taxi?"

"It's in the shop for some major engine repair, paint and upholstering. It should be back running within the next week or two. Never know when it might be needed to pick up a well-heeled Yank."

We traveled on the same London streets that I had seen the first time I visited Biff, but there was a difference. The streets had been repaired, many buildings had been refurbished and painted, and several new building were under construction.

When Biff turned on to Warwick Way, I recognized the neighborhood. The coal soot had been removed from many of the brick buildings. The wooden doors and window frames now had one or more coats of paint. The streets were clean and the scattered trash was missing, so were the rats that had run freely during that first visit. Biff turned off Warwick Way, pulled to the curb and shut the engine off.

"This is your home in London."

I looked out of the car window at the two-story brick building; the same building that had been soot-covered and dilapidated in 1948. Now it was an attractive brick building, about fifty feet across the front, no windows on the ground floor facing the street, two doors in the middle. On the second floor facing the street were four French-style windows with black shutters. From the street, the roof appeared to be flat. It was evident that a lot of work had been done on it.

Biff's expression was blank. I opened the car door with no hesitation and with a broad smile. Spending a night in this building in this neighborhood would not be a problem. I stepped out of the car—no rats lurked on the front steps. Biff opened his car door, got out, removed my suitcase from the boot, and walked up the steps to the door of the safe house. Biff inserted a key in the lock, unlocked the door and stepped inside. He turned the lights on with a switch just to the right of the door. I followed him and closed the door.

The silence was only broken by the sound of my breathing. The surprise on my face had to be the best laugh for Biff in a long time. Grinning, he walked over and turned on a table light. The light from the crystal ceiling light cast a glow over the freshly painted white walls. The room was square, approximately twenty by twenty feet. An Oriental rug covered the floor in the middle of the room; the wood floor had been sanded and varnished. Two brown leather chairs with matching ottomans were separated by a deep red mahogany table with a reading light. In front of the chairs was a coffee table with the same mahogany finish. On the table was a bottle of Balvenie Twenty-Year-Old Single Malt Scotch whiskey and two crystal glasses.

Biff dropped the suitcase and said, "Yeah," then threw his arms around me. "Welcome to London, friend."

I stepped back a couple steps, looked around and realized that Biff had been responsible for arranging this welcome.

"Let me show you the rest of the place."

Directly opposite the entrance door was an archway that led into the kitchen, the same size as the front room except for the stairs to the second floor. In the center of the room was a round maple wood table and four matching chairs with blue and white-checked cushions. On the counter was a small sink and a two-burner gas hot plate. Under the counter was a small refrigerator next to four drawers. A single cabinet hung over the counter; the glass in the door exposed dishes and glasses. On the back wall was a metal door in a metal frame secured by a metal bar. There were no windows.

"Let's go upstairs."

Biff led the way up the stairs to the second floor. There were two bedrooms separated by a bathroom with white towels on the rack and a closet with access from both rooms. The front bedroom had two French windows covered by heavy draperies. The rear bedroom had identical French windows with the same draperies. Both bedrooms had full-size beds with brass posts, a small nightstand with a lamp on one side, and a three-drawer chest against the wall. There were pillows covered in a dark maroon fabric with a gold embroidered coat of arms on both beds.

Biff was still grinning. "Let's open the Balvenie, but first I want you to look at this panel on the wall opposite the bathroom door."

I hadn't even noticed the panel. It was a crude painting of a stone archway and framed by heavy old boards, very impressive if you liked old stone pillars.

"It is the Dean's Walk through the cloister at Canterbury Cathedral—where we walked with Rev. Filpin on your visit to Canterbury."

There was that word again, *"cloister."* I held my hand up to stop Biff from talking, and asked, "Did you say cloister?"

"Yeah, a cloister is a stone archway, a passage or hallway that shelters people from the elements. They have been part of the architecture of monasteries and castles for hundreds of years. They protected the monks in monasteries from the weather when they walked in silence from one part of the monastery to another. The severe weather was responsible for their construction in Ireland, Scotland, and England as well as on the continent. All that remains standing of several ancient monasteries and castles are the cloisters giving evidence of their strength."

I stood motionless and not speaking.

"What's wrong, Rob?"

"In the middle of the night before leaving on this trip I had the strangest dream…and it was about a cloister. I had never heard the word used until the dream, and now again."

"Rob, what was your dream?"

"It was night. I was alone standing in deep snow in the center of the stones at Stonehenge. It was quiet and still. The moon was shining, casting eerie shadows of the stones on the snow. I spoke aloud, 'What am I doing out here all alone.' A voice came down from the sky, 'You're not alone, you have never been alone and you will always be cloistered.'"

The Cloisters of Canterbury

Biff looked at me with a puzzled look, but said nothing.

He raised his left arm, placed his fingers on top of the frame and ran his hand along the right edge. He moved his hand as if he was searching for something, and then a faint clicking sound came from within the wall. He paused for a second or two, and the painting started to slide to the left. When the painting had cleared the frame, Biff reached above his head and pulled the chain of a single light bulb. Behind the painting was a metal door.

Biff inserted his fingers into a recessed slot on the right side of the door and pushed the door to the left. He turned and looked at me, and then walked through the doorway. He moved his hand along the wall until the click of a switch disturbed the silence, bathing the area in a glow of light.

I followed as Biff continued to turn on lights. Opposite the entrance was a bath identical to the one on the other side of the wall. In the rear room, there were twin beds, table and lamp between them, a three-drawer chest against the rear wall. An open closet door revealed access to the front room. We walked into the front room. There were two French windows with heavy draperies. In the room were four wooden desks and chairs, two facing the left wall and two the right wall.

In the center of the room was a table about four feet by eight feet. On top of the table were stacks of folders and binders, two by three feet, three inches thick. I opened the cover of the top binder. The first page was an index, Charts of Cities and Communities in England. I moved the first binder and opened the second one, Charts of Cities and Communities in Wales, Scotland and Ireland. There were twenty-eight, four-inch thick, eight-inch-by-ten-inch loose-leaf notebooks. Twenty-four were labeled with letters of the alphabet, and the other two were labeled "Open" and "Closed." I opened the first notebook, last names starting with A, date of birth, place of birth, address if known, and organization codes.

"Rob, the names in the notebooks are under review. The information in these books was obtained from church records, city halls, passport records, school records, seaport shipping records, newspapers, immigration records, military records, court records, health departments, and informants. We are looking for any connection to known individuals who may enter the UK or the United States. The information about the twenty men in the photographs that I gave to Doud a few months ago when he was in London came from these records. We can't determine which source is the best, but informants turn in names and information for many reasons, not always for money."

I followed Biff down the stairs to the first floor. It was identical to the rooms in the first flat, except it had a small bath off the kitchen near the rear door. All the walls and ceilings were newly painted and the floors sanded and varnished.

"The reason for the two units is that they provide several options. A place for me to analyze the information obtained by others, prepare lists and reports for the Group, and a safe house for you and other members of the Group, if needed. You are also free to use it when you're in London on holiday. The owner is a barrister that lives in York and spends some time in Edinburgh, Scotland, by the name of Bifford Allen Wallace, III. Yeah, that's me. I got my wig at Oxford while I was with Scotland Yard before the war. Just follow me, but not so close that you might trip. I might have a few other surprises in store for you."

Biff turned the lights off on the first floor. The light from the second floor illuminated the stairs. I followed Biff up the stairs. "I want to show you another feature."

He went to the far side of the stairs that appeared to be a wall. He opened a small panel, unwound a rope from a block, and lowered a piece of metal that was hinged at the base of the wall. Lowering the metal plate covered the opening of the stairwell. He moved a metal bar attached to the face of the plate and moved it into a hole on the sidewall next to the floor securing the metal plate over the opening.

Biff looked at me and continued, "The first flat I can use with my family when they come to London and, as I said, you are free to use it when you're in London on Group assignments or on holiday. This flat is actually the safe house. It is secure with no windows on the ground level and a person can go to the second floor, drop the metal trap door, secure it, and be safe. The floors upstairs in both flats are reinforced with metal, as suggested by friends at Scotland Yard. The front and back doors are also reinforced metal. In the ceiling of the closets of both units are metal reinforced access doors to the roof, providing an emergency exit."

I paused to look at the clothes hanging in the closet. Biff explained. "I must change my appearance on occasions. The only other access to the flats is through the second story windows in the front and rear of the building, and with the bars across them, that would be almost impossible.

"I am the owner of four more flats, two on each side of these. When material is available, the roof will be extended on both sides. I think you call them carports in the US. Iron gates will be hung and this will provide covered off-street parking for a motor car for each flat."

We went back upstairs to the second floor in the second flat, leaving the sliding door open between the two, then down the stairs into the living room. Biff opened the Balvenie and poured two fingers in the glasses. We toasted, touched glasses and sat down. Biff certainly had good taste and the chair could not have been more comfortable.

I was beginning to understand more things now. Biff had established a realistic cover, a barrister from York with connections in Scotland who had reason to be in London and certainly would have reason for his family to visit London. It would also be realistic that a client from the United States should stay at his London flat. I was sure that there were a lot of Biff's activities that would not be shared with me.

There was no doubt in my mind that Doud knew what he was doing when he recruited Bifford Allen Wallace for the Group's key contact in the UK. I was becoming more enthused and excited about being a member of the Group. It seemed that I was learning something new each time Biff spoke.

As we sipped and enjoyed the fine scotch whiskey Biff explained that his wife was aware that he was the owner of the flats, but not aware of some of the features or their intended use. In all probability, she would never visit them. When in London, she wanted to stay at the Dorchester. She was looking forward to visiting New York City and wanted to stay at the Waldorf Astoria. She wasn't interested in decorating so he would be adding to the decor as time went by. His wife knew that he worked in the foreign office, but was not aware of his association with British Intelligence or with the Group. The fact that he was a barrister in the foreign office discretely covered everything on the home front.

Biff talked of his two young sons, both in a private school, and how his wife watched over them and her flower garden. She played golf with three women friends in the summer and read most days in the winter. They had a housekeeper who had been with them since their marriage, who also prepared their meals.

He added that his father-in-law, who was deceased, had been in the House of Commons and had been associated with one of the distilleries. He did not offer the name of his father-in-law or the name of the distillery, and I did not ask.

Biff certainly was living on the right side of the tracks. He hadn't mentioned his parents to me. It was very interesting that he had not asked me anything about my family. His only remark was that he understood I had a friend in the White House.

I recalled that President Truman told me, "Listen hard and be careful whom you take into your confidence and into your home." I was sure that the president would approve of my friend the barrister.

Biff looked at me with a smile. "It's about time we start on the purpose of your visit."

I opened the briefcase, removed the summary that I had prepared for Biff, and started reading it line by line.

"You're aware of my management consulting position with James Allen & Associates, a management consulting firm in Cleveland, Ohio? I was on several assignments with senior members of the firm for several months in northern Ohio. Then I received a consulting assignment at the Springfield Truck Company in Springfield, Ohio, not far from Xenia where I grew up.

"The Friday before I was to leave for Springfield, James Allen, the president of the firm, called me to his office to review the assignment with me. He then gave me the names and photographs of twenty men, German Nazis wanted for war crimes. At that point, he told me that he is a member of the Group. I learned that you had given Doud the photographs and information in the packet when Doud was in London. I was told to keep my eyes open for anyone resembling the men in the photos."

I turned several pages. "I am going to skip all of the details. If you want something to eliminate your insomnia you can read my field notes.

"A few days after starting the assignment, I heard a group of men talking in German. That evening, I looked at the photographs of the twenty wanted men. The photograph of Hans A. Mueller, Nazi SS officer, looked like John A. Johnson, one of the men at the plant. There was an accident at the plant, John A. Johnson was injured, and while asleep in the hospital bed I was able to take his picture."

I removed two photographs from an envelope and gave them to Biff. One was the photo of the wanted Hans Mueller and the other was John A. Johnson in the hospital bed. I removed a magnifying glass from the briefcase. Biff took it, looked at both photos. I waited for his reaction.

"There is no reasonable doubt they are of the same person," said Biff. "All features are the same. For two different men to have identical scars on their faces is improbable. Yes, they are photos of the same man."

"At the plant there is also a woman calling herself Ruth Watkins, the employment manager's secretary, who processed John A. Johnson's employment application. John Johnson, who is really Hans Mueller, lives with her. The address on his employment application does not exist. He rides the bus to work. She drives. They are never seen together, but men in the plant know that they live together and he beats her if anybody looks at her."

Biff looked at me waiting for my next words.

"I have verified that the woman is not Ruth Watkins, but Frances Murita. Both of them were in the Women's Army Corps together, received training at Fort Riley, Kansas, and Fort Devens, Massachusetts. Then, they were assigned to the American Eighth Air Force Headquarters at Bushy-Middlesex. Ruth Watkins was a secretary and Frances Murita was a driver. She became familiar with London and areas near Heston Airfield where the Eighth and Ninth Air Force Transport groups were stationed. We have obtained statements that they were inseparable while in Basic Training and in England. At some point, Murita acquired a male friend who drove an old Hillman auto. All three of them frequented The Cork Pub in Hounslow-Middlesex near Heston Airfield.

"After the end of the war in Europe, in 1945, Murita and Watkins received a three-day pass. On the third night, just before midnight, Murita returned to headquarters at Bushy and reported that Watkins had been killed in an auto accident. She reported that a lorry pulled from a side road and hit the car, and that the driver of the lorry did not stop. Ruth Watkins was riding in the front passenger's seat. The constable that investigated the accident reported that Watkins' body was found in the back seat. Her only injury was to her forehead, with very little blood on her and none in the car. No point of impact was located in the car. Murita reported that she was driving and that she been thrown from the car. She received no injuries and her uniform was not damaged, only a small amount of dirt on the sleeve of her jacket. The car that Murita was driving was an old black two-door Hillman. The accident report indicated that the owner of the Hillman was Murita's friend, Thomas Harris, and he lived near Pirbright. She told the constable that Harris loaned her the car.

"The Constable investigated the ownership of the Hillman and learned that it belonged to a Navy man who left the car in a shed next to his mother's cottage near Pirbright when he joined the British Navy. A constable in Pirbright told the investigator that the vehicle was reported stolen. His investigation determined that a man was seen living at the cottage while the mother of the owner was in Wales. Neighbors reported that the man worked on the engine of the Hillman and was seen driving it for several months. They also said that his English was poor. A note in the accident report stated that they had not been able to locate anyone named Thomas Harris after the accident.

"When Murita was questioned about Thomas Harris, all she provided was that he lived near Pirbright and she had met him at a pub in Hounslow."

"Rob, you have been busy."

I laughed, "It certainly hasn't been boring, but that is not the entire story.

"The real Ruth Watkins was raised in Springfield, Ohio, by her uncle and aunt, Henry and Rachel Wiseman. A letter from a Zurich banker stated that Wiseman died on a train to Dachau. Later a letter was received from Alvin C. Waite, a London barrister, stating that he died in Auschwitz in 1944.

"Ruth Watkins was notified of her uncle and aunt's deaths and of inheriting their estate while she was in England. The Tudor home occupied by Frances Murita and Hans Mueller is part of the estate. Lawyer Glenn Hudson probated Wiseman's will. Hudson was then killed by a hit-and-run driver as he stepped from a city bus. A couple of weeks before Hudson's death and unbeknownst to him, Frances Murita arrived in Springfield, Ohio, taking possession of the Wiseman estate. The employment manager of the Springfield Truck Company employed her as a secretary two weeks after Hudson's death without checking the information on her employment application.

"John A. Johnson, a.k.a. Hans Mueller, is now in the hospital and will be released within two weeks. He probably could walk out of the hospital on his own at any time. The Group has sufficient evidence to have him arrested now. They have someone watching him twenty-four hours a day. They will restrain him if he attempts to leave.

"Ruth Watkins/Frances Murita is financially able to leave and is expected to leave if any move is made on Mueller. She is also being watched.

"The Group would like to know more about the Mueller and Murita relationship, if possible. Ruth Watkins' death in the auto accident is very suspicious. They would like to know more about the London barrister who reported Wiseman's death and the conflicting information concerning Wiseman's death. It would be interesting to know more about the hit-and-run death of Wiseman's lawyer, but it is unlikely that anything more will be learned.

The Cloisters of Canterbury

"They would like for you to take a look at Ruth Watkins' accident report. My field reports contain all the details and statements of others. Doud thinks there may be something missing that could lead to other individuals who might not be available after Mueller and Murita are arrested."

I paused. "Doud wanted me to be sure to tell you that Frances Murita's uncle was arrested and convicted of fraud in federal court. He is serving a forty-year term in a federal prison. He was the president of a company that obtained military contracts during the war. There were several government employees involved. There were leaks about a witness who was to testify in federal court. An attempt was made on the witness's life as he entered the federal court building. In addition, I was instructed to be sure, without fail, that you know that I was responsible for the investigation and was that witness. An attempt was made on my life. The shooter and a U.S. marshal were killed. The families involved don't forget."

"Thanks, Rob. I appreciate being warned to watch my back when traveling with you. I think that it would be wise for me to read your field reports."

Sometime while I was relating the information, Biff had added a couple more fingers of Balvenie to our glasses. When we finished the Balvenie, Biff didn't offer more.

He rose from his chair. "Let's take a walk. There are a couple good places to eat not far from here."

Outside we turned left on Warwick Way. Flats lined both sides of the street. Most were four-story brick buildings, side by side, with two steps leading up to the front door, some with glass in the doors, some not. Two windows facing the street was the norm, second, third and fourth floors all had two windows.

I found it interesting that a number of flats on one side of Warwick Way had ornamental iron fencing at the edge of the sidewalk and an open space of four feet or more between the fence and the brick wall of the building. Looking over the fence, I could see that there was a floor below ground level with windows and doorways. In the US, they would be called basements. Some of them had iron gates in the fence that opened to stone steps that led to the lower level. This was certainly efficient use of land. My thoughts went back to the brick buildings in Springfield. They could have used some daylight in their basements.

Soot from years of coal smoke covered the buildings in London. There was evidence of recent cleaning and painting of doors and window frames on many buildings. Yes, England was recovering from the years of war, and people were working hard to restore their lives. There were vacant buildings with windows boarded up, but that too would eventually change.

It was apparent that the same architect had designed all of the buildings for blocks. On the front of the buildings, where the first and second floor joined, there was a concrete ledge extending about six or eight inches where the pigeons were roosting. London certainly had its share of pigeons.

Biff pointed to several small retail shops on the ground floor of buildings. "Many of the shops have been here since World War I, and the owners still live above them."

We reached the corner of Warwick Way and Belgrade Road and Biff pointed across the street at a pub. "This pub has been here since World War I. The original owner's family still operates it, and three generations live above it. They serve good food, are friendly and only occasionally have to call a bobby, and that would be on a Saturday night."

We crossed the street to the pub. The tables outside on the sidewalk were occupied. The door was standing open and the sound of laughter and a pleasant aroma of beer greeted us. Biff led the way to the end of the long wooden bar. A bartender greeted him.

"Hello, Charlie, who's your friend?"

Without hesitation, Biff, said, "This is Matt, my Yank friend."

The bartender smiled broadly. "Welcome, Matt, the first one is on the house, what will it be?

"Half of bitters, thank you."

Biff, now Charlie, said, "Yeah, make it two."

We watched as the bartender drew the bitters from the tap.

As he set the glasses on the bar, he asked, "Where are you from, Yank?"

"New York."

"My kid sister married a Yank from Brooklyn at the end of the war, and they got two kids already."

We picked up the bitters, walked to the far side of the room, and sat down at a table.

Biff looked at me. "Nice to have you back in London, Matt."

"Thanks, Charlie. I assume that I'll be known as Matt in here from now on."

Biff laughed. "Yeah."

"Is the barrister named Charlie as well?"

"No, Charlie just uses the barrister's flat on occasion."

"At what high court does the barrister plead?"

Biff smiled. "I spoke too soon at the flat, I should have said solicitor."

I didn't think that was the case. Biff never said anything he did not want to say. Everything he said or did was for a purpose. His walk changed when we started walking down Warwick Way, his body language was different in the pub, and he was a different person. After spending six weeks with him at the farm in Virginia, I knew that Biff had the ability to adjust his behavior to what he wanted people to think at any given time. Observing him, I knew that Biff was a gifted man. I only hoped to be a worthy student.

When we finished our drinks, Biff stood without saying a word, walked past the bar, said "Goodnight, Mattie," and walked out of the door.

I followed and thanked the bartender for the bitters.

Outside, Biff said, "The bartender served in the Royal Navy, a good bloke. Let's have some North Sea codfish. Just down a block they serve the best there is."

The sun had set. It was dark on the street, no streetlights. The only light shown from the windows and doorways of shops that were still open. The stores closed for the night had turned off all the lights inside, just as they did during the war.

I looked up and down the street. "Yeah, it's sure dark."

Biff laughed, "Yeah."

We walked down Warwick Way one block and crossed the street. There wasn't a car light in sight, just the sound of voices on the street from people not seen. The aroma of fish lingered in the night air, long before reaching the Fresh Fish House.

Biff led the way into the dimly-lit restaurant. Rows of bare wood tables and unpadded straight wooden chairs added to the atmosphere. We were no more than ten feet inside when a man behind the grill spoke.

"Yeah, Charlie, where you been?"

Biff approached the grill. The man wiped his hands on a towel, offered his left hand, and they shook.

"This is my Yank friend, Matt."

The cook offered his hand, "You had to come back to Brit to get good fish?"

"Yeah, and visit some good blokes."

The restaurant was busy, which was a good indication of what to expect of the food. Biff wouldn't eat where the food was not acceptable unless there was another reason to be there. The patrons were laughing and their voices expressed their pleasure of the evening over the sound of clinking glasses. I noticed the food on plates while following Biff to the only two empty chairs.

The waitress, a pleasant woman probably in her fifties, was at the table within a few minutes. "Good evening, gents. What would you like to drink?"

Biff said, "Ice tea."

I added, "I'll have the same."

Biff smiled with a "Yeah."

I watched Biff observing everyone in the restaurant, and then he paused, concentrating on a table along the far wall where four men were seated leaning over their plates of fish and chips, hands on their beer bottles. They were talking with their mouths barely opening, nodding their heads, occasionally glancing around the room, not stopping at any one location.

He was trying to tell me something. Biff started rubbing his hands together, when he stopped, the blood red stone on his ring that he had received at the farm was turned so that only the gold band was visible.

During my 1948 visit with Biff in London, we established ways to communicate with each other without speaking. Eye contact and using our rings was important in giving messages. The ring was normally on the third finger of the right hand, with the deep blood red stone visible. If it was in any other position or on another finger, the wearer was sending a message. Turning the stone under so that only the gold band was visible was the sign that there was someone of interest nearby, and to guard conversation.

There wasn't a menu, just a blackboard on the wall by the grill with "fish and chips" written in white caulk.

"Charlie, what are the options?"

"Fish and chips with coleslaw or fish and chips with beans. What more could you ask for?"

The waitress returned and set two glasses of tea on the table.

"Have you gents decided?"

Biff quickly said, "Fish and chips with coleslaw."

The waitress said, "The fish are codfish out of the North Sea and in all probability had been swimming in that cold water less than twenty-four hours earlier. During the war, it was difficult for the fishing fleet to venture into the North Sea due to the German U-Boats. Some boats did venture out and some didn't return."

I said, "Make it two."

We raised our glasses of tea and touched.

Speaking softly with the glass in front of my mouth, "What's the foursome?"

Biff held his tea glass in front of his mouth. "The one on the right provides passports and other documents for a price. We call him the paper hanger. The other three are German, and probably arranging for some forged documents. The names and pictures that were in the packets that Doud and you have came from one of his locations that British Intelligence raided. His operation has been under the watchful eye of British Intelligence and Scotland Yard for a long time. Two of our people are watching them. They know me, but have not and will not acknowledge me. These individuals will not be out of their sight until they are allowed to leave England or given free room and board."

"Why hasn't he been arrested and put out of business?"

"He is more valuable to us operating. We are aware of how he operates, and ever so often when he leaves his shop, it is raided. Sometimes everything in the shop is removed, other times they just look and record anything of interest. However, he is under observation at all times. When he sets up shop again, Scotland Yard and British Intelligence watch and wait until it appears it's time to raid again. In fact, several people think he knows that he is being watched, but so long as he is well paid, he's happy. He is not the only one in the UK in the document business, but he has been very productive for us."

The waitress served the fish and chips and asked, "Would you like more tea?"

We replied with a "Yeah" and laughed.

Biff passed the catsup. I allowed a small amount to flow from the bottle and passed it back. I glanced at Biff, he nodded. We blessed our food before eating. At the farm, we had been told to be careful about giving any sign indicating a religious affiliation in a public place, unless it was for the benefit of someone.

The fish was covered with a light golden brown crisp batter, the first bite into the fish released the most pleasant aroma, and the taste was beyond my ability to describe. I had never tasted fish any better. The chips were thick slices of potatoes that had been deep-fried, but not crisp like most places in the US.

We didn't speak for some time, just enjoyed the fish and chips. The coleslaw, the only way that I liked cabbage, was delicious too, fresh and shredded just right. As we ate our meal, Biff occasionally glanced around the room at everyone, not just at the four men across the room.

I attempted to identify the men that Biff said were doing the surveillance, but was not sure. I tried to remember the descriptions of as many in the restaurant as possible. Biff was sure to quiz me later. There was one man sitting near the door leading to the restrooms that indicated he could be one. He ate very slowly and was drinking coffee. His companion was a woman who was reading a book that was next to her plate and drinking tea with cream. They could have been man and wife, but neither wore wedding bands. Then again, not all married couples wore rings. Still, there was something about how she glanced around the room whenever she turned the pages of the book. The man sort of toyed with his food and was indifferent to the woman, but they didn't act like a couple having a spat.

The waitress returned as we finished the last speck of batter from the fish. She suggested peach cobbler with cream, which we agreed to, and two coffees.

Our conversation was limited as I learned more about how Biff operated. While waiting for the peach cobbler, Biff outlined our visit to Canterbury once our work was finished.

"It doesn't make any difference what your religion might be, the Canterbury Cathedral's architecture is always worth seeing, and besides, the journey is most pleasant, and it has changed a lot since your last visit," Biff related.

The cobbler was served and eaten just as the four men from across the room were leaving. Biff made no sign of hurrying. He picked up the check from the table, walked over to the waitress who was at the grill, paid her, and then had a conversation with the cook. I met him at the door. Looking back at the table where the man and woman had been sitting, the chairs were empty. I had not seen them leave; I must have been too deep into the peach cobbler.

When we left the restaurant, Biff lit a cigar. I filled my pipe with tobacco and lit it. We crossed Warwick Way at the corner and returned to the safe house in silence leaving a trail of cigar and tobacco smoke.

Biff opened the front door—for a metal plated door it moved freely without a sound. Inside, we returned to the leather chairs and Biff poured two more fingers of Balvenie into the crystal glasses. We touched, sipped the scotch, and continued to smoke in silence. I was thinking that there was something special about sharing this time. Time with Biff was always a learning experience for me.

Biff broke the silence, "I'll read your field reports tonight and in the morning we'll visit Scotland Yard, and see what help they might offer about the Watkins accident. And I'll also look into lawyer Alvin C. Waite. The name doesn't mean anything to me."

We finished our scotch. Biff put his cigar in the ashtray, and I tapped the ashes from my pipe into another, put it in my jacket pocket, removed the field reports from the briefcase and gave them to Biff. We both commented on the fish and chips, and Biff confirmed that the man and woman I had observed were on the job observing the four men.

Biff checked the front door, all part of the nightly ritual before retiring. When we went upstairs, I once again looked at the painting of the Cloister at Canterbury hanging on the wall, touched it and went into the front bedroom.

"Sleep well, Rob."

"Yeah, don't read all night."

Chapter 25

SEARCH FOR FACTS

Someone was singing, a male voice. It was an Anglican chant that awakened me. I soon realized that it was coming from within the house and that it had to be Biff. I got out of bed, went into the bathroom and stepped into a hot shower. As I was dressing the aroma of bacon and coffee came rushing into the room. Just before descending the stairs, I paused to look at the Cloister painting. There was something about it.

Biff greeted me when I walked into the kitchen. "Good morning, Yank."

"He cooks. He sings in a language known only to him. What doesn't he do?"

Biff looked rested and had been up for some time. He had prepared a full English breakfast—ham, no bangers for me, scones, toast, and eggs over light, just out of the skillet onto the plates.

"You must not have slept at all," I said.

We sat down. Biff said grace before we ate. After we had eaten our breakfast and started drinking the second cup of coffee, Biff's conversation turned to the task.

The Cloisters of Canterbury

"I read your field notes rather rapidly. I would like to read them again. There is no question that Frances Murita had help in the deception. She couldn't have done it alone. It will be interesting to see the complete file on the investigation of the auto accident. I called a friend at Scotland Yard and gave him the information about the accident. It will take some time before he can find what we need. This morning we will visit Alvin Waite. The address on his letter is off Bond Street."

We cleared the dishes and I washed them in the sink and put them in a rack to dry.

"Rob, it looks like your mother didn't kick you out of the kitchen."

"It looks like your mother didn't run you out either."

"It wasn't Mother, but the houseman that introduced me to the kitchen when my parents were on holiday."

I was learning more about Biff, word-by-word, piece-by-piece.

"Rob, let's take the accident report, the letter from lawyer and the photographs with us."

I removed them from the files and gave them to Biff.

Just as we were leaving Biff said, "I don't think there should be a problem, but let's put your briefcase in the safe."

He picked up the corner of the Oriental rug opposite the front door and removed a section of the wood floor, revealing a safe set in the concrete. He turned the dial of the combination lock and opened the safe. Inside was a briefcase and two handguns in shoulder holsters. Biff removed one of the holsters and put it on under his suit coat, put my briefcase in the safe, closed it, and replaced the floor panel and rug.

Biff looked at me with his usual smile, "This is the combination to the safe." He repeated it three times, slowly.

I tried to remember it, knowing that at some time Biff would ask me to open the safe.

•

It was cool, but not cold. All signs indicated that it was going to be a nice day. It didn't take long to arrive on Bond Street. Biff certainly knew his way around London. If traffic appeared to be slowing, he knew where to turn, avoiding any unusual delays. He parked off Bond Street on a narrow side street in the middle of the block, turned the engine off, and pointed to a door on the opposite side of the street.

"There's Waite's office."

On the door was: "Alvin C. Waite, Solicitor and Notary."

We walked across the street to the office. Next to the door was a button. Biff pushed it.

A male voice came from a speaker above the button, "Yes?"

"I am Bifford Wallace and my associate is Rob Royal. We would like to talk with you about a letter that you wrote concerning the death of a Henry Adolph Wiseman."

I observed the movement of a curtain in a second-floor window.

The door lock released and a voice said, "Come in."

Beyond the door there was a small foyer and stairs leading up. I followed Biff up the stairs to another small foyer. A door opened revealing a man who appeared to be in his sixties wearing a black knitted yarmulke.

"I'm Alvin Waite," he said. "Come in."

"I am Bifford Wallace and this is Rob Royal from the United States."

Biff wasted no time and handed Waite a copy of the letter that he had written notifying Mrs. Wiseman of her husband's death in the Auschwitz concentration camp.

Mr. Waite explained that he and several others had obtained the names of individuals who had died in Nazi concentration camps, and they were attempting to notify their families.

Biff said, "Rob is trying to satisfy concerns about Henry Wiseman's death. A letter from a Zurich banker stated that Wiseman had been arrested by the Nazi SS in Munich, and died on a train headed to Dachau." Biff handed a copy of the banker's letter to Waite.

"Rob is concerned. Auschwitz is in Poland and Dachau is in Germany, not far from Munich. He has a problem understanding why Wiseman would have been in a concentration camp in Poland."

Waite explained, "The allied forces discovered some concentration camp records when they liberated the camps. The records listed those killed in most of the camps each day. Henry Adolph Wiseman's name was on the list as having died in Auschwitz in 1944. I have no explanation for the report from the Zurich banker. We know that there is more than one Henry Wiseman, and that probably more than one died in a concentration camp. The names of all who died will never be known."

I thanked Waite for sending the letter and for seeing Biff and me.

Waite said, "Shalom," as we left.

We returned to the Jaguar and drove away.

"I am sure the Group wants to know that Waite is on the up and up," said Biff, "and that is the reason for their interest."

The Cloisters of Canterbury

"Biff, we will probably never know where Wiseman died for sure."

"There isn't anything that we can do until the Yard locates the accident file. So how about we drive to Bath for lunch and visit Stonehenge like we did before?"

I glanced at Biff. "What are you going to do, locate the source of the voice in my dream?"

"I don't think that we'll find the source of the voice there."

As we drove through the streets, passing buildings damaged by bombs and fire, some leveled and others under repair, I realized again how fortunate the United States had been.

"London is preparing for the coronation of Elizabeth II on June second. We need to arrange another visit for you at that time."

"What an interesting experience that would be. But, I'm not sure how that can be accomplished."

Biff obviously enjoyed driving the Jaguar, shifting the gears up and down, accelerating to pass cars in and out of traffic.

•

We arrived in Bath, had lunch at a pub on Abbey Green, and after lunch walked around the streets before returning to the car and driving to Stonehenge. When we got to the stones, the temperature suddenly dropped and it started to snow. A strong wind blew across the plain.

"Where were you standing when this voice came from above?"

Without hesitation I walked directly to a spot and stopped. "Here."

It was quiet, only the sound of the wind. I could still hear the voice telling me that I was never alone. That I was cloistered. A strange feeling came over me, one that was beyond my ability to describe.

We returned to the car in silence.

"Rob, there's another place that is very interesting," Biff said as he drove away from Stonehenge. "It's Avesbury. There are 100 stones and we'll walk around them. It's not far, and we need the exercise."

When we arrived, it was snowing. I walked behind Biff counting the stones. It was interesting, but it didn't have the same impact on me as Stonehenge. We returned to where we had started and then passed a small building, Royal Mail.

Biff pointed to a sign in the window that read: "Sandwiches."

"Rob, that looks like a good idea for the US pony express."

"Yes, I'll suggest it to the president on my next visit to the White House."

Our next stop was the Red Lion Pub. There was a fire burning in the stone fireplace and the warmth felt good on my face and hands. Darkened wood beams and ceiling recorded the smoke from hundreds of fires that had warmed many as they enjoyed a pint or more. Biff pointed to a medieval well in the dining room. We drank a half-pint of Guinness at a table next to a window near the fire. When we returned to the car, the snow had increased. The road leading from the pub was covered with snow.

Biff looked at the road and the sky. "I have a better idea than driving back to London tonight. Let's see if they have a couple of rooms here."

We went back inside and inquired about the availability of rooms. They were available. Our rooms were on the second floor, small but acceptable. Returning to the bar, we ordered another half-pint of Guinness. We sat at the same table for the next couple of hours or more.

Biff had read my field notes more carefully than he had indicated. He made comments about them as if he had them in front of him, turning a page at a time. At times, his observations and remarks were as if he had been there with me.

We ordered shepherd's pie for dinner and another half-pint. We retired to our rooms about ten o'clock.

"Rob, there won't be any heat in the room but there will be a downy to keep you warm."

I enjoyed Biff using some of the English color, expecting me not to understand. "That would be nice, I used to sleep under one at my great grandparents' farmhouse when I was a tyke, but thought that you might have arranged for a 'frump' to keep me comfy."

Biff laughed, "Yeah, lad, you have been reading that dictionary of English language you purchased at Smith's the last time you were here."

The room was cold. I certainly wouldn't be opening a window. After removing my jacket, tie and shoes, I pulled the downy up and was sound asleep in minutes.

•

Biff's knocking on the door would not stop. I finally rolled from under the downy. The sun was shining through the window. I opened the door.

"Morning, lad, it's time to rise and shine. I'll meet you in the dining room."

The Cloisters of Canterbury

I looked at my wristwatch. It was 7:30. I quickly washed and dressed and went down to the dining room.

Biff was at a table near the fireplace. "I've ordered you a full English breakfast, without the bangers." He poured our coffee. "This will warm you up. How did you sleep, Rob?"

"Very well, the downy kept me warm. In fact, it was one of the most restful nights in a long time. I slept just like I did as a kid at Great Grandma's."

After breakfast, we walked out to the car, brushed snow off the windows and scraped some ice off the windshield. The snow had accumulated on the streets until we reached the road leading to Bath. There the traffic had cleared most of it, but Biff drove with care.

While Biff continued his informative tour, we passed by old buildings and ruins that were hundreds of years old, many of which had existed before Columbus discovered America in 1492.

We stopped in Bath for petrol and lunch at the Tearoom of Sally Lund near the Abbey. There was so much to see. The Roman baths had been used hundreds of years before. As we walked through the different rooms the smell of sulfur filled my lungs. After lunch and another history lesson, we continued driving until we came into Hounslow on Bath Road late in the day.

"Here we are," said Biff. He parked in front of a darkened store and got out.

I followed.

"There it is, the Cork, the pub that Ruth Watkins, Frances Murita and the man frequented. Let's have a half-pint, see how things look."

It was a few minutes after eight and there was a full moon. Inside the pub cigarette smoke hung like a cloud. A dart game was in progress on the far end of the pub near a rear door. There were two empty stools separated by a man who appeared to have had several too many. He was alert enough that when we reached the bar, he looked at us with half-closed eyes and moved over to the next stool allowing us to sit next to each other.

Biff raised his right hand and said, "Yeah, thank you."

There were two men behind the bar. One looked to be in his sixties and the other in his late thirties. Both were six feet plus tall and weighing well over two-hundred pounds of muscle and no fat. They probably could toss most unruly customers out the door if necessary.

The older man approached us and said, "What will it be tonight, gents?"

We both said, "Half pint of bitters and a ham sandwich."

There were only two women in the pub and they were with one man at a table near the dart game. On their table were four glasses. I assumed that one of the dart players was the fourth.

The pub appeared to cater to the men in the neighborhood. There were no military people there, but it would have been different during the war. We watched the dart players who were having a good evening.

We arrived back at the safe house off Warwick Way after midnight.

"It's been a long day. I am for turning in," I said.

"I think that's a good idea," Biff agreed.

We were in our beds sleeping soundly when I was awakened by the telephone. I heard Biff answer it.

Biff came to the door, "That was my friend at the Yard, he has been trying to reach us all day. He has the information we asked for and will meet us at seven in the morning at Victoria Station. If we're up at six we can have breakfast before we leave."

•

I was awake before the alarm sounded. The Anglican chant and aromas from the kitchen were better than any alarm clock. Biff was a fine host. I wondered how to keep up with him. There certainly would never be a way of getting ahead of him.

When I walked into the kitchen, Biff greeted me. "Good morning, Yank. Breakfast is on the table—no bangers."

"You just won't forget that on my last visit I mistakenly called blood sausage bangers and told you that they wouldn't be served by any respectable cook in America, will you?"

"Never," said Biff as he put a plate in front of me.

We finished breakfast, washed the dishes and were out the door at 6:40.

It was a damp cool morning with a good chance of rain. Biff parked a block from Victoria Station. As we entered the station a man started walking with Biff on his right.

When we reached the middle of Victoria station, Biff spoke. "Winslow, this is my friend, Matt, from the States."

We shook hands.

Biff told him about the trip to Bath and that he was going to show me the sights around London and Canterbury.

"It was nice meeting you, Matt. Enjoy your holiday."

The Cloisters of Canterbury

After we walked away, Biff had a newspaper in his left hand that he didn't have before the conversation with Winslow.

When we returned to the car, Biff opened the newspaper and removed the investigator's report of Frances Murita's auto accident and the medical examiner's report of Ruth Watkins' death. He also had the constable's report of the stolen Hillman. The reports contained statements from the owner of The Cork Pub, the bartender and two men in Pirbright.

Biff began reading out loud, "The medical examiner stated, 'Has a ten centimeters open wound across forehead, one centimeter in depth. Wound appears to have had pressure applied. No accumulation of blood on the face. There is blood in ear canals, mouth and windpipe. Has a basilar skull fracture and possible other trauma, no other fractures.'"

I noted, "That certainly doesn't provide very much information. What does 'possible other trauma' mean? It sounds to me like she was killed some other place before the accident."

I read the constable's statement: "When I arrived at the accident a female in an American Women's Army Corps uniform was lying face up on the rear seat of the Hillman. Pried the door of the car open, detected no pulse, and removed the dead body from the car. There was only a small amount of blood on her forehead. There was no blood in the car and no point of impact was determined. The victim was identified as Ruth Marie Watkins. Frances Ann Murita, an American Women's Army Corps member, stated that she was driving and was thrown from the car, and that Ruth Watkins was riding in the front passenger seat. She said a lorry pulled from the side road, hit them and did not stop.

"Biff, something is wrong. Ruth Watkins received a big gash on her forehead, only a small amount of blood is on her, there is no other blood in the car and she is found lying on the back seat."

Biff nodded. "Let's go to Hounslow and talk with the owner and bartender at The Cork Pub." He started the Jaguar, revved the engine only slightly, and shifted into first gear. There was a sign of pleasure on his face.

When we arrived in Hounslow, it was just eleven in the morning. The pub's lunch customers would be arriving soon. The same two men were behind the bar that had been there the night before. We took two stools near the end of the bar.

The younger man said, "Morning, gents, welcome back to the Cork. What will you have, the same as the other night?"

Biff rubbed his chin. "No, I'll have a half pint of Guinness."

"Make it two."

When the bartender returned with the Guinness, Biff asked, "You don't happen to be Lyle Huntington, are you?"

"Who's asking?"

The older man stopped putting glasses on the back bar and looked in our direction. Biff pulled out a small leather case with a badge attached. His shoulder holster was obvious.

"Inspector Wallace, Scotland Yard." He laid the badge on top of the bar and turned his head in the direction of the older man. "Would you be Harold Kenny, the owner of this fine pub?"

The man walked over and picked up Biff's badge and looked at it, then at Biff and me. "What can we do for you?"

"This is Rob Royal from the United States and we are reviewing the death of an American woman, a Woman's Army Corps member, who was killed in 1945. You probably will remember talking with Inspector Green at the time."

Biff placed the photographs of Frances Murita, Ruth Watkins and three others on the bar.

"Do you remember if any of these women were in your pub in 1945?"

Both men looked at the pictures and pointed at the photos of Murita and Watkins.

The older man said, "These two were regulars just before the war ended. Never seen the other three."

The bartender added. "They were in on weekends."

Biff removed several other photographs from his jacket. "The Yard's report indicated that they had frequented the Cork with a man."

He sorted through the photos in his hand, placed four on the bar. Both men looked at the photos.

Kenny, the pub owner, picked up one photo and said, "This was the man with the two women."

The younger man said, "Yeah, that's him."

Biff picked up the photo and handed it to me. He then removed a paper from his jacket. "I have a paper here that states you have identified the photograph of Hans Mueller as the man seen with the two women in the photographs identified as Ruth Watkins and Frances Murita. Would both of you sign next to your names. Biff handed the owner a pen. He signed his name and then handed the pen to the bartender who also signed, without questions.

I looked at Biff's serious face.

The Cloisters of Canterbury

"We appreciate your help. Now I would like an order of that shepherd's pie and another half pint Guinness, and the same for the Yank since he seems to be speechless.

I just nodded my head in the affirmative.

We took our glasses of Guinness and moved to a table away from the bar, sitting across from each other. The bartender brought the shepherd's pie to the table.

We bowed their heads, crossed our chests and started eating.

"Biff, this gets more interesting each day that I am involved. How did Mueller and Murita meet? More and more I just have to think that Ruth Watkins' death was not an accident. It's obvious that when Ruth Watkins learned of her uncle and aunt's deaths and that she was the only heir to their estate, she must have confided in Frances Murita. We learned that they were inseparable, and it would only be natural for her to share this information with her best friend."

"That is logical. How Murita and Mueller met would be interesting to find out, but we'll probably never know. I do not like to make assumptions, but in this case, I can't help but believe that they conceived the deception here in England. We will review our records and see when Hans Mueller obtained his papers here in England and then sailed for Canada."

"Biff, I still would like to hear what the neighbors in Pirbright have to say, and if they, too, can identify Mueller as the man living in the cottage and working on the Hillman."

"I agree, Rob. We must try to confirm if it was Mueller. But of more interest to me is the scene of the auto accident. Let's go to Pirbright and find where the accident took place."

When we finished eating, we stopped at the bar and thanked the owner and bartender for their help and complimented them on the shepherd's pie.

It was interesting for me to watch Biff, the way he had presented the photographs to the pub owner and bartender. The pictures of the women all were in WAC uniforms, but Watkins and Murita were very attractive. If you saw them once it would be difficult to forget them. The photographs of the men were all in work clothes, Mueller's face with the scars would make an impression. They weren't ugly, just distinctive.

We drove several miles before Biff spoke. "When we're done with business let's drive down to Canterbury to see our friend, Reverend Filpin. He was made a Canon since your last visit. You can take a turn at the wheel on the drive to Canterbury."

"That sounds like a very good and practical idea. Just in case you get a little fuddled, I'll be able to drive us home. And it will be great to see Reverend Filpin."

The investigation reports that Biff received from his friend at Scotland Yard provided good directions. Biff drove directly to the cottage just outside of Pirbright where the Hillman car was stolen. He stopped in front, and I got out of the car and took two pictures of the cottage with the attached shed. The shed beside the house where the Hillman had been stored was now empty. I imagined Mueller bent over, working on the engine, just as he worked on the engines in the Springfield truck plant.

We drove past three other cottages and pulled in the drive of the fourth. We got out of the car, walked to the front door, and knocked. The sound of footsteps came from inside. A middle-aged man opened the door.

"Kevin James?"

The man looked at Biff, "Yes?"

Biff held his badge so the man could see it. "I am Inspector Wallace, Scotland Yard, and this is Rob Royal. We would like to ask you a couple of questions about something that happened in 1945, and would like for you to look at these pictures and see if you can identify the man who was living in the cottage down the road and working on the Hillman car."

From the expression on the man's face, it was obvious that he had not forgotten. Biff handed him the four pictures of the men that he had shown to the pub owner and the bartender.

Mr. James looked at them, removed the photograph of Hans Mueller, and gave it to Biff. "That's the man, no doubt about it. Talked with him a few times. I told the constable that when he was investigating the disappearance of the Hillman."

"I appreciate your help. We're trying to close out some old cases. I have a prepared statement that you identified this picture with the name of Hans Mueller on the back. Would you sign your name on this line?"

The man did not hesitate. He took the pen Biff handed him and signed his name. Biff thanked the man, and we walked back to the car. Biff's personality was all business, and he didn't revert to the English sports car enthusiast. He backed the car out of the drive, drove a short distance down the road and pulled in the drive of another small cottage with vines growing up the front and sides of the house onto the roof.

The Cloisters of Canterbury

When we got out of the car and started toward the cottage, the front door opened. A man about the same age as Kevin James walked out, closing the door behind him.

"I am not trying to be inhospitable, but I got a hound pup that would be all over you. He just wants to get in everyone's lap."

I wondered if Kevin James had alerted him.

"Are you Ronald Church?" Biff asked him.

"I was this morning."

"I am Inspector Wallace of Scotland Yard and this is Rob Royal. We want you to look at some photographs and see if one of them might be the man who was living at the Wells Cottage in 1945. We're just trying to clear out some old cases." Biff handed four photographs to him.

He looked at them, gave them back to Biff and said, "This is the man who was working on the Hillman. I stopped by one day after he got the old Hillman running. I was out walking the bitch, the mother of the hound in the house. He had one of those American woman soldiers with him—nice looking—think he had something on his mind other than the old car. He was in a hurry for me to leave. He must have been German or something. His English wasn't like the Yanks at the pub."

Biff removed the photographs of the four women from his suit coat pocket and handed them to Church.

He looked at the first three rather quickly and then stopped. "That's the looker, have to say that I gave her a good once over." He returned the pictures to Biff. The man had identified Frances Murita.

Biff removed another sheet of paper from his jacket pocket. "I would like for you to sign this paper stating that you have identified this picture with the name of Hans Mueller on the back, and I am going to add a line indicating that you also identified Frances Murita as the woman with him."

The man read the paper and then signed his name. Biff thanked the man and we returned to the Jaguar. The serious Biff Wallace was behind the wheel. He backed the car onto the road, returning in the direction of Pirbright.

Biff said, "It looks like Mueller and Murita had some private time to devise the deception before the accident in the Hillman."

Chapter 26

CONFIRMATION

We drove northwest from Pirbright to Byfleet. Before arriving at Chertsey, Biff pulled the Jaguar into a lay-by and stopped.

"Rob, let me see the constable's accident report." He looked at the sketch of the accident scene. "We're just about there."

Biff turned right onto a narrow road and drove slowly for about five minutes, then pulled to the side of the road and parked. The road on the right was a dead-end. Biff turned the motor off.

"This should be it."

We got out of the car and walked to the side road. Biff held the accident scene sketch up so that both of us could look at it as he read out loud: "The Hillman car, driven by Frances Murita, was traveling along Chertsey Parish Road and the lorry came from the side road to their left, according to Frances Murita's statement. There was no other witness, only Murita's statement that a lorry had run into them."

Biff glanced around and then continued. "The constable found the Hillman two-door car six meters left from the centerline of the side road against a tree. The left side of the Hillman was crushed from the center of the left front wheel to the front edge of the left rear wheel. Impact was near the center of left front passenger seat. The left door had to be pried open to check for pulse and remove the body of Ruth Watkins from the rear seat.

"The right side of the Hillman car, with the right door closed, was against a large elm tree. The right door had to be pried open. Frances Murita stated that she was thrown from the car. The constable noted that she had not been injured, and there was a small amount of dirt on the right sleeve of her uniform jacket."

Biff stopped reading. "There are several things about the accident report that concern me. From the description of the damage to the Hillman, the lorry would have to be traveling at a speed that would have made it impossible to make a left or right turn onto the road. Damage to the left side of the Hillman would indicate a direct square impact. The impact forced the car against that tree."

Biff pointed to a scar on the elm tree. "The right door had to be pried open. The report states that all of the windows in the car were shattered, not broken out but shattered. To me, this describes glass still in the window frames. The description of the damaged to the Hillman also indicates to me that the lorry pushed the car up against the tree and that it wasn't a sudden impact."

Biff shook his head, "There is no way possible that Watkins could have been in the front left seat when the car was hit by the lorry and be thrown into the back seat and land on her back. If she had still been alive after the accident and crawled into the back seat, there certainly would have been blood from the injury. Head injuries bleed profusely and you would have expected blood to be deposited some place in the car. The report states that there was no blood found in the car and no point of impact for her injury."

Biff walked across the road and pointed to the ditch. "If Murita was thrown from the car she would have landed in this ditch. It's full of rocks. Any force that would eject a body that landed in this would have received injuries and the person's clothing would have more then a small amount of dirt on one sleeve."

I walked from the centerline of the side road to the tree. "Biff, six meters, that's about twenty feet. How could the impact at the intersection have forced the car against the tree from that angle? Another thing that bothers me is that the accident report states that the accident was reported by telephone. Who made the call?"

Biff walked across the road and up the side road over twenty meters, turned and slowly returned to where I waited. "This accident was staged. Ruth Watkins did not die in the accident."

"Take some pictures of the scene from all directions, including the approach from the side road. When we get back to the flat, we will take pictures of the investigation report with the Minox. I need to return the files to the Yard and want to have a conversation with a couple of the investigators."

After I had taken pictures from all angles, Biff started the Jaguar, and put on his Brit sports car personality. However, not so much so that he couldn't rehash the accident reports and the accident scene as we drove back to London.

"Rob, it certainly seems apparent that when Ruth Watkins learned of her inheritance, she confided in Frances Murita, who then shared this information with Mueller. They then conceived the plan to get rid of Ruth Watkins. Murita returned to the United States and assumed Watkins' identity. I wonder if Murita had any help from her family in New Jersey?"

We arrived back at the safe house and went up the stairs to the workroom. Biff cleared everything off one of the desks and immediately began taking pictures of each of the documents in the file from Scotland Yard.

"When I return the file to the Yard in the morning," he said, "I'll impose on them to develop the film and make prints. I will run this accident report by them and see what they think of our conclusion. You can do some sightseeing. You'll not be able to accompany me, sorry about that."

"That's all right with me. There's so much to see, and I really need the exercise."

Biff opened the Balvenie bottle, poured about three fingers in the crystal glasses and we relaxed in the leather chairs. After finishing the scotch, we left the flat and walked up Warwick Way to the friendly pub on the corner.

The bartender welcomed us, "Hi, Charlie and Matt. Have you been staying out of trouble, Yank?"

"Yes, but it hasn't been easy," I replied.

We sat down on stools at the bar and ordered a half-pint of Guinness. Biff appeared to be deep in thought, occasionally looking around the pub. My mind wandered from one event to another. I would return to New York in three days. Tomorrow, I would go to Westminster Abby, to the tobacco shop on Victoria and replenish my tobacco supply, and walk along the River Thames. The following day we were planning

The Cloisters of Canterbury

to drive to Canterbury.

We walked without talking from the pub to the fish house where we found an empty table next to the back wall. We were greeted by the same waitress who served us on our previous visit. It was easy to order: codfish, chips, coleslaw and tea for both.

After looking around the restaurant and seeing nothing of interest Biff spoke. "Rob, I have been reviewing all of the events and trying to think of what we might have missed. Remember, there is always something else that should have been uncovered. In life one event leads to another, and then another. We never know what the end will be. What were the odds that you would spot Mueller? Only three others have been located out of the list of twenty. The meeting of Mueller and Murita in England must have been a coincidence. There is nothing to link them together. He is a German Nazi and she is from an Italian family, worlds apart. The remarks of the MPs at the airbase gate indicated that a love affair was going on in the old Hillman. Was it a chance meeting, an event that led to the death of an innocent young woman?"

After dinner, Biff lit a cigar and I lit my pipe as we walked back to the flat. The air was getting cooler. It would probably snow by morning. Coal smoke from the chimneys of buildings descended on us destroying the aroma of the tobacco.

Biff opened the door and turned on the lights. We returned to the leather chairs still in deep thought. Biff kept asking what had been missed, while I wondered how it was all going to end.

We retired with little conversation other than that Biff wanted to be at the Yard at eight. I wasn't going to leave until around nine and we planned to meet across from the entrance to 10 Downing Street at noon, unless Biff was detained. If he didn't arrive by 12:30, we would meet in front of Westminster Abby at two o'clock. We agreed that breakfast would only be coffee and scones.

Just as we started to go up the stairs, Biff handed me his gun and shoulder holster. "Please put this into the safe."

I took the holster, walked over to far edge of the Oriental carpet, rolled it back, removed the section of wood floor, got down on my knees, turned the combination two complete turns, returned to the first number, the second, the third and turned the handle. I opened the safe put the holster and gun in, closed the safe, spun the combination, and replaced the wood floor and the carpet.

When I got up from the floor, Biff handed me a set of keys for the front door and smiled. "Goodnight, Yank."

I turned the lights off and followed him up the stairs. I touched the painting of the Cloister, turned and said, "Goodnight, Biff, I am glad to be here."

•

It was another restless night. I wondered if Murita and Mueller would be prosecuted for the death of Ruth Watkins. I was dressed and downstairs in the kitchen just after seven, and had the coffee on before Biff came down.

"Morning, barrister, have a good night?"

"Morning, Yank. In fact, it was a poor night for sleeping. The more that I think about these events, the more I believe that there is something missing. Someone with a legal mind had to be involved in the States. Wiseman's lawyer apparently was not the one. His death might have been to cover up the deception when he learned about the new Ruth Watkins. Maybe there was something in the letter. Are you sure that nothing was missed in the Wiseman and Hudson files?"

I poured the coffee, removed the scones from a tin box on the counter and put them on the table with marmalade.

"When I talked with Rose White, Hudson's secretary, she said that Hudson opened a letter that she had just picked up from the post office box on the way to Hudson's home. He read the letter and said something about probating Wiseman's will too soon. He put the letter in his suit coat pocket and said that he was going to the courthouse. She did not read the letter, but said that the return address on the envelope was the Valley Bank in Dayton. It was the bank where Wiseman maintained accounts that were part of his estate. I was not able to determine the nature of the letter and did not find any unusual letters when I searched the files. I photographed everything in the files that pertained to Ruth Watkins and Wiseman."

"Rob, there are several things bothering me. After Hudson received a letter from the Swiss banker advising him of Wiseman's death, he probated the Wiseman will on September 11, 1944, transferring all of the estate to Ruth Watkins. On June 7, 1945, Ruth Watkins was killed here in England. He didn't receive the letter addressed to Henry Wiseman, the next of kin, from the Women's Army Corps, until November 1946, notifying him of the death of Ruth Watkins. The fact that the Women's Army Corps notified the next of kin is routine, but why did it take so long?"

The Cloisters of Canterbury

Biff paused, "The fact that Hudson was killed as he got off a bus by a hit-and-run driver could be coincidental, except for the fact that the car had been stolen from a car lot in Dayton the day before. Let us assume that the person who stole the car had nothing to do with the fraud, just an unlikely coincidence. That is a possibility, except we have Hans Mueller in the picture. He was probably involved in the death of Ruth Watkins here in England. Was Mueller the driver of the hit-and-run lorry?

"Where is this leading? That's what has me so concerned, Rob. I just don't know. However, something important *is* missing! I would like to know the connection in the States. They had to receive help."

Biff left for Scotland Yard at 7:35. I cleaned up the kitchen and left the flat just before nine. I lit my pipe and leisurely walked down Warwick Way to Wilton Road and Grosvenor Place, stopping to watch men cleaning the grounds around the Wellington Arch. There were men working almost every place, cleaning up, repairing, and preparing for the coronation of Elizabeth in June. I continued along Constitution Hill and stopped in front of Buckingham Palace. There was activity on the grounds and on the roof of the palace.

The weather was cool, not cold, right for a sightseeing walk. There were numerous ducks, geese and swans on the water in Saint James Park. I walked up the mall to Whitehall where more workers were cleaning the Admiralty Arch, passed a horse guard mounted on a beautiful black horse at the entrance to the horse guards' buildings. A troop of guards exercised their horses on the parade ground. I had always been impressed with the pageantry of the British Empire.

When I arrived in front of 10 Downing Street, I was early for my meeting with Biff, so I continued walking past Big Ben. I stopped in front of the House of Parliament and then walked across to Westminster Abby. There was a lot of activity, as this was to be the site of Elizabeth's coronation. Just as I was returning to 10 Downing Street, Big Ben started sounding for the noon hour. When the last sound ended, I was in front of 10 Downing Street as Biff walked across the street.

"This was timed right. Did you have a good walk?"

"Yes, there has been a lot cleaned up since the last time I was here. And with the number of men working, I think things certainly will be ready for your new queen in June." I smiled. "Biff, ever since reading about your royal family, and especially Princess Elizabeth when I was young, I always wondered if someone removes the seeds from her watermelon for her."

"Maybe we shouldn't attempt to arrange for you to return to London for the coronation. I can see the newspaper headlines, 'American Confronts New Queen — Asks if someone removes the seeds from her watermelon'."

"That's the trouble with you Brits, no sense of humor."

Biff laughed and shook his head. "I have just the place for lunch, follow me."

He opened a door next to a pub and went up some dimly-lit stairs. I was right behind him. At the top of the stairs, Biff opened a door to a restaurant. The room probably was not over twenty by forty feet, with twelve to fifteen tables, all with four chairs. Biff had obviously been there before.

He was greeted by a pleasant woman, "This way, barrister."

There was barely room to walk. She seated us at a table next to a front window that looked down onto Whitehall, and gave us a menu. It was an interesting menu, three choices, chicken pot pie, shepherd's pie, and cod fish.

"Rob, all are good, I will have the pot pie."

The woman returned and we both ordered pot pie and tea."

I noticed that Biff was not using his "Yeah," and his body language was not the same as at the pub on Warwick Way or in Pirbright.

"How was your morning, barrister?"

"It was very rewarding. I have some dates that will put some events into perspective. I also obtained opinions of others that were reassuring, and confirmation in another area," Biff replied.

The pot pie and tea were served with hard rolls. We ate without any further conversation except small talk, mainly about the weather and the coronation. The tables were close and those on three sides could hear anything we said.

When we left the restaurant, we walked to the corner and crossed Whitehall, walked another block to a parking space next to a large brick and stone building where Biff's Jaguar was parked. Standing next to the Jaguar was a London policeman. Biff said something that I did not hear.

The policeman said, "Have a good day, sir."

As Biff backed the car out, I asked, "What's that building?"

"The rear of the war rooms and, by the way, Harold Casey said hello. I am sure you remember him from the farm."

I was once again amazed at the obvious deep connections Bifford Wallace had. It would be interesting to read his peerage.

"This was a productive morning, Rob. Friends at Scotland Yard and British Intelligence were very helpful. Before we get into that, let's go

The Cloisters of Canterbury

to the flat and pick up some things for overnight and drive to Canterbury. I'll ring the Chaucer for reservations. How does that set with you?"

"That sounds like a wonderful idea. We might be able to attend evensong at the cathedral and see Canon Filpin. If he's free he might want to join us for dinner this evening."

Biff moved in and out of traffic, made turns upon turns and never delayed. He turned onto Warwick Way and into the mews, parking in front of the flat. While I packed an overnight bag, Biff called the Chaucer and reserved two rooms for the night. As Biff packed, he asked me to open the safe, get my briefcase and the top shoulder holster.

After relocking the safe and returning the wood floor panel and rug to their original positions, I laid the shoulder holster on the table, sat down and waited for Biff.

When Biff came down the stairs with his overnight bag, his eyes went directly to the table. He said nothing, just smiled. He put the shoulder holster on under his suit coat and picked up his overnight bag. "We're off."

When Biff started the Jaguar, that Brit sports car body language was in full gear. He turned around at the end of the mews, then out onto Warwick Way. Shifting through the gears only increased his pleasure—everything was well in his world. I waited for him to tell me what he had learned at Scotland Yard and British Intelligence.

We had just gone through Chatham when Biff pulled the Jaguar to the side of the road, got out and said, "It's all yours."

I did not hesitate. I was out of the car and behind the steering wheel before Biff had closed the passenger's door on the left. I pressed the clutch pedal down and released several times, and moved the gearshift through the gates. Then I tried the brake pedal. It was firm.

Biff watched with a knowing smile. "At your will."

I checked the traffic, shifted into first gear, released the hand brake, pushed my foot down on the accelerator and steered the Jaguar onto the road. I shifted smoothly into second and third. I was not concerned about driving the Jaguar from the right seat. I just had to remember to stay on the left side of the road.

Biff must have determined that his life wasn't in danger so he started talking. "When the Yard and British Intelligence raided the forger's flat, they not only obtained names and photographs, but schedules of ships leaving the UK for the United States, Canada, Australia and Brazil. They checked all of the UK ports and the passengers that boarded the ships. Hans A. Mueller, using forged papers in the name of John A. Johnson, on 18 June 1946 sailed from Liverpool for Halifax, Nova Scotia. He had obtained a Canadian passport and a Wayne County, Michigan, birth certificate according to the forger's records.

"At first it didn't make sense for the forger to keep records until they discovered that the forger was sending letters to some of his clients demanding more money, attempting to blackmail them."

I was starting to get that Brit sports car driver feeling. This was fun! I waited for Biff to continue.

"It was their opinion that the auto accident was staged. The car was a 1934 Hillman Minx foursome drop-head coupe. The car doors hinged to the rear, swinging to the rear of the car when opened. It was the consensus that the distance from the top of the front seats to the roof was not sufficient for the body of a person to be thrown into the rear seat. Therefore, it would have been impossible for Ruth Watkins to be in the front left passenger seat and forced into the rear seat from an impact to the passenger's side of the car. It would also have been impossible for anyone with such a head wound to climb over the front seat into the back without leaving blood on the seats. One of the men remarked that the rear seat of the car was small, more like a jump seat."

I down-shifted from third gear into second to slow for a car making a turn, then accelerated shifting back into third gear. What Biff was saying confirmed my theories.

"If, in fact, the Hillman had been hit on the passenger side, the driver's door on the right side would have had to open and swing back for Frances Murita to have been thrown from the car. The car door would not have been closed and wedged against the tree. Everyone agreed that she could not have been ejected from the car and not have received injuries." Biff paused and watched me drive the Jaguar.

He smiled and continued, "They were not pleased with the medical examiner's report. It should have been more complete. In fact, a physician on their staff stated that the information provided was a clear indication that the blow to Ruth Watkins' head was made by a blunt object, not a sharp edge. It was probably the edge of a wooden board. Blood in her ear canals would have resulted from the blow to her head. The blood found in her mouth and windpipe indicated that the body was laid flat after death. It was also apparent that someone applied pressure on the wound, probably to stop the blood from flowing all over her and reduced the amount of cleanup where she was killed. They concluded that her death did not take place in the car."

The Cloisters of Canterbury

We were approaching Fowersham. Biff asked, "Are you getting tired of driving?"

"I'm not sure that you'll ever get the wheel back. This is some car."

"The men at the Yard concluded that Ruth Watkins' body was placed in the rear seat of the Hillman, it was driven to the location of the accident, parked next to the tree. Another vehicle, probably an English lorry, was driven into the passenger side of the car, forcing it against the tree in a crunching action. The windshield and the glass in the doors were cracked but still in their frames. If there had been a sudden impact to the car, the glass would have been broken and pieces forced from the frames, not just cracked and shattered.

"They concluded that the Hillman was not struck by an American Army truck or jeep. The American Army truck has towing hooks and cable drums on the front. The impact on the Hillman was straight, no indentation from a wench. The front of the American Army jeep is narrower than the impact on the Hillman. Several pre-war English lorries would make the indentation. They are commonplace on the roads delivering goods in England."

Biff pointed to a structure in the distance. I recognized the tower of Canterbury Cathedral. I eased up on the accelerator, down-shifted the Jaguar, slowing so that I could absorb the beauty of the special place. Following Biff's directions, I drove through Canterbury streets and parked. We got out of the Jaguar and briskly walked to the cathedral, and were seated before the start of evensong.

As we returned to our seats after receiving communion, the radiating smile on the face of Canon Filpin in the second row was a most welcomed sight. The canon was waiting for us at the entrance after the service.

His bear hug greeting brought tears to our eyes. I had met him on my first visit to Canterbury with Biff. There had been something special about that visit, something that I had not felt at any other time in my life.

"My dear friends, what a wonderful surprise, only yesterday I lit candles for both of you. You have been in my prayers."

Biff told Canon Filpin that we were staying the night at the Chaucer and asked him to join us for dinner. The canon accepted and just before we started to leave the cathedral, Biff walked to the left of the entrance and pointed to an archway.

"Canon, what is this structure?"

"This is the Dean's walk, the passageway is a cloister, and it protects those who walk under it. Why do you ask?"

"Rob had a dream he should share with you."

We walked to the Chaucer, since three wouldn't fit in the Jaguar. Later we would walk the canon back to his residence in the Precincts.

The canon received a warm greeting when we entered the lobby. As he talked with the host, Biff and I went to the desk and checked in.

We followed the canon to a table near the fireplace where the warmth of a fire welcomed us. It was the same table where we ate lunch on our last visit. The waiter arrived, greeted us and asked if we would like something to drink before dinner. The canon ordered sherry. Biff and I asked for our usual, Balvenie Scotch.

The canon changed his order to Balvenie. "It's for warmth," he said.

We ordered roast beef with Yorkshire pudding, creamed potatoes and carrots.

"Rob, what brings you to England other then to visit old friends?"

"Several things, actually. I wanted to have some good North Sea codfish, replenish my tobacco supply in Victoria, and receive a driving lesson from Biff in his Jaguar Coupe. But mainly to visit Canterbury Cathedral and receive much needed prayers."

"I understand. Tell me about your dream."

"The night before leaving Cleveland, Ohio, for London, I dreamed that I was standing in deep snow in the center of the stones at Stonehenge. It was quiet and still, the moon was shining, casting eerie shadows of the stones on the snow. There was no one else there. I spoke aloud to myself. 'What am I doing out here all alone?' A voice from above came down and said, 'You're not alone, you have never been alone, and you will always be cloistered.' Until that moment, I had never heard the word cloister."

I continued, "I still don't understand the dream, but my friend Biff has been trying to educate me. He has a painting of the entrance to the Dean's Walk at the cathedral and, as you know, he asked about the archway at the cathedral."

The canon looked at me. "Please repeat your dream."

I repeated the dream word for word.

Biff was silent, watching and listening.

The canon placed his right hand on my shoulder and the other on Biff's arm. "I understand some of the things you and Biff have been doing and the purpose. Biff has not betrayed anything. I have been able to assist him over many years with information while not betraying any confidence of a priest."

The Cloisters of Canterbury

The canon continued, "Cloistered means protection for those beneath the archway. The voice from above could only come from One. The Lord is telling you that you will be protected in what you are doing. You cried out, 'What am I doing out here all alone?' He answered you. You're not alone. He is your cloister."

The waiter served our meal. Canon Filpin offered a prayer. The conversation was limited while we ate. The canon asked about Biff's and my families. Elizabeth's coronation in June was part of most conversations in Britain. The canon was pleased that he would be present in Westminster Abby for the coronation.

When the waiter returned, we ordered peach cobbler with cream and coffee. After we had finished Biff raised three fingers to the waiter, he returned with three more Balvenie.

The canon spoke to the waiter, and he returned with three cigars. The canon clipped the ends and handed one to Biff and one to me. He rose from his chair, went to the fireplace, removed a long straw from a holder on the mantel and ignited it from the fire embers in the fireplace. Returning to the table, he held it for Biff and me to light our cigars. After lighting his, he returned the straw to the fireplace.

We sat in silence. Three men from different worlds joined because of events out of our control. The canon had served as a chaplain during the war. He had received the Military Cross for bravery from King George VI at Buckingham Palace, and had touched the hearts and souls of those on and off the battlefields. He gave hope to those in need, the last rites for an uncountable number. Biff, a servant of his country, protected the rights of his fellowman when he could well have spent his time touring around the country in a sports car. And I, because of events beyond my design and control, had the privilege of knowing and being with these fine men.

After we savored the last of our scotch, Biff paid the waiter and we walked to the front door. There was a full moon and the air was cold. We continued smoking our cigars as we walked silently back to the cathedral. Three men comfortable in each other's company without constant conversation, especially after enjoying a good meal, Balvenie, and a cigar.

At the cathedral, the canon paused in front of the archway—the entrance to the cloister. We followed him down the Dean's Walk to the end where he opened a large door. We followed without speaking. He stopped in front of a rail in front of many burning candles. We knelt in prayer. The canon offered prayers for us and lit two candles.

Afterwards we strolled with the canon to the entrance of his home in the Precincts and said our farewells. Biff and I walked back to the Jaguar in silence. I handed Biff the keys to the Jaguar.

"I was wondering if you were ever going allow me to drive again."

Biff parked the Jag behind the Chaucer. We said goodnight and made no plans for a morning call. We would just meet in the dining room in the morning.

•

At 7:00 AM, both of us walked out of our rooms.

"Rob, would you like to go to the cathedral before breakfast?"

"Strange, I woke thinking that we should do just that. I would like to put my briefcase in the Jag first."

We stopped and put the briefcase in the Jag's boot and walked to the cathedral where we were greeted by the canon standing at the entrance to the cloister, as if planned. We followed the canon down the Dean's Walk into a small chapel for Matins. The canon said Mass.

Biff invited the canon to join us for breakfast, but he declined due to a previous commitment. The canon walked with us to Canter Street, placed his hands on our shoulders, and blessed us.

Walking back to the Chaucer, Biff said, "There are far too few men like the canon. I have been in many different churches when the canon was the celebrant and the preacher. He touches the lives of all who attend and many who do not."

The table by the fireplace was waiting with just a small fire burning. We ordered a full English breakfast, but no bangers for me. After breakfast, we checked out.

Biff looked at me. "Do you want to drive?"

"Thanks, but I would like to look at the country."

Biff pointed out numerous historical points on the drive back to London, giving me another English history lesson. I was leaving London the next morning and would be back in Cleveland in just over twenty-four hours. I had mixed emotions about leaving England and Biff, and wondered if I would ever return.

There was no doubt in my mind of the importance of the information obtained on the trip to London. Time was a factor. The Group needed the information on Hans Mueller and Frances Murita for the federal court. They had to be arrested before one or both of them ran.

We stopped for lunch in Chatham and arrived back at the flat off

The Cloisters of Canterbury

Warwick Way at 5:30.

"Try your key in the door, Rob."

I inserted the key in the door lock for the first time since Biff had given it to me. I turned the key and opened the door. I waited for Biff to go in, then closed the door.

"Biff, here's the key. I'm leaving in the morning and won't need it.

"Keep the key in case I can't pick you up when you return to London."

It was kind of Biff. It was his way of saying that I would be back. We returned to the living room after taking our bags upstairs.

"Let's review what you have to take back with you. The Cork Pub owner and his bartender identified Ruth Watkins, Frances Murita and Hans Mueller from a group of photographs. They gave statements that they did frequent the pub. Two neighbors in Pirbright identified Hans Mueller from a number of photographs that he was the man that they talked with and had observed repairing and driving the Hillman Coupe, and one identified Frances Murita with Mueller."

Biff paused and removed several documents from a folder. "Here are statements from Scotland Yard and the British Intelligence with their conclusions of the Hillman accident. This is the medical report on Ruth Watkins' death, and the signed statements from the men at the Cork and the neighbors at Pirbright. In addition, here is my statement about our meeting with Alvin Waite, the solicitor that gave notice of Wiseman's death. Attached to it is a statement from Scotland Yard attesting to Waite's activities. Here is a statement from the Yard providing details of how Mueller obtained his forged documents and when he sailed from Liverpool to Halifax.

"With these statements and your investigations, the Group shouldn't have a problem in obtaining indictments of Mueller and Murita." Biff handed me all of the documents.

I looked at the documents, put them into my briefcase and closed it.

"Now it's time for some Balvenie." Biff poured the scotch in the crystal glasses, both giving a toast to the other's health. We sipped our drinks and made small talk, both feeling satisfied.

"What you have accomplished on this assignment for the Group will make a difference. There is no doubt in my mind that Mueller and Murita will be brought to justice. Many others will not be placed in harm's way by removing these two from society. What you are doing is right. I know your personal life has been sacrificed in many ways. As the Voice and the canon said, 'You will be cloistered in what you do.'"

Biff sipped his scotch and smiled. "My life has been full—involvement in our government, excitement, meeting interesting people, and I know that I've made a difference. I have been blessed with a wife who understands more than she acknowledges. She has made a loving home for our two sons and me. They will never know everything about what I have done, things that must always be a secret. I hope that you find someone that will make your life complete."

Biff set his glass back on the table. "You have an early plane in the morning, so I think we should get some sleep. I want you to know how much I have enjoyed having you here. The more I get to know you, the more I appreciate your skills in our craft. Especially, I am proud to call you my friend."

I hesitated before speaking, "Biff, I know of no way to express how I feel about you. Observing your personality changes, from one environment to another has been an education. Watching you become the Brit sports car driver when you're behind the wheel of the Jag. Meeting Canon Filpin and getting to know him as a friend has brought me a spiritual renewal that I didn't know I needed. I am filled with the Holy Spirit's insight and God's comfort. I want to thank you for helping me to learn, and for sharing your time with me. I will miss you."

We put the lights out and went up stairs. I stopped in front of the painting of the cloister and touched it.

Chapter 27

RETURN TO THE U.S.

The sound of Biff chanting and the aroma of coffee brewing woke me. I dressed and carried my bag downstairs past the cloister painting, touching it once more as I passed.

"Good morning, Yank. Full English breakfast, without bangers for my friend," was Biff's greeting when I walked into the kitchen.

After we ate, I cleared the dishes while Biff went to his room to put on a tie and jacket.

Going out the door, Biff said, "See if you can lock the door, Yank."

I did.

The drive to Heathrow airport was without delays. We stood facing each other for a few moments and gave each other bear hugs.

"Thanks again for everything."

Biff, with his warm smile said, "Rob, you *will* return."

I watched Biff drive away in the Jaguar, giving the engine a little extra roar when he shifted gears. I carried my suitcase and briefcase into the terminal, checked the suitcase and received my seat assignment. I located a chair near the departing gate and waited for the flight to New York.

This would be a long day. I would arrive in New York LaGuardia, have a two-hour wait, and then fly on to Cleveland. Some place over the Atlantic I fell asleep. The stewardess serving dinner awakened me. After the meal, I read a few pages in a magazine and dozed off. I was awakened again, this time when the stewardess touched my shoulder. We were approaching New York and preparing to land.

The flight, as far as I knew, had been very smooth. I was one of the first to get off the plane. I walked down the steps and faced a brisk cold wind coming across the tarmac. At baggage claim there was a brief wait for my bag, and then on to customs. I had nothing to declare. I received directions for my flight to Cleveland.

At the first pay telephone I called Doud. The call was answered with the same old identification. After I advised Doud that I had the documentation they needed, he told me he was flying from Houston later in the day and that we would meet with Allen the following morning at nine.

"Nice to have you back on American soil, Rob. Be careful."

After the meeting tomorrow, I knew that it would be back to Springfield to finalize my consulting assignment. Of more interest was how the Group would proceed with the arrest of Mueller and Murita. It was going to be especially rewarding since the result of my work would take freedom from those two.

They called my flight, a direct flight into Cleveland. When the plane landed and taxied to the gate, I saw large piles of snow. It had been snowing across the Great Lakes with some airports closed when I left for England.

After retrieving my suitcase from baggage claim, I walked to the parking lot. The driveways between the parked cars were clear but cars that had been parked for several days were covered. I remembered approximately where I had parked. It was going to be a problem determining which mountain of snow was my car. After brushing the snow off seven cars' rear bumpers, I finally located it. I stood looking at the car wondering how I would be able to remove the snow when a tractor with a blade on the front stopped next to me.

The driver got off and said, "Can you use some help?"

"Yes, a lot of it."

The tractor driver removed a broom from a clamp on the tractor's fender and brushed the snow off the car. But now the snow between my car and the cars on both sides was almost to the top of the windows. The man returned to the tractor, came back with a shovel, and then started

The Cloisters of Canterbury

shoveling the snow to provide a path for me to get into the car.

When the pathway was complete, I asked, "How much do I owe you?"

"Five dollars."

I gave him twenty.

"Thanks a lot. See if your car will start before I leave." The man climbed back up on the tractor.

I put my suitcase and briefcase in the rear seat, inserted the key, and thankfully, the motor started on the first try. I let the car run and rolled down the window.

"Thanks for being a cloister," I told the man.

He looked at me as if I was off my rocker and drove away on the tractor. I thought I'd better be careful using the word "cloister."

Driving from the airport to Mrs. Gray's house in Bay Village gave me a welcome sense of going home. Snowplows had removed the snow from the roads and streets, depositing it along both sides. It was like driving in a tunnel. I was happy to discover that at the house enough snow had been removed from the driveway to park and the sidewalk was cleared.

When I walked up on the porch, Mrs. Gray opened the door. "I knew that you would be coming home tonight. Shirley at your office told me."

"I am certainly well cared for."

I unpacked and repacked my suitcase, knowing that I would be going to Springfield immediately after the meeting at the office. After laying out clothes for the next day, I enjoyed a hot shower. Just before drifting off to sleep, I remembered my dream on the night before going to England. I thought about being cloistered and went to sleep. The next thing that I remembered was hearing the alarm at six.

•

I looked out of the front bedroom window and saw there had been more snow during the night. The streets would still be slippery, and the drive into Cleveland would be slow. I dressed and picked up my briefcase and suitcase and softly descended the stairs. I brushed the snow off the front and rear windows, backed the car into the street and drove towards Lake Erie. I paused at the lake shore road before making a right turn. Dark storm clouds were rolling in from Canada. It was good to be back in Ohio, snowstorms and all.

At the office I went directly to see James Allen. His secretary greeted me and said that I was expected, and to go right in. Doud and Allen awaited me at the conference table. When I called from New York I had not provided any information about the findings in London other than it had been productive. I sat down at the conference table with Doud and Allen across from me once more. Their faces were like children at Christmas waiting to see what Santa had brought them. I opened my briefcase and removed my field report file.

"I am going to give you a summary of the information that was obtained," I began. "Biff Wallace and I showed the photographs of Hans Mueller, the one that had been acquired by the Group and the enlargement of the one that I took of Hans Mueller in the Springfield hospital, and photographs of Frances Murita and Ruth Watkins to the owner of The Cork Pub and his bartender. Both of them identified the pictures of Hans Mueller as the man who was with Frances Murita and Ruth Watkins in the pub, and they confirmed that they had frequented the pub regularly for several months.

"We reviewed the constable's report from the village who had investigated the stolen Hillman, and also talked with two of the neighbors who had talked with the man working on the car. Both picked Mueller from photographs as the man working on the Hillman. One of them identified the picture of Frances Murita as the woman seen with Mueller at the cottage with the Hillman car.

"Biff Wallace prepared signed statements for each of them. I have those statements. Biff consulted with his friends at Scotland Yard and British Intelligence. They concluded that Ruth Watkins was not killed in the Hillman when it was wrecked. The accident had been rigged and staged to cover up her death at some other location. Biff was able to determine when Hans Mueller sailed with forged documents from Liverpool to Nova Scotia. In these folders are the statements of the witnesses and documents Biff Wallace obtained."

The expressions on Doud and Allen faces could only be described as triumphant. I was enjoying this presentation. It proved that the connection of Mueller and Murita had taken place in England. I closed the file marked "Mueller/Murita," and opened another marked "Wiseman."

"Glenn Hudson, attorney for Henry Wiseman, received a letter from a Zurich banker stating that Wiseman was arrested in Munich by the Nazi SS and died on a train to Dachau, a German concentration camp. Hudson later received a letter from Alvin Waite, a solicitor in London, advising that Henry Wiseman died in 1944 while in the Auschwitz concentration camp in Poland. When Biff and I talked with Waite in London he had no explanation for the conflict in information about Wiseman's death, except that there was more than one man named Henry Wiseman and several could have died in concentration camps.

"Three weeks after notice was received of Wiseman's death, Mrs. Wiseman died. Attorney Hudson probated the Wiseman will that gave all their assets to Ruth Watkins. Watkins learned of her inheritance while in England, where Frances Murita found out about it. Murita and Hans Mueller conspired to kill Watkins. Murita returned to the United States and was discharged from the WAC. There is a period not accounted for until she arrives in Springfield, Ohio, and assumes Ruth Watkins' identity. She may have been in New Jersey receiving help on how to assume Ruth's identity. Within a few weeks after Murita was employed by the Springfield Truck Company, Hans Mueller arrived in Springfield and was employed by the truck company." I closed the folder and rested my arms on the table.

Doud spoke first. "Rob, Allen and I agree that your investigation has provided the evidence that can be presented to a federal judge, and warrants will be issued for Hans Mueller and Frances Murita. We expect to accomplish it in the next ten days or less. I will call John Myers at Village Bank and ask him to see if he can locate the writer of the letter to Hudson that he received the morning of his death. I'll advise him that you will be visiting him in the next few days."

Doud continued, "Rob, you identified Mueller at the truck plant and then uncovered his association with the woman and uncovered the conspiracy. Excellent work! It speaks well for your abilities and the way your mind works. Then, in your spare time, you completed a professional consulting assignment for James Allen & Associates. Do you remember when President Truman said that he had good judgment of men? He will want to take credit for recommending you to the Group. In fact, he might just drink a little bourbon and branch when he learns of the results from this assignment."

•

When I arrived in Springfield it was after midnight. As usual, I parked in front of the gypsy palm reader's window. I walked up the hill to the Shawnee Hotel, stopped at the front desk, picked up my room key, and rode the elevator up to my third floor room. When I opened the door, nothing had changed.

Chapter 28

Springfield

The alarm jarred me into the real world at 5:30 AM. I dressed and then removed the documents from my briefcase that were not for the eyes of anyone at the plant, put them in my suitcase in the closet and secured the door with the travel lock. I loaded new film in the Minox camera, picked up the briefcase, my brown notebook and left the room. Rather than using the elevator, I descended the stairs with thoughts of events that would soon be taking place. I skipped breakfast, deciding instead to go out for an early lunch if possible.

It was 6:30 when I drove into the plant parking lot. I parked in the first visitor's parking place, three spaces from Ruth Watkins' reserved space. A car belonging to Speer was already in his reserved space. I wondered why he had arrived so early, but it would give me the opportunity to talk with him and ask about the condition of the men in the hospital.

Speer's office door was open, and he was at his desk reading when I knocked. He looked up and said, "Rob, come in. Have a chair."

"How are the men in the hospital doing? I have been out of town for a little over a week."

"They are doing better than expected. The funerals for the two men are over, but there is still a lot of sadness and unrest in the plant. The investigation has not been completed, but the speculation by many is not helping. It will be easier to deal with the morale problem when all the facts are known."

"When is the investigation expected to be complete?"

"It's going to be several weeks, I have been told."

I did not want to show any specific interest in John A. Johnson, but I wanted to know when he would be discharged. "When will the first men be released from the hospital?"

"John Johnson's burns were not too bad and he will be the first one discharged. That could be as early as the end of next week. Even so, I don't think that he will be able to return to work for several more weeks. His hands are about healed, but his legs will take longer. They will need to be protected for a while, and shouldn't be exposed to factory dirt."

That told me what I wanted to know. Mueller was probably able to walk out of the hospital at any time. The Group needed to get moving.

"I have a few loose ends to tie down for my report and expect to have it completed in a couple of days. I have enjoyed working here. I'm only sorry that this accident had to happen."

"Your statement about the accident was appreciated by the company and the investigators."

I left Speer's office and went to my office, noting that Ruth Watkins had not arrived at her desk. I went in, sat down at the desk and started looking at the employee files of the four other German employees. They all had stated in their applications that they had been born in various places in Germany. Three of their employment applications indicated that they had served in the German Army and had been in truck maintenance units. The fourth had not been in the service, but had been employed as a maintenance man by a German manufacturer. All of the men indicated that they had relatives in the US. All four men stated that they had come to the United States from Canada through Detroit, Michigan. There was nothing negative in their files.

I copied the information from their employment applications into my notebook. I had seen all four men on several occasions, and none of them resembled the pictures of the wanted men.

My major concern was how I could help defuse Art Reilly and prevent him from doing any harm to the men. It was 7:45. With the brown notebook in hand, I left the office.

Ruth Watkins was at her desk.

"How are the men doing at the hospital?"

Her expression was passive. "They are doing better."

"I am glad to hear that. And how are you doing, getting any more rest?"

Ruth replied, with just a slight sign of a smile, "I am doing fine, thank you."

Walking away, I remembered the words of caution in the report from the Army Sergeant Major Murphy and Major Stevens describing Frances Murita as a dangerous woman. Now, just returning from England with evidence, that danger was not just probable, but factual. She had been a party to Ruth Watkins' death, erasing any concern that I might have had for her punishment. I now thought it could not be too severe.

I descended the stairs to the factory floor and started my routine tour. I listened for the musical sounds, but the rhythm was still not there. It had disappeared with the explosion. The activities of the men were different, their motions appeared strained. I spoke with several foremen in their departments. When I asked how things were going, without exception they replied, "Not good. Things have changed."

I walked through the engine test area, where signs of the explosion still existed, taking note of the lingering smell of smoke and metal columns covered with the black smoke from the fire. The burning gasoline, as it flowed across the floor, had etched a path into the concrete.

Through the opening into the motor assembly area, I saw Art Reilly talking with two men with his arms and hands in motion. As I approached the men, Reilly saw me, stopped talking and walked toward me. He stuck his big hand out.

We shook hands.

Reilly said, "Haven't seen you around for a while."

"I was at the company office in Cleveland for a few days. Yesterday when I was leaving, it was really snowing. How are things going around here?"

"We're still mad about that Kraut killing Rowell, and he'll get his when he walks out of that hospital."

I didn't respond to his statement, but did say, "After the accident you were telling me about the five other Germans working in the plant, one a woman. That interested me, so I looked at the employment files of the four men and did not find anything unusual in them. All of them said they were from Germany, came through Canada, listed their previous employment and military records. One of them wasn't even in the army. He was working in a factory during the war. All four have relatives here in the States, just like many of your Irish relatives that arrived years ago."

Reilly looked at me. "Is that right?"

"That's what I learned from their files. One thing you and your buddies don't want to do is anything crazy, like beating them and accidentally killing one or more of them. You would be in big trouble. Who would take care of your families?"

Reilly ran the fingers of his big right hand through his red hair and then across his forehead, moved his head from side to side, and looked at me. "You're right."

I continued the tour of the plant, returned to the office, and reviewed my report that was typed at the Cleveland office. It was ready for presentation to the company. I would call Allen and tell him that the report was ready to be submitted, and advise him of Mueller's condition. Allen could then schedule his meeting here in Springfield and present the firm's report.

They had not told me how the arrests were going to be accomplished. However, it would only seem reasonable that the Group had contacts with the federal court and government officials, and lawyers who would be preparing the documents for a federal judge.

There were several things that I needed to do in the next few days. The first on the list was a trip to Dayton to visit John Myers at the Valley Bank and try to learn something about the letter Hudson had received. Another thing was to dispose of the 1938 Ford. I also wanted to visit the Hudson house to tell the dear lady that I had given the information to the former friends of Ruth Watkins. I wasn't sure what that would accomplish. It might be better just to move on, but I would miss Mary Combs.

•

It was 10:30. I left the plant for an early lunch and a quick trip to Dayton. I hadn't been to the Valley Bank since my last courier assignment. I went directly to John Myers' office. His secretary remembered me.

"Mr. Myers has been expecting you." She walked to his door and opened it. "Mr. Royal is here." She motioned for me to go in.

"Have a seat, Rob. I received a call from Doud, and have the information that you are looking for. I had my secretary make a copy of the letter for you." He handed me the letter.

I read the letter addressed to Glenn Hudson.

```
Dear Glenn,

    It has come to my attention that Ruth
Marie Watkins has withdrawn more than
$300,000 from her two accounts here at
Valley Bank and closed the accounts.
There has been no change, to my knowl-
edge, in her Valley Bank stock. I
remembered that you shared with me your
relationship with Henry Wiseman and
Ruth Watkins. Therefore, I felt that
you should be aware of the activity.
When in Dayton, call and we will have
lunch.

Best of personal regards,
Lawrence Rankle
```

Myers looked at me. "I told Doud that the cashier's check issued to Ruth Watkins had cleared through a Trenton, New Jersey, bank."

"I had an idea that it would work out this way. Thanks for your help." A cold chill went down my spine. I was trying not to reveal more than necessary. I hurriedly said good bye, shook hands and left.

On the drive back to Springfield my mind pictured Hudson receiving the letter from the bank. He knew that Ruth was dead, but could not have conceived it was murder. No wonder he was upset, learning someone had withdrawn over $300,000 from the bank. He knew something was terribly wrong. Rose White mentioned that Hudson had said he had probated Wiseman's will too soon. Motivation for Hudson's bus trip to the courthouse was established. He was probably not thinking about anything else but the letter when he got off the bus and got hit by the car that did not stop. In spite of the witness's statement that the light was red and the car was driving at a high rate of speed, Hudson's state of mind must have been a factor. This was another missing piece and another motive for Ruth's murder—easy money.

•

I returned to the plant after my trip to Dayton. I walked through the plant, observing and listening. The change since the explosion and

The Cloisters of Canterbury

the death of the two men had made such an obvious difference. The music was gone.

When I left the plant for the day, I drove past the '38 Ford parked on Main Street. The only change was more dust, and thankfully no broken windows or flat tires. I returned to my regular parking place in front of the gypsy palm reader's window. When I removed the briefcase from the trunk, I looked up. The gypsy was standing on the steps.

"You have been away, I missed you. You had a good trip, no?"

I looked at her, thought about what she had just said, a leading question. "Yes, I have been visiting friends and it was a good trip, thank you."

She smiled, dropped the veil, revealing her pretty face. "You should let me tell your future before you travel."

I smiled at her and walked up the hill. Before going into the hotel, I stopped at a pay telephone and called James Allen in Cleveland to tell him that the report was ready to be presented. Allen said that he would arrange the meeting at the plant and that I should call Doud.

After hanging up the telephone, I walked to the post office. The lobby of the building was deserted. It was my choice of telephone booths. Doud answered on the fourth ring and we exchanged our coon hunting identification. I told him the details of the Hudson letter.

"Mr. Doud, it certainly provides the motivation for Hudson to be upset and to go to the courthouse that morning. Hudson believed that Ruth Watkins was dead, and learned someone had emptied her bank account. In all probability, he would have been preparing to file something regarding Ruth Watkins' estate. Mary Combs told me that Ruth had no relatives. I did not see anything in the Wiseman files pertaining to Ruth Marie Watkins' estate or having a will. In fact, I did not look for a will in the file or at the courthouse, I never even thought about it.

"Maybe Ruth Watkins executed a will while she was in England. With Hudson's relationship with Wiseman, it would be difficult not to think that he hadn't written to Ruth Watkins and sent her a will to be executed, or advised her that she should have a will prepared. If he did, there should have been a copy of the letter in the files. However, the only documents in Ruth Watkins' file were a notice of Ruth's death, and the Hudson letter requesting further information about the death and the reply from the government.

"But one thing is certain. After Ruth Watkins learned of inheriting the Wiseman estate, her friend, Frances Murita, learned about it—the motivation for Murita and Mueller to kill Watkins in England."

"Didn't you also find a connection between Mueller and a forger in England?" asked Doud.

"Yes, I did. It would have been easy for Murita to get the forged identification in England."

Doud said, "I guess we will just let the courts decide what becomes of Ruth Watkins' money, whatever is recovered from Francis Murita. Rob, do you agree with that?"

"I certainly do. However, there are other issues still open. One that I think can be closed is the hit-and-run death of Glenn Hudson. It would have been impossible for anyone to know the contents of the letter from the Valley Bank and, if so, that it was going to arrive that day. It would also have been improbable that anyone could know that Hudson was going to ride the bus that day. He didn't go to the courthouse or the bank on a regular basis.

"The stolen car from the Dayton auto dealership probably was a random car theft by some young kid out for a joyride. Now here was a young person, in all probability, scared to death, driving a stolen car. He ran a red light and hit someone. There is no way that he was going to stop and return to the scene of the accident. This was only a coincidence that provided further opportunity for Murita and Mueller to conceal their conspiracy.

"Mr. Doud, the thing that still bothers me more than anything else is the fact that no one in Springfield questioned what was taking place. Yes, Hudson all of a sudden learned something that alarmed him when he received the letter from Valley Bank. If he had not been killed, things would have been different, but why not someone else? The other thing unanswered is Ted Walsh's death, when a car forced him off the road."

"Rob, Ted Walsh's death has nothing to do with your assignment."

That ended our conversation. I still was unhappy about how the Group had not addressed Walsh's death with me. Learning that he was run off the road from a newspaper was not easy.

I walked back to the hotel. The only thing that really required my attention now was disposing of the '38 Ford. I figured selling it back to the used car dealer would be the simplest. After a shower, I went to bed. My mind was at ease, I realized that there was nothing more that I could do. My work, the proof of fraud and murder, would take two dangerous people off of the street.

•

The Cloisters of Canterbury

The next morning I woke before the alarm sounded. For a change, I felt rested. After dressing, I located the title to the '38 Ford in my suitcase, secured the closet with the travel lock, and walked down the stairs to the dining room.

After breakfast, I left the hotel and walked to the '38 Ford. Someone had written in the dust on the windshield WASH ME. That would probably be a good idea before taking it to the used car lot. I brushed off enough of the dust from the windshield so I could see, and got behind the wheel. The rancid pipe tobacco smell had not disappeared. The motor turned over several times before it started. It had served its purpose and now it was ready for another owner.

I drove East on Main Street several blocks past the used car lot, pulled into a Sinclair gas station that had a Car Wash sign attached to a street light pole. I paid a dollar for a pretty good wash and drove to the used car lot. The same salesman greeted me with a cigar in his mouth. I told him that my plans had changed and that I would be out of town and wouldn't need the car for hunting.

The cigar man strolled around the car twice and then stopped. "I'll give you fifty dollars."

"That won't buy it. One-hundred fifty is my bottom dollar. Any less than that and I'll give it to a man that needs a chicken coup." I got back in the car and started the motor.

The man's words passed by the cigar, "One hundred twenty-five."

I turned the motor off, removed the keys and followed the man into the office. He counted out the one-hundred twenty-five dollars from a roll of bills that he removed from his pocket.

I gave him the title to the car, then said, "I want the license plates off the car."

The salesman opened a drawer of the wooden desk, grabbed a screwdriver, returned to the car, and removed the plates. I started to walk away then stopped, took a cigar, one from London, from the inside pocket of my suit coat and gave it to the man.

The man looked at it, smiled and said, "Thanks, that looks like a good one."

"A friend from London gave it to me."

I returned to my hotel room, left the license plates on the table, and removed the little brown notebook and the Minox camera from my suitcase. When I returned to the hotel lobby, the desk clerk said I had a message. He removed a slip of paper from the message box and handed it to me.

I thanked him. It was a message that the hotel telephone operator had written. "Mr. Allen will arrive at the Dayton airport tomorrow morning at 9:15. Please meet him."

Well, things were moving forward. I left the hotel and drove to the truck plant. Ruth Watkins' Desoto was parked in her regular place.

I walked through the plant just like every day and talked with the foremen and several of the workers. The music of the plant was a little better, but not near the tempo that existed before the accident.

I wondered what it would be like after Hans Mueller and Frances Murita were arrested. The workers would certainly learn of their arrests and the Springfield paper would provide the details. Frances Murita and Hans Mueller's conspiracy and the Wiseman property would be the conversation in the legal circles of Clark County, and the whole town would be talking about it and the murder for years.

When I went into the motor assembly department, Art Reilly waved to me and walked away from the other men.

"Are you sure about what you said the other day about the Krauts?"

"Art, their employment records show that references were checked and there was nothing unfavorable."

"We want to be sure about them. But, I am not sure what's going to happen to Johnson when he leaves the hospital and hits the street."

"Just remember your families. They all need their husbands and fathers, and you can't be a husband or father behind bars."

"Yeah, we know that's true." Art's tone was more resigned to the real facts.

I finished my tour and went up the stairs to the offices. When I passed the treasurer's office, his secretary spoke, "I was asked to tell you that the meeting tomorrow with your firm is at one o'clock in the conference room."

I thanked her and continued to my office.

Ruth Watkins was at her desk. I stopped and asked, "What's the latest on the men in the hospital?"

"Each day they're better and some will be out soon, but not able to return to work."

"That's good, and you look like you're getting your beauty rest."

She looked at me with a slight smile, "Thank you."

I found it difficult speaking to her, but I was looking for any sign that would indicate a change in her behavior. I wondered what she would say if I asked her to stop for a drink or go to dinner... I wasn't going to risk that.

The Cloisters of Canterbury

I said, "There's a meeting scheduled for one o'clock tomorrow in the conference room with management. We will be presenting our report so I won't be bothering you any more. I want to thank you for being so helpful. I am sure that all of the files that you provided have been returned."

I went into my office and was looking through the desk drawers when she came in. "Here is the file control list, and, yes, all the files have been returned."

She remained standing in front of the desk for a second or two then said, "I'll be sorry to see you leave." The expression on her face appeared sincere.

"I really do appreciate all your help. If the company likes our recommendations, maybe they will retain us to help implement the suggestions."

She looked at me with the smile that probably was responsible for her employment. "That would be nice." She returned to her desk. Her perfume was still intoxicating and so was she. It was easy to see how any company would hire her—without question.

At five o'clock, I drove to O'Brian's, drank a beer with some of the students, then went into the dining room for dinner. After dinner I returned to the hotel. The gypsy was in the window when I parked, this time across the street. Someone had beaten me to my usual parking place. It was odd that the parking space had been available in front of the palm reader's almost every night I had been in town. She waved at me as I crossed the street. I wondered what she might see in my future.

The walk up the hill to the hotel had become part of my day. The hotel lobby was quiet as usual. This was all part of a routine that would soon change.

Chapter 29

It Would Not End Here

When the alarm sounded at 6:00, I was already dressed and on the way to pick up James Allen at the Dayton airport at 9:15.

Allen was the first passenger off the plane. As soon as we were in the car he asked, "Have there been any new developments?"

I told him of my conversations in the plant with the men and with Ruth Watkins.

Allen cleared his throat and sad, "I have copies of your report that we will distribute. You will read it to them and then ask if they have any questions. I will assist with any questions and make some general statements. They probably will not have any questions. This should take no more than two hours, probably less. I'll keep some conversation going until the meeting is interrupted."

Allen paused for a minute, "At precisely three o'clock this afternoon the U.S. marshals will be at the hospital and arrest Hans Mueller, and at exactly the same time marshals will arrive at the truck plant and arrest Frances Murita. Marshals will inform the Clark County sheriff's office and request assistance of their deputies just before three. The decision not to advise them sooner is to prevent any leaks. They will be taken to a jail in Cincinnati, and will be brought before a federal judge first thing tomorrow."

He continued, "Another team of U.S. marshals will be at the Wiseman house on Fountain Blvd and it will be under their control until they have completed their search."

"In addition, federal court orders will be presented at the banks placing a hold on all accounts in Ruth Watkins' name. Her Desoto automobile will be impounded. There will also be an order given to the truck company for all of the original records of John A. Johnson and Ruth M. Watkins to be turned over to the marshals. The copies that you made of the records will be used to verify that all records have been obtained.

"We do not want you subpoenaed as a witness, nor do we want it known that you had any part in this. We all know how dangerous the Murita family can be. The information that you have provided is sufficient for prosecution of the two. There will be articles in the newspaper. Timing of our meeting today is very important. You are a consultant, nothing more. The firm has been retained to provide a specific service that you completed and we will be paid for our work."

When we arrived in Springfield, I showed Allen the Wiseman Tudor home on Fountain Blvd. where Frances Murita was living as Ruth Watkins, and the home of Glenn Hudson, Wiseman's attorney, who had been killed by the hit-and-run driver.

"We have time for lunch. I know a place close by that has respectable food. It's also given me a change in scenery on occasion."

•

On the drive to the truck plant, Allen commented that he was confident that both the consulting work and the work for justice would reap positive results. We arrived at the plant at 12:30.

I told him, "We have time to walk through the plant before the meeting, if you'd like."

"That sounds like a good idea," Allen responded.

We toured the plant, as I had done daily, and I pointed out the various departments as they related to the report. We paused in the engine test area. The smell of smoke and damage from the explosion was evident. When we entered the motor assembly area, I stopped and spoke to Art Reilly and introduced him to Allen. We then headed up the stairs to the office area. Ruth Watkins was at her desk. I stopped and introduced Allen to her as my boss. She turned on the charm. As we walked away, Allen looked at me and rolled his eyes.

Greeting us at the conference room was Reasonier, the company treasurer. I introduced Allen to the accounting manager, plant manager, engineering manger, and production manger as they arrived. When everyone was seated around the conference table Reasonier started the meeting.

"Everyone here is aware that Rob Royal of James Allen & Associates has been evaluating the company's operation. Mr. Allen is here today to present their findings and recommendations."

James Allen stood, "We want to thank you for the opportunity to serve you. Rob has completed a thorough analysis of your company's operation. He submitted his findings to our staff of accountants and engineers who have been working directly with him in analyzing and making recommendations for the future of your company. Rob is distributing a copy of our report to each of you. I have asked him to summarize the report for you. It will require considerable time for you to read and analyze. Rob will stay in Springfield until the first of the week and will be available to answer any of your questions."

I stood, "I want to thank all of you, your staff, and the employees for being so cooperative. Everyone has provided answers to my questions and offered suggestions that have made it possible for our firm to present this report. We are confident that these recommendations will assist you in the future growth and success in the truck market."

I then, basically, read the index of the report, leaving them to read and analyze the contents. The report was factual and detailed, and could be implemented by following each and every area contained in the report.

"Gentlemen, as Mr. Allen said, I'll be in Springfield until the first of the week and will return at any time after that to assist you."

A screaming woman's voice came from the hall. "You can't do this to me."

Speer, the employment manager, came running in with a paper in his hand. "United States marshals are out here arresting Ruth Watkins. The warrant says she is Francis Ann Murita, charged with fraud in assuming the identity of Ruth Watkins, converting property to her own use, harboring a fugitive, Hans Mueller, alias John A. Johnson, a former Nazi SS officer wanted for war crimes. He is one of our employees. She is also wanted for her involvement in a conspiracy in the death of Ruth

Watkins in England in 1945." Speer stopped to catch his breath, "And they want all of the company records for Ruth Marie Watkins and John A. Johnson."

The plant manager and treasurer jumped up and went out into the hall with Speer. The others stood and expressed shock as they looked around the table at each other. From the open door, they watched two U.S. marshals and a sheriff's deputy carrying Frances Murita, screaming and kicking, down the hall.

When Reasonier came back into the conference room, his secretary followed and said, "They just called from the hospital and reported that John Johnson has been arrested and was removed by force from his hospital room."

Reasonier said, "We must attend to this problem. Thanks, Mr. Allen. Rob, please call me tomorrow and I will try to get back to your report. This is unbelievable!"

"Rob will stay in town until you can get some free time," Allen said.

He and I walked down the stairs and out of the building. There were three sheriff's cars and three other sedans just leaving the parking lot. It was impossible to count the number of employees who were in the parking lot. Art Reilly and some of his buddies were watching Ruth Watkins leave in a sheriff's car. As we walked to my car, a wrecker was towing Ruth's impounded Desoto from the parking lot.

When we were in the car James Allen said, "Everything looks like it's going according to plan. On our way to the airport, drive by the house where she was living."

I turned off Crescent onto Fountain Boulevard. There were two sheriff's cars and two other cars in front and in the driveway of the Wiseman Tudor home. It appeared that all of the neighbors were watching the activities from nearby yards or standing in the grass medium of the boulevard.

"Rob, you stay in town and follow up with the people at the plant. Also, get copies of the newspapers and do your normal looking. We want to know what is going on. Call Doud daily."

•

I stopped in front of the terminal at the Dayton airport.

Allen turned to me before getting out of the car. "Rob, there is no doubt in our minds, these two will be convicted. If you hadn't recognized Mueller and connected Ruth Watkins to him, and then uncovered her identity, these two would still be free. Your accomplishment is an example of what the Group stands for. We thank you. Not only that, the work you did on the consulting assignment was excellent and very professional."

I returned to Springfield and parked in front of the gypsy palm reader's window. I got out of the car, picked up my briefcase, locked the car and returned the gypsy's wave. The hill felt unusually steep. My load was heavy for some reason. I had expected to be delighted when Mueller and Murita were arrested. It wasn't that I was feeling sorry for them. They were cruel and dangerous people, and deserved to be punished for their crimes. However, it was apparent that Murita was under Mueller's control.

I showered and went to bed without looking at the clock or setting it.

The sound of bundles of papers hitting the pavement in front of the drugstore woke me the next morning. I knew that the papers would have been delivered to the hotel desk minutes before. I dressed quickly and went down to the front desk. The night clerk was placing the papers in racks next to the registration desk. I removed the *Springfield Sun News*, a *Cincinnati Enquire* and *Dayton News* from the racks and asked the desk clerk to put them on my hotel bill. I returned to my room using the elevator, anxious to see the papers.

All three newspapers carried bold, two-inch headlines: "U.S. MARSHALS ARREST TWO."

I read the articles in all three papers. News reporters had obtained information from unknown sources at the Clark County sheriff's office that Frances Murita had fraudulently been using the name of Ruth Marie Watkins. John A. Johnson was the alias used by Hans Mueller a former Nazi SS officer wanted for war crimes. The article covered just about everything. Federal warrants had been issued for conspiracy, fraud, harboring a fugitive, illegal entry into the United States, and the 1945 murder of Ruth Marie Watkins in England.

The reporters multiplied a few facts into hundreds of words of speculation. They had also talked with employees of the truck plant, workers who witnessed the arrest of Frances Murita, and hospital employees who witnessed Hans Mueller's arrest. The neighbors at the Fountain Blvd. address claimed their previous suspicions of the activities in the Tudor house were correct and they always knew something bad was going on there.

I cut out the articles from the papers, put them into an envelope, and addressed them to James Allen at the firm in Cleveland. I marked the envelope Personal and Confidential, knowing that Allen's secretary would not open his personal mail. I purchased two more copies of the newspapers and cut the articles from them. I sent one set to Doud and the other I put into my suitcase.

I walked slowly down the stairs and across the lobby to the dining room where Harold greeted me. After eating my usual breakfast, I walked to the post office and made collect calls to Doud and Allen advising them of the newspaper articles.

For the next three days I called the truck plant and talked with the treasurer's secretary, as she was to coordinate any meetings. I listened to the radio station, bought all of the newspapers as they hit the newsstands, clipped the articles and mailed them, and called Doud daily.

Comments from Doud were the same, "Rob, you understand if others don't why we're so concerned about leaks."

Thursday night was full of dreams and nightmares. All of the deaths that had touched my life since that New Year's Eve snowstorm played out as if I was watching a horror movie. The man who attempted to kill me on the federal court building steps in Newark was killed, along with the U.S. marshal who died protecting me. Ruth Watkins was murdered in England. Her parents, Harold and Marie Watkins, were killed in China. The deaths continued in my nightmare. The Nazis killed Henry Wiseman, and then his wife died. Glenn Hudson, Wiseman's lawyer, was killed by a hit-and-run driver. Two men died in the truck plant explosion. And then there was the mystery of Ted Walsh. Eleven deaths in some way had an effect on my life and were stored in my mind. Would I ever forget them?

I awoke wet with sweat.

There was one thing that had been bothering me that I had to do before leaving Springfield. The courts would decide what would become of the Wiseman properties, and it was time for something to be done about the living conditions in the brick buildings on Main Street. No one should be required to live that way. I removed the camera from my briefcase, put it in my jacket pocket and left the hotel.

I walked east on Main Street to one of the brick buildings, the one I had first visited. This time I didn't bother to knock. I just opened the door, walked in and closed it. As soon as my eyes adjusted to the dim light, I removed the camera from my pocket, set it for time-exposure, pointed the camera, held the button down, opening the lenses, and counted to sixty and released the button. I went down the first set of stairs to the first basement and took two pictures, and then went down the stairs to the second basement and took two more pictures. When I returned to the street I took pictures of each of the buildings.

I walked back to my hotel room and set up the film development equipment and trays in the bathroom. After reading the developing instructions once more, I closed the bathroom door, turned the light out, and proceeded with the developing process.

While the film was drying I sat down at the nightstand, removed three sheets of paper and two pieces of carbon paper from my briefcase. I wrote to the Clark County Health Department and the Editor of the *Springfield Sun*. I listed the street numbers of the buildings that Watkins owned, and then proceeded to describe the brick buildings, the two basements and the living conditions of the men. I detailed the fire hazards with only one exit from the building and health hazards due to the lack of ventilation. I signed the letter, "A Cloistered Citizen." I would enclose the interior and exterior photographs of the buildings with the letters.

I left the room, descended the marble stairs, and went into the dining room. After my meal I returned to check the film and found it was dry. I held the film up to the light bulb of the table lamp, looked at the frames with the magnifying glass, ensuring the images looked clear. I then enlarged and made prints. The finished photographs didn't equal the work that the Group or that Sergeant Murphy's staff had accomplished, but hopefully they would create some interest in the health department and the newspaper. In the morning when the prints were dry, I would mail them. The third copy of the letter and the negatives I would keep.

It was another one of my normal nights, sleep for a while, then waking up with the dream about the man falling through the skylight fresh in my mind. If I went back to sleep, the next dream would usually be of the attempt on my life. Then sometime later, I would have the dream of Stonehenge.

I was still awake when the newspapers were delivered at the drug store across the street from the hotel. While standing in the shower, I decided that there was a need for a positive change in my life.

I called the truck plant just after eight, but there was still no request for a meeting to talk about the consulting firm's report. Reasonier's secretary said the place was like a zoo since the arrests. I called Allen in Cleveland and told him of my last call to the plant and that the newspapers stories about the arrest had continued with a lot of speculation.

The Cloisters of Canterbury

"Rob, don't worry about it. Things will take their normal slow course. You need to get away, go some place different for the next ten days, just keep my secretary advised how we can contact you. But before you leave, call Doud—and be careful."

I told Allen that I was looking foreword to my next assignment, and that I would arrange for the Springfield newspaper to be mailed to Mrs. Gray's house in Bay Village for the next month.

Maybe for the last time, I walked to the post office and placed a collect call to Doud. I advised him that I would be away, and that I would return to Cleveland in ten days.

He told me, "That's fine, but when you return to Cleveland, there will be a plane ticket for you to London. I'll give you the details later. Have some fun—and be careful."

I packed my bags, checked to be sure that I hadn't missed anything, and left. It seemed like I had been calling this home for a long time. I stopped at the front desk, turned in the room key, and paid my bill.

I carried my bag and briefcase down the Limestone hill to my car parked in front of the gypsy palm reader's window, just a normal day. I opened the trunk and put in the briefcase and suitcase. When I closed the trunk, I heard the voice of the gypsy, "Tell your future before you leave?"

I looked at the young gypsy girl, paused, and walked across the sidewalk and up the steps. There was a surprised look and then a smile on her face.

She said, "Welcome." She stepped back and parted the beaded curtain in the doorway with her hand, "Please be seated."

In the center of the small room there were two chairs and a round table covered with an embroidered cloth. A dim light in the ceiling projected a soft glow over the table. I observed that there was no other exit from the room. I felt no fear.

The gypsy took my right hand in hers, gently moved a finger across the palm of my hand. "You will have a long life…there will be periods of loneliness…danger will always be present…you must always be careful…you will be protected in your journey."

I stood up and placed a twenty-dollar bill in her small hand—her eyes were moist. I said, "It's all right—I'm cloistered."

As I drove away, the gypsy smiled and waved.

From the back of my mind I remembered being told: *They may call us couriers—but we are in fact spies for a covert Group that doesn't exist.*

It would not end here…

Printed in the United States
63505LVS00004BB/43-78